PRAISE FOR DAWN METCALF

"This exhilarating story of Ink and Joy has marked my heart forever.
Dawn Metcalf, I am indelibly bound to you. More!"
—*New York Times* bestselling author Nancy Holder on *Indelible*

"[Metcalf's] rich physical descriptions create a complex fey world
that coexists uneasily with the industrialized human one. An…
engaging story of first love, family drama and supernatural violence."
—*Kirkus Reviews* on *Indelible*

"Dangerous, bizarre, and romantic, *Indelible* makes for a delicious
paranormal read, and I for one can't wait to see more of the Twixt."
—*Bookyurt* on *Indelible*

"Fans of fae fantasy, YA paranormal and modern fantasy will adore
this novel and find themselves willingly trapped within the Twixt.
Read. This. Book!"
—Serena Chase, *USA TODAY*'s *Happy Ever After* blog,
on *Indelible*

"Romance fans will melt for this new tale of the Twixt."
—*Booklist Online* on *Invisible*

"So different, so imaginative, a little bit creepy, but absolutely
wonderful."
—*Reading YA Rocks* blog on *Invisible*

Books by Dawn Metcalf
available from Harlequin TEEN

The Twixt series

(in reading order)

INDELIBLE
INVISIBLE
INSIDIOUS
INVINCIBLE

DAWN METCALF
INVINCIBLE

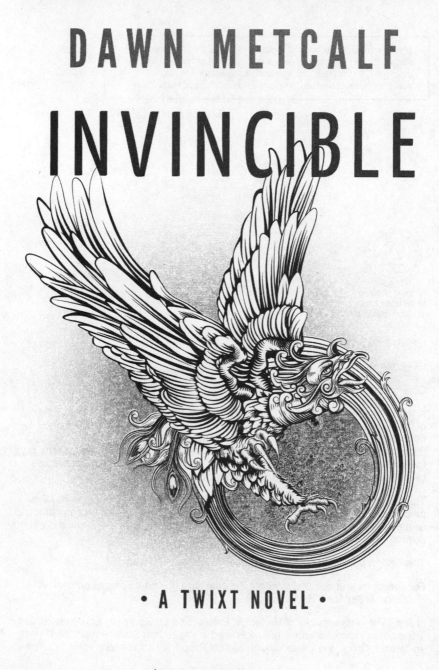

• A TWIXT NOVEL •

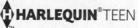

HARLEQUIN®TEEN

Recycling programs
for this product may
not exist in your area.

ISBN-13: 978-0-373-21166-1

Invincible

Printed in U.S.A.

To Barry, for all the words.

To Holly, for all the dreams.

To HollyBarry, for all the love.

Always.

ONE

JOY MALONE STOOD INSIDE THE BAILIWICK AND stared out the newly opened door between worlds. Her bare feet tingled on the illusion of grass, and Indelible Ink's hand hung loosely in hers. Her boyfriend's black, fathomless eyes were wondrous-wide as they absorbed the unbelievable sight.

Yellow banners snapped over bivouac camps spread over miles of green, grassy hills. Soldiers gathered around a large central court—elves and sprites, demons and gargoyles, gryphons and centaurs and fairies garbed for battle, all staring back at them, dumbstruck with awe. In the middle of the courtyard, nine princesses were laughing and sobbing hysterically, reunited after centuries apart. And beyond them, two crowned figures stood before their thrones, their long hair lifting like angel's wings in the wind; the Royal Majesties, the King and Queen of the Folk.

The King turned to his Queen, his words, crisp and clean, crossing the miles, slicing through sound.

"It is as you foretold," he said. "Behold the Destroyer of Worlds."

Joy swallowed. Her heart might have skipped a beat, but as Joy was only half human, her heart was still.

Ink turned to her, his voice uncertain. "Joy?"

She shook her head, not daring to look away. "I don't

know," she whispered. She had no idea what they were talking about, but their words chilled her. She shivered. Her leotard stuck awkwardly to her skin. As a former gymnast, Joy was used to wearing next to nothing in public, but right now she wished she'd kept on the elaborate ball gown. The layers of silk and crinoline might have been some small protection from the otherworldly glares, but she'd shed it while making her escape from Under the Hill. The costume was likely trampled by angry Folk searching for her back at the gala, including the rampaging dragon, the Head of the Council, Bùxiǔ de Zhēnzhū. She could almost hear the distant howling as the mob swarmed the Grand Hall.

But that was back in the real world, her world—a strange mix of the human world and the Twixt—not this pocket dimension, the "Bailiwick," hidden inside Graus Claude, which held the secret doorway to the lost King and Queen of the Folk.

The world beyond the doorway sparkled, muted like honey, motes of pollen flashing with lazy golds and greens. Purple clouds hung above jeweled fruit trees and tall waterfalls tumbled over sharp, blue-veined cliffs. There were castles in the distance with rainbow lakes and silver springs bubbling under bridges that looked spun from diamond glass. It looked like every fairy tale, every fantasy made real. This was the world of magic where the Folk had gone to hide.

Joy swallowed, forcing herself to relax, and lifted her chest and chin.

"Your Majesties." Joy raised her voice. "Your people await your Imminent Return!"

She thought that would do it, she really did. All heads turned to look at the Queen, whose face was as beautiful and terrible as the alien sky. Her skin was the color of morning glories and her eyes were as bright as stars.

The wind picked up, blowing her long hair back from her face. Her crown winked gold in a sea of amber curls. The lost Folk gathered nearer to their monarchs with a low, buzzing mumble, the curious murmur of bees.

"You are not our people," the Queen said slowly. "Come forward if you come in peace."

Ink tugged her hand gently. Joy hesitated. It was true—as a homunculus and a halfling, neither Ink nor Joy was truly one of the Folk, but, however unlikely, they were the ambassadors of the Twixt. Joy could hear Graus Claude's advice whispering in her head, *Etiquette and decorum.*

The rampaging mob Under the Hill weren't half as frightening as the King and Queen of the Folk. Theirs was power, old and absolute, serene and inviolate. They had literally spoken a world into being, gathering all the nonhuman creatures together to safeguard the last vestiges of magic on Earth in a place they called the Twixt, bound by the rules that all Folk must obey. These were the two who had done everything in their power to protect their people and their magic from human harm.

It was like looking into infinite space and having it stare back.

Joy leaned forward, but her feet refused to move. The soap-bubble barrier that stretched over the length of the doorway bowed and wobbled, rainbow reflections dancing on its surface. This was different from walking into the Bailiwick, to the safe room down the stairs under Graus Claude's tongue—this was an actual door to another world, and to step through it was to leave everything she knew behind.

The King raised his arm. He was the color of earth and

wore a cape of velvet leaves; his voice was warm and rich with hope.

"Come," he beckoned. "Tell us of our people."

Joy squared her shoulders and held her breath as the ward bowed gently to allow her passage. The barrier peeled away with a popping sound, jellyfish-slow. She felt the sudden warmth of the sun on her cheek and the cool, dewy ground under her toes. The air was heavy and humid and sweet on her lips, tasting of lavender and moss and cinnamon.

Joy drank a deep breath. She was in another world.

Ink stood in the doorway, still holding Joy's hand. She smiled back at him, radiant.

The ground cracked open.

Jagged fissures of superheated rock ripped through the grass, bleeding hot lava and billows of steam. A blast hit her full in the face. Joy reeled back. The air became dark and acrid and choked with ash. Liquid stone churned. Grass blackened. Smoke boiled. Joy stumbled forward, each step cracking and shattering beneath her like glass.

There was an inhaled gasp, then silence, then *noise*.

Volume blurred it into a visceral sound—the collective outraged battle cry and the collective thunder of weapons and claws charging full speed down the hill. Joy stepped back, tearing another wound in the earth. A gout of wet fire spewed behind her, orange-hot spatters smoking in the grass. The hillside tilted on a sea of molten rock. Joy pitched forward, using Ink's hand for balance. Winged things crested over the front line, talons bared.

Joy shouted, "Ink!"

His hand fastened over her wrist, his face a mask of terror. "Joy!"

The ground crumbled underneath her. She jumped,

grabbing his biceps, suspended over a glowing chasm. Heat baked her heels. Joy screamed, "Don't let go!"

"I'll not let go," he assured her.

"Don't let go!"

"Never."

He twisted sharply, pulling her up with impossible strength, her body arcing through the air with a familiar feeling of weightlessness before piercing the fine membrane of the doorway and crashing against Ink. His arms wrapped around to catch her as they landed in the Bailiwick's hazy meadow with a punch of breath. They both turned to look back at the army hurtling toward the open door.

Joy opened her mouth to shout and nearly gagged on the taste of limes as Ink snapped open his straight razor and slashed a door through space, whirling them through the flap of nothing hanging in midair.

They reappeared on the edge of the Bailiwick, at the base of the stairway to their own world.

Ink urged her upward. "Go!"

They ran up the stairs in a blur of slapping feet, heavy boots and heavy breathing, racing toward the muted light. Ink flipped his straight razor as Joy cleared the top stair, the back teeth, and the line of red fire as she sprinted out of the Bailiwick—the magical entryway's wards flaring blue as Ink ran close behind her.

They landed on the floor of the Atrium in the Forest wing of the Council Hall.

Joy spun around, gasping. "I formally withdraw from the Bailiwick!"

Graus Claude's jaw closed with agonizing slowness. She pictured the army of lost Folk pushing their way through the door and up his throat. Joy prayed for a speedy trans-formation as the Bailiwick's skin lost its stony pallor, his mouth shrank to merely wide and his eyes changed from cataract-white to their normal icy blue. Reanimated, Graus Claude slumped forward, tired, weak, but looking more like the hunchbacked, four-armed frog she knew. She grabbed one of his elbows.

"Up!" she commanded.

He stumbled to his feet. "Where is the princess?" he murmured, blinking around the greenhouse room. "Where are the King and Queen?"

"Don't talk!" she snapped in panic. "Keep your mouth shut!"

Shocked, he did. She could hear the sharp click of his teeth.

Joy glanced up at the skylights above the treetops, the Atrium's ceiling filled with colorful butterflies and exotic birds spooked by their arrival. There was one way out, into the long hallway flanked by open stairwells, obvious to everyone searching on several floors. She glanced at the shadows between the trees, wondering if Briarhook still lingered there. Her skin crawled. Joy had bribed the giant hedgehog to help rescue the Bailiwick, but the deal hadn't included anything about him not turning them all in afterward. Knowing how much Briarhook hated her, Joy wouldn't be surprised if he'd betrayed them to the Council in order to gain the last piece of his heart.

Joy ground her teeth. *Focus!* She grabbed her scalpel and purse from the floor. Shattering the Amanya spell had let the Folk access their lost memories of their forgotten King and Queen, but now there was an angry mob of Twixt socialites and a deposed Council likely looking for answers or, even more likely, Joy's head on a stick. Invisible Inq was out of action, Joy's brother, Stef, was with his satyr boyfriend,

Dmitri, and she'd have to trust that Filly and Avery and Ys-abel and Kurt would get themselves out.

Right now, the three of them had to escape.

"Ink?" She reached for him.

He flinched away. She dropped her hand. Joy tried to em-pathize—he'd just found his mother, the princess, lost his sister, Inq, freed his monarchs, the King and Queen, and was currently running from a vengeful army who had been trapped for more than a millennium in another dimension. It was enough to spin anyone's head, but they didn't have time for an existential crisis right now.

"Listen, getting to the Atrium was the fallback plan to get Graus Claude out in case anything went wrong," she said. "And ever since we found out that Aniseed made a graftling clone of herself, *everything's* gone wrong!" She dropped her voice, wondering if saying the dryad's name aloud might somehow alert the Forest Folk. "How do we get out?"

"Miss Mal—"

"Not you!" Joy shushed the Bailiwick, who glared at her from beneath his deep postorbital ridge. "How far are we from the East entrance? That's where the car's parked. How far outside the Hill do you need to be before you can slice a door home?" She squeezed her clutch purse full of keys. Indelible Ink looked unfocused, lost. Joy's feet still burned. "Ink?"

He turned to her, blank, all-black eyes drowning.

"I—I'm—" he stammered. He was in shock.

A manicured claw tapped the flagstone path and Joy looked down. Graus Claude had drawn a large *E* in the dirt and pointed over his shoulder. Joy ran to the thick glass windows that warped the light outside. She couldn't see a thing. They could be four feet from the ground or four hundred—it was impossible to tell. Flowering trees and vine-wrapped branches nearly obscured the skylights on this side of the room. Her panicked reflection stared back at her.

There was a rustling in the Atrium. It shivered the hairs on the back of Joy's neck.

The door opened. Everyone spun around.

Filly poked her head in, her ornamental horse mask from the gala still perched on her head like a hat.

"Ah," she said, grinning. "Everyone together now? Good! I'll just hold them off, then."

"Wait!" Joy cried. "How do we get out?"

The Valkyrie shrugged and licked the blue spot under her bottom lip. "Haven't a clue," she said. "This is Forest floor and I only know Air." She flicked the mask's trailing horse-hair mane over her shoulder. "The plan's gone sideways, in case you haven't noticed. I lost Kurt in the hubbub, but that'll serve as cover for your retreat. There's many keen to speak with you, Joy Malone, and double that for our noble toad, so you'd both best be off."

Joy cringed. "But what about you?"

"I don't mind staying—you're missing a beautiful row!" Filly beamed as tumultuous noise gathered behind her, approaching fast. "Must go. Call me when you need me." She raised a fist. "Victory!"

"Victory..." Joy answered, but the door had already shut. Both Ink and Graus Claude stared at her. Joy glowered back. "Okay, I'm thinking!"

There was only one door from the room—one *obvious* door—but Joy couldn't believe there would be only one way out. They were in the Grand Hall Under the Hill, the hub of the Twixt, the central government stronghold of the Folk, and the Folk *always* had a loophole, another way out. She made her way around the perimeter of the Atrium, feeling along the trees, along the glass, tracing the sills with her fingertips. What she wouldn't give for one of Dmitri's glow stick beacons, or, for that matter, the glyph preventing Ink from cutting a door out. If she could find it with her Sight, she would erase it with the scalpel. If she couldn't bend the rules, she'd break them.

There was a great *slam! slam! slam!* as the Atrium door buckled and smashed in. Filly bowled backward, curled around a Minotaur. A scrabble of Folk in ball gowns and feathered masks streamed in after them, pushing and shouting in outrage. Butterflies scattered in haphazard clouds. Kestrel appeared, straining against her leash. She hissed, her long tongue snaking out to taste their scent. The tracker's eyes dilated. Her stiff eyelashes blinked with a scraped-metal *shing*!

Joy flattened against the wall as a group of bird-masked guards rushed the Bailiwick. Graus Claude roared a battle challenge—halfhearted at best, but enough to stall the horde and push them, stumbling, back. He clambered to his feet, propping himself up on his knuckles like some great silverback beast. Filly grabbed the Minotaur's nose ring and yanked down sharply, kneeing him in the face once, twice, then wrenching him sideways, bowling over two fairies with a shout of triumph. Ink skipped out of reach, lithe and limber as a swallow, dancing along the edges of the mob, dodging his way between the trees toward Joy.

She watched the attack with a strange, distant awareness. A tingle crawled up her arches and the backs of her calves, deliciously burning up her thighs, warming her vitals, boiling her blood. Her head felt heavy and she turned her chin to one side, considering the masked faces of those rushing nearer. Her neck cracked. A smile came easily to her lips. The voice in her head—the one that seemed to resonate from deep within the earth, pitched ten times louder and surer than her own—thrummed in her rib cage and echoed in her brain.

THEY CANNOT DESTROY US NOW.

Filly staggered as an antlered man materialized out of the foliage and fastened his arms around her chest. She gave a grunt and smashed the back of her skull into his pointed chin. The horse head mask split, the mane flung wild.

A face appeared in front of Joy, hanging upside-down from a low tree branch.

"Got you!" Hasp hissed, his impossibly long fingers wrapping around her wrists and yanking her arms above her head. The aether sprite laughed from his perch, drawing her face closer to his. His breath smelled of exhaust and malice.

But her feet still touched the ground.

She could feel the tingling afterburn of the world beyond the Bailiwick and beneath that, the tempting whispers of land and stone, rock and soil, metal and dirt and old, old ice. The voice inside her snarled as Joy latched on to Hasp's knuckles and *pulled.*

She felt his hands crack in her palms. He howled a high-pitched scream and let go.

Joy dropped to the ground as giant stick-like creatures snapped their wrists, shooting barbed splinters through the air, slicing birds sideways. Ink torqued his body, evading the shower of darts. Filly twisted, using a Green Man for a shield. Joy drove her arms into the ground, grabbing something sharper than the scalpel, older than stone, hotter than hell; the taste in her mouth was copper and blood.

A wave of darkness fell around her, muffling the cacophonous roar inside her head. A voice hissed at her from under a fluffy shield of white feathers. *Avery,* she thought dimly. *The Tide's courtier and Councilman Sol Leander's spy.*

"Go!" he said. "Go now, Joy Malone!"

The world slowed to a crawl. Avery's voice dulled to a hum and the screams blurred into a distant din. Faces turned comical as lips curled, cheeks stretched, brows furrowed and mouths formed words. Butterflies waved lazily by like water weeds and Ink soared between two trees, suspended midleap, ballet-like and beautiful, his naked blade sweeping in one hand like a scythe. Joy watched another bird explode, its soft blue and pink feathers puffing in a burst of arterial red.

Joy turned her head. Graus Claude extricated himself from his size-thirty shoes, his giant webbed feet unfurling and slapping wetly across the floor. Joy watched in fascinated horror as he drew claws down the seams of his trousers, slicing them lengthwise, freeing long, bowed legs from their tailored confinement. His knees bent outward, exposing striped limbs banded in black. His sharp toes gripped the dirt as the long muscles bunched beneath him.

One arm shot out, grabbing Joy, and clamped her to his chest. A second hand gripped Ink's forearm and yanked him out of his arc. The Bailiwick folded his upper arms over their heads, shielding them under a helm of rubbery flesh. His jowls trembled. His body tensed.

He sprang, leaping hard and fast through the eastern window, shattering the glass with the force of his skull. The crash was deafening. The cold was a slap. The impact was enough to choke out all breath. Joy gagged as they soared upward through a cloud of spliced light and broken glass, the wind whistling in her ears and flattening her hair across her face. Gravity tossed her stomach as they crested and fell, time rushing up to greet them at fast-forward speed.

WHUMPH!

Graus Claude's massive legs absorbed the landing, bobbing them up and down like a spring. Releasing his grip, he dropped Joy and Ink and then staggered, his six limbs trembling, his torn clothes hanging off him like rags. The Bailiwick blinked watery blood from long scratches above his eyes.

"It's been a while..." he muttered, glancing back at the gaping hole in the Hall. His flat frog feet slapped the ground uncertainly. His empty hands shook.

"I guess that answers the question of how it went."

Raina emerged from behind Ilhami's shiny black Lamborghini. Luiz and Ilhami stared past them, up at the broken windows in the Atrium wall. The three *lehman*—Joy's friends and Inq's human lovers—slowly lowered their bottle of champagne and thin glass flutes.

Luiz frowned. "Where's Inq?"

"She's still inside," Joy gasped, peeling her purse from her skin—the beading's imprint would leave an interesting bruise. "She—"

"Tell us later," Raina said. "Now you go." She grabbed her thigh holster and aimed her gun into the air. Ilhami and Luiz popped the trunk and pulled out more guns to follow suit.

"What are you doing?" said Graus Claude, alarmed.

"Providing a distraction," Raina said, shooting six times in quick succession. Thick clouds boiled out of nowhere, coating the underside of the world. "Iron triggers the Hall's defenses," she said. "It's attempting to cloak."

"The Avalon mists," Graus Claude stammered. "Brilliant."

Raina smiled, flipping back her Pantene hair.

"Time to go!" Joy said. She fumbled with the clutch, dug out her keys and punched the fob's blue button. The Ferrari materialized right where she'd left it.

Ilhami cackled. "I *knew* you'd love that car!"

Raina slapped him good-naturedly upside the head. "Circle around in formation, punctuate fire every five, rendezvous at high noon. Go!" The Cabana Boys split up, diving into the mist. Raina waved at Joy before the clouds swallowed her up. "Good luck!"

"Bailiwick!" Ink urged the great frog forward as Folk began pouring out the hole in the Atrium windows, leaping, running and flying through the misty sky Under the Hill. "We must leave."

Graus Claude's head shook with more than its usual palsy quiver. "I cannot."

"Not arguing," Joy said as she popped the locks and flung open the door. "Get in."

The Bailiwick sighed. His voice a thin baritone compared to his normal rumbling bass as he spoke carefully through clamped shark's teeth.

"I cannot *fit*, Miss Malone."

Joy groaned. He was right—the Ferrari couldn't accommodate the massive, four-armed frog. She fell into the driver's seat and wrenched at the seat belt, swearing and trying to think. Ink dropped into the seat beside her and cracked the windows.

"Get on," he called out as something ricocheted off the hood.

Graus Claude leaped, belly flopping onto the roof and splaying across the back windshield. Four sets of claws sank into the plastic molding through the partially opened windows and his toes gripped the trim above the back wheels. A thin trickle of blood dripped down the windshield.

"Go!" ordered Graus Claude.

Joy floored it. The wheels spun beneath her. Zero to sixty—*gone*.

She shifted quickly, flying through three gears, the heavy *chunk-thunk* almost lost in the roar of the wind by her ears.

A howl chased them just behind the exhaust. Joy didn't bother checking the mirror; she pressed her foot firmly to the floor. Graus Claude's claws tightened. His nails popped through the metal. She winced and gritted her teeth. Enrique would never forgive her for wrecking his car. Then she remembered—Enrique was dead. Inq was unconscious. Kurt and Filly and Stef were back at the gala. Ink was in the passenger seat, and Graus Claude was on the roof.

"I imagine that's not the way a traditional Welcome Gala is supposed to go?" Joy's voice, high and hysterical, sounded alien to her ears.

Ink glanced at her as if weighing her sanity against his. He gripped the seat cushion as if unwilling to let go.

Joy caught a glimpse of movement in the rearview mirror—a lot of movements, too many to count. "They're coming after us," she said, turning deeper into the mists. "I'm starting to lose track of exactly who wants us dead."

"The Tide, Hasp, Briarhook," Ink began. "Sol Leander, possibly the Council, probably the whole of the Twixt now that you've broken the Amanya spell and they've realized that you've kidnapped the only means to reach their King and Queen..."

"Yes. Thank you. Very helpful." Joy interrupted him, slamming into fifth gear. A red dragon curled the mists under the mighty beats of his wings. It seemed to spy her through the mirror, its reptilian eyes glinting. A chill ripped down her spine. She yanked the car to the right, plunging them into the frosty fog. Silence enveloped them as they sped through the soft blanket of white. Only the car's engine purred.

"I need a little distance," she said more to herself than Ink. She remembered that terrifying ride with Enrique after they'd rescued Ilhami from Ladybird's drug den. This was worse. She thought about the tiny switch that lay just under the dashboard lights. She didn't know what it would do to the Bailiwick clinging to the roof of the car, but it was the only way they were getting out from Under the Hill.

"Ink," Joy said to the dashboard. She didn't dare take her eyes off the lack of road. The eerie fog parted around them like ghosts. "I need you to flip the switch next to my knee when I say so." She tried to keep the squeezing panic out of her voice, but she couldn't pry her death grip off the steering wheel. She could all but feel the dragon breathing down her neck. Out of the corner of her eye, she saw the tips of Ink's hair barely move as he shook his head. His hands stayed locked. He'd stiffened, immobile and silent.

"Ink, you have to hit the slip drive!"

Ink didn't move.

The fog parted. Pointed teeth filled her rearview mirror.

"Ink!" she cried. *"Hit it!"*

His hand darted forward and flipped the switch. The indicator light blinked. The back of the car ignited with a roar.

Joy's shoulders tensed. Her ears popped. The windows went dark, then everything went white.

TWO

JOY SCREAMED AS THEY SWERVED INTO THE PARKING lot of her apartment complex. Her legs locked as she hit the brakes, the back of her head slamming into the headrest and turf flying into the windshield as the car's buffer field engaged, bouncing them off the nearest Honda and spiraling to a stop. The engine rumbled threateningly.

"Out!" Joy barked. She hit the cloaking shield. "Off!"

There was a creaking snap as Graus Claude pried his claws out of the molding, leaving deep, pointed gouges in the padding and frame. He groaned from where he appeared to be hovering several feet above the ground, flattened against the roof of the now-invisible car. Joy stumbled onto the asphalt, knees shaking, still wondering what was real.

There was a sound in the bushes.

Joy froze.

Ink appeared beside her, grabbing hold of the Bailiwick's elbow and flicking his straight razor free.

"Come," he said.

Ink grabbed Joy's hand. The Bailiwick grunted. There was a flash of spliced light, the scent of limes, and the three of them appeared inside the condo's foyer, the house alarm set, the wards sparking gold and Joy's head spinning.

Ink marched quickly around the kitchen, checking the

wards he had placed to keep Joy safe inside her home. His face was stern, gaze piercing, tense and intense.

"Ink?" Joy tried to follow, but she felt dizzy, her thoughts whirling. "Graus Claude?"

The Bailiwick sagged against the closet door. His glistening frog's feet were red and weeping, blisters standing out against the thin webbing between his swollen toes. Joy ran to grab towels as the giant amphibian sat heavily on the floor, half in the foyer, half in the kitchen. Her brain took quick inventory: it was barely Monday morning, Stef was supposed to be driving to U Penn, Dad was visiting his girlfriend, Shelley, and therefore they were alone in the house, protected by Ink's wards. Safe, for now.

She hoped that her brother was somewhere safe, too.

She dropped the pile of towels and knelt before the Bailiwick, wrapping his feet gently in layers of fluffy cotton. He'd gone from pale to ashen.

"Water," he croaked through cracked lips. Joy ran to the fridge and shoved a tall glass under the spigot, filling it with water. She filled another glass with ice.

Graus Claude drained the first in a shot and grimaced, but healthy patches of olive gray bloomed on his cheeks. He opened his hands for another three glasses. Joy kept filling them, exchanging the empties, and tried not to think about the smears of blood on the floor.

He drank six more glasses of water in quick succession, two of his arms alternating glasses and the other two hands fastening towels over his feet. Joy couldn't believe he'd ever squashed them into human-shaped shoes. No wonder he limped.

"Keep drinking," Joy said. "You shouldn't talk."

He swallowed. "Miss Malone, I assure you that if the King and Queen were to make their appearance, the strength of my jaw would do little to stop them. I can only assume from our current circumstances that they are not yet able to make their Return." He rubbed his jaw near the crux of his eardrum. "Therefore, my being mute serves no overt purpose and there is much that needs to be said."

Ink entered the kitchen, the claw-toed boots of his gala costume clicking against the tile. There was no smile in his black, fathomless eyes. He stalked like a predator and Joy felt like prey.

"Master Ink," Graus Claude rumbled. "I trust the wards are in place?"

"Yes, Bailiwick," Ink said. He was as tense as a bowstring, nearly quivering in place.

"Very well, then," the noble toad said, attempting to gain his feet and wincing with the effort. "I would ask that you return me to my domicile so I might make necessary arrangements. I shudder to imagine what things have been like since my incarceration, not to mention after tonight's festivities." He cast a glance at Joy. "As your mentor, I feel that I ought to scold you for your actions, Miss Malone—from the debacle of your Welcome Gala to aiding and abetting a known prisoner of the Court." He sighed and his demeanor relaxed around the pain. "However, I find myself quite at a loss to do so and confess that I am rather proud of your efforts on both of our behalves. Subtlety was never your strong suit and humility was never mine." His wide head dipped perceptively. "I owe you many thanks, Joy Malone." He repeated the gesture to his associate. "And to you as well, Master Ink."

Joy went to stand next to Ink, but he shrugged away, cutting off her touch. She hesitated, hurt and confused, but he purposefully ignored her as he addressed Graus Claude.

"Then permit me to ask a boon of you," Ink said with a tightly added, "sir."

Graus Claude slowed his ministrations. His browridge quirked. "Indeed?"

"You must swear upon your honor and the honor of the King and Queen that you will not harm Joy Malone in any way. You will neither hinder or hamper her efforts nor will you aid any other party in their intent to do her harm, by word or by deed, else your True Name be forfeit," Ink said all at once. "Do you so swear?"

Joy and the Bailiwick both gaped at him.

"What—?"

"Master Ink," Graus Claude said, his voice punctuated with his usual ire. "Why would you suspect that I would do anything that would necessitate such a terrible oath?"

Ink remained resolute, as solid as a wall. "That was not a 'yes.'"

The great frog's face darkened to a steely mottled gray. "Your ears appear to be in fine working order, although your sense of humor—not to mention propriety—may have suffered since our last meeting," he replied. Joy might have imagined a twitch by Ink's eye at the rebuke. She remembered his warning when she first met the Bailiwick: *Humor me. Respect him. Always.* Joy shook her head, wondering what Ink was doing.

"You took an oath," Ink said by way of explanation.

Graus Claude lifted his head, the jowls at his throat stretching around his collar. "I have taken a number of oaths," he said. "To which are you referring?"

"First this one," Ink said fervently. "To me. Do you so swear?"

"I cannot—"

"You *must*," Ink insisted, his fingers curled into fists. "I will answer your questions when you grant me my boon. Or is your blind loyalty stronger than your word?" Ink was nearly shaking, his voice cut like a blade. "Swear it."

Graus Claude's gaze slid between Ink and Joy through shaded eyes. "I do so swear." The Bailiwick sniffed. Ink relaxed an inch, if that. "Now," he said icily. "Which oath have I now countermanded by agreeing to this tidy charade?"

Ink recited, "'*Sampo ei da Counsallierai emantanti der dictuunuim, es payanciim, es emonim der teriminatuum ou da cloite sei grachenscuta pandeimaenous delvanessi.*'"

Graus Claude's expressive glower went slack. Veins pulsed along his eardrums as his teeth ground together with the sound of scraping saws. His surprise bloomed into a deep, red outrage.

"YOU—!" he roared, forcing Joy to step back. The blood rushed from his face and colored the towels with spots of red. "That *CANNOT*—!" All four hands grasped the air, fisting open and closed in impotent fury. His massive head swung back and forth. "It is simply imp—" The words gagged him. He swallowed gulps of fury. Joy knew what was happening—he could not say that which he knew was untrue. She touched the wall behind her cautiously, carefully, making no sudden moves.

His breathing slowly settled into a low, bellows thrum. His bloodshot gaze flicked between Joy and Ink. His voice was a deep accusation, "You are certain of this?"

Ink nodded. Joy barely moved. She had no idea what was going on, but it didn't sound good.

Graus Claude leaned back on his haunches and crashed to the floor, his legs splayed beneath him.

"By the Swells..." Graus Claude murmured, discreetly translated by the *eelet* in Joy's ear. Her strange gift from the Siren's widower, Dennis Thomas, had proven to be more than just a pretty shell—the tiny creature inside it could translate Water Folk Tongue into English. She'd learned quite a few of the Bailiwick's favorite curses.

Joy reached for Ink again, but he flipped the straight razor like a shield between them. She stopped, stunned. The silver chain swung gently at his hip like a warning.

"Ink—?"

"Don't!" Ink snapped. "Do not come near me. Do not..." His anger cooled as his arms sagged. His voice softened. "Do not come closer. Please."

Tears welled in her eyes. The Tide's betrayal, the gala, their harrowing escape—something had happened to Ink and she'd missed it. He looked torn, pained, ready to bolt. Joy wanted to touch him but feared his reaction.

She spread empty hands. "Ink, please—"

"I cannot stay here," Ink said.

Graus Claude rumbled. "Of course. Mistress Inq is missing. I quite under—"

"I cannot stay," he said again without lifting his eyes. He swept a line of fire through the air, peeling back a flap of nothing at all. "I have no oath to bind me," he said to Joy. "And you have foresworn all armor." He turned and stepped one foot through the breach. "Bailiwick," he murmured. "You are bound by your word, your claim and your Name."

The frog inclined his head. "I have foresworn it."

"Wait! No! Ink!" Joy cried. *"Stop!"*

He didn't turn, but paused on the edge of the void, the lip of this world flapping in a foreign breeze. His crisp, clear voice slipped over his shoulder. "Find the loophole, Joy," he whispered. "Do it soon."

The door zipped closed behind him.

Joy stumbled forward, touching empty air. Hot tears dripped off her cheeks.

"He can't—he can't just *le*—!" She gagged on the word *leave*. He could and had. She desperately fumbled to hold on to their last words like a frayed thread. She spun on Graus Claude. "What's going on? Why did he—?" She could barely put words to the look on Ink's face. She'd never seen him look at her that way—not when he'd caught her in an act of betrayal, not when she'd stood between him and revenge. He'd been holding himself back, warring with himself, warding her off for safety's sake, but she wasn't sure whom he'd been trying to protect: her or him. He'd left her without an explanation, leaving behind only riddles and an injured frog. Anger obliterated her hurt confusion and she slapped her hand against the counter. Hard. "Who does he think he is?"

The Bailiwick sighed. "Your enemy."

THREE

JOY FROWNED AT THE HUNCHED PILE OF CLOTHES and towels and bloody frog.

"Ink is not my enemy." She didn't know much, but she knew that better than she knew her own missing heartbeat.

Graus Claude heaved himself up on swaddled feet. "Perhaps it is more accurate to say that he believes you are *his* enemy," he amended. "And not just his enemy, but all of the Twixt's."

"*What?* Why?" Joy demanded, following the Bailiwick as he squeezed into the bathroom and fiddled with the taps. "Is it because I'm the most dangerous human—or half human— in the world? Because I was born with the Sight? Because he gave me his scalpel? Because I can erase Folk marks?" Her voice rose above the splashing water. "We know all that already! It's why I accepted a *signatura* to protect my True Name—to take my place and be part of your world, to prove that I'm no danger. It's why I agreed to join the Twixt!"

Graus Claude turned off the water and patted his hands dry as his upper two hands rubbed the hand towel over his brow. He ignored the mirror. It ignored him back, showing no evidence of a giant frog in its reflection.

"There may have been some misinterpretations concerning your person that had been previously unimagined or unnoticed, and have therefore gone unaddressed," he said.

"As your sponsor, the fault is mine, although I can honestly say that the possibility was quite beyond my capacity to theorize or even imagine, given the circumstances." His icy blue gaze regarded her uncomfortably, his four hands wringing the hand towels into ropes. "In fact, I must confess that without the oath that Master Ink required of me, I would find myself sharing his conflicted loyalties." He folded the towels into squares and set them down in a neat stack. "But you can rest assured that you have nothing to fear from me, Miss Malone, as he has ensured that you have at least one ally, one neutral party, until we can sort out this sordid affair."

Joy exhaled slowly. "I have no idea what you're talking about and I am *really* getting tired of it."

The Bailiwick sniffed through flat nostrils. "Tired? Indeed, I imagine you are." He glanced out the window at the paling blue sky. "It must be only hours until dawn. It has been a long night. A *very* long night..." The Bailiwick plucked at his ruined clothes. "Might I request that we sit down for the remainder of this conversation? I find myself quite exhausted by the evening's events."

She knew—*knew*, mind you—that he was manipulating her by using the proper rules of etiquette, decorum and polite society that he'd drummed into her head during their tutoring sessions in order to prepare her for the gala, but she still felt guilty for badgering him when he was clearly in pain. Joy bowed slightly and led him into the hall in silence.

The Bailiwick might be invisible, but even with Dad gone, she didn't feel comfortable sitting out in the open. She pushed open the door to Stef's room and stepped aside to allow Graus Claude to enter. After contorting himself gently through the door frame, he ambled into the bedroom on toweled feet and eased himself onto the bed. The springs groaned in protest. He sighed in relief.

"Can I get you anything?" she asked.

He leaned back. "No, thank you, I think I can—"

"Good," Joy said, cutting him off and shutting the door. "Explain."

The Bailiwick threw her a rueful glare, but it was harder to wield an aura of commanding authority while sitting on her brother's bed.

"Very well," he said. "You might as well make yourself comfortable. It is likely the last time you will be able to do so again."

Joy grabbed the desk chair and dragged it closer. "That sounds ominous."

Graus Claude nodded. "It is." As she settled into her seat, he lifted his legs into an odd sort of lotus position, pillowing his bandaged feet beneath him, his knees bent behind. He rocked forward, putting the bulk of his weight on his belly. "Master Ink was good to remind me of my oaths, both to you, as your sponsor, as well as those mandated by the King and Queen as a member of the Council." He paused. "As you know, there is no oath that requires loyalty to the monarchy—it is part of the rules they spoke into being, the very words that created the Twixt."

"Yes." This was nothing new. So why did Graus Claude look so serious/uncomfortable/afraid? His gaze didn't look so much at her as through her, as if he was avoiding direct eye contact, speaking to her from a great distance.

"The oaths we take when we swear allegiance to the Council are designed to align us to the safekeeping of our world." Graus Claude hunched farther into his squat. "Do you know what we say about the origins of the Twixt? Even without the memory of the King and Queen who spoke the world into being, we somehow managed to remember enough to know that the Twixt was a place of safety, of rules and order cleaved from the Elemental Wild." Joy nodded. She'd heard the phrase before. The Bailiwick looked at her expectantly. She raised her eyebrows. He demurred. "It is an apt description, if not expressly clear when employing proper nouns."

Joy frowned. He'd lost her. "I thought 'Elemental Wild' meant that the Twixt was made back when Earth was form-ing, full of volcanoes and glaciers and stuff—mountains growing, oceans receding, dinosaurs dying and all that."

Graus Claude was surprised enough to chuckle. "The Twixt is hardly *that* old," he said. "Remember, humans and Folk used to share this world and there was a peace between us, reflected in your stories—we shared magic and technol-ogy, knowledge and medicine, land, children..." He sighed. Joy knew there had not been children born to the Folk for nearly a thousand years. "There was a time when there were alliances and oaths and bonds between us, before our True Names were used to force us into servitude and retaliations became swift and dark and dire. That is when myths were born. The brightest daydreams became the darkest fairy tales, horrors whispered around the fire. Those were the dark times, when there was war between us." He shook his head. "No, that is not when the Twixt was made. It was made when the King and Queen decided to create order, rules to govern the land and our people in order to protect both hu-mans and non—before we tore the world apart. Those who agreed to obey these laws became the Folk," he said. "And those who rejected order, preferring chaos and the battle of wills, they were called Elementals and their part of the world was called the Wild."

Joy tried to wrap her brain around this new information. She swallowed before speaking. "So they were Folk?" she asked. "Wild Folk. Folk without rules?"

"In a sense. Yet they were like another thing entirely—older, primal, powerful and proud, with deep ties to the physical world, preserving the shape of what's real. From them, we took our courtly names: Earth, Air, Fire, Water, Aether...you are familiar with these." His gaze slipped to the window where morning painted the clouds late-summer colors, pink and purple and bronze. "They were the first ones, crafty and cruel. They did not seek to ally with humans nor did they have any interest in peace. On the contrary, they enjoyed sowing chaos and encouraging wrath among mortal creatures." He sighed again, sounding tired. "The Old Ways were forged in that time when life was lawless, swift and absolute, when mischief presaged violence and violent ends. The Elementals were eager to stoke the fires of dissent and sought no compromise. They would not bend to the rules." He undid a button at his collar, which was equivalent to the noble toad collapsing into an inelegant heap. "They were prepared to undo everything forged between our peoples, everything the King and Queen hoped would protect future generations on both sides from folly and death. But the Elementals were unapologetic, rigid, unwilling to be tethered by logic or laws." He paused. "Once the King and Queen declared themselves sovereigns, the Elementals were deemed enemies of both human and Folk."

He was speaking in excuses, platitudes. Joy felt nauseous. "What happened?"

The Bailiwick lifted his eyes to hers. "They were hunted down. Destroyed. Rooted out for the good of us all." He rumbled like a whisper of distant thunder. "It brought about the Age of Man. The Twixt was forged in their blood and on their bones."

Joy shuddered. *Genocide.* Her voice was very small, her fingers twisted into white knots. "I thought the Folk didn't kill one another." The words fell like bricks between them— the beginnings of a wall.

"They were not Folk. They were *Elementals*," he mumbled gruffly. His fingers squeezed his shins and the points of his knees. "We needed peace. We needed rules to govern and protect. We needed to create order out of chaos if any of us were to survive. That is why Master Ink reminded me of my Council oath—not simply to serve the Folk of the Twixt but, specifically, to stand against the 'Elemental Wild,' to protect our world from the threat of Elementals and the chaos they sowed in their wake." He shook his head again. "I did not think they meant it *literally*—it was a figure of speech, an old saying left over from the days of my mentor Iron-shod and his kin."

"Sort of like the Imminent Return?" she guessed.

"Yes," Graus Claude said. "That traditional salutation survived Aniseed's spell of forgetting, but we were ignorant of its deeper meaning until you broke the chandelier in the Grand Ballroom, releasing our collective memories of the King and Queen. We had forgotten about the promised Return of our people from their refuge beyond this world." The Bailiwick looked heavier, grim. "We forgot that they were waiting for the Council to send word that peace had been restored and to open the door." He touched a palm to his belly. "Centuries of waiting, wondering what had happened to the world they'd left behind, their families and friends... I cannot imagine the suffering I caused."

Joy wanted to remind him that it was Aniseed who had tricked him into casting the Amanya spell, erasing the memories of everyone in the Twixt so that she could lead her coup against the Council, violating the Folk's unswerving loyalty...but she couldn't. It was true—Graus Claude was the one who'd cast the spell for his lover, Aniseed, not knowing of her planned betrayal. Joy twisted her fingers together in silence.

He looked at her strangely. "But you saw it, didn't you?" he asked with a spark of hope. "The world beyond the Bailiwick?"

"Yes."

"And you opened the door?"

"Yes."

He leaned forward, his voice low. "Did you see them?"

Joy flushed, uncomfortable with the memory. "Y-yes."

His eyes were barely slits of sapphire light. "Tell me."

She did, and the story came spilling out as if she could explain away everything that had happened. "After I removed Aniseed's *signatura*, I used the scalpel to cut through the other sigils that locked the door..." Joy trailed off, uncertain how Graus Claude would react to her erasing the Council's sacred safeguards, but he didn't comment. "The princess ran through as soon as the door was open. And there was an army camped on the hills." She knotted her fingers in her shirt. "The King and Queen saw us—Ink and I—in the doorway. They said—" She faltered, but they were not words that she would ever forget. "They said, *'Behold the Destroyer of Worlds.'*"

Graus Claude sat up, his spine pressed against the wall. He blinked twice. "I admit that does not sound like the most fortuitous of greetings," he said slowly. "What happened then?"

"They said to come closer," she tried to explain. "I didn't want to, but I—"

"You obeyed," he said. "You could not help but obey. They are our monarchs, after all. Those are the rules." He tilted his head at her expression, which felt oddly lopsided on her face. "And yet...?"

"I don't know. I stepped through the doorway," she said. "And the ground *cracked*." Joy could feel the give of the earth under her toes, the sudden lurch of lost balance and dread. "It split right under my foot. Ink grabbed me and pulled me back."

The Bailiwick stayed silent for four long breaths. "And then?"

"The army charged," she said. "We ran."

He folded two sets of arms. "A wise course of action."

"And you know the rest," Joy said, shoulders slumping. "The door is open, the Folk remember, but the King and Queen have not Returned. Now Ink is upset, the Council's pissed off and you're giving me a history lesson in my brother's bedroom."

"Yes, well..." Graus Claude had the grace to look uncomfortable, shifting his towel-wrapped toes against the mattress. "Circumstances are hardly ideal, but I have graver concerns." His gaze slid sideways. "Do you know what that place was beyond the door, those verdant fields and succulent mists under a milk-and-honey summer sky?" Joy shook her head. The Bailiwick hung his. "You were in Faeland, Miss Malone."

"Fairyland?" Joy said. "I thought that didn't exist."

"Not Fairyland like some children's tale," he snapped. "*Fae*land. Where all Folk eventually make their Imminent Return."

Joy frowned. "What? Like Heaven?"

"Heaven is a human concept," Graus Claude said mildly. "And—who knows?—perhaps it is a human reality. However, none who cross those pearly gates ever return to confirm or deny its existence, yet all the Folk know that they have a place in Faeland when all is said and done." He turned his massive head with a palsied shiver. "Immortality is a concept that far exceeds our physical firmaments."

Joy's limbs went numb. "You mean... I was in *Folk Heaven*?"

"It's not as if we have worlds within worlds at our fingertips, Miss Malone," the Bailiwick said. "There were few options available to the King and Queen in order to avoid human persecution and, given no human can cross into the afterworld, asylum in Faeland was the logical recourse." He sounded matter-of-fact. "This is our world as well, and we have access to our afterlife just as you have with yours, theoretically speaking, although there is no magic there save that of the word of the King and Queen."

Joy squeezed the back of the chair like a shield between them as she digested the news. "Your King and Queen escaped this world with the majority of your people and took them to *Heaven*?" Her voice broke a little on the sacrilegious notion. "You mean to say there's a doorway to the Folk's afterlife *inside your body*?" Her thoughts were jumbled and fractured, cracking against themselves. "But...they're in *Heaven*! Why would they ever come back here?"

The Bailiwick looked disappointed. "We gave our word to protect this world's magic and honor the bonds to those whom we owed allegiance," he said. "We, as a people, shall always keep our word and our integrity as well as the magic of this world intact. Always."

This was clearly an absolute. Joy nodded dumbly. The breath lodged in her chest came out with a whoosh. "Well..." Her sentence dissolved into silence. She tried again. "Wow."

"Indeed," Graus Claude said. "So you understand the gravity of our predicament and Master Ink's conundrum?"

Joy tried to gather the threads together, but the pattern still eluded her. "Um, no." She loosened her death grip from the chair back. "I mean, I get that I probably shouldn't have stepped into Faeland, but I have no idea why Ink would be more freaked out than I was after what happened, and what any of that has to do with wild Elementals..."

The Bailiwick rested his head in two of his hands, the other two smoothing the edges of the towels with exaggerated calm. "Miss Malone, it is difficult to comprehend how you can be so adept at maneuvering through many of our subtlest societal niceties and yet be so grossly inept at grasping our most obvious taboos. Have you failed to understand anything I have labored to teach you?" He lifted his head and spoke through shark's teeth. "You stepped into the Folk's most sacred territory and it physically *rejected* you. The King and Queen themselves named you the Destroyer of Worlds." He struggled to keep his composure, his face flushing olive gray with the effort. "I suspect that you, Joy Malone, are descended from Elementals—the sworn enemy of all the peoples of our world."

She stared at him, dumbstruck.

"But—no," Joy said slowly. "I'm one of the Folk. You said so yourself!"

"Yes, well, while it is true that you were obviously not entirely human, what other conclusion could I have drawn?" Graus Claude said in his defense. "The Elementals were purged from this world aeons ago, and no one would have suspected they would interbreed with humans. They quite despised your lot, save as base amusement." He snorted. "If you think the Folk can be cruel, you cannot fathom the depths of the Elementals' depravity." One low eye ridge quirked. "Then again, perhaps we can." He shook his shoulders as if ridding them of a chill. "If your lineage originates from one of the most primal sources of magic...it might explain much." He leaned back on his haunches. His tone grew professorial. "It would account for your heritage going unremarked in our annals, as well as your latent magics coming to bear once you came in contact with the Twixt. It might also explain the Sight itself—the ability to see those in the Twixt would be an advantageous inherent defense against the Folk. That might also cause your proto-*signatura* to be misshapen or malformed since an Elemental would never accept the yoke of the rules that bind us..." His eyes grew wide. "By the Swells, an Elemental taking on a True Name, bound by oath to the King and Queen?" He gaped. "It's unheard of!"

"So I *am* one of the Folk," Joy said. "I swore my oath and sacrificed my armor for my True Name. Our word binds us to the rules, right? I am one of you!"

"Yes! No. That is—no!" Graus Claude squeezed his hands into fists. "It is imposs—" But he couldn't finish the sentence, because he knew it wasn't true. He gave a long-suffering sigh that ended in an almost smile. Almost. "You never cease to amaze me, Miss Malone." He adjusted himself on the mattress. "However, this latest riddle is not a passing game for intellects—it is likely to get you killed."

"Why?" Joy said. "What did I do?" She refrained from adding, *now?*

The Bailiwick stretched his spine, eliciting deep pops and cracks. He exhaled tightly. "It is not what you did or did not do," he said. "It is your *ancestry*. It is what you *are*. The very nature of your being flies in the face of the Accords, the Edicts and the rules that shaped our world. No wonder that the King and Queen did not come with you!" he murmured. "The Elementals represent our baser instincts, the primordial chaos from which we evolved, and yet we needed to be rid of them in order to leave that world of anarchy and destruction behind, to forge a new path within the human world, one of culture and compromise and a commitment to live in peace. The Elementals are no more..." Graus Claude gestured toward her with a genteel dance of many hands. "Theoretically speaking."

Joy crossed her arms protectively over her chest. "That means you could be wrong, theoretically speaking."

"Indeed," Graus Claude agreed. "And yet here you are, against all odds and precedence, cloaked in half humanity and bearing a True Name." He shook his head ruefully. "Whatever the truth of it, I can feel My Lady's hands upon both our backs." The Bailiwick straightened both pairs of shoulders. He was known as Fortune's Favorite—his auspice was luck. "May we be guided toward the light that presages a new dawn and not, as I fear, an oncoming train."

He threaded his hands together and cleared his throat. "Now then, let us suppose Master Ink is correct and that you are a descendant of Elementals. Perhaps all those with the Sight could, in fact, trace their lineage back to those primal creatures. Well, what then? It might explain our long-standing traditions to eliminate those with the Sight, if not out of fear of human interference, then out of an instinctual sense of self-preservation against our ancient foes. Then, also, such a rationale might explain why those such as Sol Leander would not lay claim on those with the Sight who had been victims of an unprovoked attack, regardless of its outcome. He might not be compelled to claim them nor acknowledge their qualification." He raised his chin. "Hmm. Interesting. For no one would claim an Elemental under their auspice—they would have to stand and protect them under their Name." He snorted. "Ridiculous! Preposterous! No one would agree to give succor under our laws to those who refuse to obey them." He eyed her again sharply. "Grimson would be quite put out."

Joy rubbed her shoulder, the spot where she'd been marked. "I've never met him." Inq had marked Joy as a Scribe in Grimson's stead when she'd erased the Red Knight out of existence.

"Pray you never do," Graus Claude said. "He is a humorless sort behind that black cowl and scythe."

Joy wondered if the Bailiwick was joking. "So...that disproves it, right?" she said. "Grimson would never have claimed me if I were an Elemental."

Graus Claude sniffed. "I would never presume to guess another's motives, but perhaps that is why Grimson accepted this as his auspice, marking those who murder one of the Twixt, for the Elementals would have surely qualified and the mark might have served as a warning to the Folk. A Grimson's mark does not so much brand those who are under his protection as those who are considered criminal. Interesting."

"Fantastic," Joy said, getting up from the chair. She wrung her fingers around a twist of leotard. "Well, I don't see why it matters what type of Folk I'm descended from or what any of that has to do with Ink."

"The Elementals are not Folk, Miss Malone," Graus Claude said patiently. "They are two entirely different things—"

She stopped her pacing. "How?"

The Bailiwick's eyes darkened from icy blue to gray. "They were barely more than animals, Miss Malone. Lawless, ruthless creatures who lived to destroy."

Joy thought about their escape from the rampaging mobs of costumed Folk Under the Hill. "Doesn't sound so different to me."

"Miss Malone—"

Joy crossed her arms. "Well, that doesn't make them a different species."

"Neither does the color of skin, but human history has long claimed otherwise," he said with deep rebuke. "But if you are indeed an Elemental changeling, then the change must be stopped."

"It can be *stopped*?" Joy said incredulously. "But that's what I've been *trying* to do since you first told me about being a changeling! You said it couldn't be done!"

"Stymied, then. Repressed." Graus Claude's gaze slid aside. "You must *not* be permitted to become an Elemental!"

Joy was way ahead of him. She had planned to rescue the princess, return the King and Queen and then ask them for a boon as reward—namely to stop the change and stay human or, at least, half human. Being an immortal enemy of the Twixt made that less likely. She bit back her own bubbling anxiety. "Okay. How?"

"I am not certain," he said. "Although I know it can be done." He slapped his hands against his knees in a chord of finality. "I will need access to my not-inconsiderable resources before I can sufficiently answer that question." He coughed politely into one fist. "And, first, we will need some confirmation of fact."

"What does that mean?" Joy asked.

"It means—" Graus Claude sighed as if loathe to admit defeat "—that such mysteries lie beyond my ken and that you will have to seek out answers from one who presides over the appropriate domain. You are a claimant, after all, fairly acknowledged, whose favor was undeniably witnessed by hundreds of Folk at the gala—"

Joy knew he was babbling. "Graus Claude?"

"Maia," he said abruptly. "You must go ask Maia."

"Maia? The Council's High Earth Seat? The head of the Court of Earth? The one who's in a private game of one-upmanship with you?" Joy pressed down on each of her fingers. "The one who claimed me at the Naming? The one whose jeweled hair comb I destroyed? *That* Maia?" she squeaked. "She'll kill me!"

"Not if you manage to swear her to the oath to which Master Ink bound me," the Bailiwick muttered. "You are still of Earth, acknowledged and witnessed, and therefore she should abide by House rules and grant you sanctuary. She knows more about Elementals than I, being one of the original members of the King and Queen's Council." He straightened his spine and glanced around the room. "The trick will be in getting you there."

Joy fidgeted. While she did not like the idea of seeking out Maia, who would no doubt be seeking *her* along with the Head of the Council, the dragon, Bùxiǔ de Zhēnzhū, she liked the idea of leaving the warded condo even less. "Don't you think I should have Ink come with me?"

"No," Graus Claude said flatly. "As far as Master Ink is concerned, you are to remain here, with me, under his own protections until we can find a solution to your...predicament." The Bailiwick fiddled with his buttons as he considered the rest of the room. "You know that the primary role of the Scribes is to be a buffer between the Folk and any undue risk, namely humans, who—at the time of their making—represented the greatest threat to our peoples' safety. But it was understood that the Scribes were to safeguard us against *all* enemies, including our first enemy, those of the Wild. It was written into his being, his body, blood and blades." Graus Claude turned his great head to one side. "I imagine that Master Ink is struggling with a conflagration of duty and emotion, of instinct and the heart." He caught her expression and dropped his voice. "Have pity, Miss Malone. Master Ink had enough control to withhold his suspicions long enough to place you here, in my keeping, but I fear he cannot disobey his basic function—to protect those in the Twixt, which, in this case, might again include the likes of you." Joy hugged herself miserably. The great frog attempted to soothe her distress. "He had the strength to resist blinding you at first Sight, did he not? By his own assertion, he has chosen to interpret his wards as both protecting you from the Twixt as well as protecting the Twixt from you until we can find an interpretation that will suit the rules enough to forgo his having to kill you."

"Great! So I'm safe as long as I stay here, but now you want me to go?" Joy said with an angry, hysterical tremble.

"To remain here is to remain caged," Graus Claude said. Having only recently escaped from his imprisonment, the Bailiwick was uniquely qualified to speak with authority on the subject. Joy bit the inside of her cheek, face flushed. "I sympathize with your distress, yet you fail to appreciate what your paramour has done for you—no one else in the Twixt suspects your true nature, and he has bound me by my oath. Otherwise, be assured, I would feel obligated to kill you myself, *which I shall not,*" he hastened to add at Joy's look of horror. "I understand all too well that circumstances concerning your person are hardly ever what they seem and that, as you have noted on previous occasions, you often embody a rather exceptional exception to the rules." He pressed sincerity into his words. "I have set aside many luxuries and amenities in my time in order to retain my personal integrity. To shelter you is to damn myself utterly, but look—" he glanced around at the walls of Stef's bedroom "—it is you who have given me shelter, as well as my freedom, both from the spell of forgetting as well as the Council's justice Under the Hill." He raised a single manicured claw. "Therefore, no matter what else may be said, you have proven yourself a trusted friend and that fact, more than anything, countermands any theoretical debate." He lowered his hands to rest in his lap, a Zen Buddha on a lotus of cotton towels. "I have never met an Elemental, so I must admit that my knowledge is based on hearsay and second-hand myth, but I know *you*, perhaps better than almost anyone else in my world. I ask that you trust me, as you once asked me to trust you." He paused, his speech closing with finality. "I will help you, Joy Malone."

She ran up and hugged him, collapsing against his squashy body, and his many arms wrapped around her like an afghan. "Thank you," she whispered. He sighed a bass rumble in his throat and gave an *oof* of effort as she let go.

Joy winced. "You're hurt."

"I am well aware of it," he muttered, releasing her slowly with each of his hands.

"But how can I convince Maia when I can't convince Ink?" Joy said, looking at the lightening sky. "And I can't leave you here. What about Stef? My Dad—?"

"Calm yourself," the Bailiwick said. "You know your father's whereabouts, and your brother is in the company of the satyr lad. Both your family and your friends are still protected under the Edict as long as no one else discovers what we suspect. Your secret must remain safe."

Joy avoided looking at him as she thought, *Which one?* Joy had a number of secrets that would likely get her killed. Graus Claude knew at least two of them, but there was still one more that he did not—*the Red Knight*—and Joy doubted that he'd still be helping her if he knew that she could erase Folk out of existence. She was the Twixt's worst nightmare, the Tide's proof of human evil.

"As for Mistress Inq," the Bailiwick continued, "she will remain incapacitated for some time, given what we know of Master Ink, and he will wisely be avoiding you until we come up with a credible solution." Graus Claude tapped the side of the bed. It lacked the satisfying *click-click-click* of thick nails against his mahogany desk. "He should avoid all contact with the Folk, especially those on the Council. I suspect they are already overly eager to extract news of you and I." He nodded to himself. "Let us pray that the Scribe's bravado and chivalry do not eclipse his common sense. If he's smart, he'll busy himself by working in the field. He accrued an impressive backlog of assignments while he lay unconscious those few days."

Joy frowned. "*You're* the one who knocked him unconscious."

Graus Claude looked pained. "Needs must, Miss Malone," he said. "To be fair, he was going for my throat."

And it had all started with Joy accusing Graus Claude of being a traitor to the Twixt. She decided to drop the subject. "So what do you want me to do?"

"It would be wisest to remain within the wards," he said. "However, when have we limited ourselves to pursuing only the wisest course?" His browridge quirked. "Instead, I propose you visit Councilex Maia with all due haste and secrecy—thus requiring that you go without either Master Ink, Mistress Inq, young Filly, myself or the like—then report back here and we shall endeavor to concoct a well-researched strategy of next steps."

"But how am I supposed to do that without Ink?"

Graus Claude grinned with his many teeth. "Magic, Miss Malone. Observe." He lifted his four hands before the door-length mirror and twisted each one just so—the image of Stef's empty bed and bare wall shifted slightly, a warp in the aluminum that rippled like a tickle of a pond. The giant amphibian eased himself forward, hesitant to touch the glass, but his fingers disappeared as he rummaged around inside the quicksilver before extruding a familiar-looking velvet bag.

"Ah!" he said as the mirror solidified into a single sheet. He untied the strings and rolled a set of familiar chalky-yellow knucklebones into one of his left palms.

"How—?" Joy stared at the mirror, then at Graus Claude and the bag.

"The bottom of the stained glass box is mirrored," he explained. "In case of such an emergency."

Joy juggled realities in her head. "I thought you said you weren't a spellcaster."

"I'm not," he said, inspecting each die with a jewel cutter's eye. "I used Water magic. Mirrors are reflections, which is an inherent property of the thing itself and thus under our domain. That is not a *spell*. That is magic intrinsic to our House." He sniffed austerely. "There is some advantage to being the High Water Seat, after all."

Joy gaped at him. "But then couldn't you have escaped from Under the Hill yourself?"

His icy glare was damning. "Do you truly think that I would have been delivered in such a state if they had lent me a mirror?" He sounded aghast. "Besides, they not only knew my skills and limitations, but how best to humiliate me. All my meals and my toilette were performed in the dark so as to enhance my discomfort in subtler ways than the Council's usual base methods of inquiry." He growled. "We learned some things from humans, after all."

He massaged the bone dice between his palms, warming them. "Now then, we will send you to Maia's back door, which is used by me as well as the other members of the Council, so should be both accessible and vacant given their current pursuit, namely you. First, request sanctuary. Once granted, ask that she swear by the King and Queen and her

True Name that she will not cause you harm by word or deed or intent to hinder or hamper your efforts nor aid any other against you. Now repeat that back to me." It took Joy three times to get it right, but it was the best she could do without a Pearl of Wisdom. She still had one in her handbag, collected after Hasp had broken her double-stranded necklace of magic cheat sheets. She'd promised to grant a boon to whoever brought her every single pearl and didn't want to owe a promise she couldn't keep, so had kept one herself. She'd learned *something* from Graus Claude, after all.

After her third attempt, the Bailiwick nodded, satisfied. "I will use these to open a gate," he said. "When you are ready to return, call your house phone, let it ring twice, then disconnect. That will be my signal to reopen the gate."

Joy tried to remember how the knucklebones worked. "Don't you need a laser beam? And coordinates?"

The Bailiwick shrugged, fingers fussing with the sheets and the dice. "The photon effect isn't strictly necessary," he admitted. "Consider it a precondition for the appropriate sense of drama. However, one always needs coordinates, or else you might end up anywhere in creation. Fortunately, as I've explained, this is a property of Water and once one of the Water Folk has slipstreamed, there remains an echo of a trail, like a rivulet tracing a path through stone, weathering a course through which it can easily flow once again." He pointed a clawed finger at her. "You have traveled to Maia's before, as Kurt explained to me upon my escape, so the coordinates are already available in you."

"But I'm not Water Folk," Joy said, twisting her fingers. "I'm Earth."

"I am well aware, Miss Malone," Graus Claude said, "Hence 'in you' is less a turn of phrase and more a literal fact." He tapped the side of his head near his eardrum. "The *eelet* inside your inner ear is one of the Siren's royal breeds, if Dennis Thomas was to be believed. This would make it one of the Water Folk's creatures and since it has traveled this route previously while anchored to your skull, it should be able to carry you back along the route as well."

Joy blinked. "You want me to be dragged through the Twixt by a worm in my ear?"

Graus Claude grinned. "You must admit, no one would think of it." He didn't laugh. Neither did she. The Bailiwick arched himself forward, the bed groaning in protest. He enunciated his words to give them the proper weight and severity. "The longer we dally, the greater the chances of our being discovered. Master Ink, as well as the Council, demands that we take swift and decisive action before that time." Joy hesitated, losing the feeling in her fingertips. The great frog's eyes softened. His nostrils flared a final sigh. "Trust me, Miss Malone."

She took a deep breath and licked her lips. "I trust you."

He tossed the handful of dice, which rolled across the floor and landed in a rough circle.

"Go," he said.

She stepped forward with none of the appropriate drama and, between one step and the next, disappeared.

FOUR

JOY STUMBLED INTO THE DARK, HANDS BOUNCING off a wall. Her ear popped. She clapped a hand to it and hoped that the *eelet* was still attached, but without Graus Claude swearing under his breath in Water Tongue, it was impossible to tell.

Joy swore in fluent, fluid English.

She touched the wall again. The soft warmth was familiar; the golden glow of one smooth, unbroken sheet of polished bird's-eye maple. Joy wasn't certain if this was the front door or the back door, but the darkness beyond the soft glow of the wood convinced her that she didn't want to linger on the doorstep any longer than she had to. She stood on a ledge that circled the building—or tree root or trunk or whatever—and she had the sense that she was either very far down or very high up, and to fall off that ledge would be a terrible thing, either way.

She slid her fingers over the shiny surface, feeling for a seam or a button or a knob—anything to indicate a way inside. Finally she decided to knock with her fist.

"Hello?" she said, and was scared silent by the way her voice traveled in the shadows, as if her words had gained wings, fluttering into the black. She knocked again. And again.

The door opened. Councilex Maia stared up at her, blinking owlishly.

"I request sanctuary," Joy gasped.

The squat, mushroom-y woman stretched herself to Joy's height and beyond, looming taffy-like above her head, squinting down through eyes that were barely slits, her rubbery frown smeared over her chin in a scowl. Joy cringed on the threshold of the Court of Earth.

Maia deflated like a balloon, blobbing back into a wobbly shape. "I imagine ye do," she said, and stepped back. "I 'ereby grant you sanctuary, Joy Malone." The pale, round woman shuffled to one side and gestured into the den. "Care for a cuppa?"

Joy walked into the high-ceilinged house full of draping plants, carved furniture and glowing, bulb-like lamps. She nearly collapsed into one of the squashy moss-colored chairs, but held herself firm. "I need to ask you something first."

"More'n one something, I'd wager," Maia said with none of her gummy smiles. She was serious-looking even as she kicked the length of her dark hair out of her way and plucked one of the wilting flowers from the wreath on her head. She sniffed it once and ate it. "We've been combing the realms for the likes of you t' throw you before the Council on yer knees. Done us a service and an insult and a favor all at once, reminding us of our King 'n' Queen, an' not a soul knows what t' do about it. But Folks figure it'd be good t' catch ye first an' ask questions later."

"I don't blame them," Joy said, still feeling as if she were treading on eggshells made of razor blades. "I made a mess of things, but I want to fix it...if they'll let me." Neither Joy nor Maia needed to say the name *Sol Leander*, but it hung in the air like rotten perfume. "Still, first things first." She looked up at the shelves full of flowers and vines and vases and boxes with Maia's *signatura* painted or carved onto every locked surface, its curling teardrop shape surrounding them both. "I need you to swear by the King and Queen and your own True Name that you will not cause me harm by word or deed or intent, nor hinder or hamper my efforts, nor aid any other against me."

Maia pursed her lips. "You sprang the Bailiwick," she said matter-of-factly. "Or've spoken wi' him recently. That's his words in your mouth."

Joy didn't dare answer. "Do you swear it?"

The Earth Seat gave her the fish-eye. "Or else...what?"

"Or else..." Joy said as a furry creature waddled in pushing a tea tray, its frilly apron askew. Joy shrugged, pinching her eyes against an oncoming headache. "I don't know," she confessed, falling into a chair. The cushions coughed up a *whump* of dust bunnies. "I have no idea. I came here because the Return is important. Because I don't know what else to do, but I'm trying to stay safe long enough to make things right." She glanced at the squat woman in her cupped armchair. "I came to you because you are Earth and you might be the only one that can help me."

The furry creature served Maia a cup of tea and burbled as she scratched its fuzzy ears. "An' where's your boy bodyguard, then?"

"Like I said," Joy muttered, "I'm trying to stay safe."

"Ach, is that right?" Maia took a sip and settled back in her own chair, perching the warm cup on her belly and wriggling her chubby toes. "All right, I do so swear upon our recently rediscovered King an' Queen an' on my own True Name at that." She slapped the top of her armrest. "So be it." She took another contemplative sip as Joy melted into her chair with relief.

Maia's fingers traced the woodwork as her servant snuffled about. "Ye didn't need such a fearsome oath to bind me for sake of that old frog, nor for the gala, neither," she said.

"I wager this is somethin' else—somethin' bigger?" Her dark eyes sparkled and her stretchy smile split sideways. Maia's eagerness reminded Joy of Filly, who was always excited at the prospect of gossip or mayhem.

"Perhaps," Joy said, watching the furry creature dust the drawers.

"One moment." Maia gave a few quick grunts in the back of her throat, and the animal obediently dropped on all fours and waddled out the door. Maia rubbed her nose. "Was due for a day off, anyways. An' now we're alone wi'out extra ears." She clicked her tongue and winked. "Now talk an' we'll see what's what."

Joy hoped that Graus Claude knew what he was doing. She sat up straight. "What do you know about Elementals?"

A long string of syllables tumbled out of Maia's mouth like a crumbling avalanche. She poured a flask of bright amber liquid into her cup. Joy was glad that her *eelet* only translated Water Tongue. The Councilex took a long drink and started pouring another.

"I'd say 'twas nonsense, but I suspect we know that ain't so." She eyed Joy with a squint. "I'd say 'twas impossible, but that'd be my head in the sand. An' I'd say it'd be a miracle or a curse or an omen, but who can say that wi'out a sooth-sayer, an' I'll be damned if I'd let one get a right sniff o' this!" She drank again and smacked her lips, a rosy glow warming the tip of her nose. She shook her head and blinked back tears. "I can't say it ain't so, though I dearly wish t'..." Her voice whispered in her country dialect, the *a* drawing out like a bovine *o*. "But I *can't!*"

Because she knew it was true.

"I was hoping we were wrong," Joy said.

"Still could be," Maia said, wiping her nose and draining her cup. "Ye haven't changed yet. The frog might still be righ' that yer too dilute t' manifest, an' that may buy you time."

Joy seized on the hope. "So it might never happen?"

"Aye, but I doubt many Folk'll be content to dwell in the land of 'might.'" Maia said. "More like they'd end ye quick 'afore somethin' bad happens." She drummed her fingers in caterpillar waves. "Well, y'have until ye form a chrysalis. After that, s'all over." Maia pushed herself to her feet, which plopped on the floor with the sound of raw dough. She waddled through the room, bending and stretching, checking this shelf and that. Joy watched her with a queasy wariness. Maia could unlock any object that bore her *signatura* and who knows what she might have hiding within easy reach?

"A chrysalis?" Joy mumbled after her.

"An Elemental is born of the elements, ye ken? It's an instinct tha' grows inside you t' burrow deep within the earth, pull the soil around you 'til yer encased in rock. The protective layer's like a suit o' armor an' allows the metamorphosis t' happen." She twisted around to stare at Joy, squeezing an eye in her direction like a zit. "Yer flesh melds with the Earth, yer bones melt and yer insides change t' match the outside. The chrysalis becomes the part o' yer body attached t' the world." She nodded to herself as she took her usual shape. "I hunted Earth Elementals back in the Old Days, being of Earth m'self. I had t' watch their habits, foller their patterns, learn their ways—s'only way t' beat 'em." She shot Joy a sideways glance. "I'd know how t' kill you if ye hadn't bound me. Smart thing, that." She waved her hands as if drying them. "Well, so, if we can keep ye from bein' bound in stone, there might be time enough t' let it run its course. Ye can die a mortal death, a natural lifetime before anything 'appens." She tugged her lips. "Maybe."

"I've been encased in rock before," Joy said. "And nothing...like that happened." The words squeezed out of her mouth. She couldn't say "nothing happened" because something *had* happened when she'd been captured by mud golems while camping with her father and brother at Lake James. She'd been wrapped in a tomb of stone, asphyxiating in the dark, when she'd realized that she could breathe through her toes. They'd burrowed into the earth, touching something awesome and ancient and cold with fury. She'd tapped into that power and foreign fury and blown the golem-cage to pieces. Stef thought it had been Filly, who had come to rescue her, and Joy hadn't corrected him. She'd never told anyone what had really happened, remembering the rush of anger and the taste of old, old ice.

And it had happened again in the Atrium.

"Ye've felt it, haven't you?" Maia said shrewdly.

The answer was easy but flavored with something dark, shameful. "Yes."

"Ach, it's a heady wine, power like that," Maia said. "They were of the Wild, y'understand, drunk on life, with the power to birth and destroy at will, to smash down the world an' drink it back up, crush it all to dust an' shape it into life again. Aye, that's what it means t' be Earth." She eyed Joy with a calculated wariness. "Anything else changed, then?"

Joy hesitated, which spoke volumes in the quiet. "I...lost my heart."

"Not to the Scribe?" Maia said casually. "Oh! Ye mean literal-like?"

"My heart stopped beating." Joy said the impossible words and, because she spoke them aloud, she knew it was true. It trembled on her tongue. "I don't have a heartbeat anymore! I don't know how it happened, but it's gone." She rubbed her eyes and felt a pinch in her nose. "At first, I thought it was Briarhook who'd done something, but now...I think it's this."

"Oh, aye," Maia said, sounding unconcerned. "Makes sense. An Elemental is part o' the earth, the skin an' bones of the world. What need you for heart and blood and such? You'll be feelin' the beat o' the planet, the pulse o' the Earth, the shift of land and lava and salt. You can eat an' drink an' breathe through the soil. Yer becomin' part of the world—the great Maker, the All-Mother—what need you of a mortal heart?"

"But I *want* my heart!" Joy said. "I need it to stay human, to be mortal, to be *me*."

Maia toasted her with an empty cup. "Well, good. Not so far gone, then. Still, like as not, Folk'll not take th' news well, so best not share it lengthwise. If the Scribe suspects, he's not said a word, nor will he if'n what you say's true, an' ye've got the Bailiwick and I in yer confidence. That's no small thing. But the Council..." She circled the chairs and tapped Joy on the back with a wormy finger. "Ye wear your True Name on your flesh—you'd be better off if ye had more friends than foes at yer back, I warrant." She stuck out a fat lower lip. "Might have an idea 'bout that," she said slowly. "Know someone who knows somethin' about such things as this. Not many would spare you a word, mind you—ye left the gala in quite a state, but mark me, they won't forget it soon!"

Joy twisted her fingers in her lap. "Sorry about the hair comb."

"Why?" Maia sounded genuinely puzzled. "Tha's what it was for—t' keep ye breathing." Her smile stretched from ear to ear. "Yer *mine* an' some Folk need be reminded that Earth is nothin' t' take lightly. We're this world's hearth and home. We might be portly an' matronly, offerin' up a warm cup, a hot meal an' a playful bed, but let them not forget that we birth mountains and swallow rivers, bury forests and shatter lands—Earth can be terrible as well as terribly kind, but both words're rooted in terror an' awe." She winked. "Aye, yer one o' mine an' I'm proud t' have you so long as ye keep yer skin intact." Her voice left no doubt that there was an unsaid, *Or else*. Councilex Maia blinked and the threat was gone, leaving a portly, kindly matron with an empty cup in her hand.

"Never expected the bit wi' the lamps, o' course." She sniffed and tossed the mug over her shoulder. It hit the floor and rolled thickly against the rug. "But that's one o' the joys in life—the unexpected!" Her face brightened. "Aye! I bets I know *one* who knows 'bout fending off the change, but ye should let me make the call. If you tried it, like as not you'd be turned in to the Council, an' not a thing I could do 'bout it 'afore you're thrown six ways to the wind." The stumpy woman eyed her, lips pursed, looking smug. "What say you?"

Something in Maia's eyes made her leery, but Joy found she couldn't think of one reason to say no. "Okay," Joy said. "Arrange a meeting. I—" She tried to say "I trust you," but found she couldn't do it. Embarrassed, she swallowed back her polite lie. Maia pretended not to notice.

"Thank you," Joy said instead.

"Aye," Maia said. "You'll be thanking me plenty before this is over." She patted Joy's arm. "Now ye better get goin' t' yer safe house right quick."

Joy nodded and picked up her phone, dialing her home number, letting it ring twice and hanging up. It was mere moments before there was a sound like a low gong emanating from the wall. Maia toddled over and opened the door.

A hum of energy spun on the threshold, a Spirograph in space. That was her ride. Joy stood up quickly and bowed.

"Thank you, Councilex Maia, for all of your help."

Maia patted Joy on her doorstep. "I envy you, girl," she said softly, outlined in the ward's ghostly light. "Yer on the lip o' something grand, no mistake, but I wouldn't trade places wi' you for all the world." Her gaze burned as she whispered, "Not for the *world*."

"A cautionary tale, a shred of hope and an arranged meeting with a mysterious benefactor," Graus Claude concluded. "Hardly conclusive, but it certainly could have been worse." He surveyed Stef's bedroom sourly. His stomach grumbled. "Much worse."

In Joy's absence, Graus Claude had managed to find a tarp, a large bucket and sponge from under the sink, and was currently squatting in the middle of the blue plastic, patting his exposed skin to keep it moist. Their conversation was punctuated with soft, delicate squishes and the pitter-patter of droplets hitting the tarp-covered floor. Joy tried to ignore it. Graus Claude's eyes dared her to comment.

"At least we know that Councilex Maia cannot work against you in this matter, given that she swore her oath," Graus Claude said as two hands wrung out the sponge. "She is honorable...in her own way."

Joy might have said that the same could be said about him, but not within earshot.

"So, what? We're back where we started? Sitting around waiting?" Joy glared out at the sky. It had been almost no time at all.

"No, Miss Malone. We have an ally of sorts, a possible expert in your area of inquiry and proof that even without my vast resources at my disposal I remain a force to be reckoned with." His smile was guileless and proud. "However, I do not believe that Maia has the breadth of experience and understanding of the possible ramifications as I do. Foresight is a skill that comes from large quantities of data that have been meticulously studied for trends over hundreds of years—hence why my investment portfolios often prove so lucrative." Joy was glad that some of her earnings had been included in one of those portfolios back when she had been working for the Bailiwick. She'd never asked to see what amount Enrique had left her in his will, but had turned it over to Graus Claude at the first opportunity, knowing he would manage it until her twenty-first birthday. Engaging the Bailiwick as her broker was the most grown-up thing she'd ever done, and neither of her parents knew about it. "Yet between Maia's confirmation of the Council's position and the King's declaration, I fear that we are not where we began, but far worse off."

Joy stilled. "What do you mean?"

"The Elementals were beings of chaos, you understand, creatures of the Wild that were true to their most primal nature and disavowed the limitations of rules and obligations." The Bailiwick squeezed out another sluice of water, wringing the sponge between two of his hands. "The King and Queen removed them from the world, safeguarding both our people and yours. They spoke the Twixt into being and so it was." He hesitated, a guarded look hooding his eyes. "Similarly, the King and Queen declared that once freed of Elementals, the world would know peace."

Joy waited for the rest of the sentence, but there was only silence. "That doesn't sound so bad," she hazarded.

"Yes, but you see, whatever they spoke into being became the rules under which we survived, absolute and inviolate, as I've previously described. Therefore, if there were no Ele-

mentals, we would be safe. Ergo, if the opposite were true..."
He sighed, a deep rumble of regret. "Then I am afraid that
the reverse would also be true, in accordance with the
rules." His icy eyes flicked up to look at her from beneath
his prominent ridge. "If a true Elemental returned to our
world, then the Folk and the humans would no longer be
safe. There would be war between us, and there would be
no hope of Return." His voice crumbled her pride to dust.
"If you are a descendant of Elementals, then you would thus
qualify as the Destroyer of Worlds."

Joy stared at him, ice racing through her veins. "No," she
whispered. "No, that can't be..." And yet the words echoed
Maia's. The implications sank in. "But I'm not!"

"Not yet," Graus Claude agreed. "And that is why it is
imperative that we bring the King and Queen back to ensure that it shall not be." His four hands slapped his long,
banded thighs. "Your initial theory of how to best reverse
the change is, in fact, our best option—to convince the King
and Queen to Return and undo their proclamation and
your state of being is our best hope. In fact, I would wager
that you may be the only one who can do it, as there are
few who possess the knowledge of what may be to come,
and I cannot accompany you through the door. No one else
save Maia and Master Ink know the extent of these implications as omens of a next Age, and they have both been
neatly bound." The Bailiwick ran a clawed hand across the
length of his chin. "I admit I am greatly impressed by his
ability to have accurately assessed the situation—another
coup to my credit, I suppose."

"The next Age?" Joy echoed. It sounded like something
Aniseed's clone might say in her thin, wretched voice.

"Time is a long, winding river road," he said. "The Folk
have come to know its tides and swells, its tributaries, its

swamps and switchback turns. Years have a shape to them, a pattern, an era, and each of our eras have been marked by an Age. Perhaps it is time for the Age of Man to finally be at an end. Perhaps the Golden Age that Aniseed promised has begun?" Joy froze at his words. His eye ridge quirked. "But not yet, I think. And I would not welcome it any more than you."

She exhaled in a rush, adrenaline skittering down her limbs. She shuffled back and forth on her heels, unable to pace, taking half steps and turning back, unsure where to go or what to do. She felt caged, trapped. Her fingers wrung nothing but air.

"So what now?" she squeaked.

"It would behoove us to consider that the best course of action may be to 'lie low' until Kurt or Maia or one of your other associates makes contact. It has not been long enough for us to accrue formal charges to speak before the Council—my preemptive freedom from incarceration notwithstanding—but they will no doubt be very interested to speak with you," he said archly. "Your voluntary cooperation will likely be considered optional."

"Great. So we're just supposed to sit and wait, praying my father doesn't bump into you in the meantime?"

The Bailiwick squeezed the sponge over his head. Water coursed down his jowls and off the crest of his chin. "Indeed, that would be best for both of our sakes," he said. "However, I suspect you and I both chafe at the idea of 'doing nothing' and, given the severity of our situation and the instability of our positions reminiscent of our preparations for your gala, I believe you already know what course of action I would advise."

Joy stopped pacing. "Yeah," she said, remembering. A slow smile spread across her lips. "We cheat."

FIVE

JOY CHECKED THE PEEPHOLE BEFORE OPENING THE door and gratefully accepted a large latte from her best friend.

"You are a wonderful human being!" Joy said, and sipped the edge of drizzled foam.

"It's true," Monica agreed. "And I know for a fact that you can't lie."

Joy grinned. "Thanks for coming." She shut the door and locked it with the bolt, the chain and set the alarm.

"Always," Monica said breezily. "Although perhaps four o'clock on Monday morning isn't my finest hour. I'll be expecting a call from Gordon, 'cuz I kind of left him hanging and he was *not* happy, but sisters before misters." She licked her whipped cream. "I figured this was an emergency, but I didn't know what to bring besides coffee and this—" She took the ox bone letter opener out of her purse. Joy had borrowed Monica's gift from her aunt Meredith in order to sever the Amanya spell at its source: Graus Claude.

Joy gulped. "Why did you bring that?"

Monica frowned. "It's the only thing that I know works in this Twix world of yours."

Joy laughed. "It's the Twixt, like 'betwixt' this world and another one. Twix is a candy bar."

Monica smiled. "Mmm. Just like my caramel mochaccino."

Joy shut the cover on the alarm. "Did you get in okay? Did you see anyone?"

"Normal people are sleeping. Although there are some crazy joggers around at this hour..."

"I meant did you *See* anyone?" She raised her eyebrows meaningfully.

"Oh," Monica said with sudden understanding. "No. I mean, not since I saw you and your boy leave the baseball field yesterday. I even looked on my way home," she confessed. "In the park, in the garden and in the cemetery on East. I admit I still think you could be pulling my leg." She wagged the letter opener at Joy. "I also saw that funky arrow thing on my face—*not* an attractive feature." Joy felt a curl of guilt twist her gut. Now that Monica had the Sight, she could also see the *signatura* embedded in the scar that marked her as being under Sol Leander's auspice. It was Joy's fault that Monica had been wounded by the Red Knight and thereby claimed by the Tide's representative. Sol Leander was the guardian of victims of unprovoked attacks. "Last I heard, you were headed to a big to-do in an invisible Ferrari." Monica took a long look at Joy. "Please tell me you didn't wear *that* to some fairy-tale ball."

Joy plucked at her T-shirt and shorts, her toes waggling in mismatched socks. "No," she said. "I changed when I got home. You would have approved of my ball gown, trust me."

"Pics or it didn't happen."

Joy shrugged. "Sorry. No flash photography." The Folk didn't have reflections, so they didn't show up in mirrors or cameras. Joy waved around the empty kitchen. "Dad's at Shelley's, Stef's gone and my date's not here. Consider this the after-party."

"Swanky," Monica said. "So how did it go?"

"The word *pitchforks* comes to mind."

"That good, huh?" Monica winced. "Ouch."

"Yeah. It's a long story." Joy swallowed more warm, sweet caffeine. The throbbing in her temples could have been the beat of her heart if she'd had one anymore. Her smile faltered. *One conniption fit at a time*, she reminded herself. First, survive impending doom. Then, stop changing into something inhuman. For dessert, get the King and Queen to come back from Heaven and save both the worlds. *Oh yeah. Piece of cake.*

Monica pointed toward Joy's room with the ox bone dagger. "Well, I freed up the morning to hang out with my bestie and left a message for Gordon to ping me later so we could rearrange plans, so in the meanwhile we can *OH JESUS!*" Monica rankled like a cat hit with a boot, spying Graus Claude squatting in front of Stef's old TV. "DOWN!" she screamed. "GET DOWN!" She grabbed a pen off Stef's nightstand and made a shaky cross with the letter opener.

"Whoa! Whoa! Whoa!" Joy jumped in front of Monica, hoping to shield her friend from Graus Claude's response. The Bailiwick didn't take kindly to disrespect, and surprise could be mistaken for an insult. Joy cringed, expecting a bellow or a stern lecture as she waved her arms in front of Monica's eyes. It took Joy a moment to realize that the Bailiwick had prostrated himself obligingly against the floor, all four arms spread-eagled in meek submission. She was obscenely grateful that he was willing to play along. She'd forgotten to tell him that she'd given her best friend the Sight.

"It's okay," she said aloud, to herself and Monica and Graus Claude. "Everybody calm down."

"What *is* it?!" Monica shouted.

"*It* is wondering if anyone bothers to dust beneath the

furniture," Graus Claude said. "The filth is appalling." He sneezed. The explosive shudder shook his massive body and flopped his burly arms. His head swiveled to glare at the two of them in the doorway. Monica's breath hitched at the sight of his baleful, blue eyes. "Am I permitted to get up without further incident?"

His ire was like cold syrup. Joy nodded. Monica, too.

"Yeah," her friend said weakly. "Yeah. Sure."

The Bailiwick very slowly got to his feet, unfolding his impressive height like a magician's trick. He straightened out his stout limbs and the long, winding chain of his spine, settling himself into his usual, impressive hunch—his scoliosis hump stood seven feet at the shoulder. His head retained its palsy shake as two hands straightened what was left of his suit shirt and the other two tugged at the four stained and crumpled cuffs. His gaze never left Monica, exuding his usual impression that he was a grand and noble amphibian, the infamous Bailiwick, comptroller between worlds, and no one to trifle with.

A few droplets of sponge water pattered against the tarp.

Monica stood rigid, terrified. Joy sighed. This was not the best first impression in the world.

"Monica, this is my mentor and friend, the Bailiwick, Graus Claude," she said smoothly. "Graus Claude, may I present my best friend, Monica Reid."

The icy blue glare never wavered. "Miss Malone has spoken highly of your friendship."

"Y-yeah," Monica stammered. "Thanks. She's the best." Monica grabbed Joy's biceps. "Will you please excuse us for a moment?" She dragged Joy back into the hall. Graus Claude watched them go, intense as a cat.

"Indeed," he rumbled as they fled into Joy's room. Joy just managed to get inside the door as Monica slammed it shut.

"HolyMaryMotherofGod," Monica spat. "You never said there was something in here!"

Joy winced. She hadn't. "To be fair, I never told him that you could see him, either," she said as she glanced back at her door. "He's got to be pretty freaked out."

"*He's* freaked out?" Monica squeaked. "I nearly swallowed my tongue back there!" She dropped the pen and the letter opener on the desk and fussed with her hair. She'd gotten extensions, long, dark waves like chocolate curls. Her hands trembled.

"I'm sorry," Joy said. "Really. I'd hoped to introduce you under better circumstances." Although she had to admit, any circumstances would have been better than these. "I thought you two would really get along."

"I'm taken, thanks," Monica said with a hint of her usual smarm. Some of the umber color was coming back to her cheeks. "What *is* it?"

"A giant frog, I think," Joy said. "Maybe a toad? I confuse the two."

"I mean is it..." Monica sat on the edge of the computer desk. "Is it a *demon*?"

"What? No! He's the Bailiwick," Joy said. "And he is one of the most powerful people in the Twixt. He's a member of the ruling Council—or, at least, he was before his arrest—or maybe that doesn't matter now that the King and Queen are about to Return...*if* they agree to Return...which I now seriously doubt." She dropped onto her bed and curled a pillow into her lap. "I'm not sure it would be a good thing, anyway, having them Return, considering they've got an angry army at their back ready to attack the human world." Joy buried her face in the pillow, muffling her words. "I seriously screwed up."

"Yeah? I get that," Monica said, her voice slipping into Peer Counselor mode. "Do you want to tell me about it?"

Joy rested her chin on her pillow, her face wet. *"Yes."*

"...and when we got out, we left Stef behind with Dmitri; Kurt, Graus Claude's bodyguard, was looking for Inq; Filly and Avery were fighting our way out and we barely made it to the car in time before Raina, Luiz and Ilhami had to shoot down some cloaking magic to cover our exit." Joy was almost all talked-out, dimly realizing that Monica probably couldn't follow half of what she was saying, but it was good to say it out loud, anyway. She rubbed her eyes with the back of her hand. It was almost six in the morning. "For all I know, Briarhook led the mob straight to us." She wrung her pillow in her fists. "We may have bargained for him to find and free the Bailiwick, but we never said anything about helping us escape Under the Hill." Joy blinked up at the ceiling. "Or maybe we did. Kurt did the negotiations, and he's pretty thorough. Maybe I'm just being paranoid."

"Being paranoid doesn't mean that everybody's not out to get you," Monica said wryly. "And, in your case, both sides of this thing sound like they might be itching to do just that." Her best friend gave a deep sigh that ended in a yawn. "I tell you, Joy, you don't do things by halves."

Joy rubbed her face. "Yeah. When I screw up, I go all out." She blinked up at the ceiling and pressed her hands to her stomach. Lying on her bed made her think about how little time had passed since her family's camping weekend, since the gala and the jailbreak and opening the door into Faeland, the last glimpse of a charging army and Ink's bitter leaving. Time did funny things when you were zipping between the real world, Folk Heaven and the Twixt. "Just keep your voice down," she said quietly. "I don't want Kermit the Hutt knowing every gruesome detail."

"Miss Malone," Graus Claude's powerful voice called down the hall. Both girls sat up straight. "I find it laboriously inconvenient to maneuver down your narrow hallway, so might I request an audience that does not require shouting?" There was a pause as Joy and Monica stared at one another, exchanging silent questions with their eyebrows. Monica pointed a suggestive thumb out the window. Joy mimed hanging herself by a noose. "And honesty forces me to add that your walls are paper thin," he grumbled. "I can hear the both of you breathing."

Joy covered her face in her hands. Monica let out a sigh. Together they stood up and crossed the hall with all the enthusiasm of visiting the principal's office. Joy peered around the doorjamb; Monica peeked over her shoulder, keeping the ox bone blade in one fist. Graus Claude sat in a lotus position, a picture of calm serenity, until he saw them staring. A tic twitched at his eye.

"I gather that we are now all up-to-date on current events?" His deep bass voice rumbled. Joy flinched. A grin softened the corners of his lips. "Very good," he said. "Our alliances are our strength." He pointed a claw at Monica. "You will stay here and keep Miss Malone company until such time as we can find a suitable escort for her future travels." Monica planted her fists on her hips. She'd obviously been planning to stick by Joy anyway; she just didn't want to be *ordered* to do it. She turned to Joy, ignoring the enormous frog.

"And your boy, Ink, isn't here, why?"

Joy groaned. "Until I can convince him that I'm not going to Hulk out and turn into an Elemental, he thinks it isn't safe to be near me, or vice versa."

Monica smirked. "Yeah, Gordon says he feels that way every twenty-eight days."

"Ha!"

"Ladies, *please*," Graus Claude gurgled, clearly pained by the topic of women's hygiene. "If we theorize that the change is slowed due to your distant, diluted heritage, then perhaps human magic might succeed where Folk magic would not?"

"You mean like wizard magic?" Joy said.

"I have heard such magics cannot cancel out one another, but they can adjust results to suit."

"Ooo! Like the fairy godmothers in Sleeping Beauty?" Monica asked.

Graus Claude looked at her levelly. "Quite," he said, over-enunciating the *t*.

"Well, Stef's not here, but his master's nearby." Joy tried to ignore Monica's *'Scuse me?* face.

"Yes. But you should not seek out the Wizard Vinh until we can locate a capable bodyguard." He turned his face toward the window, ignoring Monica's insulted *"Hey!"*

"It is past dawn, yet I doubt it is safe to contact Kurt at this time. We cannot know when we can expect his being available, but I trust in his unique inventiveness and I know that we can trust his unswerving loyalty." He didn't bother adding that Kurt was bound to him in servitude due to the Bailiwick's saving him from the Black Plague. "However, his current absence is both unavoidable and inconvenient. Therefore, I shall endeavor to perform my own ablutions and toilette." Graus Claude grunted as he got to his feet and unwrapped the towels with brisk efficiency before stepping gingerly onto the floor. The bleeding had stopped, but his wide, webbed feet looked much abused—gouged, patchy yellow, glistening with runny fluid and peeling, pale pink skin. He grumbled as he shuffled forward. Monica backed up into the hall.

"Um," Joy said, picking up the towels. "I'll just go wash these—"

"No!" Joy froze. Graus Claude loomed in the doorway, his voice grave. "They must be burned." The Bailiwick glanced at Monica's frightened face and adjusted his volume, sounding apologetic, but insistent. "We must leave no evidence of my being here, Joy Malone," he said reasonably. "They must be burned."

"O-kay," Joy said and grabbed the laundry basket out of Stef's closet. "We can burn these in the bathtub." She hitched the basket up on one hip. "Just open the window so you don't set off the smoke alarm."

"A bath," Graus Claude said wistfully. "Yes. Perhaps things will look brighter after a dip in the pool."

Monica's eyebrows rose. Joy hesitated. "Um, we don't have a pool."

He chuckled. "Well, I very much doubt that I could fit in your tub."

Joy nodded. "True enough."

Graus Claude paused, considering. "A shower, perhaps?"

"You'd have to squeeze," Joy said, eying his bulk. "A lot."

The Bailiwick lumbered forward, his vest draped over one arm and his chin at a stubborn angle. "Very well. Simply lend me a few more towels, if you please, and I am certain I will manage somehow."

Joy opened the bathroom door as Monica pressed herself against the farthest wall. "After you."

The eight-foot, four-armed amphibian steadied himself, turning his body sideways and shuffling through the door, mincing into the narrow space between wall and sink and toilet and tub. Joy placed a book of matches near the scented candle atop his pile of laundry, nabbed a couple more towels and squeezed out the door. Graus Claude watched her contort her way past him, his head cocked at a curious angle, one hand on the doorknob.

"Anything else?" Joy asked weakly.

He paused. "Do you, by chance, have any cold-pressed avocado oil?"

Monica stifled a laugh. The Bailiwick glared.

Joy shook her head. "Sorry."

"Pity," he sighed and closed the door.

"Honey, I'm home!" Dad fought to free his keys from the lock. Joy checked the clock. It was 6:55 a.m. and the caffeine was losing its edge.

"Hi, Dad!" Joy called.

"Hi, Mr. Malone!"

He paused. "Monica?" he sounded surprised as the girls came out of Joy's bedroom. "What are you doing here? It's Monday morning." He checked his phone, just to make sure. "Yes. Says here, Monday morning. Seven a.m." He crossed the hall, oblivious of Graus Claude standing in the bathroom, covered in towels. The Bailiwick's browridge lowered. Monica tried not to stare.

"I'm just leaving," Monica said quickly. "You can pay me for babysitting later."

"Ha ha," Joy said.

"You know I love you." Monica squeezed her purse against her body as she hugged the opposite wall, giving Graus Claude a wide berth. She smiled back at Joy's dad. "Welcome home, Mr. Malone."

"Thank you," He gave a tired smile. "You're welcome here anytime, obviously."

Monica took out her keys. "You good?"

Joy nodded. "I'm good."

"Good. Stay good." Monica jingled her key chain. "I got you covered. See you later!" She waved as she ducked out the door.

"Thanks, Mon!" Joy called after her.

"Bye, Mon." Dad said, closing the door. They were now alone with a half-naked Bailiwick in the house. Her father frowned, curious. "So why was she here, again?"

Joy shrugged, trying to lure her father out of the hallway and away from Graus Claude. "Girl talk. We were catching up—" she yawned and stretched her arms, elbows-out "—I couldn't sleep."

Her father sighed. "Well, now you look like you could sleep for a week."

Nodding, Joy scratched her shoulder. "Good idea."

"Not so fast," Dad said. "Don't you have work today? I just stopped home to change."

"Ungh," Joy groaned. "I'm supposed to be—" She trailed off at the look Graus Claude threw at her as he crossed the hall, shuffling quietly into Stef's room. She tore her gaze away from the steamed amphibian and quickly switched gears. "Ah. I'll have to check the schedule."

"Get there early," Dad advised. "Remember, Joy, if you can't be a 'Yes' man—"

"—be indispensable. I know. I know." She jerked a thumb over her shoulder. "I'll go log in right now and check."

"Good idea," her father said as he strode toward his bedroom. He stopped midway down the hall. He was standing in a puddle. "Did you a take a shower?"

Thou shalt not lie. "Um, is there a problem with that?"

"Less attitude, please," he warned. "No, nothing's wrong, but next time wear your slippers. You got water all over the floor." He shook his dripping foot. "Clean it up before you head out."

"Okay. Sorry. No problem." She grabbed a rag from under the sink, one that no one would miss. If she was going to have to burn all the evidence that the Bailiwick had been there, she'd better try to salvage what towels they had left. She dropped the rag on the floor and smeared it around with her foot, glancing sideways through Stef's open door. Graus Claude had draped himself in one of Stef's bedsheets, toga-like, with one towel perched atop his head like a turban. He looked ridiculous and unapologetic. Joy picked up the wet rag and debated throwing it at him.

"Are you going to see Mark tonight?" her father called from his room.

"I hope so," Joy said sadly, mopping up spots.

Dad poked his head out. "What? Did you two have a fight?"

"No," Joy said, mentally adding, *Not yet*. She didn't want to think about it.

"Well, that's good," he said. "It's the last week before school..." He glanced at her uneasily. "I mean, I know you two have had a lovely summer, but I don't want you losing focus your senior year." He sighed at the look on her face. "Don't 'Dad!' me. I think it's fair that I don't want your self-employed, financially independent, tattoo-artist boyfriend distracting you from your school studies, okay?"

"Dad!"

"What did I just say about the 'Dad!' thing?" he said, fixing his tie. "It's bad enough knowing I've got Senioritis to deal with as a single parent. I don't need an added assault in tight pants messing with your grades. I thought I'd have to drag Stef through his last year to keep him on track!" He groaned at the memory. "And while I know you two aren't the same, you're more alike than you think. Believe me. I've lived through this once and had high hopes that this time would go smoother." He tightened the knot of his pin-striped tie. "Things have been coming together around here and I don't want you getting sidetracked."

"Sidetracked?" Joy said. Ever since she'd quit gymnastics and her dream of Olympic gold, she hadn't *had* a track. "From what?"

"Life," he said, grabbing his briefcase. "*Your* life, specifically, which includes school, job, college, career, marriage, kids and Happily Ever After, in that order."

Joy crossed her arms and stared at him from the hall. "Do I get to be happy now?"

Dad returned the couple of steps and chucked her under the chin. "Are you kidding? Happiness costs extra." He gave her a kiss on the forehead and headed out the door. "Love you."

Joy smirked. "Love you, too."

The door closed. There was a pregnant pause.

"Your father is a wise man," the Bailiwick said. "And Miss Reid, a good friend."

"Yeah," Joy said. "I know a lot of smart people." In fact, she knew *a lot* of smart, loyal and crazy-strong people, which was exactly what she needed right now. Scooping up her purse, she dug out a pouch of vellum notes and matches and squeezed it in her hand. If she needed a bodyguard and, next to Ink, there was no one better.

"You know me," she said, smiling. "No Stupid."

SIX

"HOY! JOY MALONE!"

Joy pushed back the bedroom blinds and saw Filly kicking the edge of the ward by the gate, gold sparks erupting under the tip of her boot. Joy waved. The young Valkyrie waved back, her metal vambrace shining in the sun. For all that they'd parted during the greenhouse brawl, the blond warrior looked no worse for wear.

"What's the password?" Joy shouted across the courtyard.

"Asinine," the blond warrior said drily. "Are you going to let me in or not?"

"Do you solemnly swear that you mean me no harm and will attempt neither to bind me, subdue me, punish me, render me unconscious or abscond with the whole or any part of my person from these premises without my express permission, by the Blind Eye of the All-Father?"

Filly licked at the blue spot below her lower lip. "You've got the Bailiwick there with you, eh?"

Joy shrugged, evasive. "One way to find out."

Filly tipped back her chin and laughed, exposing her horse head pendant necklace and a new pink scar down her throat. "Very good! They'll make a politico of you yet if you're not careful." She raised her fist in salute. "I do so swear it upon the Blind Eye of the All-Father." She let her fist drop.

"Good enough for me." Joy severed the loop Ink had left in his ward—the specific, conditional exceptions that allowed Joy to choose who might safely enter or leave. First Inq, then Graus Claude, now Filly. Joy nervously wondered if she shouldn't just let a whole brass band march through the front door. The Folk were looking for her now, and they couldn't be allowed to find out what the Bailiwick suspected. If she were really descended from Elementals, she'd be on everybody's hit list and if anyone could sniff out a secret, Joy would lay bets on Filly.

The armored Norsewoman twisted some errant strands of hair back into their braids as she waited for the ward to part. She kept a foot touching the gate, testing the edge, until the tiny sparks of light around her dissipated in a static haze. She strode forward as if without a care in the world, her short cape of finger bones rattling behind her as the gate clanged closed.

Joy left the window and ran to wait by the door, imagining her brash friend taking the stairs by twos. At the flippant knock, she opened the door and came face-to-face with a bright sword's edge. Joy stumbled back. Filly glared at her from behind the hilt.

"Don't let your guard down," she said, deadly serious. "Are you a warrior or not?"

"Um," Joy said, fixated on the blade between them. "Not."

"We'll have to work on it, then, if you live that long." Filly sheathed her sword and spread her empty hands. "Well, can I come in?"

Joy debated saying no, but she was the one who'd called the Valkyrie for help. No one besides Ink or Kurt was better suited to be her bodyguard. Joy stepped aside. "Welcome."

Filly nodded, sweeping her gaze around the room, taking in all the likely exits, partial views, handy weapons and salient details. It was a professional once-over. "It does look like the place where we fought Aniseed's shadows in the dark," she admitted. The illusion had been part of Aniseed's plan to capture Joy and bargain for Ink's *signatura*, but no one had bargained on the Valkyrie's interference. "But it doesn't *feel* the same. It feels like cardboard and custard. The *segulah*'s spellwork felt like bees. Best take note of it so you can recognize the difference." She turned a full circle. "Where's the frog?"

"In here." Graus Claude's voice drifted around the corner of Stef's room. Filly followed Joy into the hall and burst out laughing. Graus Claude still wore the bedsheet and a moist towel over his head. The Bailiwick's wardrobe had been reduced to barely functional rags so he'd opted to burn them along with the towels. The bathroom still smelled of Lysol and smoke.

Graus Claude frowned as Filly doubled over in laughter, cheeks red, eyes tearing as she slammed an open palm against the door. He removed the towel and tugged the sheet discreetly into place with three of his four hands. His makeshift toga slipped farther off one shoulder. Filly wheezed as she struggled for air, snorting and slapping her thighs.

"If you are quite through," the Bailiwick murmured. "There is important business to attend to."

Filly wiped her tattooed eyes and nodded, still laughing, gleeful and uproarious as she collected herself. "Yes. Yes. Important, no doubt!" She laughed again and punched herself in the chest. "Oh, I am glad you summoned me, Joy Malone. I would not have wanted to miss this for the world!"

"Miss Malone requires an escort to the Wizard Vinh," he said primly. "Someone who can guarantee her safety and possesses impeccable loyalty and *restraint*." Graus Claude shifted his steely gaze. "I can only assume she chose wisely selecting you."

Filly still looked merry-eyed as she crossed her arms and grinned. "Oh, aye," she said, chipper as anything. "I can see her safely from here to wherever she might need be. But if it is to be a wizard's lair, then we'll have to hoof it. I cannot call down the skies to bring us there with a wizard's wards in place."

"It isn't far," Joy said.

"It rarely is until you start the journey, then you never know where you might end up," Filly muttered, but then brightened. "Still, it will give you a chance to tell me all that has transpired since we last parted company. As I recall, you were last seen launching through a window, traveling by toad." She chuckled again, her shoulders bouncing with mirth. "Where is Ink?"

"He is unfortunately unavailable at present," said Graus Claude.

The horsewoman scowled. "You didn't shut him off again, did you?"

Joy gaped. "How did you know about that?"

"Hard to miss once," Filly said. "Impossible to miss twice. When both Scribes fell, it took very little guesswork to make two and two four." She nudged Joy with her elbow. "I am awfully good at riddles, after all!"

Joy sighed. Filly had been the first to figure out that she wasn't entirely human and that the mysterious mark on her back was her own developing *signatura*—a fact that neither Graus Claude, Inq nor Stef had shared with her, although they had guessed; each one of them had been guilty of withholding information as well as manipulating Joy by her True Name. For all her wild and wily antics, the young

Valkyrie was very clever. Maybe Joy should have had her swear on Loki instead.

"Very well," Graus Claude said with his usual brusque efficiency, the effect somewhat ruined by his ridiculous appearance. "Move swiftly and brook no delay until you are safely ensconced within the wizard's protections. Make the necessary inquiries and depart with all due speed—the less you are seen or your whereabouts known, the better off we shall all be." He rocked on his haunches. The bed frame groaned in a poor parody of his throne back in the brownstone. "It is simply a matter of time before we are discovered and for once, time will not be bent in our favor. I will attempt to place any necessary plans into motion while you are away." One clawed hand flowered open. "Give me your phone."

"What?" Joy said, scandalized.

"Your phone," the Bailiwick repeated. "I know for a fact that you have my number, and I do not wish to leave any further evidence of my having been here by delegating my instructions using your home phone." He frowned, but continued politely. "I am attempting to maintain your thin illusion of familial normalcy here, Miss Malone. And I do so for both our benefits." She still hesitated. Without her phone, she felt disconnected from the world. Naked and vulnerable. Graus Claude looked unimpressed. "The phone," he growled. "Now."

She dropped it in his hand. He'd sounded absolutely paternal.

"Grab your things and let's go," Filly said, giving Joy a merry slap on the back. "Before he next sends you to bed without supper!"

Joy walked down the familiar path to the C&P, pausing to glance up at the streetlamp. The glass had been replaced since that night she'd been chased by the *bain sidhe*, before she'd taken an unexpected trip to Ireland and watched Ink's mischievous trick with the milk. Her smile at the memory faltered. Having Ink out there somewhere, thinking the worst of her, made her footsteps sound extra loud to her ears. Especially when Filly walked so silently beside her, eyes scanning the landscape, hand on her hilt.

"You sure you can't pop us any closer?" Joy said, squeezing the strap of her purse. "It'd be a lot less risky."

"So you say," Filly countered. "I wouldn't want to be on the receiving end of whatever your resident wizard uses as a deterrent for unexpected visitors. From what I can tell, wizard's magic loathes other magic. Best announce ourselves graciously and walk in on foot." She flashed a smile and widened her blue eyes. "Besides, you have nothing to fear— I shall keep you safe while your lover dallies elsewhere!"

Joy groaned. "It's not the dallying that worries me."

"Oh?" Even though her attention was on the walkway, Filly's voice curled with interest. As one of the Folk, she couldn't help being as curious as a cat. "I'd heard the name 'Raina' became tiff-worthy only recently."

Joy stopped, flushing. "Who told you that?"

Filly grinned. "The wind."

"The wind ought to learn to keep its mouth shut," Joy grumbled. Filly laughed and pushed her forward. Joy allowed herself to be dragged down the path, if only to keep moving. The trees looked harmless, the shrubs moved with the breeze, but everything *felt* malevolent—like eyes and ears were behind every leaf's shadow, watching her, studying her, biding their time. Graus Claude was right: she had to get to Vinh's quickly, get in, get out and get back home, safe behind wards. She hoped her last-minute call in to work begging for a recovery day from her trip wouldn't cost her her job. Of course, she hadn't managed to hold a job for more than a month since February, when she'd first met Ink. "It was...a misunderstanding," she muttered, fishing for her scalpel. Holding it made her feel better. "Everything's fine."

"Fine?"

"Fine."

Filly shrugged. "Fine."

"Better than fine—one might say, *excellent*," Ladybird said as he stepped out into the path. The drug lord grinned wildly, doffing his plumed pirate hat. "I do so love being right." Behind him a posse of creatures emerged from the ground, the trees, the folds of a flag; a few fell from dangling branches while others zipped out of thin air. Ladybird adjusted his brim. "Fetch her."

Joy jerked back with a gasp.

Filly leaped forward with a battle cry.

The first fighters clashed together, exploding in a crash of spittle and spray. Filly punched one beaked face, hooked an imp around the neck and levered herself, delivering a solid kick to a hairy yeti chest; the sasquatch doubled over, pawing at its matted green fur. With a twist, Filly flipped the imp over her shoulder and used its wing as a shield, clamping the membrane together and trapping a clawed fist between bones, wrenching it swiftly with a sideways snap.

Ladybird grinned.

Two flying pixies, shag-haired and sooty, circled Joy, armed with wicked-looking pikes the size of fondue forks. A grizzly thing approached her with lazy, loping strides—a boarhound on two legs with bandoliers of daggers crisscrossing its blue-gray chest and knobby clubs hanging from the scrappy belt on its hips. It looked intelligent and dangerous as it snarled at her scalpel.

"Donne prathiea toun de mallabra," he said in a low growl. "Drop it, girl, or you might get hurt." The hunter spread his scarred arms in an exaggerated gesture. "We've only come to escort you back to the Hall. The Council wishes to have words with you."

She should have said something brave, but the words dried up on her tongue.

"Just talk," the boarhound said. Both pixies leveled their weapons. Joy raised her scalpel and bent her knees.

There was the crunch of bone breaking, a high shriek and another "HA!" as Filly tore past, a blur of vambraces and finger bones. A horned black rabbit flopped onto the grass. A multitailed fox tumbled end over end, teeth gnashing and snapping. A cloak of mist with floating eyes settled over the melee like a blanket. Filly grabbed both its eyeballs and slammed them together. The thing wobbled and dissipated.

Joy squeezed the scalpel. Filly's bravery fueled her own. *"Duei nis da Counsallierai en dictie—"*

The boarhound barked out a laugh. The pixies tittered. "You've got guts, girl, I'll give you that, but the Edict won't spare you this time."

The pixies swarmed forward in a blur of wings, weapons pointed directly at her eyes. Joy inhaled sharply. They couldn't *blind* her—not now! Not when she was one of them! Or did they suspect her already? Did it show? Did they *know*? Joy gagged on a tight knot in her throat, imagining her tongue turned to stone.

The pixies said something low and menacing, barely more than an angry drone. The *eelet* in her ear was useless for Air Folk speech, it was only good for Water, but she understood the threat, if not the specifics. She backed up warily. Panic rippled under her skin like sweat in reverse.

"I don't understand," she whispered.

A crimson sleeve came from behind her and folded gently across her throat. A voice hissed in her ear. "Let me elaborate." Ladybird's voice hinted at giggles and malice. "These hirelings want to kill you, but I was here first."

Ladybird tightened his grip. A fine spray of spots pulsed along the edge of his profile, black against a glossy, chitinous sheen. His plumed hat pushed against her ponytail. Sparkling rings flashed on his fingers.

"Miss me?" the drug lord whispered like a song. "I'm flattered. I confess, I've spent a great many nights thinking about you!" He pressed her against his chest, grinding against her hip. Joy flinched against her trapped throat. "Did Ilhami tell you, my little Turkish thief, what I said would happen if we crossed paths again?" His exhaled breath was smoky-sweet and it shuddered against her ear. Her insides clenched. She missed the angry thump of her heart. "Ah, but such pleasures will have to wait," he said. "There are those who would pay quite handsomely for such a rare, pretty bird to be delivered—" he squeezed and Joy gagged "—*safely* into the Council's waiting arms." He nuzzled the side of her face. He smelled like crude oil and cloves. "I may not be good at math, but I can divide a bounty by one!" He slipped a length of gold chain from around his wrist like a magician's trick. "What say you, Nightingale? Ready to take a spin?"

Joy flipped the scalpel's handle and brought the blade down, slashing quickly across his arm. It bit through the crimson greatcoat, and hot liquid gushed over her skin. She wrenched out of his elbow and spun into the boarhound, who grabbed her shoulders, surprised. Ladybird held his wounded arm, grinning like a demon.

"Blood for blood, eh?" he cackled, and took a long lick

of his forearm, painting his tongue red. The drug dealer's eyes yawned. "Mmm. Needs salt."

There was a mellow *crump* noise and the clawed hands on her arms loosened. The boarhound fell boneless behind Joy's ankles. Filly popped the clasp and whipped her cape sideways; the net of fine finger bones caught both pixies and tossed them to the ground. She was body-slammed by two burly elves sporting multiple piercings. Filly struggled, then backslapped her forearm, knocking them flat.

"Run!" the horse warrior shouted. "Run now!"

Joy spun around, but Ladybird cackled and whipped his gold chain around Joy's throat, yanking her backward and catching her arm.

"Well, this was fun," he said, tipping his hat with a bloody hand. He spun the end of the gold chain in a humming circle. "We'll have to do it again, sometime! Until we meet again, *ást!*" Filly charged, but was tackled by a wall of bodies. She screamed in defiance as Ladybird winked and stepped back. Joy dragged her feet against the sidewalk. Giggling, Ladybird lifted her bodily over the breach.

Between one flash of the gold chain and the next, they were gone.

SEVEN

THE GOLDEN CHAIN WHIPPED FROM HER THROAT, SER-
rating her skin in a sharp, thin rash. Joy rubbed her neck,
swallowing convulsively. Even before her eyes cleared, she
knew where she was—the shade of the light, the smell of the
air, the angry mumbling surrounding her, which shattered
with one bitter cry.

"Now we see what happens when our desperation for
progeny eclipses our reason!" Sol Leander's voice rang
through the Grand Hall. The sound of his voice slapped her
ears as she stood on the smooth, central dais. "This *changeling* has brought nothing but chaos and ruin since she was
first allowed to retain her Sight and dally with the Scribe."
Joy's eyes focused on the flat hand stabbing in her direction. The Council members mumbled among one another,
some of them still wearing their gala finery. The stands
behind her were packed with every creature imaginable.
She wondered if Ink was somewhere in the crowds. A hot,
tight coil of dread twisted her insides as she felt everyone's
eyes on her.

Ladybird bowed crisply, doffing his hat and collecting a
small bag from a dryad on his left before making a smug-
faced escape. Joy watched him take the bounty, vaguely
wondering what she was worth.

Her secrets. Her power. And the whereabouts of her friend, Graus Claude.

The Bailiwick's chair was empty. Sol Leander was on his feet. Maia frowned but said nothing as the leafy dryad whispered something under its breath. A shape stalked along the back of the dais, plunging the jeweled walls into shadow as it passed. It prickled something inside her.

The rap of a gavel brought a muttering silence. Bùxiǔ de Zhēnzhū presided over the Council in humanoid form, but there was something of the dragon in his long mustaches, which twirled alongside his face in the nonexistent breeze. "The indiscretions and indignities of the one known as Joy Malone are far too numerous to list, exacerbated no doubt by her continuing loyalty to her mentor, the Most Honorable Councilex Claude." His head undulated sinuously over his shoulders; hints of scales flashed along his throat. "However, these crimes must be weighed against the immeasurable gift she has brought to our attention by freeing the Twixt of its unknown enslavement under the Amanya spell, restoring the knowledge of our beloved monarchs and kin."

"Which she has abused by absconding with the Bailiwick!" Sol Leander sputtered. "A crime of epic proportions and in direct defiance of the Council, our laws and the very rules regarding sovereignty by proxy set into being by the King and Queen themselves!"

There was a roar at the Tide leader's pronouncement. Joy looked around for an ally among the bleachers, but Ink, Inq, Filly and Graus Claude were all far away. She didn't even know whether Ink would try to help her if he were here; his withdrawal still felt like rejection, like she'd failed him once again. Joy clenched her teeth and her fists against the din. Her enemies far outnumbered her friends here.

Sol Leander flicked his sparkling cloak of galaxies and

sat down. Joy spied Avery just beyond him, standing by his master's side. The young courtier, aide to the Tide, was expressionless as stone. Only the feathers of his cloak moved. He would not even look at her.

Crap.

The gavel banged again patiently. Bùxiŭ de Zhēnzhū's reedy voice was calm but firm. "At this time, we are concerned only with those particulars as they might pertain to the Imminent Return."

"To that end, now that we are all in attendance, let us discuss the matter plainly." The Low Air Seat, a ruby-lipped fairy with twin spears, glared down at Joy. "We, the Council, have reason to suspect that you, Joy Malone, willingly and with knowledgeable intent, removed the locks securing the door between worlds. Is that correct?"

What else could she say but the truth? "Yes. I'm sorry, but—"

"And did you witness what lay beyond the door?"

Joy sighed. Her breath echoed in the sudden silence. "Yes."

Murmurs gained volume, like a trickle before a flood. "And did they acknowledge you?"

Behold the Destroyer of Worlds. Joy swallowed. "I'm sorry—" and she was. That much was true. "I don't understand what you—?"

"Did they acknowledge your presence?" the dryad asked slowly.

"Oh," Joy said, relieved. "Yes. And they—"

Noise filled the Hall as everyone started shouting and pointing, waving arms and wings and wands and staves. The Council Head banged the gavel, but it was lost in the uproar. Maia's face had gone ruddy with shouting, spittle flying from her rubbery lips. Joy watched the thing lurking closer, slipping like a whisper between the gaps between seats. It glared from the shadows and wore a black, hooded cloak. Joy's stomach curdled with fear.

She raised her hand like a child in grade school, patiently waiting to be called on, staring intensely at the teacher, praying that he'd see.

"—and that makes her the courier, does it not?" The last speaker shouted at full volume, surprising itself in the sudden silence. Joy's fingers tingled pins and needles. Was that true? Did being the first to see the King and Queen make her and Ink the new couriers? If so, then...

Bùxiǔ de Zhēnzhū inclined his head, tacitly acknowledging his position and admonishing further interruption. The Grand Hall stayed respectfully silent.

"You have something to add, Miss Malone?"

It was worse knowing that her voice would carry perfectly throughout the Grand Hall for everyone to hear. "Yes," she said, and took a deep breath. "I saw them. I saw the King and Queen of the Folk." The Council Head held up a hand to forestall any person from interrupting her words. "And I saw an army—a vast army that rushed the door." She hoped that she was making sense; that she could make them understand. "That is why we left the Bailiwick," she said, thinking of Ink. She could picture him hauling her to safety, pulling her out of Faeland, pressing her against him, safe in his embrace. She felt his absence like an ache. "That is why we ran."

Silence had a flavor now—sharp and tinny and taut as wire.

"An army, you say?"

The voice dripped from the bulbous droplet that hung above one of the chairs. Joy had never seen the face of whoever occupied the Low Water Seat, but Graus Claude once told her it was a Leviathan and that the crystal held the shape of him, which was larger than the entire Hall. Joy could only nod. A few of the Council members exchanged glances.

"It verifies her claim," the fairy said, crossing her bare ankles.

The androgynous High Fire Seat leaned forward, its crystalline body snapping with tiny pops and cracks. "Nonsense," it hissed like a fissure of steam.

"It's fallacy." Sol Leander sniffed.

Maia snapped, "It's proof!"

The Council Head looked interested, his curiosity piqued. "How?"

Councilex Maia grinned. "They've been waitin' for the courier to bring word," she said. "I say we let her! It suits the conditions o' their Return an' will get them here all the quicker." Her dark eyes twinkled as she rotated in her chair. "Them's the rules."

The dryad groaned. "After the last disaster—"

"Stay in the now, please."

"If she really qualifies, then—"

"You'd let her go?"

"You'd keep the others from their Return?"

"She'd have to be the one—"

"—cannot fathom a worse—"

"The attack proves *my* theory," Sol Leander insisted, gesturing emphatically in her direction. "They recognize her for what she is."

Fear stabbed Joy's gut. *Was he right? Did they know what I am? Are they all after me?*

Maia fumed. "If there's a chance—"

"Turn her over to the law and be done with it," Sol Leander snapped with a contemptuous wave. "To ignore the evidence of her guilt is to condemn ourselves to death." He glanced discreetly over his shoulder at the shape in the dark. "Which, in this case, might prove most fitting."

Avery twitched very slightly. His arm stirred beneath his cloak.

"Silence," Bùxiǔ de Zhēnzhū intoned, his reedy voice slicing through the Great Hall. "If Joy Malone has indeed stumbled into the role of royal courier, then it would now be her duty to bring the proof our monarchs require to Return to this world and therefore we cannot risk restraining her efforts for the good of us all."

"That is unacceptable!" Sol Leander shouted, jumping to his feet. "We cannot allow this lunatic to run rampant! We must consider carefully our actions that precede the Imminent Return. To be unfaithful to the promise that it is safe for all those who took refuge beyond the door to come back to this world is grossly irresponsible!" he thundered. "Look at the world! Beyond our borders is death! It creeps ever closer with each passing year and we must ask ourselves if we are willing to expose our only King and Queen to this wreckage of iron and steel and human filth. Entrusting *her* with the future of our people is—"

"Her fate." Bùxiǔ de Zhēnzhū said quietly. Sol Leander gaped. The murmurs began again. His serpentine gaze slid to Joy. "And therefore I conclude this matter is now closed."

"No!" Sol Leander insisted. "I call for a motion of *Duei noq Counsul*, requiring that all representatives meet with their designated—" His voice was drowned out as the stadium seats emptied, Folk swarming down to the floor level as each Council member rose to address their constituents. Joy stood anchored to the giant, smooth stump as the crowds parted around her, not trusting herself not to bolt or that the Folk wouldn't tear her to pieces if she moved.

"Restrain her!" commanded Sol Leander, bolstered by the delegates around him who could only be members of the Tide. Joy had never seen their faces, but she knew that these were her enemies, those who were committed to human genocide to bring about Aniseed's promised Golden Age. She would have never guessed that these people who barely knew her would hate her so. She stood her ground and did not look away. She was staring so hard, she jumped at the boneless touch on her back.

"There now, dear," Maia said gently. "Come wi' me."

"I object!" Sol Leander turned to Bùxiŭ de Zhēnzhū, who still presided over the Council seats. "Councilex Maia is High Earth Seat and has claim for Joy Malone."

"Ye know my proper title," Maia sniffed haughtily. "Tha's an improvement!"

"I fear she may show leniency or favoritism toward the subject of these proceedings."

Maia huffed, plunking her pudgy hands on her squat hips and drawing herself upward until she towered like a spire of taffy over them all. "She's *my* responsibility, as you so rightly point out, an' I'm not takin' her anywhere other than jus' beyond that door." She jabbed a thumb back over her shoulder. "I've got to inspect her for m'self as she reflects on all us Earth." She nodded to the crowds of Folk, who must have included many of her House. "But if ye 'ave issue with my doin' so alone, then lend me one o' yours to take up the task as well." She nodded as if that closed matters. "Your aide, then?" Avery stepped forward, soldier-straight. She lowered herself to his height with a piercing eye. "Do you accept the task I set t' ye of yer own free will?"

The frosty-haired courtier waited for his master's nod before answering. He did not look at Joy. "Yes, Councilex, I accept."

"That do?" she huffed. Sol Leander nodded, at least partially mollified. Satisfied, Maia bubbled back down to size. "Come away, then," she said, hooking her chubby fingers in the crook of Joy's arm and grabbing a hold of Avery's cloak. She dragged them off the dais and down an empty aisle to a set of carved doors flanked by thick velvety curtains. The crowds funneled and dissipated behind similar doorways, the private conference rooms of the various Houses of the Twixt. Bùxiŭ de Zhēnzhū gave Joy one long glance as she passed, his mustaches waving past his lips. She might have imagined he'd said something, but it was lost in the commotion.

Maia brought them into a green room, pale and cool as a grotto. She closed the door behind them and clapped her hands together with a bang.

"Ah, there now. Tha's better!" Neither Joy nor Avery seemed to share her enthusiasm, but it didn't dampen her smile one bit. Maia hummed a little as she circled Joy, puttering and muttering like an old hen. Avery stepped back, keeping professional watch, face tight and tense. "Now ye've got yer *signatura*, Grimson's mark, yes, yes, the Scribe's blade— now yours—and ooo, a message bag! Tha's handy!" The Councilex poked Joy's purse as she kept circling, patting Joy here and there. It was eerily reminiscent of Idmona's ministrations when the master tailor had carefully inspected Joy's dress before the gala. It was equally humbling and creepy. "An' you still have the satyr's dowsing rod t' smell out spells, do you? Mmm-hmm. Okay. Good." The mushroomy woman patted Joy companionably on the back. "Tell the old frog we're countin' on him, make no mistake." She winked.

Joy blinked in shock. "Wh-what?" she stammered.

"Good luck," Maia said. Pat-pat. "An' goodbye."

Without a word, Avery swirled the hem of his great feathered cloak over Joy's head, pulled her against him and let it fall.

They fell together through a swirling cloud of white.

EIGHT

JOY LANDED HARD, HER FEET SLAPPING AGAINST A wooden floor. Her knees bent automatically, accustomed to recovering a botched dismount, her nerves on high alert. She didn't recognize the room, which was sparsely furnished and dim. It might have been a cabin, or a servant's quarters in a bigger house. The place smelled of old, dry firewood and something spicy, like pine. Avery strode about the room opening drawers and removing their contents. He kicked open a trunk with the heel of his boot.

"Where are we?" Joy asked as Avery dropped a stack of things into the trunk.

"My home," he said. "Or it was. Things will be much different now."

Joy rubbed her arms. It was cold—much too cold for August. She had no idea where they were, but had a feeling it was north. Far north. Like Greenland. How far away was she from her home and safety? How far away was she from Ink? She shivered, remembering his last, parting look and wondered what he'd think of her now.

Avery continued packing, swiftly gathering the paintings and maps hanging on the walls.

"We left the Council Hall," she said.

He nodded. "Yes."

"You broke me out."

"Yes."

Joy paused. "Won't you get in trouble?"

He rolled his eyes. "Gods, yes."

Joy folded her arms tight. "Then why?"

Avery paused with an armful of fine coats, the tails draping off his wrist. "I have often asked myself the same thing," he admitted. "Ever since Maia came to me saying that you needed my advice."

"*Your* advice?" Joy said, walking around the butcher-block table in the center of the room. Everything was utilitarian and made of thick, solid wood. "About what?"

"I imagine it pertained to staving off the change," he said, folding his clothes carefully into thirds. He concentrated on the task at hand, neatly avoiding her startled gaze. "There are not many changelings in the Twixt any longer, and even fewer who have struggled half-in, half-out of the transformation—" He stopped folding one-handed and lifted his gaze. His eyes seemed oceans away. "Anyway, I imagine that was her intention. Communication was difficult."

Joy gaped. "You're a changeling?"

"Of a sort," he said. "I was born human, transformed by magic. There are few of us at Court, and it is considered... embarrassing. Not to be discussed in public."

Joy circled the table. "And so you brought me here to tell me about changelings?"

"No," he said, hugging the clothes against his chest. "Maia tasked me with getting you out of the Hall should anyone on the Council try to hinder you. I agreed with her that every effort must be made for you to bring about the Imminent Return. Bùxiǔ de Zhēnzhū agreed." He ducked around her and continued gathering objects, folded bags, wrapped packages and small boxes tied with twine. It looked as if he might have been preparing to leave. Or that he'd never un-packed to begin with.

"That's...against the rules," Joy said. "The Council's rules. Sol Leander's rules. The Tide's—" The look he gave her made her stop. She shook her head. "Maia I can understand, but you always believed in the law."

"I believe in what is right, for our people and yours—*that* is the law that takes precedence," he said. "The Council no longer matters. Our monarchs await their Return, and to forestall that is to play games of power and intrigue that are no longer theirs. Some of the Folk accept this, others do not." He tucked a quilted blanket into a soft square. "When Councilex Maia asked me to accept the task she'd given me with the entire Council as witnesses, it was my final act of obeisance under their governance. I am loyal to the Twixt, to the King and Queen," he said. "And therefore, to you."

Joy almost smiled. "You were loyal to me before then."

Avery closed a book by the mantel, his back to her. "As you say."

There was an uncomfortable silence. "Why?"

Avery turned around, cradling the old book in his hand. His face was carefully blank, his voice, quiet. "Do not ask questions that you do not want answered." He ran his thumb lightly over the tattered spine. "Some truths should remain unsaid."

Joy glanced away. Nodded. She'd learned that lesson all too well.

"Now, then," Avery said, piling books into what Joy suspected to be a bottomless chest. "My particular case involves an elixir, one that can reverse the change and allow me to retain my hand and arm for one hour out of every twenty-four." He swept the top of his cabinet clean. "I can choose when to take it, but it is only good for that one hour—no more, no less." He picked at something on his cloak, preening. "I do not know if the elixir will stave off your change, but it may slow it down considerably. Perhaps you can be human or Folk for one hour out of twenty-four? I am no alchemist, but at least it may provide a start."

He pulled a roll of paper out of a drawer and handed it to her. "I have written down the ingredients and their measures, but you will need to find someone to draft it—a hedge witch or herbalist." Avery stepped past her, dismissive and hurried. "It is human magic," he admitted. "And not gotten lightly."

Joy touched the scroll. The stiff paper felt sharp. "You were human once," she said. Her voice was harsher than she intended. "Did your family find the cure?"

Avery laughed, sounding both surprised and surprisingly hurt. "No. My family died long ago, living out their human, mortal lives." He lifted a wooden box from under the bed and pressed his hand to each of four clasps. They sprang open, and the room filled with forest scents. He lifted out a shaggy tunic of spiky nettles that was missing one sleeve. It crackled as he held it. His face turned grim. "My sister tried to save me," he said. "She tried to save us all, but I was the only one—" He stopped and sighed. "The last one who couldn't fully change back. So I lived and they died, because they were mortal and I was not."

"And your auspice—?"

"Being betrayed by a family member? Yes, I believed that once," he said. "But I was angry and alone, and it was untrue." Avery squeezed the woven fibers. They cracked and crumbled in his hand. "It was true enough for me at the time and easily fed my hatred for humanity, my bitterness at betrayal, but I have since learned that failure does not justify fear."

He draped the prickly shirt on the white bedsheet and folded it up neatly, then tucked the bundle gently into the trunk. The room felt suddenly empty. Whatever had been Avery's was gone.

"We cannot linger," he said. "They will be here soon. There are few places in the Twixt I can fly."

Joy gaped. "You can *fly*?"

He gave her a sour look. "I can slipstream short distances. Air Folk call it 'flying' or 'loqcution.'"

"Ah." Joy glanced around the abandoned room. "All done packing?"

Avery smirked. "Unlike you, I don't have a great love of furniture."

Joy gave him her own sour look and declined to comment. Despite Avery's favorite dig, Ink was a *person*, not an object—he was a thinking, feeling being and not just a convenient shape. Joy swore that if Avery ever called him a chair again, she'd kick him in the shins. But thinking about Ink made her anxious. What would he do now that she'd escaped with Avery? She fumbled with the zipper pull as she tucked the scroll into her purse. "So where are we going?"

"To the Bailiwick," he said. "If you are the courier, then the King and Queen are awaiting your word, your assurance that it is safe for them to Return in order to abide by their rules." He closed the trunk with a snap. The lid folded in upon itself, becoming a smaller trunk, then a box, then a packet, then a cube, which Avery picked up and tucked into a small pouch on his belt. It was neatly done, just like the scroll and the rescue and the offer to bring her back—everything she needed to succeed and escape—but the Folkish part of her balked, wondering if the elixir could be poison, the rescue might have been staged and the offer to return her to the Bailiwick was a ploy to expose where Graus

Claude was hiding. If she was going to stop the change, wish back her heart and free the Folk trapped in Faeland, she was going to have to stop thinking like a human and start acting more like the Folk. Her human half wanted to trust Avery, but the Folk half knew that she couldn't. Too much was at stake. He was a rival, a ranking courtier and an agent of the Tide.

"I left Filly on the sidewalk outside my house," Joy said, hoping that the fight back in the real world was over even though it'd been only a moment, if that. "She's probably having fits. You should take me there before she breaks something valuable."

"Very well," he said, glancing once more around the bare room. He opened his cloak, exposing his rapier and the snowy left wing curled against his side. "Come. We haven't much time."

She stepped closer, squeezing her purse strap, feeling his nearness like a betrayal. She kept her eyes forward, wishing for the smell of rain, the *shing!* of a razor, the sharpness like limes. She tried not to feel the soft feathers embrace her as his cloak fell warm about her shoulders. "Where will you go when they come for you?" Joy asked for something to say.

"Not far," he said, his voice by her ear. "I have my duties." His wing unfolded, lifting the cloak high over their heads. Avery whispered into the feathered quiet. "And you have yours."

His cheek touched her face. Joy held her breath. The cloak dropped in a flurry of feathers. And they disappeared.

Avery dropped them onto the grass just within sight of the path. Filly stood among the wreckage looking smug. Long gouges ripped through the topsoil, a stone bench lay cracked in half and monstrous bodies littered the ground like scattered, broken toys. Joy shrugged off the cloak and stepped quickly away from Avery. She felt his gaze prickling behind her. She didn't look back.

"Hoy!" Filly waved, rattling her half cape of bones. "There you are. Figured you'd be back here quick enough when the hirelings ran off. Left the Council in a ruckus, I'd wager." The blond warrior eyed Avery over Joy's shoulder. "Popped her out right from under their noses, did you?" Robed in feathers, Avery could only nod. Filly's face split in a grin. "I *knew* I liked you! Well met indeed." She nodded to Joy. "And you? Are you well enough?"

"I'm fine," Joy said, amazed at Filly's quick deductions.

"Oh, yes, *fine*." Filly snorted. "You keep using that word like a well-worn boot."

"If that is all," Avery said crisply, "I will leave you in the Valkyrie's capable hands."

Joy spun around. "Avery, wait!" She stopped twisting her fingers and tucked them behind her back. His blue-green eyes seemed to alternately harden and swim as she drew closer. She tried to put the heart she didn't have in her words. "Thank you."

The tips of his feathers and his hair ruffled in the breeze. It was a long moment before he spoke.

"Make it worthwhile," he said. "Bring them home."

He ran down the sidewalk, away from them, his cloak billowing behind him, almost level to the ground, before he lifted his wing and arm and disappeared in a swirl of feathers and down.

Filly stepped beside Joy and scanned the surrounding carnage. "Well, that was fun, but I'll admit it's not what I was expecting."

Joy glanced at her sideways. "Why? Were you expecting something else?"

"I always expect something to happen around you, Joy

Malone." Filly tossed her head, snickering. "And I am rarely disappointed." She snapped an arm across Joy's chest, stopping her flat. "Wait," she whispered, smiling, expectant. "Wait for it—*there!*"

The air tore sideways and Ink appeared, silver-shirted, razor drawn and wallet chain swinging. Joy couldn't help but feel excited to see him—beautiful and *here*—but it was followed quickly by a wave of wariness and guilty shame. She was afraid to look at him.

"Ah! There you are!" Filly barked. "You're late."

Joy reached for him. "Ink—"

"*Stop!*" he reared back, black eyes wide. Joy froze.

His arm rose at the shoulder, snaking out in a short burst of speed...

She was back in the Carousel, back against the Red Knight, back standing between Ink and Maia's door. Joy stumbled backward, scalpel held high. Their blades met in a burst of black-on-white sparks that pinwheeled in a firework cloud. Ink jerked back, stung.

"Ink!" Joy screamed as shock turned to terror. He swept forward again, blade flashing, eyes flat, face tight. He looked like a thing possessed—an angel of death.

Fear punched her breath. Her brain shrieked. *Ink, no!*

A buckler knocked them apart, crashing into Ink's face.

His head snapped back. Joy stumbled aside. Filly laughed as Ink spat at the ground and shook his head. Oily wetness stained his teeth. The straight razor danced a whirling, flaring loop like a shield between them. Snorting, Filly advanced, dodging the blade and landing two kicks and a solid punch to his gut. Ink buckled, but kept his weapon raised high as if trying to keep it out of reach. His elbow locked. His muscles quivered in effort. He glared at Filly, looking annoyed.

"Here!" He slapped his left breast. "Hit me here!"

"What?" Joy cried. "No!"

Ink's arm sliced down, guillotine-straight at Filly's leg, but she danced a quick fade, and sprang upward under his guard, landing a deep rabbit punch right on target. Something clicked and Ink crumpled, eyes open, mouth slack.

Horrified, Joy screamed.

"INK!"

Filly glanced back at Joy, a grin smeared across her lips. The thin tattoo lines on her eyelids curled in a wink. "Don't worry—he's *fine*."

NINE

JOY STUMBLED OVER THE THRESHOLD AT THE C&P, triggering its two-tone *hello* chime. She knew the security cameras would see her, but not the invisible warrior woman with the unconscious Scribe slung over her back. Joy held the door open behind her as Filly stepped to one side and rested her load on a squat freezer full of ice cream sandwiches and frozen Dove bars.

The owner's son, Hai, sat behind the counter. He didn't bother looking up.

"He's in the back," he said, and flipped a page in his textbook.

Joy nodded wearily, heading toward the Employees Only door. She glanced back. Filly strode behind her, nose wrinkling against the stale smell of air freshener and old coffee. Ink hung like a limp sack over her back.

"This is either an excellent illusion or a terrible wizard's lair," she complained.

Joy was glad the aisles were empty. "How many wizard's lairs have you been to?"

"Oh, a few," Filly said. "More than my fair share, truth be told, and less than I ought!" Laughing, she hoisted Ink higher on her shoulder. His arm knocked cans of salted peanuts off a shelf. Joy stopped and picked them up, getting a close-up look at Filly's buckskin boots. The toes and heels were spattered with grass stains and blood. Joy's skin prickled with equal parts fear and guilt.

"Come on," she said quickly. "Let's go see the wizard."

She knocked on the storage room door. It opened. Mr. Vinh was checking his inventory against a thick sheaf of spreadsheets. Stacks of juice flats, power bars, toilet paper and candy filled the shelving units nearly to the ceiling. A lunar calendar tacked to the wall hung next to the mandatory Employee Rights posters and an altar decorated with faded photographs and tiny bowls of sweets. Joy turned a close circle. It was a tight squeeze, and she was conscious of Filly and Ink standing invisibly behind her.

"Hello, busy girl," the wizard said while ticking off a column of boxes. "I hear you've been *very* busy lately."

"Yeah," she said. "Tell me about it."

He flipped the sheaf closed and tapped its corner to his forehead. "I was about to ask you to do that very thing." He reached behind the shelving unit to pull the lever that Joy knew would spring a hidden door to his back office, but he hesitated. "Do you wish your friends to come with you?" he asked casually.

Joy paused. "Yeah. Can you see them?"

"No," he said. "I just wanted to make sure you knew that you were being followed." He pulled the lever, and the secret door cracked open. "The *tien* are not allowed to bother you here—it is against my magic and their Accords. My shop is considered neutral territory so that I may conduct business without interference." He tapped a small gong with his fingernail, which gave a tiny *ping*. "Always best to announce yourselves before entering someone's place of business," he said to the open air.

Filly raised her eyebrows, stretching the blue tattooed lines in question. Joy said nothing as the wizard pushed the door open wider, allowing them to enter as he flicked on the lights.

The back room was lined with bamboo slats. Bundles of dried herbs and wrinkled things hung from the ceiling among oddly twisted lightbulbs that gave off a golden glow. A large painting table dominated the room, strewn with scrolls of paper, inkwells, brushes and wax stamps. A dark red armoire with rows of tiny drawers stood beside a glass case filled with all sorts of strange equipment made of lenses, dials and twists of wire, rock and brass and bone. The shelves were lined with pickle jars and ceramic jugs, each crammed full with unidentifiable things. A dark mirror hung on the opposite wall, reflecting everything in shades of gray.

"I'd think you'd be able to brew up something to give yourself the Sight," Joy said, stepping onto the tatami mat floor. "It might be useful in your line of work."

Mr. Vinh shook his head as he fastened the frog buttons on his long, black robe, his official wizard gear. "No," he scoffed. "Why buy my glamours if customers know that I can See them? Depletes my own market value. Supply and demand!" He grabbed a flat, black cap from a hook and placed it on his head. "Besides, the Sight is more trouble than it's worth." Mr. Vinh leaned forward, dark eyes sparkling. "Tell me I'm wrong."

Joy said nothing. He nodded knowingly.

"You can't," he said, swirling a long stylus in a pot of paint. "Because it's true. And you cannot tell a lie."

Joy was conscious of her many changes since last they'd met. "You know, then."

"I do."

Changeling. Part-Folk. Destroyer of Worlds. Joy swallowed. "And Stef?"

His brush stilled. He held his long sleeve out of the way of the ledger and took a deep breath. "Yes," he said sadly. Joy was not the only one worried about her brother. His master clearly knew something about his apprentice and the *tien*. The Wizard Vinh made a few, last sweeping notes with his brush and set it aside, balanced perfectly across the pot. He opened the cabinet and picked up a small instrument with many lenses, twisting a half dome of milky crystal with a thoughtful expression. "May I see the company you keep?"

Joy glanced at Filly, who shrugged and dropped Ink on the mats with a muted *thump*. The horsewoman grinned at Joy's pained expression. Joy didn't know whether to go to him, to touch him, or not. The push-and-pull of imagining Ink as her love or her enemy was torture.

"They're there," she said, and pointed Vinh in their general direction.

The store manager held the apparatus up to his eyes, adjusting a small magnifying lens and a rock with a rough hole so that they became eyeholes. He twisted the knobs to gain focus and fiddled with a dial above the grip.

Filly draped her cape of finger bones back over one shoulder as she stood over Ink's body, spread out like a rug. She saluted the wizard with one fist. "Hoy!"

Mr. Vinh's lips pressed in a thin, professional slash. "I do not perform healings, amputations, surgeries or disposals."

Filly tossed her head. Joy's stomach sloshed sideways.

"No one's asking you to," Joy said. "He's—" She glanced at Filly, who arched her eyebrows. Joy finished her sentence with a resigned sigh "—fine."

"Fine?" Mr. Vinh said with mild surprise. Filly snorted a laugh. He lifted the strange spectacles from his eyes. "Very well, then. Why come to me?"

"I need...something," Joy said, twisting her thumb in her

shirt, feeling Filly's eyes like sunburn on her skin. She had to be careful. The Valkyrie was far too sharp and much too curious. Joy handed over the scroll that Avery had given her. "It's a potion, an elixir—something that maybe can slow the change, if it can't be stopped altogether. I don't know if it will work, but I thought you could take a look." She glanced at Filly, who was listening with an eager, obvious hunger, drinking fresh gossip like wine. Joy mumbled, "It's *really* important."

"Mmm." He grunted as he scanned the scroll. "Do you know what you are changing into?"

She couldn't answer. Not with Filly there. The Valkyrie might have sworn her oaths, but if she learned the truth— the whole truth—Joy doubted that she could stop the Norse warrior from trying to destroy her for the sake of the Twixt. She looked at Ink in a heap on the floor. She wanted to brush his hair away from his blank, pooling eyes, but didn't dare.

"Something...inhuman." Joy swallowed. *True enough.*

Mr. Vinh circled her slowly. Filly's gaze followed his path. "But that is the price you paid for this." He tapped her back lightly with the tip of the stylus, right where her *signatura* burned. "You sold your humanity when you traded your life to the *tien*." He sounded stern and unforgiving.

"No," Joy said, the word wrenched from her gut. She didn't know if it was denial or revulsion. "That's not true. My ancestor wasn't human, so I've always been this way— potentially, in any case—I just didn't know it yet." She turned her head, watching him circle her curiously. Joy knew she was speaking for Stef as well as herself. "When Ink marked me, it ignited the magic in my blood. I needed to accept my True Name so that none of them could control me. It was too dangerous, and I was vulnerable without one." She caught Filly's eye. "I wasn't forced into anything, but that's because

I didn't *want* to be forced to do anything against my will."
Filly nodded. She'd been the one to tell Joy and give her the
choice. "No one wants to be used as a slave."

Mr. Vinh fastened the oculus around his head with an
elastic band. His face was impassive. "My ancestors were
survivors of Hỏa Lò, a POW prison camp. I am a child of
refugees. I know something of that which you speak." His
voice was rough. He turned on his heel and walked to his
alchemist cabinet, opening and closing its tiny drawers.
"This cannot cure you, nor halt the progress of your transformation," he said over his shoulder. "But I believe I can
adjust this formula to slow it down until I know more." He
tapped bits of leaves and scraps into a small scale and used
the stylus to tap the counterweight. "It will not be perfect,"
he warned softly. "But it will be better than giving up."

Joy ignored his warning, homing in on the hope. "But
it can slow it down?" She just needed more time. Time to
get the King and Queen out of Faeland. Time to ask them
to change the rules. Time to remain human and not become an Elemental. Time to avoid becoming the Destroyer
of Worlds.

Mr. Vinh made another noncommittal noise as he ground
the herbs and twigs into a chunky powder that he poured
into a Ziploc bag. "Steep one tablespoon for two minutes in
boiled water. Drink hot, once a day." He placed the baggie
in her palm. "Brush teeth thoroughly afterward. The taste
will be unpleasant."

Joy closed her fingers around her stay of execution.
"Thank you." She felt the grit through the plastic. "What
do I owe you?"

Mr. Vinh was writing in his ledger, holding his sleeve
away from the wet calligraphy. "We will discuss payment
when my research is complete," he said stiffly. "The final

formula must be up to my standards, which carries my personal guarantee. I have a reputation to uphold." Joy wasn't sure whether to be grateful or terrified, but she had no room to bargain. He lifted his head, the wrinkles deepening behind the strange lenses. "You will use the dowsing rod and follow your brother's *mana*—his magical energy— and you will bring Stefan to me," he said. "We can do the same for him."

Joy didn't care to explain that Stef wasn't changing—that even if he now realized that he wasn't wholly human, the process of becoming whatever they were hadn't happened to him yet. Whether it was because he hadn't been marked by one of the Folk, or been a *lehman*, or crossed through the Twixt as often as she had, Stefan had not changed after he'd discovered he had the Sight back when he was five. Did it have something to do with his apprenticeship in wizardry, with Great-Grandma Caroline, or something else entirely? Thinking of her brother brought a fresh wash of worry. She'd last seen him at her gala in the final moments before chaos had broken out Under the Hill. She hoped he and Dmitri had gotten out okay. He *had* to be okay.

Mr. Vinh pointed his stylus at the wall. "What about your friend there?"

She glanced at Ink's body. "He's...fine." Filly smirked and nudged his hip with her boot. He flopped lifelessly. Joy winced, thinking about the last time he'd been shut off. He'd faked it then, pretending to collapse when Sol Leander had struck him, humiliating Ink and undermining Joy at her own Welcome Gala. It wasn't until later that she learned that Ink had fooled them all, that he'd built an internal block over the trigger, swearing that no one would ever shut him down again. And then he'd all but ordered Filly to do it. It didn't look like he was faking it now.

As if hearing her thoughts, Filly clucked her tongue to get Joy's attention. "Ink told me what to do," she said, looking around the room. "But it will be messy. We should move him elsewhere in the lair."

Joy went from uncomfortable to alarmed.

"Um," she mumbled. "May we use your bathroom?"

"The key is on the counter up front," he said, raising the multispectacles again. "Do not take offense if I walk you out."

Filly lifted Ink by one arm and bent forward, hauling him over her back and then tugging him into place. "A wise precaution," she said, approvingly. "Good tactics. I like this magician of yours!" She nodded in the wizard's direction as she followed Joy out the door. His eyes were magnified into strange shapes as he watched their passing. Filly hesitated in the doorway.

"Can you ask if he—?"

"You want to do business?" Mr. Vinh said. "Buy glamour first."

The Wizard Vinh wasn't born with the Sight so could only see the Folk with his invented oculars, but Joy wondered whether the old man could read lips.

Filly shut her mouth as the storage room door opened into the multicolored aisles of candy bars and salty snacks. Joy walked uncertainly to the front of the store as Filly waited by the chips.

"Need a bag?" Hai offered as Joy came closer.

She nodded. "Thanks," she said, dropping the baggie into the Have A Nice Day bag and paying for a bottle of Gatorade to wash it down. "And can I have the key to the ladies' room?"

He picked up a short dowel painted pink with a key dangling off the end. "Around the corner to the left."

Joy took it and the bag. "Thanks again."

* * *

Joy pushed the bathroom door open and let Filly in first. Fortunately, it was a single large bathroom with handicap access. Joy shut and locked the door.

"Did you two plan this?" Joy asked.

"Oh, aye," Filly said, lowering Ink onto the tile floor. "This was it, the grand plan!" She poked him with the toe of her boot. "At least Ink had his priorities in order—first free the Bailiwick, *then* try to kill you." She grinned as she arranged his loose limbs. "Ink and I used to plan stunts like this all the time for fun—makes a dull workday brighter. Although most often, I'd be bait." She elbowed Joy. "Remember when we met? I'd been priming a brash young bull at the bar? Ink needed him knocked senseless in order to mark him and asked me to egg him on. What a lark! Wasn't hard, truth be told. All it takes is a long sigh and a short skirt." Filly whistled through her teeth and punched herself in the leather-plated breast. "But that boy was fighter through and through! A good catch!"

Joy thought back on it. "So you already have a glamour?"

"No," Filly said with a smile. "I borrowed Hildr's. She never missed it!"

Joy gazed at Ink, puddled on the floor. It made her sick to see him slack against the scuffed tile. She hugged her arms and glanced at Filly. "So now what?"

"We wake him up," Filly said as she knelt beside him. "All part of the plan." She rubbed her palms together eagerly. "Like I said, he told me what to do."

She ripped his silk shirt collar, exposing his chest, and pushed her fingers straight into his flesh up to the wrist. Joy covered her mouth, feeling ill. Filly licked the blue spot under her lip as she fished around inside, the putty-like skin gaping out the wound. Wet, sucking sounds squelched off the walls.

"There we are, then," Filly muttered to herself. "Almost got it—" There was a popping noise and something jumped under his left pec. The Valkyrie eased back on her thighs and stood up. "That should do it."

Blood dripped off her fingers, leaving gruesome splashes of black neon light on the tiles.

There was a *click* and Ink started breathing, his chest slowly filling with air. The beat of his heart was thick, even and loud, and he blinked open/closed/open/closed, shutter-speed quick. The sparks of light in his eyes stopped swimming in circles, then focused on Filly. His mouth shut with a snap.

"You are in the wizard's lair," Filly said. "You were right—inside his protections is neutral territory, so you're in a confirmed safe zone. Oh, and you are on the bathroom floor." She wiped her hand on her legging, smearing Ink's blood. She glared down at him sternly. "Now patch yourself up. I'm done carrying you."

Ink pressed a hand to the yawning hole in his chest and sat up slowly, vaguely massaging the skin back together with long, slow strokes. Joy stared—she couldn't help it—wondering if he was really alive, if he was really okay, if he'd lost too much blood or if he'd attack her again. Ink glanced up. A rose-colored blush crept over his cheeks.

"Joy," he said, quiet and disarming, unable to look away.

The sink sputtered and splashed as Filly washed her hands, then shook off her fingers, spraying water like a dog. She curled her lip at the towel dispenser.

"As if I'd wipe my hands on dead trees!" The blond warrior turned around and smirked at the two of them. "I'll be outside," she said. "Call me if anything needs beating."

The door closed behind her with a *snick*.

Joy kept staring. Ink didn't move. The floor was a mess, spattered with dark, rainbow light. With a lightning jolt, Joy realized Ink's blood couldn't be replaced while the princess was still in Faeland beyond the door.

Joy hurried to the towel dispenser. "Let me help..." She yanked the handle repeatedly, making a long, beige-colored spool. The crunching sound was oddly normal, comfortingly real.

"Wait," Ink said and pressed his hand on the floor. Joy watched the splashes of blood tremble, forming tiny beads that rolled over the tiles, gathering around his handprint and siphoning into his skin. He lifted his palm. The floor was clean. Joy scrunched the wad of paper in her hands, useless.

"Oh," she said weakly. "Right. Neat trick." Every time she thought she was prepared, she was reminded once again that he wasn't human. In that moment, it was hard to believe that she wasn't, either. She twisted the ball of paper towels in her hands. What were they doing? What was he thinking? Why did she both feel like running to him as well as bolting out the door? Everything felt dangerous and precarious, off balance and strange. She couldn't make sense of what she was feeling. She couldn't quite meet his eyes.

"Joy, I am sorry," he said, rising to his feet. "I had to leave. You would not be safe from either the Council or me until we could manufacture a caveat that would satisfy the rules," Ink said. "I had to stay away, for both of our sakes. I could not bear it if I..." His voice trailed off, echoing in the room. "But I was not the only one who knew that you would come here, eventually, so I requested Filly's intervention should I appear." He tried to catch her eye. The paper towels crinkled in her fists. "I knew that the Wizard Vinh protected his neutrality and therefore I would not be beholden to the Accords within his domain. If I could get inside, you would be safe from me."

Joy lifted her face and swallowed, falling into his wide, black eyes. Her voice betrayed her, warm and hopeful. "Sounds risky."

"It was a calculated risk," he admitted. "But one worth making." He took a tentative step closer, his fingers tracing the wallet chain by his hip as if hesitant to trust either his hands or hers. "It is safe now."

"As long as we're here," Joy said slowly, watching his hands, envying the silver links under his touch.

Ink nodded. "As long as we are here."

"In the bathroom."

He smiled. "In the wizard's territory," he said. "All such places are declared neutral, noncombative zones where both human and Folk can coexist without fear of reprisal or retribution. I obey the letter of the rules." He gave a little shrug, a human gesture. "Filly assured me that she could manage things if I held back."

Joy raised her eyebrows, a smile tugging at her lips. "That was holding back?"

Ink grinned. One dimple. "It was not much harder than holding back now."

"From trying to kill me?"

"From trying to kiss you."

Joy blinked. "Oh," she said softly. Ink came closer. Her head filled with the scent of spring rain.

"It was worth this," he said again, circling her edges, her forearm, her waistline, her shirt, not quite touching but drawing closer, near enough to brush the fine hairs on her skin. "I needed to talk with you without the fear that I would be forced to act upon my knowledge, as is mandated by the rules that protect the Twixt."

"Sort of like blinding humans with the Sight?" Joy said. She could feel her breath bounce off his face.

"Yes," he said. "I hesitated. And so I missed." He took another cautious inch. It cost him something to do it, something precarious and brave. "I *wanted* to miss." His voice dropped to a whisper. "I fought the mandate. I fought the rules and made a mistake that was no mistake." Ink hesitated to touch the side of her face, his fingertips barely brushing the baby hairs by her ear. His voice trembled. "I am confident that I may do so again."

"So...we're here?" she asked hesitantly.

Ink cupped the side of her cheek. "We are very, very here."

She turned her face into his palm, hardly daring to let go of her fears, her uncertainty. She took a long, shaky breath. "I thought you'd left me, that we'd become enemies—" she confessed. "That I disgusted you. That you hated me."

"No," Ink said, pulling her close. "But you are only safe from me as long as we are here, until we have proof that you pose no threat to the Twixt, and that is only until you walk out those doors."

Joy curled in his arms, feeling both safe and afraid. "Are you my enemy?" she whispered.

"No. But I am bound by my Name." He drew back, searching her eyes, and steeled himself. "Mark me," he said. "Bind me to your Name and then I cannot turn against you."

The shock was like a splash. Joy pushed him back. "No!" she said with honesty and horror. "I can't. I mean, I don't even know how..."

Ink sighed. "Do you not know your auspice yet?"

"No," she said. "I don't even know how I find out."

Ink smiled tiredly. "It calls to you. It is who you are and

what you believe in. You will know it like you know yourself. And I know *you*, Joy Malone." He brushed his bangs from his eyes. "Tell me it will not happen, and I will believe it."

Joy hesitated. "What?"

"Say *it will not happen*." It was a demand, a request, a plea. "Your words will make it so, as per the rules. You cannot tell a lie and therefore you will make it come true." He squeezed her shoulders and gazed deep into her eyes like he was the one drowning. "Say it, and I will believe you."

She trusted him, unsaid and said.

"It will not happen."

Calm slowly seeped through his body, smoothing his face, his arms and the tight curve of his spine. As his tension melted, Joy felt hers grow. Were they talking about the same thing? Did he suspect or did he *know*?

"Ink?" she asked. "What do you think *isn't* going to happen?"

He rested his forehead against hers, his voice barely a whisper. "I think you are *not* becoming an Elemental."

Joy swallowed. "That's right," she said firmly, pulling their arms tighter. "I'm n—" But she couldn't say it for certain. The word gagged on her tongue. "I won't."

Hope wasn't the same as a lie.

"The Elementals are the sworn enemy of the Folk, decreed to be destroyed for the sanctity of the Twixt and all its peoples." His fingers fisted on her arms, kneading and needing. "Please," Ink begged. "Tell me how I can keep you safe."

Joy leaned back enough to focus on Ink's face. "Vinh gave me an elixir to help slow the change," she said. "Either he will find a cure, or he will buy us enough time to bring the King and Queen back into the world." Her words were coming faster, giving Ink the hopes and truths he needed. "If we can bring them back, then they can change the rules—they can stop this from happening." She licked lips gone dry. Joy tilted her chin. "How's that?"

Ink nodded slowly. "Very convincing," he breathed, the words caressing her mouth. She could taste them on her lips.

"Are you convinced?"

He kissed her, a deep, wanting kiss that reached all the way inside her and squeezed.

Her arms looped around his shoulders, pulling him closer. Their arms tightened, their breathing changed, their kisses became desperate, grasping, gasping for air.

There was a pointed knock at the door.

"Are you well in there?" Mr. Vinh's voice called.

"Yes," Joy said, disengaging her lips from Ink. "Just a minute."

"A minute," Ink whispered thankfully in her ear and held on tighter. "My world has forever changed in less."

TEN

FILLY SMILED KNOWINGLY AS THEY WALKED OUT OF the C&P, Joy and Ink almost touching, hovering a breath away from not being able to keep their hands off each other.

Once beyond Vinh's boundaries, Ink sliced a passage directly into Joy's foyer, bypassing his wards, the alarms, the door and the stairs. Joy zipped into the condo, prepared to see Graus Claude, but completely unprepared to find Stef shouting at him.

Her brother stood in the disheveled remains of an Armani tuxedo, tie gone, jacket torn and sleeves pushed up to the elbows, displaying charms and wizard's marks along the length of his forearms. He stabbed an accusatory finger at the four-armed amphibian, who squatted resolutely, eyes hooded, looking grim.

"I don't care *who* is after you," Stef shouted. "They can search all they want *outside this house!* This is still *my* domicile and its borders fall under the established Accords—"

"Stef!" Joy snapped. Her brother spun around.

"Joy? Joy!" He looked incensed, confused and relieved all at once. "What's all this?" He pointed around the room, starting with the Bailiwick dressed in a bedsheet and moving clockwise. "What is *he* doing here? What is *she* doing here?" He waved past Filly and trained his glasses on Ink.

"And where have *you* been?" he said. "You were supposed to be protecting her!"

Ink stepped calmly beside the Bailiwick. "I could say the same thing of you," he said as he considered brother and sister together. "But she is safe now."

Graus Claude gave an almost-imperceptible nod.

"Safe?" Stef almost laughed at the word. Almost. He spread both arms riddled with magic and scratches and wine. "Does this look safe to you? Is this a safe house now? Or a zoo?" He turned to Joy. "I rushed home after a rather significant riot Under the Hill to find a wanted fugitive *wearing my bed*."

"Oughtn't you be away at university or Hogwarts or something?" Graus Claude asked mildly. Joy watched her brother's face turn various shades of purple, but even he knew the Bailiwick was no one to trifle with. The great frog's browridge rose as if he were struck by sudden understanding. "Ah! You believe that you are not being shown proper deference? That you are due some modicum of respect even in the face of less-than-ideal circumstances." His eyelids lowered to half-mast. "I can only imagine what that must feel like."

Filly snorted a laugh, poorly disguised as a sneeze behind her wrist.

Stef jabbed a finger at her. "Don't *you* start," he warned. "Last I saw, you had to blast Joy out of a hunk of rock after she'd been buried in mud golems. And before that, you were chasing after that Red Knight, dragging Joy off to God-knows-where. Through a *tree*." His voice climbed. "You're complete havoc waiting to happen!"

"And I thought you a stubborn, pigheaded spellcaster with a mouth full of bad air and a brain full of cheese," Filly said simply. "Good to know we're both excellent judges of character."

Joy hurried to change the subject and distract her brother. "Where's Dmitri?"

Stef swung back to glare at Ink. "He's stuck outside the wards," he said flatly. "Neither of us could break them." He crossed his arms. "Mind letting him in?"

Ink shrugged. "Ask Joy."

Her brother frowned at her. "You didn't place these wards, did you?" he said, pained. "You're not dabbling in magic now, right?"

"Me? No!" Joy said hastily. "Ink placed the wards to keep the Folk out of our house. I asked Ink to make exceptions for those who could help us. Those I'd trust with my life."

Stef marched up to Joy and whispered hotly into her face. "You trust these guys with your *life*?"

Over his shoulder, Joy saw her friends gathered together in the kitchen. Graus Claude. Filly. Ink. "Yeah," she said. "I do." She turned to match Stef stare for stare. "Do you trust Dmitri with my life? With yours? With Dad's?"

Stef stiffened and then sighed through his nose. "Yeah."

"Okay, then," Joy said quietly, then with a little more volume. "Ink, can you please let Dmitri in? Filly, can you make sure the boys behave?"

The Valkyrie raised her brows. "Well, now, *that's* an order I've never heard before!"

Ink withdrew the silver quill from his back pocket. "I can put a clause on a window," he said to Stef. "Preferably yours."

Stef growled, "Fine." Joy punched her brother's arm. He added a halfhearted "Thank you."

"It will be temporary," Ink said. "And, therefore, delicate. It would be wise if both you and your friend watch your step."

Stef seemed to hear the double meaning and held his tongue. Her brother nodded and led the way into his room, presumably to unlock his bedroom window for the satyr. It didn't seem worth mentioning that they were two floors up.

"I see you have managed to rally Master Ink to your cause," Graus Claude said smoothly. "As if there were any doubt."

"There was *some* doubt," Joy muttered.

"Mmm," the Bailiwick purred knowingly. "Were you as successful with your original endeavor?"

That was a longer story. Joy tried to tell it as quick as she could before the others returned. Hitting the highlights took a surprisingly short time.

"The good news is that Maia is clearly on our side and, evidently, so is Avery. And the Council seemed inclined to believe that by being the first to open the door, I've become the new courier by default, so it's up to me to tell the King and Queen that it's safe to come home, so they're better off leaving me be." Joy sighed. "You can imagine how Sol Leander and the rest of the Tide liked that idea."

"I imagine the Council's new clemency does not extend to the Tide," Graus Claude intoned. "Stopping you is still their best hope to achieve their Golden Age. As soon as the King and Queen Return, Aniseed's plans are all for naught. None of the Twixt could be disloyal." He tapped his claws on the counter. "I wonder if they know about the graftling?"

Joy shook her head, trying to get the image of that bulbous, fetal *thing* out of her mind. "Ugh! I hope not," she said, quelling the urge to scratch the goose bumps off her arms. "Aniseed's clone is enjoying the Grove's protection, secluded in the nursery." Her voice hitched higher, tighter. "How long do you think it'll be before she comes after us and tries to take over the world again?"

Graus Claude grumbled. "Hysterics will not do, Miss Malone, and are entirely unnecessary. Firstly, the graftling is not the same as Aniseed, no matter its resemblance or what you might think. It is an entirely different entity altogether."

"But—!"

"Secondly," the Bailiwick interrupted smoothly. "It will take years before the graftling is grown enough to be safely separated from its stump. And in the interim, it will be guarded by the satyrs of the Grove and therefore be both closely observed and zealously protected. It can do you no harm and poses no threat. To react otherwise is to be paranoid."

"But—"

"Baseless paranoia is, forgive the phrase, stupid," the Bailiwick said flatly. "And remember what Miss Reid said— No Stupid." It surprised Joy enough to shut her up.

The Bailiwick nodded. "Now then, what is Maia's solution to our little problem?"

Joy lifted her bag from the C&P. "Maia sent Avery to speak with me—he had a formula for an elixir to adjust the change. We took it to the wizard. He mixed up a batch." Joy rattled the baggie and went to fill a mug with water. "Mr. Vinh says it ought to slow down the effects until he can come up with something better."

The Bailiwick frowned, which was no small thing—his mouth was as wide as her arm. "That is not as promising as I'd hoped."

"It's all I've got," Joy said, pressing buttons on the microwave. "Which is better than giving up."

"Indeed," Graus Claude said. "What did it cost?"

The microwave beeped. Joy dropped in a tablespoon of

dried herbs and started stirring. "He said he'd bill me once he figured out a cure."

The giant frog pressed three hands against his chest in alarm. "You opened a tab with a *wizard*?" he squawked. "Without any prior binding agreement? Did you make a contract? Was it witnessed? Notarized?"

"It was more like a verbal handshake." Joy stirred the powder into a vile-colored mush. She added more water. "Why? Is that bad?"

"Look at his face," Filly snickered as she reentered the kitchen. "You're doomed."

"What else is new?" Joy said, and took a gulp of the stuff— it tasted like crushed mustard, wasabi, charcoal and Freon. Her mouth flooded with saliva. Her throat burned. Her nose stung. The glob dodged her tongue and stuck to the roof of her mouth. She slammed her palm into the counter and blinked back tears. She made a fist and swallowed, gasping for air.

"Gah!" She unscrewed her bottle of Gatorade and drank half of it down. She wiped her mouth with her wrist. "Ugh! That's awful!"

"Well," Graus Claude said, relaxing slightly. "At least that sounds like it will work." He filled a large glass of water in each of his hands. "If he'd wanted to poison you, it would likely taste better. The foulest concoctions are the trademark of proper witches, wizards, herbalists and midwives and are widely considered to be ruthlessly effective."

Joy swallowed again, testing her teeth to make certain they hadn't dissolved. "Fabulous."

"Consider yourself fortunate. I had to contend with your brother's abominable behavior in your absence," he said. "It is a wonder that you weren't in worse shape when we began your tutelage. Disgraceful." He downed each glass in quick succession. "It is good to see that at least one good thing came out of your efforts."

"A proper wizard's brew," Filly smirked. "And we had to fight to get it!"

"Two good things, then," Graus Claude said, approvingly. "May the Council see your escape as a show of strength! I dare say they should not underestimate you or your resources. They would be wise to grant you a wide berth."

Joy scraped her tongue against her teeth. "Really?" she said. "Is that what you think they'll do? If you were sitting on the Council and I had just escaped, having not only the key to the Imminent Return, but also the door, would you just let me go?"

The Bailiwick gave an affronted sniff. "Don't be ridiculous. I would have you killed in your sleep."

Ink froze in the doorway, casting a black look at his employer. Graus Claude had the decency to look embarrassed.

"That is, of course, speaking purely hypothetically and is completely irrelevant," the Bailiwick hastened to add. "They will be looking to skew their decision in view of the Twixt's reaction to the gala."

"Great," Joy said, and finished off the last of her Gatorade. She still couldn't get the vile taste out of her mouth. The idea of doing this once a day was nauseating and the best motivation she could have for wanting to get the King and Queen back as soon as possible. She opened the fridge looking for something that might help kill the taste. Salami? Pickles? Blue cheese? Nothing. What a time for Dad to be on a diet! She closed the door. "I think the Council's had it in for me ever since I removed my mark, and certainly since I took on my True Name. Screwing up the gala was just the icing on the cake," she said, glancing at Graus Claude. "I'm really very sorry about that. You worked so hard. I tried, but..."

"On the contrary," he said, reaching around her and opening the fridge. He removed various containers and condiments and placed them on the counter in a steady stream. "You gave an excellent performance—quite beyond my wildest hopes, truth be told. You handled yourself with poise and decorum, showing wit and favor, humor and grace and completely damning those who tried to force their wills upon you, quelling any and all attempts to maneuver you into a less-than-strategically advantageous position." He took a knife from one of the drawers. "You proved that you are no one to be underestimated, Miss Malone, and that does us both credit. That nimble knot with Sol Leander? Beatific. Striking his aide on the dance floor? Sublime. And your answer to Hasp and the broken pearls? Well, I could not have dreamed better." He chuckled. Ink stared at Joy—this was all news to him. Joy prayed the Bailiwick would stop talking even as he smacked his lips. "It was, I must say, *most* rewarding." His hands began a complicated dance, assembling a massive sandwich with the dexterity of shuffling cards. "And though I may humbly take most of the credit for your transformation into a passable debutante, I was pleased to hear that most of the unexpected improvisation was uniquely yours." He nodded approvingly at her and his towering lunch. "To which I say, brava, Miss Malone! Masterfully done."

Joy gaped at his snack. He'd put half the fridge between an entire loaf of bread.

"Thanks," she muttered as he took the plate to the kitchen table and sat on the floor—no chair could possibly hold his weight. "You could hear all of that from your holding cell?"

"Most of it, certainly," he said, tucking his sheet underneath him. "But there were many eager to pass me news about some of the highlights before Briarhook arrived."

Joy frowned. "I thought that none who were your friend could get close to you," she said.

"I did not say that it was *friendly* commentary," Graus Claude said, plucking a long steak knife from the block. "I think it might be more accurately described as gloating." He grinned a mouthful of teeth. "Look who is laughing now!" He lifted the knife like a jeweled dagger. "Well done employing the Forest Guardian, by the way," he added, sawing the massive sandwich in half. "He was hardly friendly in the least. Brutish, but effective. I am only sorry what it cost you." He placed half the sandwich into his mouth and started chewing. Joy didn't want to think too much about the iron box that held the last slivers of Briarhook's heart. The filthy Forest Guardian had kidnapped Joy and branded her as a message meant for Ink, which the Scribe had returned with bloody vengeance. Ink had bequeathed the heart he'd cut from the giant hedgehog's chest to Joy, ensuring Briarhook would keep his distance. Joy had reluctantly been returning his heart, piece by piece, buying off Briarhook's debt with favors like helping them free Graus Claude, knowing that the moment Briarhook earned back the last scraps, he'd promised to kill her. Slowly.

Stef reappeared with Ink, eyes widening at the impressive spread. Dmitri followed, admiring the layout of the condo. Stef leaned an elbow on the counter. "Anything else we can get you?" he asked. "A roast pig, perhaps? Maybe a keg?"

"A hogshead of wine would be delightful," the Bailiwick said out of the corner of his mouth. "A Greek white or a bold rosé." He chewed thoughtfully and gazed at the sandwich. "Needs more olives."

"Olives!" Joy shouted and dived for the jar on the counter. It was empty. She drank some of the oily brine. It helped scour away the aftertaste of Mr. Vinh's tea.

"Really, Joy?" Stef said. "Stop acting like you're half-animal."

Dmitri slapped his arm. "Hey!"

"In a not-nice way," Stef amended.

Dmitri tsked. "You're going to have to do better than that."

Stef grabbed a hank of Dmitri's shirt. Laughing, the DJ grabbed a bottle of wine. The two of them left the kitchen wearing identical smirks.

Ink waited for the bedroom door to close and glanced at Filly. "Guard them," he said. Joy opened her mouth to protest, but Ink shook his head. "We have little knowledge of the satyr's loyalties outside of his love for your brother and the Grove. His troop are still the keepers of the Glen who are guarding Aniseed's graftling clone." He checked the wards by the doors and the air vents. "You may trust him with your life, but I do not."

Filly clapped her hands together with a bang. "*Finally* someone who thinks like a warrior and not a politician!" She raised a fist in salute and bounded happily down the hall.

"Only for the moment," Ink said. "For soon we must think like diplomats."

Graus Claude finished the second half of his sandwich and dabbed at his lips with a folded napkin. "Fortunately, that is a particular arena in which I excel."

Ink paused. "Unfortunately, you cannot come with us," he said, taking Joy's hand. "We demand entrance to the Bailiwick of the Twixt."

They descended into the Bailiwick, Joy's stomach clenched as tight as Ink's hand in hers.

"Are you sure this is a good idea?" she asked.

"No."

Joy stopped on the stone steps. "What?" She hadn't

wanted to come back down here, back into the pocket universe embedded in Graus Claude—not until they were ready, not until the chaos on both sides of the world had died down. She'd half expected there to be an army waiting for them under the Bailiwick's tongue. Had it only been a day since they'd fled?

Ink tugged her forward. "Come," he said gently. "We bring the courier of the Twixt—they are waiting for us. It would be impolite to tarry." He tried to project a smile through the dark, crossing the median where the light from the kitchen faded to black and the artificial sunlight had not yet leaked up from the base of the stairs. "There were once a great many things I felt with certainty that I now know was merely blind obedience, programmed loyalty, empty thoughts that were barely my own. I have grown to question much of what once I considered true, which left me with very few things I would consider 'certain.'" He squeezed her fingers as they approached the bottom of the stair. "But I am certain that I love you and therefore it is imperative to bring the King and Queen back, not just for the Folk, but also for you."

Joy loved him so much, heart or no heart. It filled her completely. "Thank you."

Ink stepped into the clearing, boot heel crunching on the grass. "You do not have cause to thank me yet," he said. It seemed strange to hear him quote his employer while they were traveling down the giant frog's throat.

The clearing was as they'd left it, the small copse of woods, the trickling stream, the muted play of light and dappled shadows, the meadow of wildflowers and tall waving grass. Every inch of it, every detail, had been created by the forgotten princess while she'd been trapped inside this pocket between worlds. Joy tried not to step on anything, hyperaware that the princess, as a Maker, had written this world into being just as her parents, the King and Queen, had spoken the rules that created the Twixt. Joy prayed if they could make the rules, they could break them as well, or at least rewrite the ones responsible for her change.

She was counting on it.

Joy squinted at the hazy horizon whose edges seemed to blur, the images of the forest and field tucking under themselves like bedsheets. "Is the door still open?"

Ink searched the sky, an optical illusion that was no space at all. "The fact that the army hasn't moved to occupy the Bailiwick could be considered a good sign," he said. "It means that the King and Queen have not decided to declare war on the humans and have chosen to remain within the confines of Faeland for now."

"Is that what they've been doing all this time?" Joy asked with a hitch in her voice. "Just waiting to attack?"

Ink walked into the meadow. The grasses parted before him. "I imagine after a long time passed without word from the Council, the King and Queen might have concluded that the Twixt had fallen, the remaining Folk besieged or enslaved by humans. Once the last member of the Council died, the door between worlds would open, allowing those in Faeland to avenge their kith and kin. They swore an oath of vengeance should that ever happen," Ink said, walking unerringly toward the hole in the sky. "It is quite possible that they have been waiting to strike first and fast for hundreds of years."

"So maybe they didn't mean what they said?" Joy said hopefully. "That no one is really a Destroyer of Worlds? They saw a human—or what they thought was a human—and jumped to the wrong conclusion?" Then Graus Claude might be mistaken and there was no need to worry about Elementals or being hunted down by Folk...or anything.

"Perhaps," he said. Although the way he said it did not make it sound all that likely.

Ink raised his straight razor, drawing a series of lines that glowed in the air like sparklers, cutting through his mother's illusion of what looked like earth and grass and sky. In the distance, a circle flared. Joy's breath caught. *There it is.*

Neither spoke as they stepped forward, the scenery sliding beneath their feet like a zoom lens. A crackling glow sketched the edges of the unlocked door into Faeland, behind which an army awaited along with hundreds if not thousands of Folk itching to come home. Joy shifted nervously, her feet crunching on the illusion of roots.

Standing on the precipice, Joy didn't know what she wanted, what she hoped for, what she was doing here; she knew only that she *did not* want to go in. For the first time, she felt that returning to Folk Paradise might be very, very wrong; something she should never do. It was a new sensation, a new word for her: *sacrilege.*

Ink stepped onto the edge of the doorway, the fractal light playing off the shiny, black leather of his boots. He pressed her hand close to his side. "We will remain on this side of the doorway," he said. "There will be no cause for you to fear."

Joy stared at the portal, which flared like a solar eclipse. "What if the King calls me again?" She knew in her bones that she'd have to obey.

"I will be here," Ink said, squeezing her hand and turning to face the light. "I will be very, very here."

Joy took a deep breath. "Okay," she said, and gently opened the door to Folk Heaven.

ELEVEN

ARMED GUARDS STOOD ON THE THRESHOLD, STERN-faced and solid. Joy jerked back but Ink held her hand firm, and so she remained where she stood, dwarfed by two towering soldiers haloed in a corona of alien sunlight.

"We wish to parlay with the King and Queen," Ink said with a confidence Joy envied. The sound of it sliced through the air, crisp and clear.

The guards did not move or acknowledge their presence. Their armor did not so much as creak. Joy had a very close-up view of the elaborate breastplates and polished helms, the ornate clasps and jeweled hilts. She could smell the scents of summer and spring—pollen-thick with honeycomb and berries from the one on her right and more delicate scents of buttercups and eggshells from the elf on her left. Their eyes were multifaceted and sparkled darkly. Joy tried not to look like a Destroyer of Worlds.

The guards parted, swinging open like saloon doors, and a centaur—armored from neck to tail—glowered at them as he crested the hill. This was unmistakably their general. He stopped, the breeze teasing the grass underfoot and the stiff hairs on his head that trailed down his spine. He glared at them as tiny will-o'-the-wisps danced around his mane. Something about him reminded Joy of the eldest satyr in the Glen.

"Stay where you are," he said. "In accordance with the rules of parlay, you may speak your piece and they will hear you." He gestured to the bivouac camp where the royal family had gathered once again on that familiar stretch of land on the hill. The King and Queen sat in the two tall thrones flanked by attendants and banners and nine young women wearing matching gowns. Joy knew that the princess, Ink's Maker—his mother—was among them, but it was impossible to make out which of the King and Queen's daughters was her. The centaur's voice was a command, accustomed to being followed without question. "Any false word or move will be your last."

Joy didn't doubt it for an instant.

Onlookers gathered on either side of the rolling hills, creating a long, open aisle from the royal family to the door. Armored soldiers lined the perimeter like a police brigade, a living wall between Ink and Joy and Faeland's civilians, many of whom craned their necks, lifting small ones above their heads, trying to get a better view. The crowd was a calliope of feathers and furs, wings and horns, claws and paws and snouts, as all eyes stared—their faces hopeful, fearful, earnest—the lost look of refugees imploring for home.

Joy faltered under their collective gaze. Something about them nagged at her, but she couldn't place why. She kept her attention face-forward so as not to appear rude. She doubted the King and Queen tolerated rudeness any better than the Bailiwick did. Graus Claude's advice whispered to her, *Etiquette and decorum.*

"We have returned as couriers of the Council to welcome your Imminent Return and to apologize for how long it has been," Joy said, using as many Folk terms as she could think of. "The Twixt has suffered under a terrible curse that stripped them of the memory of your exile and the door inside the Bailiwick. We have come to tell you—" Joy gagged. She couldn't say it. She didn't believe that it was safe to return. She panicked, words tripping off her tongue "—to *welcome* you to take your place once again as rulers of the Folk."

There was a murmur among the crowd like a rustling forest.

"You are not our courier," the Queen said. "Where is she?"

"The last courier died," Ink said with a diplomatic bow. Joy marveled how that was both true and not. "We come to you as representatives of the Bailiwick."

"Who now bears Ironshod's title?" asked the King, surprised.

"Graus Claude," Joy said. "He is the current Bailiwick of the Twixt."

The King and Queen exchanged the barest nod. "You speak true."

"Then the Council's proposal was successful?" the King asked. "Our True Names are protected by sworn sigils?"

Ink bowed again. "Indeed. I am one of the Scribes crafted by the hands of one of your own," he said. "My sister and I were created to inscribe the True Names, the *signaturae* of the Folk, upon those humans and places that fall under their auspice, preserving the magic and safeguarding them from harm, thus securing our world in safety as well as upholding the honor of the Twixt." Ink's words slowed a fraction as he watched the monarchs, but those who did not know him might have missed it. The hairs on Joy's arms prickled. "We have kept the magic alive, as per your Decree."

There was a short, calculated pause. "What of the Council?" asked the King. "Those left to rule in our stead?"

"The Council still stands," Joy said. "Some of the faces may have changed, but those who serve await your Return."

There was more than a murmur now, a rising hubbub through the crowds, the collective mutterings of an entire nation of exiles, looking to their leaders for hope. Joy could just imagine them talking among themselves, wondering whether their long wait was over and that today might be the day when they finally Returned.

Ink dared not move his hands, but he gestured with a slight rise of his chin. "Cross the Bailiwick, Your Majesties. Come and lead your people."

The King and Queen rose, formal and foreboding. Their long hair lifted behind them like unfurled wings.

"No," the Queen said simply.

The King continued without pause. "We shall not return until we are assured that the world is *safe* for our people," he said with a look directed straight at Joy. "What assurance is there that we may have safe passage through the Baili-wick into the wider world and that, once returned, the Folk may live in peace?"

Joy glanced at Ink. What could they say? There was no such assurance. And with Aniseed, the original courier and traitor to their throne currently reborn as a graftling clone, Joy doubted she could reassure them without gagging on the truth. But the system of *signaturae* was in place and the Folk were dwindling without their monarchs and kin. Shouldn't that be enough? Ink's lips creased in a thin, tight line. One of the young ladies whispered into her mother's ear. *That must be the princess.*

The Queen raised a single palm, a gesture that reminded Joy of Inq.

"We charge you with this, couriers of the Twixt—bring us proof that it is safe to return. Prove to us that the humans will not abuse our favor and that we may live among one another as we did in ages of old. Show us that magic is still our purview and that our bonds remain unbroken." The Queen's words settled like a blanket over the crowd. "These are your tasks, Scribe and Sundered. If you succeed in this, then we shall Return and reunite the world as one."

The vague musings and mutterings changed to a chorus of approval, everyone marveling at her wisdom. Joy watched the subtle ripple course through the gathered crowd. *Of course, who would side against their King and Queen?* Joy felt herself uncomfortably siding with Aniseed against their forced loyalty. What was it like to live without choices? To blindly follow and put faith in whatever they said? And now these monarchs had given her an impossible task—to prove the world was safe or else there'd be no Return. Joy felt hope dying like a burned matchstick.

The King called to Ink. "To you, my daughter's creation, I charge you with our safe passage." His galactic gaze turned to Joy. "And to you, the foretold Destroyer of Worlds, I charge you with devastation."

Ink stiffened. Joy paled.

"Go," the King and Queen said in unison, and the door slammed shut.

Joy let out a shaky breath as feeling tingled back into her fingers and toes.

Ink blinked at the door. His voice was matter-of-fact.

"That went well."

"That did *not* go as well as I'd hoped," Graus Claude admitted.

Joy paced the den, arms crossed. "You think?"

"Impertinence does not suit you, Miss Malone," the Bailiwick reprimanded her gently. Ink glanced at her sideways. *Respect him. Always.*

"Sorry," Joy mumbled, taking a seat. "But I don't see how

we're going to coax them out if it's contingent on some sort of proof that it's safe to come back." She gestured around the kitchen that had been an illusion for one of Aniseed's traps, including a blood-soaked coffee cake and monsters in the dark. "How can anyone prove that the world is safe? Nothing's safe! Life isn't safe!" The truth was that even when you thought everything was fine, life had a way of ripping the rug out from under you. She'd learned that all too well after the Year of Hell when Mom moved to Los Angeles with her boyfriend, Doug, leaving Joy and Dad to pick up the shattered pieces of their lives. Now, post trauma and past depression, Joy had figured out life was many things—surprising, scary and wonderful—but rarely was it safe.

Filly nodded curtly. "Well said! Safety is for buckles and pins." She licked the blue spot beneath her lower lip and took another bite out of her peeled apple. "Which makes me wonder why your wizardling brother isn't in here clucking over you like a mother hen."

Joy and Ink had found the Valkyrie banished to the main rooms, listening to music through earbuds and attempting to turn on the TV. Graus Claude had reanimated and downed several more glasses of water. His eyelids sank to a half-mast glaze. "Prudence forbears me from mentioning specifics, but I believe we can safely assume he is abed," he said mildly. "If there is any mercy left in the world, he and the satyr lad are sleeping. It has no doubt been an exhausting affair, thumbing their noses at authority and adventure. Let them rest."

Joy rubbed her eyes, which had become bleary and unfocused, painting everything in watercolor wash. The very mention of sleep made her head spin, and her proximity to the kitchen made her stomach grumble.

"I need to eat something. It's been..." Hours? Days? Slicing through time messed with her internal clock. She didn't even bother excusing herself as she plodded toward the fridge. Hunger made her grumpy. She couldn't afford to be grumpy.

"Well, you're hungry—that is a good sign," said Graus Claude.

Joy paused with a handful of green grapes. "Why?"

The Bailiwick pushed himself out of the couch. "Because Earth Elementals gather sustenance from the ground. Eating and drinking are an autonomic system—food and water are leeched from nutrients in the soil. Elementals feel no hunger as they can ingest and expel while moving or at rest, making them formidable, tireless foes. Therefore, the fact that you feel hungry and tired means that you are still more human than not."

Joy swallowed the sour juice on her tongue. "Lovely."

"Do not fret," he said. "Once I am back within my offices, I will endeavor to construct a worthwhile argument for you to deliver to the King and Queen." He sniffed. "Pity that I cannot join you, as my role seems to be limited to that of a convenient conveyance, but I have the utmost confidence in your ability to be both capable and prudent." He arched one side of his browridge. "Don't tempt me to doubt my veracity." Joy stuffed a slice of cheese into her mouth and shook her head. "Indeed. Fortunate, then, that it is my time to depart as I have arranged to meet the Bentley at the appointed hour." He cast a baleful look at Stef's closed door. "I believe that I have overstayed my welcome and must confess that I am eager to be elsewhere. Not that I have not appreciated the accommodations, Miss Malone, and for that I thank you, but I have duties that require alternate arrangements—" he plucked at his sheet with distaste "—which include sufficient clothing and assorted amenities." He winced at his chipped manicure and hid the offending hand in a fold of his improvised toga. "I will dispose of these drapes at such time and will make due compensation." He breezed past Joy's fledgling protest and turned to the blond warrior leaning against the couch. She removed the earbuds with a yank of the cord. "Would you be so good as to escort me to my rendezvous point? It would be remiss of me to take my leave without taking the necessary precautions to see it through. I do pride myself on keeping my person as well as my personal integrity intact." He straightened the sheet unnecessarily as he regarded Joy and Ink. "Do see that you are like-minded, with yourselves and one another. Our side can ill afford further fracture." His icy gaze swept over them both. "See to it."

"Yes, Bailiwick," they chorused.

"Very well," he said. "Then I shall bid you good day. I will contact you when appropriate." The Valkyrie fell into step beside the Bailiwick and began checking the front door with a warrior's expertise. The great amphibian paused on the lip of tile between the kitchen and the door. He turned back to Joy, his wide face a mask of solemn humility. "I must thank you again for your part in these affairs—for bringing me my truth, honoring my word and then breaking it in order to serve the greater good to free our people, reuniting the Folk at last," he said. "I have considered you a student, a collaborator and friend, and in all ways you have far exceeded my expectations. It has been an honor and pleasure assisting your efforts and I will do everything in my power to be worthy of your association." He bowed a fraction. "Until next we meet, Miss Malone."

Joy was speechless, the taste of air drying on her tongue as the Bailiwick swept majestically out the door.

TWELVE

JOY STOOD IN HER KITCHEN AS THE FRONT DOOR closed behind Filly and Graus Claude with a final click. She frowned at Ink.

"So...what are we supposed to do now?"

Ink tested the edge of his blade on his thumb. "We are supposed to wait here until we receive word from the Bailiwick," he said mildly. "He will come up with a solution of proof, which we can present to the King and Queen, convincing them to allow the Folk to Return. Then our obligations will be over, the Folk will be free, you will have your boon and we shall all live happily ever after."

Joy couldn't help smiling. "Is that what you think is going to happen?"

Ink tucked the blade back into his trifold wallet. "I think that is what is *supposed* to happen," he said with a grin. "But there are those who may have other ideas."

The house phone rang. Joy jolted, half expecting Filly to reappear in a chime of bells. She jogged into the kitchen and snagged the receiver, not even checking the caller ID.

"Hello?" she said.

"It's me," said Dad. "Look, I'm going to be working late tonight and I thought I'd stay over at Shelley's."

Joy blinked. She'd almost forgotten about Dad. "Oh. Um. Okay."

Ink glanced at her across the counter and smiled.

There was a slight pause, as if her father didn't know what to say—the rehearsed part of their conversation exhausted, he'd come to a complete standstill. "I didn't want to ditch you for a second night in a row," he said. "I know how you hate being left alone in the house and I didn't want you worrying or thinking I didn't care…"

"No no no. It's fine. I'm fine!" Joy said a little too loudly. Left alone with Ink? That was probably the best news she'd heard all day. "No problem, Dad. Really. I'll just be home—" she wandered next to Ink and slid a hand down his arm "—keeping myself occupied." Ink smiled wider. "But thanks for calling." Ink cupped her hips in his hands, placing a kiss at the spot above her clavicle, and she shivered at the sudden tingle. She felt his breath on her skin, smelling of spring rain. "Have fun," she said weakly as Ink kissed the side of her neck.

"You, too, honey. See you tomorrow. Good night."

"G'night," she murmured and hung up as Ink's lips closed over hers.

She dropped the phone on the counter and raked her fingers through his hair, pulling his face closer so that she could taste his mouth on hers. This wasn't a kiss—just a kiss—it was more. Much more. This moment was their moment, and it felt like they had been waiting a lifetime for it to arrive.

She made a small sound in the back of her throat as he gripped the pockets of her shorts. He answered with something deep in his chest, pressing closer as if they could meld through their clothes. She slid her hands down his back, running her fingers over familiar muscles and runnels, bones, hair and skin, the canvas where they'd carved one another's marks, craved one another's touch. She could feel spicy tingles straining under her skin. Her nerves were on fire. She *burned* for him.

A tiny voice nagged in the back of her brain. It had a name: Stef.

"My brother's home," she whispered into his mouth. He didn't need to breathe between kisses, his words slipped into the spaces between her tongue and teeth.

"He's sleeping," Ink said.

Joy moaned. "It's too risky."

"Some risks are worth taking."

She smiled, pulling him closer. *True.*

Joy dragged him past the counter, down the hall, into her room and shut the door. It happened so fast, she surprised herself. She was being pushy, impatient, wanting this, wanting him—embarrassment was an ember flash and then it was gone, because Ink was in her arms and they were kissing again, somewhat slower this time; a lovely dance of lips and limbs, shedding clothing and crawling across her bed, supine in the dark. They tumbled into blankets, folding over and under them like a sea of soft caresses, touching cool fingers where their skin burned on their shoulders, their backs, their arms, their legs. Their bodies slid closer, her bra strap fell off one shoulder, her knee twined tight behind his as they touched—belly button, singular, belly buttons, plural. Such a simple, precious thing shared by two not-quite-humans, perfect as puzzle pieces fitting together.

"Wait," Ink's whisper sliced low. Joy wound her hands through his hair.

"Don't you dare," she said, her lips kiss-swollen and buzzing. "You stay right here."

He laughed then, both dimples. "I am not going anywhere," he said, reaching out into space and clicking on her lamp. She squinted at the sudden colors, the soft bedtime glow etching the outline of his body in white gold. He was shirtless—how did that happen?—his chest rising and falling, his pulse jumping at his throat, his smile laid bare. He reached out a hand and touched her face, warm and heady with a thin dew of sweat. His thumb traced her jawline, trailing fingers down her throat. Her senses rose to meet him. His fathomless eyes drowned in hers.

I love him. She floated in the thought. *I love Ink.*

"I want to see you," he said. "I want to see you see me. I want this to be ours, together." His palm stroked her body, memorizing her by touch alone, his gaze simply tagging along for the ride. "Whatever happens, whatever is next, I want to be with you." She watched him watching her, watching him. He tilted his head to the side, his long bangs drifting over his eyes and the side of his nose. "I am here with you, Joy," he said softly. "I am very, very here."

There was a moment when Ink stopped, his arms locked at the elbows, apologetic panic in his voice.

"I don't know what to do."

It was a quiet confession, open and bare. Joy touched the side of his face and whispered, "It's okay."

And it was.

There was a moment when Joy pushed back.

"Wait," she said breathlessly. "Wait."

Ink stilled, eyes drowsy, lips swollen. He blinked as if under a spell. She snagged her purse from the floor and removed the scalpel. Ink watched with growing concern.

"Joy—?"

She sliced a thin line below her belly, breaking the sigil

drawn there. The circular glyph of warding flared once and disappeared.

Ink's eyes asked a question. Joy's kiss answered it.

Joy lay against her pillow, tired and replete. Her head rested against Ink's shoulder, her leg slung across his knee. His hand lay against her thigh, the other twined in her hair, still as a hovering breath. He blinked. She felt it like a butterfly's wing against the inside of her wrist. She felt the motes of dust in the air like kisses. Everything felt drowsy and woozy and warm.

"What is it?" Joy whispered.

"You didn't," he said simply.

She snuggled closer. "Didn't what?"

"Didn't squeak." Joy sat up and looked at him. He sounded boyish, confused. "The Cabana Boys said if you were happy, you'd squeak."

Joy laughed out loud, tugging the blankets over them both. He smiled, both dimples. She rubbed the spot over his heart. Resting her ear there, she could hear its rhythmic *thump-thump, thump-thump*. She closed her eyes and patted his chest.

"Maybe next time."

Joy woke to small noises: shuffling feet and clinking plates. Ink lay next to her—not sleeping, but pleasantly, comfortably still. His eyes opened as her gaze fell on him. His smile spread like sunshine across his lips—inviting her to kiss.

But she had to pee and brush her teeth.

Joy lay against the pillows trying to stave off the inevitable, staring into his eyes, yet the sounds from the kitchen made her wonder, was Dmitri still there? Was Stef awake?

Was he waiting for Joy to come out of her room? Which one of them was going to acknowledge the other first? It was an unspoken dare, a contest of brotherly/sisterly wills. Joy didn't want to get up, didn't want to give in. Ink was smooth and beautiful and warm and here.

But Joy *really* had to pee.

"Be right back," she whispered as she crept out of bed. She rolled delicately off the edge of the mattress, unfamiliar with having another body in her bed. She held the bedsheet against her body as she shimmied on a tank top and yanked on capris. Joy peeked over her shoulder. Ink was smiling, both dimples.

"Again, please," he said.

Oh boy.

She held a finger to her lips and tiptoed across the room, opening her door just enough to squeeze into the hallway and close it with a quick *click* behind her back. She tried to keep an eye on whoever was in the kitchen—Stef was taking a carton of eggs out of the fridge and Dmitri was sipping coffee, wearing one of Stef's shirts. They looked comfortable, happy, like they'd been doing this for years.

Dmitri's ears twitched against his mop of tousled curls. "Good morning," he said loudly, toasting Joy with his mug. She pulled her hair back from her face and nodded politely, all the while her brain chanted, *This is weird. No, it's not. It should be, but it's not.*

"Morning," she said. Stef cracked eggs into a bowl and started whisking them into a bubbly froth. He was the only one in the house who ever used a whisk.

"Want some coffee?" Dmitri said, taking another sip. "Turkish blend. Thick as mud. *Serious* joe."

"I'm making eggs," Stef said overcasually. "How many should I make?"

Joy ran her fingers through her hair, scrubbing her scalp. "Is this a quiz question?"

"What he's asking," the satyr said, sidling up to Stef, "is whether your boy will be joining us for breakfast?" He took another sip and gave a theatrical "ah" of pleasure and a wink. "I bet he's worked up an appetite."

Joy felt herself turn various shades of pale.

"Whoa. I mean, what? He's not—um." Too many words crowded to fit on her tongue. Her mind raced through possible excuses like a mouse in a maze.

"Don't," Stef said, cracking more eggs. *Bang! Crack!* "I don't want you making yourself sick trying to wheedle your way around the truth. Is he still here or not?"

Joy tried evading the question. Evasion was good. "This isn't about him being Other Than, right? Because—hello?" She pointed at Dmitri. "Pot, kettle, black?"

Dmitri grinned and bit a piece of toast. "Oh, I doubt it's that, little lady," he said cheerfully. "More like rocking the cradle."

"Hey!" Stef snapped. "She's my *sister*."

Dmitri's ears flicked. "She's barely illegal and looks killer in a dress," he said. "And I do not use that phrase lightly in this case." He snagged an apple and took a bite, then clapped his free hand on Stef's shoulder. "Face it, *agapétos*, your little sis's hot."

Her brother grumbled, but didn't shrug off the satyr's hand. "Remind me to kill you later," Stef said, slopping eggs into the skillet. Dmitri placed a sly kiss between Stef's shoulder blades. Her brother jumped like static shock.

"I can make you forget," the satyr leered.

"O-kay," Joy said, turning around. "I'm going to the bathroom."

When she got back to her room, Ink was still in bed,

wrapped in sheets, face pillowed in her pillows, smiling up at her. His eyes were wondrous-wide and black as starless night. She felt herself falling into them, deeper and more willingly than when they'd first met.

"Joy?" he said softly.

She sat on the edge of the bed and smoothed back his hair. "Yes?"

"Are you in any threat of immediate danger or death?"

Joy balked. "Um...no."

He smiled suddenly, both dimples. "Good."

He pulled her close and kissed her deeply, hungrily, like he was trying to crawl back into her skin. Her body responded like a thunderclap, all senses roaring, pressing against him, hands holding on tight. It was fireworks all over again, but this wasn't just a kiss—this was the opening chords of a symphony, rushing toward a crescendo of strings. She could feel his heartbeat pounding against her, demanding to be closer, to hug tighter, join together, delving deep and down and boiling over. It was primal, urging, dancing like sparklers in her blood. Electric fingernails raced along her insides, searing, raking, reaching for something hot and strong and...

"Tea!" Joy said, pushing away, gasping. Her whole body throbbed. "I have to make the tea!"

Ink fell against the pillows, blinking rapidly. He swallowed, stunned. "If this is revenge for my leaving that once, I'd consider us even."

"Ha ha," Joy said, sitting up, gaining inches and breath. She pulled back her hair, as if that'd keep her hands from grabbing him again. "It's important." She let her eyes linger on the rise and fall of his chest, the lines of his body, the want in his eyes. "Really, really important." She swallowed against the sensation of falling, that first foreign flicker she'd felt Under the Hill, the rush of heat and change that would make her into a liar because she'd promised Ink that *it would not happen*. Joy took a deep breath. *I won't change! I will not become an Elemental!* She squeezed her fingers in her hair. She tasted his mouth on her lips. "Okay." Joy shook her head and wiped the sweat from the back of her neck. "Get dressed. Come into the kitchen. Just to warn you, we've got company."

He snagged her elbow and pulled her closer. "Then let's stay here."

Joy sighed, lingering. The first flush was over, she was safe and he was here. Ink raised his eyebrows in question. She laughed at his look. "Tempting, but we've been made. Time to face the music. You want breakfast?"

"I do not know," Ink said honestly, propping up on one elbow. "Do I?"

"Probably not," Joy said. "But something tells me that I'm going to need some serious joe."

Ink frowned. "Who?"

It wasn't the most awkward breakfast in history, but it probably came close.

"Good morning," Ink said, taking a seat at the kitchen table. Joy smiled, grabbed four napkins and sat down.

"So he *is* here," her brother said, passing the toast.

Dmitri swatted the back of Stef's head playfully. "You knew."

"I *suspected*," her brother corrected as he scooped a serving of eggs. "*Now* I know."

Joy snagged the butter knife and picked up her toast.

"Well, *I* knew," Dmitri said, stealing a pinch of scrambled egg from Stef's plate. He popped it into his mouth and breathed around the steam. "I can smell him all over her."

Stef choked. Ink blinked. Joy's face flamed. "Not. Help-ing."

Dmitri ignored her, head swiveling around to stare out the window and his ears perking up like antennae. "And now there's another gentleman caller at the door." He curled his chin beard over one knuckle. "Another notch in the bed-post? My, my, someone *is* a busy girl!"

Joy ignored him and ran to the door. The idea that Dmi-tri talked with Mr. Vinh enough to know her nickname was more than a little alarming, but not as much as the idea of Dad coming home right now. Why couldn't he eat breakfast at Shelley's? Why not move some of his clothes over there? Why bother coming home? Before she started seriously considering the idea of moving him into his girlfriend's apartment, she peeked through the peephole. It was Kurt standing stiffly in full butler-slash-bodyguard mode. A mo-ment later, Ink's twin sister appeared at his side.

Invisible Inq glared into the tiny peephole lens.

"Let me in," she said. "Now!"

Joy opened the door. She was glad to see Inq, who'd been switched off at the gala by Sol Leander's supporters and then dragged off to a storeroom somewhere. Kurt must have found her after Graus Claude had escaped. The fact that Kurt and Inq were here now meant that things were getting back to normal.

Inq barged through the door. Ink stood up.

"YOU!" she shouted and grabbed his head in both hands.

Her clawed fingers fastened on either side of his head, squeezing, yanking his hair and forcing their foreheads to-gether. Her face was wild, full of grimacing and grinding teeth. Ink staggered, struggling in her grip, scratching at her hands, which had sunk into his skin. He made a word-less sound as they grappled. Stef and Dmitri jumped back from the table as Joy screamed. Kurt didn't move, watching the siblings grapple with mute disinterest.

"Joy—?" Stef barked. *Should he use magic or not?*

Joy shook her head, dumbfounded, stunned. She watched the Scribes wrestle and claw one another, bouncing off the counter and slamming into the fridge. The two of them were locked together, grunting, head-to-head.

"Stop it!" Joy shouted, waving her arms. "Inq!"

Inq wrenched away. A gaping hole on her forehead closed, leaving a smear of inky fluid. She gasped, stumbling sideways, then caught her balance on a chair. She shook her head like a wet dog, then popped the side of her neck, eyes calm.

"Thank you," she said crisply.

Ink was gasping, bent over, hands on his knees.

Joy touched his shoulders. "Ink!"

He shook his head, trying to clear it. He rubbed his forehead with one hand. Joy glared at his sister. "What's going on?"

"Just making an adjustment," Inq said, pushing her hand straight into her chest, fishing around, pulling and pushing unseen things into place. She pressed her other hand against the spot as she withdrew, closing the wound behind it. She smoothed her skin with strong fingers and licked runnels of black off her wrist like a kitten. "That ought to do it."

"I'm sorry." Ink coughed, standing up. He wobbled on his feet. "I am sorry I did not tell you before," he apologized sincerely. "It was my fault."

Inq brushed her dangling bangs out of her face. "Well, you can't take *all* the blame. It seems the Tide had something to do with it, after all." She fussed with her sleeves. "Sol Leander and his precious *rules*. Nothing's worse than a literalist in a position of power." She shook out her hair and tipped her heart-shaped face to one side, "Now, if *I* were on the Council, well, let's be honest, I'd've never let me past the door."

"Excuse me?" Stef sounded indignant. "What just happened here? *In my house?*"

Inq crinkled her nose at him. "Oh. Hi, puppy."

"'Puppy'?" Dmitri smirked. Stef turned crimson.

"Down, boy." Inq said as she glanced around the room. "Is it morning already? Or is it Tuesday? I'm all out of sorts. But I guess that's what happens when you're knocked unconscious at a major social event by a righteous sycophant and his lapdog coup." Her lips pursed as she noticed Joy's dumbstruck stare. "Are you all right, Joy?"

"What?" Joy stammered. "No. I mean—*what*?" Joy was having trouble processing. Ink didn't seem angry, just contrite. She didn't know how to react or what to feel. He hadn't told his sister about the Council's kill switch, and Inq had been understandably pissed, but now her rage was gone like a summer storm and Joy was left trying to switch gears. "I, uh, just didn't think you would be up—back—so soon. I thought..." She kept seeing Inq crumpling onto the ballroom floor in her bejeweled beetle gown, but here she was back in her gunmetal-gray corset and layers of black Goth chic as if nothing had happened. Joy shook her head, clearing some of the cobwebs. "You're safe," she said, finally. "I'm glad you're safe."

"No thanks to you," Inq sniffed. "But now I know how to fix our little snooze problem, so no harm done. However, I would have *much* rather known that information before I took a nosedive into the canapés." Her voice was light, but her gaze was steely.

"And now you know?" Joy asked.

"Of course," Inq said. "We share *everything*." She shot a sly look at her brother and winked at Joy, whose face burned red. "Welllllll," she amended, "*almost* everything." She waved a hand airily and took a piece of toast. "We've learned to filter a few things over the centuries—blood is thicker than water and it only takes a drop." Inq licked a dab of jam off her thumb. "And it's so much quicker than *talking*."

Ew. Joy's stomach flipped. Ink reached out to touch her, but she flinched. *He isn't human,* she kept reminding herself. *And neither am I.*

Inq tore off pieces of crackling bread. "You should be glad," she said casually. "Otherwise, I'd've attempted to kill you, too, as per the rules." She smiled while chewing. "But I'm pretty sure I would have felt bad about it afterward." Inq raised a hand to Stef's fuming face. "Tut-tut. No worries. We're good. You're all safe. From me, anyway." She pointed at the table. "Could somebody pass me the butter?"

Stef, Joy and Dmitri exchanged looks. Kurt picked up the butter and the knife and handed it to her, hilt-first. Ink squeezed the edge of the counter.

"How did you get out?" he asked.

"See previous—no thanks to you." Inq said. "Kurt came and got me after the place went completely widdershins. Raina and the boys filled me in on the rest." Her foot bounced over her knee. "Heard I missed quite the party. Too bad I wasn't around to enjoy it."

"You didn't miss much," Joy muttered.

"Are you kidding?" Dmitri said. "It's the talk of the Twixt from the Hill to the Wild!"

Inq frowned at the satyr, slit-eyed. "And you are—?"

"Arm candy," Dmitri said, hooking Stef's elbow. "Don't mind me."

A hint of a smile tugged at Inq's lips until she cocked her head at Joy. "Well, boys, this has been fun, but Joy and I need a little Girl Time." Inq wiped the crumbs from her fingers and hopped down off the chair, grabbing Joy's arm. "Excuse us for a minute." Inq dragged her down the hall. Joy glanced nervously over her shoulder, wondering if any of them were going to help her, but Inq shoved her into her room and shut the door before anyone moved.

So, obviously, the answer was no.

Joy sat down, resigned, in her desk chair and waited for the threats to start.

"You've gathered quite an assembly," Inq noted. "Happy worshippers, all."

"In the twenty-first century, we call them 'friends.'"

"Don't be silly," Inq said. "Friends are a click of a button. Minions follow orders. But worshippers will do anything you want without you even having to tell them." She patted Joy's arm. "Trust me, I know the difference." She sat down, bouncing on the bed. "But that's not why we have to talk. Before I took my unscheduled nap, I'd heard a rumor at the gala that someone had a secret for sale."

Joy twisted in her desk chair. "So?"

"A secret about *you*," Inq said, eyes snapping. "Something big enough that they were willing to sell it to the highest bidder at an obscene starting price and there was already interest. Seems the gala was the best place to start the bidding, given the dinner and a show." Inq stabbed a finger in her direction. "Someone has got something on you."

Joy's insides burned cold. Her first thought was, *Elementals?* The second thought was, *The Red Knight?* The third thought was to wonder if she was being blackmailed by Inq—*again*.

She ventured a guess. "Is that 'someone' you?"

"What?" Inq said, looking honestly shocked. She gave a light laugh. "Don't be ridiculous, Joy. I'm the one telling you this so that you know what's going on in the Big Bad World while you've been holed up in your little love shack here." She waved her manicure around the room. "Just tell me who you told, and I'll take care of it." Inq sighed at Joy's look of alarm. "Really, Joy! I *said* that it should be a secret between us girls and I meant it."

She means the death of the Red Knight, the fact that I can erase Folk out of existence. Joy started breathing again until it hit her—someone else knew that she'd erased the infamous unstoppable assassin and was willing to sell the information to anyone willing to pay!

Graus Claude. Sol Leander. Ladybird. *Anyone.*

"I didn't tell anybody!" Joy said all in one breath. *Not even Stef. Not even Monica. Not even Ink.* The guilt burned in her stomach and the back of her tongue. She'd been very careful with her secrets. Having Inq holding this one over her head was what had gotten her into this conspiracy mess in the first place. If the Council found out that Joy could erase anyone in the Twixt, she'd be hunted down and killed faster than if they found out she was part-Elemental.

Maybe.

"Well, someone knows something and the Folk don't lie," Inq said, inspecting Joy's odd collection of fertility dolls, all gifts from Ilhami. "Fortunately, if a secret is officially sold, the original owner cannot divulge it to anyone save the person who bought it, so it's a self-sealing contract. Only one owner per purchased secret—that's the rule." Inq glanced at Joy over her shoulder. "I could have stopped this before it started, but then—" She mimed a nosedive with her hand. "It may already be too late. But if you really don't know who it could be—?" she fished.

Joy crossed her arms. "I don't."

"Hmm. Last chance," Inq warned. Joy squeezed her arms

tighter and shrugged. "Well, then..." Inq kicked her heels and stood up. "I guess the lucky winner will let you know soon enough. The numbers being bandied about were nothing short of blood money, so I'd beware of any strangers bearing strange gifts."

That would have been good advice last year—before the Kodama at the kitchen window and the *guilderdamen* at the door and the *eelet* in a shell by her ear—but then again, if she'd been leery of strangers, she probably would have never met Ink.

Joy pinched the bridge of her nose. She was getting a headache. "If it's just a matter of money, can't you outbid them or something?" At one time, Joy might have been able to try to buy it back herself when she'd been working for Graus Claude, but all of her savings not invested in mutual funds had been rescinded by the Bailiwick as punishment for erasing the Scribes' work on the sly. "Maybe Ink—?"

"Ah, but then Ink would possess your secret, and neither of you want that, do you?" Inq said in mock innocence. "*I've* managed to keep it from him so far."

Joy cringed. Inq was right. That was one thing Joy *really* didn't want Ink to know—he took his job of protecting the Folk very seriously. For a long time it hadn't been what he did, it had been who he *was*—his purpose, his entire reason for being—and he'd only recently evolved to become a person instead of a tool used between humans and the Twixt.

Part of her wanted to just tell him, like ripping off a Band-Aid, and have it be over and done with, but the rest of her wanted to keep that one, worst secret quietly under wraps. She knew Ink would be devastated if he ever found out what she was really capable of. He was made to protect the Folk from harm—specifically human harm—so that made Joy's ability to erase Folk out of existence exactly what the Tide had always claimed: the most dangerous girl in the world.

Dangerous. Devastated. The Destroyer of Worlds.

"Besides," Inq continued blithely. "I'm not eligible to conduct formal negotiations, being not 'technically' one of the Folk." She mimed the air quotes. "Just a second-class citizen, after all." Her sarcasm had an edge to it. Unlike her younger brother, Inq had long outgrown her automaton status, and she not-so-secretly longed to be more than equal to the Folk. She wanted to master them, a subtle game that required equal parts guile, passion, ruthlessness and patience—all things that Invisible Inq had in spades. Joy twisted her fingers on the edge of her shirt. When Inq was in evil-mastermind mood, it was best to get clear.

"Well, I didn't tell anyone," Joy said bitterly. It was a horrible memory, one that still gave her nightmares at night— that feeling of falling into the thorn bush as the armored knight suddenly disappeared beneath her, the sick realization of what she had done. It wasn't something she ever wanted to repeat.

"Well, neither did I," Inq said, sounding slightly perturbed. Inq did not like someone getting the best of her in anything. "It could be a ruse, a way to make a quick fortune, but I doubt that many would dare to bluff with the Council so hot on the prowl. They would give anything to have some leverage over you, our most famous wild card." Her eyes fairly glittered, pink-and-green flashes in the dark. "And you're certain the Bailiwick doesn't—?"

"No," Joy said. "Definitely not." Graus Claude had discovered that it was Joy who could erase *signatura*, and not some magical property of Ink's scalpel when he'd manipulated her into helping Ysabel Lacombe. He'd watched as Joy had erased the abusive Henri's mark from the enslaved river sprite. Joy didn't regret freeing her, but it had been enough to out Joy. She doubted the Bailiwick would ever sell that secret to the highest bidder, but he didn't know what would happen if Joy erased someone's *own signatura*. Erasing a living being was worse than murder. *So many secrets...*

"And where is Graus Claude now?" Inq asked.

"I thought he was back at the brownstone," Joy said. "Filly escorted him to the Bentley."

"No," Inq said curiously. "We were just there."

Joy frowned. "Wouldn't Kurt know?"

"Kurt's gone out on errands for him. He's received messages, instructions, but no summons yet," Inq said. "Hmm. I imagine the Bailiwick's holed up in one of his safe houses."

"Safe houses?" Joy asked, surprised. *Then why did he stay here?* "Where would he go?"

"Who knows?" Inq shrugged. "That's the point of safe houses."

Joy sighed. "Well, he told me that he'd contact me when he got settled, so we'll just have to wait until then." She stood up abruptly. "In the meantime, let's assume that someone's bluffing or has some other secret until we learn different." *One conniption fit at a time...* "Do we know if anybody's bought it yet?"

"I don't know," Inq said. "I'll find out."

"Good. That'd be good," Joy said, taking a deep breath. She mentally walked through her calming routine, the one she used to practice before hitting the mats before gymnastics. Nothing was worse than mentally spiraling before a Level 9 competition, when every tenth of a point counted—except, possibly, when it involved the Twixt and her life was on the line. "If we can isolate the buyer, we can stop that problem before it starts. What we really need to do is prove that the world is safe, find the Bailiwick, convince the King and Queen to Return before Sol Leander finds out about Aniseed's clone and keep Ink and the rest of the Twixt from finding out any more about me before I have a chance to undo it all."

Inq slapped Joy's shoulder good-naturedly. "Well, well. You're finally starting to think like one of us." Inq grinned. "I *knew* I liked you!"

Joy tried her best to take the compliment and ignore the vomit moths fluttering in her gut.

THIRTEEN

JOY HEADED BACK TO THE KITCHEN WITH INQ IN TOW.
Ink and Kurt both stared as they approached, unasked questions in their eyes. Stef glowered in a corner. Dmitri was peeling grapes.

The buzzer sounded. Joy stopped. Everyone stared at the call box.

"It's not Dad," Joy said, more to herself than anyone else.

"Well, go answer it," her brother said. "I'm not supposed to be here, remember?"

The buzzer sounded again.

Joy slowly pressed the button. "Hello?"

"Hey there!" Monica chirped. "I'm stopping by to check in on you, as promised. And I come bearing bagels!"

Joy's skin tightened in panic. Monica was outside, unprotected—again—and the condo wasn't warded against humans. She glanced around the room, finger stuck on the button.

"Uh—"

"Don't let her in!" Stef said.

"I heard that!" Monica said. "Is that Stef? I thought he was supposed to be halfway to college by now."

"You go to college?" Inq said, surprised. "I thought you were a wizard."

Dmitri snickered. "Some of us working stiffs still have to get jobs topside."

Monica's voice dropped. "Joy—?"

Joy let go of the button, cutting her off. "We *have* to let her in!" she hissed. "Monica's vulnerable out there beyond the wards."

"She'll be fine." Stef said. "Just tell her to go away."

The buzzer sounded an angry, rapid staccato. Joy answered it.

"Don't you hang up on me!" Monica said. "Now buzz me in or so help me, I will bust down that door with my Jimmy Choos."

Stef shook his head. Dmitri's ears flicked. Kurt may have cracked a smile as he walked by Ink and Inq on his way to the window to inspect the perimeter by the gate.

"Right," Joy said. "Hang on." She buzzed Monica through.

"What are you *doing*?" Stef snapped, grabbing multiple dishes to throw in the sink.

"Ditching her will just make her more suspicious and if she's standing out there yelling, someone's bound to notice," Joy said, grabbing more plates. "Even if she hadn't already been a target once because of me, I'm not leaving my best friend out there in danger." She waved her hands over the breakfast mess. "Can't you just cast a spell or something to *whoosh* this all up?"

Her brother looked disgusted. "You don't use wizardry to 'whoosh' things up."

Joy grimaced. "Well, what good is it then?"

"She has a point." Dmitri said, pouring stems and crusts into the trash. "It would make things hella easier."

"Have you ever considered stand-up?" Inq chirped. "This is very entertaining."

There was a knock at the door.

"Check the peephole," Stef whispered.

"I am!" Joy whispered back. Monica stared straight back at her, hands on hips, one leg cocked back, lips screwed into one cheek, looking hella annoyed.

"Open the door, Malone!" she called from the hallway.

Joy waved her hand behind her, shooing them all away. There was a scramble of sounds as she slowly gripped the doorknob and turned it, opening the door an inch at a time. Her best friend eyed her like she'd gone insane.

"Is anyone else here?" Monica asked.

Joy wasn't sure if she meant Graus Claude or Ink or Stef. "Um—"

"Well, you're dressed," she said. "That's a good sign. At first I thought that maybe you'd—" Her face broke into a sparkly smile. "Oh my Lord! Don't tell me—it happened! You *did*! You *have*! EEEEE!" Monica's girlie squeal made Joy's face flush and she was too stunned to do much of anything as Monica bear-hugged her, the bagel bag slapping her back. Her friend rocked her back and forth, then let go with a bubbly laugh. "I'll grab us a plate and you can give me all the juicy details—" Monica stopped dead, staring around the kitchen.

Dmitri, Stef, Ink, Inq and Kurt stared back.

"Hel-lo." Monica bit her lips together and made a small humming sound in her nose as she turned to Joy. "Has it always been this crowded around here, or have I just been too blind to see it?"

Joy groaned and waved her arm furiously at the group. "When I do *this*, it means *hide*!"

"She can See us?" Dmitri whispered theatrically out the side of his mouth. Stef's eyes bugged out behind his glasses. He looked like he'd been hit in the head.

"You can See them?" her brother roared. "Joy! You gave her *the Sight*?"

"I h—" Joy gagged on the "had to," since she didn't *have* to. "It was her choice!" Joy said, which was true. "It was right before the gala. I didn't want to leave her unprotected—"

"Whoa," Monica muttered as Dmitri's ears lay flat. He flashed a wicked grin.

"You must be smokin' crazy to jump aboard this ship of fools," he said, tying off the trash bag.

Monica gave the satyr a second once-over. "Don't I know you?"

He swore something low and squiggly. Stef was furious beyond swearing.

"Monica," Joy said quickly. "You know Stef. That's Dmitri and this is Inq, Ink's sister, and Kurt. They're from the Twixt."

"I guessed as much," Monica said, squeezing her purse strap against her chest. Monica could never grow pale, but she looked a little ashen around the eyes. Of course, after Graus Claude, a satyr, a muscleman bodyguard and a black-eyed Goth pixie chick might look normal by comparison. Monica smiled stiffly. "Nice to meet you."

"Same." Dmitri reached forward and shook her hand. Kurt followed suit. Inq nodded politely and draped a hand over Kurt's arm, considering Monica from every angle.

"Are you another one of hers?" Inq asked.

Monica's voice sharpened. "Hey, lady, nobody *owns* me."

Joy smiled. Inq did, too. She whispered in Kurt's ear, "I likey."

Stef growled and slammed the fridge closed. "Joy. Your room. Now."

Stef closed the door behind them. "You *gave* Monica the Sight?" he said, the words low and furious. "What were you *thinking*?"

Joy moved to block the rumpled bed with her body and prayed that he didn't notice the smell. It was far too late in August for the cool scent of spring rain. "I was *thinking*," she said, kicking her underwear under the bed, "that she'd been hurt by the Red Knight once already and since I'd been attacked by mud golems over the weekend and had no idea what was going to happen at the gala, that it might be nice to make sure my best friend had some idea what was going on in case someone else from the Twixt came after her. I couldn't—" She shook her head and crossed her arms tight across her chest. "I was *trying* to keep her safe!"

"By giving her the Sight?" he said again. "Joy, you *know* how the Folk treat humans with the Sight! It's how our family got into this whole bloody mess in the first place! It's how you ended up getting stabbed in the eye! It's why I've been wearing the same damn pair of glasses since I was fifteen! It's how Great-Grandma Caroline ended up in an institution, blind and insane!" His voice flattened. "Do you want that for Monica? Her mother already thinks you're nuts—do you really want her looking at her own daughter that way?"

Memories of Mrs. Reid raising her e-reader over her head, shouting at Joy to get away from her baby girl, raced through her mind with awful clarity—the tears on Mrs. Reid's cheeks, the wildness in her eyes, the feel of hitting the wall, backpedaling as Joy tried to explain, the flash of fear/running/panic/guilt... Joy knew that Mrs. Reid was only trying to protect her daughter; she'd seen the blade in Joy's hand inches away from Monica's face. Even though Monica had invented a bogus voodoo excuse, blaming it on a promise to her own witchy aunt Meredith, things hadn't been the same between their families ever since.

"You're wrong!" Joy insisted. "It's not like that at all!" But for a fraction of a second, she was hard-pressed to think of why, exactly, her brother wasn't right. She scrambled to figure out what had changed. "The Council ruled not to touch humans with the Sight until it could be determined if they were halflings or changelings, mortal descendants of Folk or whatever..." She trailed off. That was before Graus Claude's arrest and crimes of treason—before he suspected that they might all be Elementals. Would the ruling still hold? Was their case still valid? Had her actions at the gala put everyone with the Sight at risk? Had she managed to put Monica in danger *again*? She glanced up, and Stef nodded at the fear dawning on her face.

"Yeah," he said, sarcastically. "Now you get it. She was protected under the Edict, remember? But, by giving her the Sight, you *broke the Accords*!" He waved back at the door. "It's an agreement that the knowledge of magic between humans and Other Thans would be regulated. An exception would be those born with the Sight, and the Council never liked that particular loophole! When you decided to share with your BFF, you broke the agreement and quite possibly gave these jokers an excuse to throw all of our protections under the bus!"

Joy shifted on her feet, feeling miserable and small. "Oh," she said weakly.

"*Oh!*" Stef mocked. "You're damned right, 'Oh'!" He wiped his hand over his face. Joy watched him, mentally whispering another quick prayer that Ink had taken all of his clothes with him. But it gave her an idea.

"The Cabana Boys—"

Stef spun on her. "Who?"

"Sorry," Joy said. "They're a bunch of guys, *lehman*, mortal lovers, who belong to Inq." She was extra careful to overemphasize the *q*.

"They're humans, and she gave each of them the Sight

with the same elixir and no one's said or done anything about it."

Stef glared at her like she was six kinds of stupid. "Inq is one of them," he said. "You're not."

"Well, technically, since Inq and Ink were made, not born, they're not exactly Folk..." She trailed off. Clearly, Stef couldn't care less and it wasn't earning her any points, so she dropped it. "But anyway, this is all beside the point. Monica is under Sol Leander's auspice and it's my fault for letting that happen, so I wanted to give her a choice to know what was really going on, since he might go after her at any time and I might not be able to do anything about it. Monica doesn't want to be rescued. She wants to stand up for herself. She deserves to know what's going on." Joy twisted anxiously under his stare. "Okay, yes, it was selfish, and yes, it's dangerous, and I'm sure it's not going to win me any more popularity contests Under the Hill, but it's done and it can't be undone so let's move on, okay?" She swallowed against her dry tongue. "Right now I'm a little more concerned about what's happening with the Tide."

"Well, after that disaster at the gala, I don't blame you," Stef said. "And harboring the Bailiwick in our house wasn't a particular stroke of genius, either."

Joy humphed. "He's gone now and we have a houseful of... everyone. It's a circus." She grabbed her doorknob, taking her exit while she could. "Let's just clear them out before Dad comes home."

The kitchen looked like some strange after-hours party, a Halloween affair in the middle of summer that had devolved into half-worn costumes and eating bagels out of the bag. The chatter was friendly, lively, even fun, with Dmitri's easy laughter and music pouring from the den. Ink and Inq murmured quietly in one corner as Kurt stood by the door. Monica silenced her phone as she described the last concert she'd attended to Dmitri, who was taking out water glasses, wineglasses, mugs and bowls while opening random bags of pretzels and chips. Inq wiped her fingers on paper napkins. Ink smiled at her. Stef poured orange juice.

Joy leaned across the counter. "What do we do if Dad comes home right now?"

"Don't look at me. I'm somewhere across the Pennsylvania border," he said as he poured. "He can't See them and you can't lie." He handed her a glass of orange juice and clinked it against his. "Good luck with that."

"Thanks." She drank the juice in several gulps. The sugar rush helped ease the pounding in her head. "Dork," she muttered behind her cup.

"Dweeb."

Joy smiled and grabbed one of the mugs for Vinh's tea, refilling her juice in anticipation of washing it all down. She glanced over the crowd. They were missing Graus Claude and Filly, and possibly Avery, but otherwise, the gang was all here. Where *were* the others now? How long had it been? What happened to time when it ran simultaneously between this world and the Twixt? Her eyes skipped from Ink to Monica and the scar above her eye. Some days felt like a blink and others felt like forever. Would she ever feel like she belonged in one world or the other?

Behold the Destroyer of Worlds.

She drank her vile, bitter tea.

Stef stretched. She heard a dull pop. "Okay," he sighed. "I'm going back to bed."

"What?" Joy said, suddenly left at the helm. "You've been sleeping all morning!"

"I've been *in bed* all morning," he said. "There is a difference. And I'm tired."

Dmitri appeared at his side, twirling his beard around his finger with a wide grin. "Sorry, sis, things to see, people to do." He slid his hand into Stef's back pocket.

Stef pulled away grumbling as they disappeared down the hall. "You're impossible."

Dmitri laughed, "You know it."

Joy downed the rest of her juice.

Ink sidled up to Joy. Even the nearness of his body brought an electric rush to her skin. It was as if she'd had the first taste of a drug she didn't know she craved and she envied her brother for seizing the moment first.

Monica fished out her phone for the nth time. "You know, this used to be cute, but my boy can be—" She stopped, eyes widening in alarm. Grabbing her purse, she killed her screen and tossed her cup in the sink. It bounced around, clattering, shattering the mood. She locked eyes with Joy. "I gotta go."

Joy snagged her friend's arm. "What's wrong?"

"I thought...it was Gordon," she stammered. "I thought he kept calling me, but it's Mom." Fear tinted her words. Hysteria nudged her pitch higher. "It's the family code for 911." She yanked back her arm and fumbled for her keys. "I have to go!" She dropped the keys, cursing, and tripped over her feet.

Joy signaled Ink. "Forget the car," she said. "We can get you there faster."

Ink leaned closer, his voice a crisp whisper. "I have not been there," he said.

"I have," Joy said. "And so has the *eelet* in my ear so there's a path, right? One you can follow?"

Ink looked impressed, an expression mirrored in faces around the room. "Yes," he said. "That should work."

"Okay," she said. "Party's over." Joy glanced around at everyone who had come to help her, to warn her, to protect her. She wouldn't forget that, but these two people were her closest friends in the world. "Thank you," she said sincerely to Inq and Kurt.

"You should not go," Kurt said.

Ink took Joy's hand. "They'll be safe with me."

Monica held on to Ink and Ink held Joy as they stepped forward through a sudden breach with the sharp scent of limes.

FOURTEEN

MONICA LIVED IN A NEAT BLUE COLONIAL ON A STREET with other neat Colonials of varying neutral colors lined with young trees and trim little shrubs. Normally, it was hard to tell the houses apart, but today it was easy—Monica's was the one with the police cars in front.

The three of them appeared at the edge of the driveway where the mailbox was obscured by plumes of decorative grass. Monica exhaled like a cough, letting go of Joy's hand as she bolted toward the house. Joy moved to follow, but Ink caught her arm.

"Glamour or no?" he asked.

Joy hesitated, watching Monica dive through the open front door.

"No," she said. "Stay close and keep an eye out." Joy frowned at the long, empty road. "It's going to be tough to explain how we got here. We should've taken the car." She wasn't eager to get back in the Ferrari; it felt too much like the need to escape. The upholstery still smelled like Enrique, a reminder that she was fragile, mortal and out of her league.

Ink considered this. "We can go get it," he said. "It'll only take a moment."

Joy grinned. "If that."

"Joy?"

Joy spun around, surprised to hear Mrs. Reid's voice. Monica's mother stood in the doorway, looking pinched and worried, neck craning to spy Joy through the shaggy decorative grass. Joy felt the same guilty, scared hesitation tightening her insides whenever Mrs. Reid was nearby. Ever since she'd caught Joy in the hospital with the scalpel poised over Monica's face, she'd been politely not-seeing Joy, erasing her as effectively as if she had a magic scalpel of her own. Hearing Mrs. Reid speak her name while looking right at her pinned her like a deer in headlights.

Joy swallowed. "Yeah?"

"Please come in," Mrs. Reid said. "Monica needs you."

Joy nodded. "Of course." What else could she do? She started walking up the driveway toward the house. Ink followed invisibly at her heels.

"I can get the car," he said.

Mrs. Reid was watching. Joy pretended to sneeze. "You can't drive."

"I can drive," Ink insisted. "But I do not like leaving you. Even for a moment."

Joy climbed the steps as the reality of the situation sank in: she was entering Monica's house and there were police in the living room and yellow tape across the doorways and Mrs. Reid looked grim. There had been an emergency. Joy needed to be here now.

"Thank you for coming," Mrs. Reid said, and gathered Joy to her in a one-armed hug. Joy sank against her suit jacket, feeling more grateful than she had since she'd busted out of the golem's stone cage. She'd earned a hug! She felt like she could finally *breathe*. "There was a break-in," Mrs. Reid said. That was when it finally registered that the place had been tossed—furniture moved, drawers emptied, their contents spilled across the hardwood floors. It was unsettling, like a natural disaster confined inside the house. "The alarms didn't go off. It must have happened when we left this morning. I came home after my meeting and found it like this." Mrs. Reid shook her head. "I sent Monica upstairs to see if there's anything missing."

Ink hovered in the doorway, straight razor in hand, senses alert.

"Should I stay?" he asked, unheard by Mrs. Reid.

Joy stopped in the foyer and chose her words carefully. "Go ahead," she said. "I'll find Monica."

Mrs. Reid nodded and walked slowly toward the two officers talking in the kitchen. Ink nodded, sliced a doorway, stepped backward and disappeared.

Joy made her way upstairs, snatches of conversation following her up the stairwell. "Sweeping for prints," "Nothing taken?" and "Looks like a professional job." The words urged her upward and around the corner into Monica's room.

The place was a disaster. The mattress had been ripped open, propped against the far wall where the dresser drawers had all been emptied, clothing strewn across every surface and puffs of synthetic pillow fibers were scattered everywhere like dandelion fluff. Every shelf in her room had been swept clean, their contents on the floor. The closet was empty, shoes tossed in a pile and boots turned inside out. Her makeup mirror was buried in upended bags. Her picture frames had all of their backs torn out. The bed frame slats were broken. Her flat iron had been split in two. Monica stood in the middle of it all, ankle-deep in broken trash, with an eviscerated doll in one hand and an oversize calculator in the other, her whole being asking, *Why?*

"Oh, Mon—"

"Look at this!" Monica said. "My Cabbage Patch? My clothes? My *bed*?" She waved her arms helplessly at the room, overwhelmed. "I mean, what *is* this? I get drops in my eyes, and two days later my house is tossed? Coincidence, much?" Monica crossed the room, tripping over a small mountain of books to hiss in Joy's face. "I thought you said I was protected by this almighty Edict thing!"

Joy didn't say what Ink would have said. *No one was injured. It was a threat, nothing more.* She knew that, while true, it was less than comforting and no help at all. While her best friend had been protected under the Edict that cloaked Joy and her family and friends, she did not have any wards on her house protecting it from invasion. The Folk could do what they pleased. Joy had known this and, just as stupidly, had forgotten to ask Ink to help protect the ones she loved the most.

Monica was right. It wasn't a coincidence—and it was Joy's fault. Again.

"I'm sorry," Joy said. "Let me help—"

Monica raised both hands and shut her eyes. "No. Don't. Just—don't." She exhaled through her nose and opened her eyes. "I can do this." She tossed the doll and the calculator onto her ruined bed. "The good news is, no one was hurt," she said aloud, sounding like Ink. "And at least they didn't take this." She picked up a compact pink plastic tote whose zippers had been opened and pulled out a long, white shape. She handed it to Joy. Joy frowned, turning the thing over until it suddenly made sense.

There was a vague shape of a head and breasts and a waist in the long, slippery tube of wax. A knot of brown tangles had been plastered on top of its head and two cloves stuck where the eyes should be. A small, red dot trailed smears of dye from deep inside the thing's chest. Joy could feel the slight give of the wax and the tiny ripples left by Monica's fingerprints.

"I made it from a candle and some hair from your hair-brush," Monica said apologetically. Joy stared at her. "I read about it on the internet. I figure if Aunt Meredith was onto something and all this magic stuff is real, maybe I could do something to help." She tapped the blot of red in its chest. "I didn't know what to use, since 'missing heart' wasn't on the drop down menu, so I put in a Bleeding Heart seed and a Red Hots candy from my Valentine's stash." She sounded uncharacteristically quiet and shy. "I think," she said, breathing softly, "I think the *intention's* the thing."

"You—" Joy could barely believe it. She blinked back sudden tears. "You're trying to help me grow a heart?"

Monica nodded, but didn't look Joy in the eye. "I don't believe in witchcraft, okay? But I believe in God and forgiveness and fixing mistakes." She ran a finger over the little red bump. "I don't know if it will work—I mean, I have absolutely *no* idea what I'm doing—but I figured I had to try." She said it almost in a whisper. "You're my best friend."

Joy wrapped her arms around Monica, squeezing her in a hug until the tears that had been threatening to come spilled over. The two of them clung to one another for one, long happy-sad cry, breaking apart slowly as their feet crunched down on things in the carpet.

Sniffling, Joy tried to hand the wax doll back, but Monica shook her head. "Oh no—it's yours. Mom will freak out if she finds it." She glanced around her room with a sigh. "If she could find anything at all in this mess."

Joy held the doll gently, pressing its heart against hers. "When did you do this?"

"I started researching right after you left Sunday night," Monica said, peeling her pillowcase inside out and filling it with unbroken things. It was Tuesday. Had it only been two days? "I got the hairs at your place yesterday and then scrounged through Mom's gardening stuff for the seeds and the pantry for the cinnamon candies from last February." Monica considered a torn book and tossed it in the trash. "It was a mix of a healing spell and a love spell, so I wasn't sure if it would do what I wanted. The text was pretty vague on the details, but I finished it last night."

"Um, *last* night?" Joy said.

Monica paused. Joy blushed. Monica clapped a hand over her mouth. "Was last night when you and Ink—?" She sounded horrified. "I mean, don't tell me that I—"

"I don't think so," Joy said, coughing on a laugh. "But let's keep that little theory from Ink—just in case."

They both paused and then burst out laughing, the flipside of their earlier cry. It was ridiculous and a relief a release of the tension they were both under, but they could share it honestly—a knowing between friends.

There was a pounding of shoes up the stairs outside the door.

"Monica!" Monica's boyfriend, Gordon, filled the doorway, his wide shoulders pressed against the jamb, his face a mask of panic and relief. He stopped at the mess on the floor, shearing his fingers through his crew cut. "You okay? What happened?"

Monica flung herself into his enormous embrace. "Vandals? Burglary? Haters? Who knows?" She sighed against his chest as he murmured into her hair. Her shoulders shuddered for an instant. "They didn't take anything. No one was hurt." She sniffed and looked back at her room. "Maybe the fashion police finally caught up with me, huh?"

Gordon didn't look amused. His eyes were stormy and scared. "I texted you. I called you like a million times. Your mom called, but you didn't answer—"

"Sorry." She cut him off with another strong hug. "I

should have. I've just been—" She glanced sideways at Joy
and shook her head. "Things have been crazy. But I don't
think I knew what that word meant before now. I mean,
seriously, look at this!"

Gordon unfolded slightly, swaying her gently in his arms.
"It's just stuff," he said as his gaze swept over the room. "I'm
just glad you're okay."

"I'm okay," Monica said. "Pissed off and freaked out, but
okay."

He nodded. "I thought, at first…but then I heard what
happened, and Mark said—"

"Mark?" Joy echoed.

"We brought coffee," Ink said from inside the doorway.
He held a recyclable four-cup tray awkwardly in two hands.
His eyebrows raised below his long, black bangs. "Gordon
said it might help."

Monica grabbed one gratefully. "Yes! Thank you. You
are a god."

Ink smiled, one dimple. "It has been said before."

Gordon took the next cup, one arm still wrapped around
Monica. "Ah, how fickle godhood, how fleeting fame." He
took a large swallow and plonked it down on the dresser.
"C'mon—let me help you pick up your clothes. At least you
know I can do that well."

They helped clean for the rest of the day, taking orders
and hauling trash, making lists for the insurance company
and lending willing shoulders, hands and ears. Joy sat on
the floor sticking labels on plastic bins while Ink discreetly
set wards around the house. It wasn't much, but it was
something—members of the Twixt could no longer claim
ignorance of the Edict that protected the Reids; it would be
written in glyphs, undeniable evidence. Just as *signaturae*

warned the Folk about who was marked under someone else's auspice, anyone approaching Monica's home would know that both Ink and Joy were watching.

Where is Sol Leander? Joy thought angrily, stuffing a black garbage bag into the bin. Wasn't he supposed to protect Monica? She was under his auspice, after all.

As the survivor of an unprovoked attack, Monica had walked away with a scar through her eyebrow and the mark of the Tide's representative on her face. If she had to endure the pain, she ought to get the benefits, too. Where was he, if he wasn't on the job?

"No one was hurt," Ink reminded her as she passed him in the hall. Joy nodded. He was right. Sol Leander wasn't a house alarm, but she couldn't help thinking that maybe he'd let it happen. *Maybe he did it out of spite. Maybe he did it to hurt me. Maybe this is all my fault.* Joy ripped the masking tape. And even if it wasn't Sol Leander, it could have been any one of her enemies sending a message through her friend, as surely as the Bailiwick's clients had once sent messages meant for Ink through her. This could be a warning from anyone—any one of the Folk who wished to do her harm— the Tide, Briarhook, Hasp, Ladybird, even Aniseed herself, wrinkled and malformed on her stump in the Glen. Any one of them had the means and the motive to do something like this.

Joy was really starting to hate "something like this."

Anger bubbled beneath her ribs, a hot, roiling acid that slid along her limbs. Her eyes winked with spots of light. She clenched her hands so hard, they shook. She wanted to step outside, take a breath, calm down...but no, that wasn't really true. She didn't want to calm down, she wanted to *explode!*

She thought about making some excuse, running to the car, zipping out to Abbot's Field, flipping across the grassy plain and letting it all go. But she didn't crave the release of her free-form routine, the flips and leaps and three-sixty spins, it was the feel of the earth breaking apart, shattering, embracing her like stone serpents, squeezing her like a cocoon until she burst. Joy could *See* herself becoming something both powerful and pure—a thing of vengeance, rage, unstoppable, invincible.

YES!

The keys were in her pocket. She was a dozen steps downstairs, nearly out the door. A short ride. A quick trip. No one would know. No one could stop her. And then— And then—

A montage of violent, explosive images flashed across her brain: red-eyed golems, orange fur coats, black earth spewing, the Carousel toppling, spinning glow sticks, smashed glass, broken fairy lights—and some deep instinct held her back.

Joy stopped on the stairs. It was an addict's dilemma—to leave it all, shuck her shoes, wade through the lawn, delve through the earth and soil and layers of rock, reach down with the greedy, fiery feel of freedom yet knowing that it would be very, very bad. She wanted to rip the world open, search the planet through the roots of the world, find her enemies—make them hurt, make them pay—and *CRUSH* them...!

A drop of sweat trickled down her spine.

"Hey, Joy?" She turned. Gordon waved from the dining room. "Give me a hand?"

She dropped the keys in her pocket and took a shaky breath. "Yeah. Okay."

He pointed to where all the drawers had been emptied of silver and cloth napkins were now repacked, the dishes had been piled neatly in stacks on the table and the pictures were once again arranged on the walls. Only the chandelier hung at a disconcerting angle, half-yanked from the ceiling, dangling by thick wires. Gordon pointed up.

"I don't want to stand on the table, but we have to feed the wires back into the drywall and hold the whole thing up while screwing it back in place." There was a short stepladder next to the wall. "I can hold it up or you can hold it up, but it's a two-man job."

"Or woman," Joy said. "Any prefs?"

"You any good with tools?"

"I have opposable thumbs," Joy said.

Gordon chuckled. "Excellent. You hold it. I'll screw."

Joy bit the inside of her cheek as she stood on the table and lifted the heavy light fixture. "You've been hanging out with Monica too long," Joy grunted. "Haven't you heard of innuendo?"

"Innuendo in, innuendo out..." Gordon muttered as he stood on the top step of the ladder and began tightening screws with quick twists of his wrist. Joy could feel the threads catch as they sank deep into the wood. It shook the glass crystals by her face. Gordon smiled and continued thumbing screws into the ready-made holes. "Can I ask you something?"

Joy shifted her grip. "Sure."

"Do you know what's up with Monica lately?"

Joy was glad—briefly—that she didn't have a heart because she was afraid it would be beating triple time and he would hear it, but she wasn't part-Twixt for nothing. She knew how to dodge. "What do you mean?"

"I mean, first Monica's in the hospital, then she gets all secretive—stops talking, stops texting, breaks some dates—then her house gets tossed and you—you're always there," he said with a hint of suspicion. He shook his head as he twisted the screwdriver. "I mean, is it just me?" He shifted his grip. "I know she's not the together-all-the-time type, and I get that, which is good, but there's this distance creeping in and I don't know what to think." He ground the screwdriver harder. "But I feel like if I don't do something, it's over." He shot Joy a quick look over his elbow, checking her face. "You're her BFF. So I'm asking you, friend-to-friend, if there's somebody new." Gordon sounded grim. "Is she interested in someone else? Was she really at your house or am I just an idiot?"

"You're not an id—" Joy said.

"Look," he said, cutting off her protest. "This isn't an ego thing. I just want to know if she's going to break up with me again, because we already did that once and it was *not* my idea of a good time, so if I could avoid that, I'd like to do it ahead of schedule."

Joy frowned. "By preemptively breaking up with her?"

Gordon paused, muscles taut. "Should I?"

"No," Joy said quickly, feeling the weight of the chandelier lift by inches. "I don't think you should because yes, she was at my house with me and no, I don't think there's anyone else and PS, I don't think she's planning to break up with you, unless, of course, you act like an idiot." Joy tried to sound stern as the chandelier wobbled and chimed. "If you're going to blame anybody for her weirding-out, it should be me—I've been soaking up a lot of her time with my drama and dragging her into my mess. She's been checking in on me, stopping by, putting me first, mother henning—you know how she is."

"Yeah, I do," he said, helping Joy let go. The crystals twinkled back and forth as they steadied its swing. Gordon looked right into her eyes. He was a straight-talker, down-to-earth and vulnerable. So very human. "I know you two are tight, but I also know she's not one to go looking for trouble...unless it's with you." He stepped down off the ladder. Joy dropped off the table. Their feet met the hardwood floor with a double-strong punch. "Do you know anything about what happened here?"

Something whizzed past the bay window. Joy was grateful it was just a robin and not a pixie or a banshee or an aether sprite. Did she know anything? No, but she suspected it had something to do with the Twixt, and she'd hate to have to try to lie when she really wasn't sure. Instead, she watched the bird peck the grass and take flight.

"No," she said before turning to him fully. "I don't know what happened or who did this or why and, by the way, I hate feeling helpless about it as much as you do." Joy tugged her shirt and twisted the hem around her fingers. "I wish I could stop feeling like a lightning rod for bad luck."

Gordon laughed, down-playing his worry. "Ever thought of getting a four-leaf clover?"

Joy snorted. "Already got one."

He hooked the ladder over his shoulder and scratched his cheek. "You know I love her, right?"

"Yeah," Joy said, surprised. "I do."

"Then watch out for her, okay? The way she would for you." He pointed a finger at her and it stabbed something inside her, just to the left of guilt. The gesture reminded her of Monica. "I'm trusting you, Malone," he said. "Remember— No Stupid."

Joy smiled weakly. "Right," she said. "No Stupid."

Ink emerged from the basement, arms empty, his wallet chain trailing a thin wisp of dusty spiderweb. He'd come upstairs quickly. There was something urgent in his eyes.

"We should go," he said.

It was what he didn't say that scared her.

Joy took the hint and called upstairs, "Hey, Mon? We have to head out."

There was the drumbeat of Monica's feet taking the stairs double time. "Already?" she said, checking the grandfather clock. "Yikes! Did you call your dad and tell him that you were here all day?"

Joy hesitated. Ink's mouth was a tight, thin line. Her guts clenched like a fist. "Um..."

Mrs. Reid came down from the master bedroom in jeans and a dust-smeared T-shirt, wiping her hands on a rag. "Not a stitch out of place, not a piece of jewelry missing, nothing wrong with the safe..." she muttered as she descended the stairs, stopping to put on her Beauty Queen smile, rich and sweet. She was way better at it than Joy. "You sure you don't want to stay for dinner?" Her eyes reached right into Joy's with a familiarity that ached. "You're more than welcome."

It was the forgiveness she'd been craving, the moment Joy had prayed for since that terrible day at the hospital, but she knew that this wasn't the time. Not now. She could feel Ink's impatience.

"Thank you," Joy said, grabbing Ink's hand. "But I've got to get home. We left in kind of a hurry and I didn't tell Dad where we were."

"I understand," Mrs. Reid said. "Thank you both for coming." She put an arm around Monica. "It's good to have good friends." She nodded to both Joy and Ink. "Be good, now. God bless."

Monica grabbed Joy in a hug. "Thank you," she said.

"Thank *you*," Joy whispered back. "Remember, you're *my* best friend, too." They let each other go. "I'll call you soon," Joy said as Ink opened the door. Gordon lingered near Monica and pointed a warning finger at Joy. Joy pointed a finger back. *Got it. No Stupid.*

She made a beeline for the car. By some miracle Ink had parked it on the curb and not on the sidewalk. Joy made certain to run on the asphalt, even avoiding the tiny bits of grass eking up through the cracks. She didn't trust herself. She didn't trust the Earth. She wanted it too much. She could taste the tang of metal on the back of her tongue.

"What's going on?" she whispered.

"Something set off the wards."

"Here?" Joy said. "Already?"

"No," Ink said, circling the white Ferrari 486. "Your house."

"My house?" Joy said, jumping into the driver's seat and slamming the door. "What's at my house?"

"I do not know," Ink said, buckling in. "But it is most persistent."

Joy gripped the wheel. That didn't make sense. She wasn't there and neither was Graus Claude. No one could have tracked them there. The only one home was—

"Stef!" she yelped.

She yanked the car into gear, peeled into the street and hit the button on the dash that slammed them into slipdrive; but not before a familiar twinkle caught the corner of her eye.

Sol Leander stood by the azaleas, glowering in his starlight cloak.

The car appeared on the grass, slamming with a sudden break of g-force and magic. Joy barely shut off the engine before she grabbed her scalpel. Ink circled the car quickly, razor in hand, and they both ran straight for the gate.

Ink laid a hand on the keypad. "It is not a counterspell," he said. "Nor a breach." Ink flipped his grip. "The wards have activated. Therefore, it is an intruder."

Joy ran through the courtyard, scanning with her Sight. "But they didn't break the wards?"

Ink paused. "They did not have to," he said. "I made a gap. For the satyr."

Joy gagged, tasting bile. "Dmitri's doing this?"

"He would not give me his True Name," Ink said. "So I opened the window for the Forest born."

Forest. Satyrs. Golems. Dryads.

Aniseed.

Joy's throat squeezed shut. *"Stef!"*

Slicing downward, Ink yanked her through the nothing that smelled citrus-sweet. She blinked in the sudden indoor darkness, the momentary vertigo splintering at the explosive crash of breaking wood. Joy ran down the hall and wrenched open Stef's door.

The golem took up most of the room, shoulders braced against both walls, hemmed in, growling, its ruby-red eyes burning in its flat slab of a face. The wall had been torn open, bits of wood and plaster and glass hung off the frame. Its face was in shadow, but the glyph on its brow burned. The mud golem had gathered an impressive mass before hauling itself through Stef's window, but now it was stuck.

Joy's anger boiled. She knew this thing. Golems had found her in the woods, in the Carousel on the Green, and she'd found one squatting at the feet of that horrid thing in the Glen.

Aniseed's pet.

"You," she whispered.

It turned its head sharply. Joy looked down.

Stef!

He lay on his bed, motionless, fetal, face turned away.

With a grunt, the golem lifted its foot and brought it down on Stef's skull.

FIFTEEN

JOY SCREAMED AND KEPT ON SCREAMING.

The golem ignored her, its foot grinding down.

"NO!"

Ink braced himself. "Get d—"

The thing shrieked, a hollow sound that punched her body with the force of gales, knocking Joy into the hallway, slamming her onto her back. She rolled and came up quickly, her fingers scrabbling against the floor. She squinted. Ink shouted something, the words whisked away by the buffeting wind.

The golem ran out of air. Between one breath and another, Joy pounced.

It raised one club-like arm and smashed the wall. Cracks shot through the paint like veins. Chunks of plaster fell from the ceiling, powdering against the floor. Ink switched the straight razor for his obsidian blade, drawing a hasty barrier; a smoky antilight corroded the air with a low, dental buzz. Joy clenched her teeth against the uncomfortable humming in her head. The golem reared back and struck again. A bookshelf shattered. Joy saw nothing but her enemy, its flat face, its burning sigil and its red eyes, hot as coals.

Joy tried to reach for Earth before she even realized it, but she was indoors, trapped inside the human world of plastic and paint—they didn't even have houseplants—so she gathered the feeling of the grass outside in the yard, the bits of dirt, the living world that knew her well. She touched the golem, its body of mud and branches, soil and clay. She fisted her power around it and *pulled*.

Pinhole lights skimmed her vision, the distant voice whispering in her ears. She concentrated with all the hate and fury she felt for its master, the *segulah* witch.

Aniseed!

Joy was suffering, people she loved were suffering, and the suffering wouldn't end until she CRUSHED EVERYTHING THAT STOOD BEFORE HER! *HER ENEMIES WOULD BURN!*

The golem bellowed another roar as it beat at the gray, buzzing barrier, the impacts exploding with hissing sparks. The homunculus reeled back, stung. Joy snapped her hand sideways. She felt the coursing, focused energy pour through her, flicking along the baseboards, skittering over the floor like a static shock.

A thousand electric crackles lit up its body, fracturing it from within.

The golem raised its head and *howled*, mouth open, lips peeled back, red eyes bulging like bubbles of lava. Joy slammed her palms against her ears as if she could blot out the noise, but it pierced her brain like the scalpel, driving her to her knees. Ink cringed, then just as quickly, stood up, unaffected—Joy envied that he could shut off his ears.

There was a *crack* of sound and light, and the golem collapsed, disintegrating into steaming hot dust.

Joy pitched backward, the steam baking her face. The buzzing hum continued as Ink slashed the thick clouds. She coughed as her lungs tried to sieve out the air. Falling to her knees, she scrambled, searching the floor...

"Ink!" she screamed, coughing on waves of heat. "Stef!" she cried, fumbling blindly, not knowing where he was.

Spears of light spliced the fog, stabbing sharp arrows through the room. Silence slapped like a bedsheet. Her eyes teared, blinking rapidly against the dust and her mounting fears.

Joy pawed through the blankets, the broken bookcase, the bed.

"Stef?" she choked. "Stef!"

The fog lifted. Her brother's room was a wreck, but there was no sign of him. Joy froze, fingers splayed over the carpet, powdered in clay dust. No body. No blood. Ink stood in front of the ruined window, backlit by the sun. The glyph on the windowsill still shone, intact. Moisture dripped off the end of the knapped and pitted blade.

He dropped to his knees beside her. The room was hot and empty.

"Where is he?" Ink asked. "Did it take him?"

"No," Joy said slowly, her thoughts whirling. "No, I don't think so..."

She sat down heavily and started laughing. Joy curled over her stomach, suddenly hysterical, keening for breath. Ink touched her tentatively, a gentle brush of frictionless skin. She caught his worried gaze and laughed harder, crying and tugging his arm.

"He's not here!" she gasped. "It wasn't Stef. It was his doppelganger!" She'd recognized the curled position of her brother asleep in his pajamas. "It was magic! An illusion!" she said between breaths. His magical decoy double had fooled someone other than her! "It's a spell that looks like him. He left it asleep on the bed! He must have gone somewhere with Dmitri." Joy exhaled, relieved, her voice still hoarse and sore from screaming, her fury disappearing with the mist. She surveyed the damage, contained in the one room, and was ridiculously thankful that it wasn't worse.

Ink hovered near her, still clutching the arrowhead and watching her cues—he was still new to things like nuanced facial expressions and the extremes of human emotion. He didn't look reassured by her laughter or her tears or the intense gleam in her eye. She turned and gazed out the broken wall. There was a scattered pile of drywall and glass two floors down.

"Where do you think they've gone?" she asked.

Ink tucked the obsidian blade back into his wallet. "If the wizard wished them gone, they might be anywhere on Earth—I am unfamiliar with the breadth of your brother's power. However, he has yet to display the ability to travel by magic, so they may not be far."

Wiping away tears, Joy glanced over the mess, stopping when she saw the pile beneath the knocked-over nightstand. There was a clock blinking twelve, Stef's wallet, a box of condoms, his Fossil watch and a broken plastic hook on a bit of string. Joy picked it up. She'd know that piece of plastic anywhere.

"They used a beacon," Joy said. "I know where they are."

Something was wrong. Joy felt it the moment she stepped into the meadow on the edge of the Grove. The creepy, magic feeling reminded her of being inside the Bailiwick—which reminded her of the princess, the King and Queen, and Graus Claude. The grove in the Bailiwick was an exquisite copy of a real, living forest but this—this was real, as real as anything, as wild as any fairy-tale country, a wildness that wasn't hemmed in by fences or projects, cities or farms, or anything human. This was the world as it had been, as it once was, as it had every right to be, and that was both freeing and terrifying.

She didn't belong here.

Ink hovered by her side. There was a sharp *click* as the straight razor snapped open. It would have echoed if the Grove had had walls.

"You feel it, too?" she whispered.

"Yes," he said simply. "In there." He indicated the deep woods with his chin.

Joy led the way across the field into the Forest Grove.

The air cooled as the canopy grew thicker, the underbrush cracking under heels and snapping as they passed. Shadows deepened from spring green to emerald, and evergreen to black. She half expected a party of satyrs to come boiling out of the trees, but given the eerie silence, maybe not.

And that was far worse.

She wished that she could somehow sense Stef, but all she had to go on was the gut feeling that Stef would have gone with Dmitri, and Dmitri would have come here. Maybe they'd recognized the golem, too, and come searching for answers. The last place she'd seen one was here in the Grove.

Guarding Aniseed's graftling.

Joy stood in the meadow on the edge of the wood, feeling like she *ought* to have some way to find her brother; they were connected by blood and Earth, after all. *Blood is thicker than water.* Inq was onto something. Joy was used to demanding the impossible from herself and recently, she'd been able to get it.

She slowed, listening. Her body tingled. She felt her senses extend, searching for her brother like a red spot in her head. It wasn't until she was halfway through the for-

est that she realized that while it felt like she'd been moving, her feet were standing still.

She didn't remember taking off her shoes.

The world flowered open, offering color and fragrance
and a taste she could touch.

"Joy?" Ink's voice came from far away, but she shushed
him with barely a breath, the air leaking from her lungs.
Her eyes unfocused as she sifted through the warm layer
of topsoil, sending tentative tendrils spiraling out and she,
at the center, drinking it in. Depth had a scent, direction
had a flavor, and all that passed through these woods lingered like a ghostly aftertaste on the tip of her tongue. If she
could sort through them all, she could find him. She knew
it. The thought tickled like delicate ferns and clover, a giggle
of movement that brushed the leaves like a breath of wind.

She laughed, her voice pitched low.

"Joy?"

Ink's voice held a hint of warning, but not enough to call
her back from exploring the roots of a tree that seemed to
recognize the shape of Stef's passing, some odd tidbit of
hair or skin or blood. It chilled her and fascinated her and
the scent of him was almost within reach...

"Joy!"

She blinked. Trapped, she looked down. She was thigh-
deep in earth; a rough hillock had formed around her like
an anthill, an avalanche in reverse. Rocks and stones and
clods of dirt had gathered to cluster at her feet, surrounding
her ankles, pushing together, climbing over one another to
worship at her knees. A dry crust had formed, riddled with
cracks, protecting her in the center of the moist, brown soil.
It was warm and rich and brown and *alive*. Joy fell backward, kicking hastily at the dirt and landing hard on her

hip. She extricated herself, flailing and clawing. The connection—if there was one—snapped, broke, gone.

Joy lay on the ground, panting. Ink wound a hand around her forearm and hauled her to her feet. She clung to him, pulling him hard against her, grasping him with both hands and gasping.

"What happened?"

"You called Earth to you," Ink said. "And it answered."

"I—" She faltered and slid her hands down her arms, over her stomach, touching her legs. "I didn't—?"

"Change? No," Ink said. "It stopped. You stopped." He weighed his words carefully. "I waited to be sure."

Joy stared at his eyes, endless pools of fathomless black flecked with flashes of neon light. Would he have killed her if she'd changed? Become an Elemental? Broken her promise? What would he have done to protect the Folk from the Destroyer of Worlds?

His eyes begged her not to ask questions she didn't want answered.

"Did you find—?" he asked.

"No," she said, looking toward the Grove. "I sensed him, but I would have thought we'd be greeted by now."

Something stirred beyond a distant tree, rippling the leaves. Joy pulled on her shoes and held her scalpel. Ink raised his blade likewise, eyes on the approaching slither of movement. Joy felt the familiar patter along the top of the earth a moment before it reached them in a burst of branches.

Two spears hit the ground with a meaty *chunk-chunk!* Ink whirled around, dropping a ward with a sweep of his razor, golden glitter sparkling as the satyrs came to bear.

Last time she'd seen the troop, they had been alarmed, but Joy had never seen them *livid*; she had no doubt from

their faces that the keepers of the Grove would have gladly
stabbed her first and asked questions later. They glared at
her through the sparkling ward, their serrated spears and
yellow teeth bared and glinting.

Joy turned slowly, squinting through the ward's golden
veil, taking in the many spears, bows and machete knives
pointed straight at her. The satyrs seemed to have materialized from the woods themselves. It made sense, in a way,
as they were the keepers of the Grove.

Ink held out his straight razor like a warning between
them, staring around the troop through the curtain of his
long, black bangs. "What is this?" he asked simply, his voice
slicing smoothly through magic and malice. "Why are we
greeted in this manner? We mean you no harm."

Breathing heavily, angrily, and shifting their weapons,
the Grove's keepers did not seem inclined to talk. They'd
steeled themselves for silence. Most of their faces were
wretched. A few bearded faces held back tears. One auburn-
haired satyr, younger than the rest, scrubbed a grubby fist
against his eyes, leaving a childish smear of grime across
his nose and one cheek. Joy hesitated, empathy softening
her confusion.

"Please—"

Snarling, the young satyr flung himself at her and was
physically restrained by two of his comrades from rushing
the ward. His bare chest strained at their heavy arms, his
hooves pawing at the ground, his screams drawing spittle.

"She did it! She took it! You did this! *You!*" He lunged in
impotent anger. "Where is it? Tell us! *Where?*"

Joy was too surprised to feel anything besides shock. She
was more confused than afraid. "What?"

"Tell us where it is," another voice barked. "Now!"

Joy squeezed the scalpel and tried to keep the quaver out of her voice. "I don't know what you're talking about."

"*I'll kill you!*"

There was an angry surge of assent.

A sharp, humming drone split sound lengthwise, rendering them silent. A buzz saw whine sliced the air as Ink dragged a long gash in the world, jagged and raw, his arms fighting the air itself, thick and resistant to his blade. He finished his glyph with a wrenching twist, yanking the razor free from the gutted wound. The sigil hung in midair, ominous and powerful.

"She is under my protection," Ink said quietly. "As all that which lives here is yours. We should respect one another in this." His gaze shifted to touch each of the satyrs in turn. "Your loyalty is admirable. Therefore, I will forgive you your fervor if you can forgive me mine." The terrible rent in the air fizzed with unspent energy. Joy felt a coolness leaking from it, frosty and fine. She had the unsettling sensation that when she looked at it, it was looking back at her. Ink's voice was calm, yet severe, promising many bad things might happen should his reasonable request be denied. "Now will someone please explain what has happened here?"

The troop leader shouldered his way through the band to stand at the ward's edge. The gold light played off his graying hair and the puckered scars on his chest. He flicked his eyes to the malevolent sigil and back at Joy and Ink.

"Do you claim ignorance?" he asked.

"Yes," Joy said quickly, trying to ease the tension. "I came here looking for my brother. We just arrived moments ago."

The crags of the elder's face deepened and parted with a sneer. "Uninvited."

Joy nodded. "True," she said. "I'm sorry. I was worried."

The old satyr exhaled through his nose, tickling the whiskers of his mustache. "Worry not," he said darkly. "We have him."

"Joy!"

Stef was running through the underbrush, Dmitri hot on his heels, joined by at least four other satyrs with staves and seed bags slung over their shoulders, accompanying them down the winding paths between trees. Ink straightened slowly and with a sharp swipe, collapsed the jagged sigil upon itself. The world swelled back to normal, perfumed in kinder scents of pollen and young wood. Another deft gesture and the ward disappeared, just in time for Stef to grab her in a slam-grateful hug.

"Oh my God," she said into the weird texture of his skin. Shirtless, her brother looked scrawny and pale. "Stef! I thought you'd been killed!"

He squeezed her, rocking back and forth. "I have never been so glad to be out of that room in my life," he said. "It happened just after you left. When I saw what was happening, I freaked out and we bailed, but I forgot the doppelganger spell resets automatically when I leave my own bed. Once we got here, I had no way to warn you and they wouldn't let me leave—they thought I was a decoy and the golem attack, a distraction."

Joy pushed away enough to glare at Dmitri and the troop leader behind him. "A distraction?" she snapped. "Are you kidding? What's going on?"

The elder scowled. "We are keepers of the Grove, its caretakers and protectors—it is on our lives to guard the graftlings. Our collective auspice is to keep alive the First Forest and its kin." The troop leader spoke low, strained and tight. His voice cracked like ancient stones. "It is our sacred trust."

There was a scuffle near the back, and the auburn-haired satyr gave a wordless, choking scream before being cuffed hard across the face and sent sprawling to the ground. He landed hard, heaving and sobbing. Joy twisted her fingers in her shirt.

The troop leader sighed. "You saw the guardian."

Joy tried not to grin. The fire-eyed golem was nothing but a mound of clumped dirt. "It was hers, wasn't it?" Joy said. "The one Aniseed left to her heir."

"It was bequeathed to the graftling, yes," the satyr said. "In order to guard it from harm."

His eyebrows drew down. His ears lay flat. Joy squirmed, not understanding why all of them were glaring at her. Then it clicked.

"Wait. You think I—?"

"The graftling is gone," Dmitri said quietly. The rest of the troop ground their teeth in unison.

A chill of fear twisted in her gut and bloomed, squeezing the air out of her lungs. *"What?"* She imagined the tiny, wrinkled thing tearing itself from the moss-packed wound, falling from the willow stump to crawl hand over hand, dragging its bloated brown belly though the dirt, its veined eyes spinning madly in its bald baby head. Dread burned like bile in the back of her throat. "She's loose?" Joy screamed. "She's *free*?" Ink's hand was on her arm. Her brother was at her back. She spun around and grabbed them both, hyperventilating. "She's coming! She sent it to kill you! To kill me! Ink, she's *back*!"

Ink held her arms if it that could quell the panic. "Joy!"

"No. It's too young," the troop leader said, shaking his horned head. "It will not survive long outside its surrogate stump." He growled. "The last of the *sobto*-dryads will wither and die, and then they will truly be lost."

Drooping, limbs buzzing, Joy said nothing. She could not say she was sorry because it would be a lie. She wanted to believe it, but she didn't. *Aniseed was alive!*

"Extinction of any one species depletes us all," the troop leader said darkly. "The world suffers and knows remorse." A murmur rustled through the troop, acknowledging their shame. The troop leader rested the butt of his spear against the ground by his hoof. "Now perhaps you understand the gravity of the crime," he said. "Please take us to wherever you've hidden the graftling before it is too late."

"What?" Joy said. "I didn't take it!"

A voice snapped, "She's lying!"

Ink faced the troop calmly. "She cannot lie."

A satyr slammed the end of his spear. "He could have!" he said, pointing at Stef.

Stef shot back angrily. "Why would I take it?"

"To save your sister," the satyr said. "To save your people."

Angry voices joined the throng. Joy's voice, hitched high, shouted over them all.

"It's Aniseed!" Joy insisted, pleading to deaf goat ears. "She's behind this! She's up to something! She's *not* dead!"

The troop leader leaped forward. "Is that a confession?" Wild animal scent poured off him, pushing her back.

"No!" Joy said. "She's escaped—"

"Ridiculous!"

"You don't know Aniseed."

Dmitri spoke up timidly. "It's not Aniseed—"

"It *is*." Joy said sharply. "It *remembers*. It's *her*."

The troop leader didn't flinch. "And you wanted to kill it," he said.

"*Of course I did!*" Joy screamed. "Aniseed tried to kill me—to kill off *most of humanity*—by sending her disease through *signaturae*, using everyone the Scribes had ever touched."

Her voice broke off as hopelessness seeped in, returning her to the here and now. She shook her head. "But you said it yourself—the Council sentenced her, tried her and found her guilty. Her sentence was carried out. She was killed on the battlefield. I saw her fall."

Of course, she'd also seen Kurt kill Aniseed and then fall under a pack of feathered bears, so maybe Joy should not have been surprised to find that the *segulah* had also managed to cheat death by cloning herself before the final showdown on the warehouse floor. Aniseed wasn't stupid; she was smart, patient, manipulative, insidious and evil. Unfortunately, she also was a master at twisting the rules that bound the Twixt.

"The rules state that a graftling, even if it retained any memories, cannot be held accountable for the actions of its parent. It was under your protection and the rules of the Twixt," Joy said, glaring at the grizzled satyr. "I respected that, and you, and your rules. And I walked away."

"So you sent your brother instead?"

Joy's "I did not!" chorused with Stef's "She did not!" Their leader did not look impressed. He pointed the spear at each of them. The troop held up arms. Joy tensed in her shoes.

"One of you knows where the graftling is," the elder said gruffly. "The golem must have followed it to your abode. We cannot waste time tearing your house down to its bones. You must return it now!"

Joy shouted. "We don't have it!"

"The golem was bequeathed to the graftling," Ink said solemnly, crisp with reason. "If the graftling gave it orders, would it be bound to obey them?"

The elder paused and many grumbles rose behind him. "The graftling is not old enough to give commands," he said. "But once it reaches maturity and cleaves from the stump, then, yes, the golem guardian would be beholden to it. That is its inheritance."

Ink raised the razor. "And what if the golem was ordered to raid Joy's domicile?"

The troop leader strode forward and hovered as close as he dared with Ink's blade drawn. He showed no fear, the cords of his neck tight as a bow. He was a warrior and a leader and an elder of the Folk who had seen too much; it was painted on his face. He loomed over them, cracking his neck to either side as if sharpening the curling horns on his head.

"That is a lot of 'ifs,' Master Scribe," he said. "Far more likely this girl hungers for revenge."

Joy cringed. It was true. But not the way he meant it.

He spun on Joy. "You—you must tell the truth, and I must believe you, but this one—" He pivoted slowly, eying Stef. "This *wizard*," he spat. "*He* can lie." It was an insult, the worst of all the Folk's Deadly Sins.

"No," Dmitri said, stepping forward. "He's telling the truth. He's been with me the whole time. On my honor."

"And what worth is that? Your honor?" the old satyr said over his shoulder without looking directly at the young buck. The other satyrs similarly avoided Dmitri's gaze. A couple of them shifted aside. "Why do you think your post is on the Hill and not here in the heart of the Grove where we belong?" He sniffed. "You lost your place among us long ago." The old satyr's voice dropped to a harsh whisper. "You lost your faith and you lost your way."

Dmitri lifted his bearded chin, spots of color on his cheeks and chest. "I am not lost," he said. "I chose this."

"You 'chose' it?" The troop leader snorted. "You *have* been among humans too long." He stepped nearer to Stef, glaring at his glyphed rectangular lenses. "Especially this one." Her brother didn't speak a word, glaring hotly back.

"He has a name," Dmitri said.

The troop leader snarled, "I know his name."

The threat hung in the air like smoke.

Joy held her breath. Stef hadn't locked his True Name into a sigil, a *signatura*, so he was vulnerable to anyone to whom he'd willingly given his name—every time he'd introduced himself, he'd offered up the chance to be enslaved to their will. *He didn't know. He's still human.* Joy glanced at Ink.

But if this was his chance, the troop leader did not abuse it.

"I'm sorry," Ink said. "None of us know what has happened to the graftling, Grove Elder. If it is as you say, then the graftling is gone. She is dead. I am sorry for your loss."

The leader of the troop chewed furiously on his tongue, words clearly aching to be spat out roiled behind his teeth and the spear trembled in his grip. Finally he signaled to the others to lower their weapons.

"It is not safe for you here," he said. "None of you can stay. Go back from whence you came and do not return!"

Stef sighed, deflating his chest, raising his hands palm-up. "I'm all for leaving," he said. "Consider me gone."

"What?" Dmitri asked, ignoring the black look from his superior. "Where're you going?"

"Pennsylvania," he said. "I'm going back to U Penn."

"You can't go back to *college*!" Joy said. "It's not safe—!"

"I'll go with him." Everyone stared at Dmitri, who looked surprised himself. "I'll go," he said again. "To Pennsylvania. I'll keep him safe."

Joy gaped at Dmitri. "Are you *crazy*?" she said, and turned to her brother. "You can't do this."

The troop leader inhaled, ready to roar, "You cannot—!"

"I swear it. I'll swear on anything—by rowan and ash and be ironwood bound—I will stay with him." Dmitri looked over at Stef. "As long as he'll have me, I'll stay with him. I'll be there."

"Madness!" The troop leader snarled and stamped his hooves into the earth. "You'd chain yourself to a human just as surely as if you'd given him your True Name! Have you learned *nothing*? Have we taught you *nothing*?" He spat in disgust.

"Oh, I have learned many, many things, Pappoús," Dmitri said. "Enough to know that I'm done. I'm out. I have to live my own life."

"Your life is not yours to give like coins or riddles or promises in the dark!" the graying satyr growled. "You, the young, are all we have left—you are the last of our years, our final hope for the future—your life is your bond." He tried to impress his words upon the young buck. "The King and Queen are due to Return and we will show them our loyalties have stayed true—that we did not shirk our responsibilities. You owe us that much, at least!"

Dmitri was wide-eyed and solemn beneath his mess of chocolate curls. He brushed Stef's forearm lightly with the back of his hand. "I owe you nothing, Pappoús. I have given my life and name to the Twixt, to my duty, to the troop and to you." He glanced sideways at Stef. "I have been chained to him for a quarter of a lifetime," he said. "Now that I've found him again, I will spend the rest of my days and my nights doing the same."

Stef smiled, blushing. The troop leader back-kicked the dirt with a scarred hoof. "Idiocy!"

Dmitri shrugged. "Call it what you want," he said. "I choose to be happy."

"You're young and foolish," his elder grunted, sweeping his spear wide to encompass all the outsiders. "If you think the rules don't apply to you, you are sadly mistaken." His eyes narrowed as he glared at Joy. "It begins and ends with you."

She couldn't deny that.

He righted his spear. "Get out," he said. "Get out of my sight."

"So what are we going to do?" Joy asked as Stef packed the last of Dmitri's things into his car.

"About what?" Stef said.

"About the satyrs, the Grove, the King and Queen, Graus Claude, the Council—all of it." *And the change*, Joy thought but didn't dare say. *How are we going to stop me from changing into something that might destroy the world?*

"Joy, this is what happens when you mess with Folk politics. You don't *have* to do anything—this isn't about you." Joy didn't bother correcting him by saying that it *was* about her, about the Council's ruling, the King and Queen's Decree, and the possibility of changing into an Elemental—mostly to avoid sounding like the most childish person ever, but it also wasn't something she wanted to say in front of witnesses. Stef shook his head, misunderstanding her silence. "Listen, you broke the spell, you played by their rules, they have their memories back and their King and Queen can come home—what else do you want? You did it. It's done. *You're* done. It's over." He adjusted his glasses. "It's time to move on. Life goes on, and I, for one, am all for getting back to the real world." He glanced at Dmitri. "Plus one."

Dmitri dared a small smile, but his ears still drooped. Stef reached out a hand and took the DJ's, less a meshing of fingers than an offering of strength. Joy averted her eyes, slipping her hand into her purse, finding the smooth shape of the wax doll with her fingertips, seeking out the dark bump in its chest. She ran her thumb over its surface, the simulacrum of her heart, and felt a stirring in her chest, something like hope. Was it possible it was working? Was she growing a heart? Joy felt a little flutter. She touched the spot in her chest, trying to believe in an answering echo— perhaps it was nothing. Perhaps it was too soon.

What does time mean to one of the Folk? Dmitri and Stef had met and lost each other years ago and had been reunited only very recently. Was that a long time or no time at all? The way that they looked at each other, it was like it was the first time and also forever.

Stef helped Dmitri push the last box into the car. The thing was packed right up to the front seat. They closed the trunk and sat on the back fender, leaning on one another's shoulder, sharing a beer.

And that was when Joy figured it out.

Ink smiled at her. "What is it?"

She grinned, eyes sparkling. "I just had a perfect idea."

SIXTEEN

"THIS IS A TERRIBLE IDEA," STEF SAID, STANDING OUT-side the Bailiwick's grand brownstone.

"What he said," Dmitri agreed, craning his neck. "This is insane."

"Shut up. It's brilliant. And it solves all of our pr—" Joy stumbled on the stone steps. Wind shivered the urns of bamboo. "Well, most of our problems, anyway. But we have to find the Bailiwick first." She rapped the door knocker again sharply. She'd never had to knock twice. No answer could mean anything, but she gave Ink a worried glance—they'd never been left standing in front of the building for long.

Joy swallowed back her worry and a mouthful of spit. She was dying for a Clif Bar and a blue Gatorade. Maybe some pizza. And pretzels. Anything with salt.

Ink inspected the doorway with a critical eye. "The wards are in place," he said. "There may still be a chance that I could appear inside, but it would most likely be—" he chose his words carefully "—messy and unpleasant."

"Two of my least favorite adjectives," Dmitri said drily.

"Hang on," Joy said and pulled out her phone, scrolling through contacts and tapping Kurt's name. She hated to call on him for anything short of an emergency, but if she was right, this might qualify. If she was wrong, well, she was already outside.

The phone rang once and connected.

"Joy."

Kurt sounded not-at-all pleased. She'd kind of preferred it when he was mute.

"Hey," she said. "We're outside the brownstone. Anybody home?"

"The Bailiwick is unavailable at this time," Kurt said. "He will contact you at his convenience."

"We need to see him now," Joy said looking at the others gathered on the steps. "I have an idea how to get the King and Queen to come back, and better sooner than later."

"Miss Malone—"

"Aniseed's loose," she said, cutting him off. "She's out. She's escaped. The satyrs think her graftling's going to die now that it's off her stump, but I think you and I know better than that." There was a satisfying pause on the other end of the line. She'd gotten his attention. "We have to stop her. And for that, we need Graus Claude."

The front door opened. Kurt glowered at the rabble on the doorstep. Stef got to his feet. Dmitri's hooves clomped up the stone stairs. Ink fished behind his wallet and held out his card. Kurt frowned at it; his muscleman body blocked the door. The Bailiwick's butler was as immovable as iron.

"The Bailiwick is not in residence at this time," Kurt said.

"I know," Joy said. "And I know that you must know where he is."

"I do," Kurt said. There was no sense in denying it. "However, he has made it clear that he does not wish to be disturbed."

"Yeah?" Stef said. Joy shushed him. Her brother ignored her. "Let's say that he owes me one. I found the Bailiwick in my room wearing my bedsheets—which, I assure you, certainly qualifies as being 'disturbed'—so I'm certain he can put up with us dropping in unannounced to tell him that we're trying to save his world."

Dmitri's eyebrows shot up. Joy bit the inside of her cheek. Kurt did not shift his eyes from Stef. A muscle moved, a twitch in his arm. Ink stroked his fingers nervously along his wallet chain. Kurt stepped aside.

"I would have *loved* to see that," Inq quipped from inside, materializing in the dark corridor as if emerging from the wall. Joy knew she'd actually used the secret elevator at the end of the hall. Inq smiled at the assembly, grinning hugely when she saw Joy. She clapped her hands girlishly. "Look! You brought me presents." She beamed. "And here, I didn't get you anything."

Stef rolled his eyes as Dmitri leered a foxy grin. Ink greeted his sister by touching her shoulder.

"We need to see the Bailiwick," Ink said.

"He isn't here," Inq said, sliding a hand down Kurt's chest. "And we're quite enjoying the place without him."

"Joy believes she has found a way to convince the King and Queen to return," Ink said.

Inq's eyes lit up with interest, all green and purple fire. "Really?" she said. "Tell me."

Joy gestured to her brother and Dmitri. "Meet Exhibit A and Exhibit B," Joy said. "If the King and Queen want proof that it's safe to return to the world of humans and Folk, then why not show them how well we get along?" She flashed her Olympic-class smile. "Ink and I have already made our first impression, and I considered asking you and Kurt but, as you've pointed out, you're not *technically* Folk." Joy shrugged helplessly at Kurt. "And, frankly, you're not so human yourself. So, I figured the best thing is to show them the two lovebirds, here."

Dmitri licked his lips and whistled a twittering, lively tune. Stef slapped him in the stomach. He stopped.

"Well, well," Inq said approvingly. "A very compelling argument. And quite a handsome pair, too! In fact, we should dress them up properly—you know how much royalty loves pretty things." She gave Kurt a sly smile. "By all means, then, we should find the Bailiwick at once."

"The Bailiwick left explicit instructions regarding his wishes," Kurt said flatly.

"Then he should have been a djinni," Inq said with a haughty wave. "Honestly, he couldn't have known that Joy would find a solution so quickly or that Aniseed's offspring might escape the Grove." She sat herself in one of the flaring wingback chairs. "Time is of the essence. They need to see Graus Claude. Give them the coordinates and Ink can take her to him with their prize specimens in tow."

"Hey!" Stef managed, but Dmitri hushed him quickly. Joy's brother looked murderous. Inq grinned.

"Good puppy."

"That's it!" Stef snapped. "I'm out of here."

"Seriously?" Joy said, a tired edge in her voice. She turned to Kurt. "Can you tell us where he is or not?"

Kurt's spine straightened an inch. "No."

"You mean to say 'yes,'" Inq simpered under the butler's black glare. "Well, it's true—you *can* tell them, you just won't." Inq stage-whispered to Joy. "Hence, the usefulness of having a manservant who can lie."

"You mean slave," Kurt said flatly. The word dropped like lead.

Inq stopped and placed a hand on his chest. "One day, my love, we will all be free." She said it like a promise without words, because she, unlike him, could not lie. Joy wondered how long Kurt had to work off his debt to the Bailiwick or if it would ever end.

Inq forced a lightness into her voice as she hooked Joy's elbow. "Excuse us, boys, we have to go powder our noses."

Kurt glowered at them but didn't move as Inq sauntered past, dragging Joy in her wake. They walked down the sconce-lit corridor with its old mirrors and oil portraits in gilt frames. Joy felt Kurt's gaze sizzle on her back.

Joy stumbled on the carpet runner. "You don't pee," she whispered.

Inq huffed. "Details. Get in."

She pushed their way into the powder room with its salmon-and-gold-striped wallpaper, fluted sink, claw-foot tub and matching couch and ottoman. It was eerily surreal how often Joy had experienced life-changing moments in this all-too-familiar room, most of them medical and many of them painful. She wondered if Graus Claude had gotten around to installing a Rod of Asclepius outside the door.

Joy eyed the fainting couch. "Are you going to get Kurt to tell us?"

"Ha!" Inq barked a laugh. "No. He's had enough of being manipulated, don't you think? However, I believe I know how to find our absent amphibian with minimal effort." She bumped Joy's hip and tilted her head coyly to one side. "Do you have the dowsing rod with you?"

Joy rattled her purse. "Don't leave home without it."

"Good," Inq said. "All you need is a bit of the old frog, a little incantation, and off you go. Fortunately, I know just the thing."

Inq let go of Joy's arm and crossed the room to the medical chest. Joy recognized it from when Kurt had tended her wounds. Inq opened the chest with an almost-sacred reverence before gently extracting some of the trays and clasped boxes, a biohazard bag and a heavy glass jug filled with a dark, viscous fluid. The lid was smoked glass in the shape of a squatting toad, balefully glaring and gloriously fat. Inq lifted the lid. The ring of glass scraping glass echoed in the room.

"Give it here," Inq whispered, and Joy handed her the Y-shaped stick, the device she'd used to track down the source of the Amanya spell—the mass spell of forgetting—that had condemned Graus Claude, exposed the true traitor, Aniseed, and reawakened the Folk's memory of the King and Queen of the Twixt. For that, Joy had been accepted, assaulted, hunted, humiliated; chased from her own gala Under the Hill; and attacked in her home, across Faeland, the world and the Twixt, placing herself, her family and friends at risk. She twisted her fingers as Inq worked, thinking that a simple "Thank you," would have sufficed.

Inq placed the dowsing rod on the floor and popped open a box of Band-Aids, choosing the smallest strip. Peeling a sterile syringe from its wrapping, she reached one hand into the dark, murky goo and carefully lifted out a single dark globe. Oily juices dripped off her wrist.

"What are you doing?" Joy asked, alarmed.

"No harm," Inq said, turning the thing over in her hand. Light shone through the thick membrane, revealing a darker shape at its heart, like a pit or seed. Inq bit the cap of the syringe between her teeth, pulled it free and pushed the needle into the orb, then drew back the plunger, sucking out the thick indigo liquid. The barrel filled slowly. Satisfied, Inq pressed her thumb over the point of insertion as she withdrew the needle and stuck the Band-Aid over the tiny pinhole before dropping the orb back into the jar with a *plop*. She dropped the syringe on its plastic wrapper, rolled to her feet and washed her gooey hands in the sink. Joy stared at the mess, feeling vaguely sick.

"Please don't tell me—"

"Then don't ask," Inq said, wiping her hands on the towel and draping it primly through its ring. "Now, the important thing is to have everyone holding on to the rod at once—that will decrease the chances of anyone getting lost in transit. You remember what happened last time." She sounded mock-stern. "You left Filly bleeding under a tree somewhere north of Rovaniemi." Inq neatly capped the needle and wiped the plunger with a cotton ball before offering it to Joy. "Use this to track him down. Blood calls to blood." She paused, considering what was in her hand. "Or whatever. Close enough." She waggled the syringe. Joy took it by the flanges. The liquid looked like prune juice and smelled like brine. *Egg albumen. Ew.*

"Are you sure this will work?" Joy said weakly.

"It'll work," Inq said, grinning. "Trust me."

It was not exactly comforting. Joy kept her eyes on the purple liquid as Inq replaced the supplies in the chest.

"So what am I supposed to do with it?" Joy managed, swallowing thickly.

"See this divot here?" Inq said, lifting the dowsing rod so that Joy could see the tiny dip in the wood, no bigger than the pad of her pinkie. "Squeeze a few drops into the reservoir, whisper the word and hang on tight." Inq tapped the syringe with a lacquered nail. "The spell is 'Anvesana.' Say it like you mean it. Like you want to find him."

"I *do* want to find him," Joy said. "I want this to be over."

"Well, once the King and Queen are back, you can wipe the slate clean—or rub it in everyone's faces, which is what I'd do." Inq rubbed the towel between her fingers. "I checked on your secret, by the way—there hasn't been a sale yet. There's talk of bargains and bartering, negotiations, trade deals, offers, counteroffers—you're a hot ticket item and your secrets are as good as gold."

"My *secrets*?" Joy yelped, fear dribbling through her nerves.

"Secret, singular," Inq corrected. "My bad." The Scribe paused, her curiosity piqued. "Why? Are there more?" Inq sounded positively delighted.

Joy scrambled to think of something crass or flippant, anything to divert Inq from following that particular line of questioning down a dark rabbit hole. She didn't need Inq to have another excuse to threaten her life.

The Scribe watched her squirm, then straightened with a laugh, flashing the silver necklaces at her throat. "Oh, Joy, you are a treasure! I really should have taken you for my own." Her nose wrinkled in glee. "This is going to be *such fun!*"

She held the door open and Joy stepped out, tucking the dowsing rod and syringe back into her purse. Joy had the feeling that she'd just gone from the frying pan into the fire. Her face was hot and flushed as they entered the foyer. The menfolk were in a rough circle, glowering at one another in silence.

"Did you get what you need?" Inq asked politely.

Stef's frown deepened. He glared at Kurt. "No."

"Ah well," Inq chirped. "Stubborn to the last. Nothing to be done, then, so you'd best be going." She shooed Joy toward Ink and tucked herself next to Kurt, a kitten curled against his side. "We'll notify you as soon as the frog deigns to call." She looked up at her lover. "Those were his instructions, correct?"

Kurt said nothing. Inq took his silence for assent.

"Well, then," she said. "Off you go. You were interrupting our private playtime."

Dmitri looked like he might say something, but Stef ushered him out the door with Joy and Ink's prompting. They filed out in a tight cluster.

"Until then," Ink said. Kurt barely nodded and shut the door.

Stef sighed angrily. "Well, that was pointless."

Ink turned to Joy. "Do you have it?"

She nodded. "Yep."

Ink scanned the street, confirming the coast was clear. "Good."

Dmitri raised a finger. "Wait a minute. What?"

"Kurt cannot act against the Bailiwick's orders, but we Scribes have no such restrictions. He is our employer, not our master," Ink said, acknowledging Joy's success with Inq. "Are you ready?"

"What, right now?" Joy said.

Ink glanced at Stef and Dmitri. "We cannot afford to delay."

Joy took a shuddery breath. "Okay." She removed the dowsing rod, the scalpel and the syringe. She tucked the blade into her pocket, grabbed the rod by the handle and flipped the needle point-down. Dmitri pointed at her collection of odd objects.

"Isn't that...?"

"Yes."

Stef frowned. "Do I want to know?"

Both Joy and Dmitri answered, "No." She held the dowsing rod level to the ground. "Everybody needs to hold on. When I say the word, it'll pull us straight to Graus Claude. Ink can cut a series of doors to get us there, but we have to keep running, so don't slow down and *don't* let go." She swallowed. "It's a lot like being pulled by a tracker, and Kestrel didn't make it easy. This thing doesn't even come with a leash." She glanced around. "Everybody ready?" They all nodded and fastened their hands on the Y-shaped wood. "Okay," she said. "Hold it still."

She uncapped the syringe and squeezed a dark bead into the divot above the bifurcated branch. It wobbled for a moment with surface tension, then sank, absorbed into the wood. Joy almost forgot to speak as she stared.

"Anvesana," she said quickly. "Take us to Graus Claude."

A familiar shiver buzzed under her palm, shaking her wrist and shuddering up her bones. She gripped tighter, feeling the others do likewise. Her feet moved without permission as the magic dragged them forward.

"Hang on!" she said as Ink slid his straight razor free, opening a gateway through the world, a trapdoor of nothingness perfumed in limes.

Together, they stumbled through the torn air, gone.

SEVENTEEN

THE AIR WAS BALMY, AND THE PAVEMENT WET AND sticky with liquid pooling under the nearby heaps of trash. The gray stone alley smelled of fish and cigarettes. Paper lanterns trailed red tassels that spun lazily in the wind and the bustling sound of many people was right around the corner. Joy glanced behind them and up the rusty fire escape running along the back of the nearest building, craning her neck to look up at the mismatched rooftops and their crisscrossing telephone wires. Dmitri had a strange expression, half amazed, half cowed, his brown eyes wide in a pensive face. It made him look vulnerable, innocent and childlike. Joy, ever the performer, hoped that might work in their favor when they encountered the King and Queen.

But they had to find Graus Claude first.

"This is it?" Joy asked. "Is he here?" The dowsing rod still quivered, but it was locked solidly in place as if held by an invisible fist in midair. Ink tapped his boot against the curb. An ornate Chinese character flared.

"He is here, beyond the ward." Ink examined the length of the enchanted line without letting go. He nodded at Joy. "We will find him. But we will have to do so without any *mana* disturbance." He put his thumb into the divot and pressed down. Purple liquid squirted across the wood. The dowsing rod went still.

"So where is he?" Stef asked, popping his knuckles. "It's not like you can easily hide a giant, four-armed frog."

Ink crept out of the alley into the busy street. The others soon followed. It was a shock of color and noise, people and honking traffic, hawking to one another in a babble of languages Joy didn't recognize; the signs were all Chinese or English, sometimes both, and the streets were festooned with lanterns and flags and red banners with yellow writing flapping in the wind. A flicker of orange made Joy jump, but it was just a traffic cone on the curb.

In the distance, a green-roofed gateway flanked the main street. People slipped between cars and skirted the crowded sidewalks, hurrying to get wherever they were going with shopping bags and cell phones and backpacks and rolling carts. Storefronts full of plastic-wrapped clothes and china figurines and paper goods spilled into the street along with trays of fruits and nuts, herbs and plastic souvenirs. Postcard towers turned above racks of silk wallets. Figurines of Betty Boop and Homer Simpson stood over big-eyed dinosaurs and small-mouthed cats. Halved piglets and chickens hung next to whole roasted ducks dangling by their necks under red-gold heat lamps. And people were absolutely everywhere, pushing strollers and hand trucks, bicycles and walkers, jostling wheels and carts and mostly each other. They gathered around whole fish on crushed ice and lucky bamboo in water-filled pails.

The foot traffic parted easily around them, unconsciously moved by the invisible Scribe.

"Oh my God," Joy breathed. "We're in Chinatown."

"San Francisco," Stef said. "I don't believe it."

"We know the Bailiwick is nearby," Ink said, pointing at the carved glyph in the sidewalk. "He's somewhere inside the wards, which are preventing unexpected visitors from barging in unannounced."

"So what do we do?" Dmitri said, watching a couple of teenage schoolgirls bounce past, arm in arm.

Ink checked the storefront with a sweeping gaze, a familiar gesture Joy recognized as he took in sigils, seals, glyphs and other magics. He blinked. "We announce ourselves," he said. "Politely." He walked inside, and the others followed him through the door.

The narrow aisles were full of vases and pottery, round fat cats and porcelain boats painted with blue dragons. Paper parasols crowded the ceiling and wooden planter stands cluttered the floor. Ink led the way past the display cases of jewelry and bits of jade on black velvet toward a beaded curtain near the back door.

"Can I help you?" asked a saleswoman as they passed.

"No, thank you," Joy said. "Just looking." She was careful not to bump anything and to keep her head down. A security camera in the corner pointed directly at them. It was no doubt recording her and Stef walking in alone.

Joy felt the sizzle as they got closer, the shiver of a spell crackling between the beads. It was something like the curtain separating Ladybird's drug den from the rest of the building in East New York, but it was stronger, more powerful. It tickled the hairs in her nose.

She sneezed.

When her eyes cleared, Filly was standing in the doorway. The beaded curtain did not so much as twitch behind her.

"Took you long enough," she said over crossed arms, her vambraces flashing in the cold fluorescent light. She tossed her head. The tight net of blond braids at her nape didn't budge. "I told him that not telling you where he was outright would be much the same as laying out a welcome mat

and setting fire to the sky. But would he listen? Not likely!"
She sniffed. "Stubborn old toad."

Joy didn't dare speak since, to everyone else in the store,
she'd appear to be addressing empty air. She pretended to
look at the framed pictures on the wall. Stef checked his
phone. Dmitri tugged the strings of his hoodie over his
head.

"Will you escort us in to see him?" Ink asked.

"No," Filly said. "Afraid not. I'm not to allow anyone inside."

Joy's heart sank. It wasn't as if they could fight Filly—not
only was she a seasoned warrior, but they were hemmed
in on all sides; it would be like letting loose a blond bull in
a Chinese china shop. Joy glanced behind them, but it was
as if everyone in the store was too preoccupied to notice
anything unusual.

Ink considered the young Valkyrie with a tilt of his head.
"It is quite important."

"I've no doubt," Filly said agreeably. "When is it not, when
it involves the mighty Joy Malone?" Joy felt her face flush.
Filly winked. "You surpass my every expectation. We'll
make a warrior of you yet!" She glanced around at every
breakable thing in the store with ill-disguised relish, the
tip of her tongue caught between her teeth. Stef picked up
a pen near the credit card machine, ready to draw combat
spells on his skin. He held the ballpoint tip to his wrist like
a dare. Filly nodded with a grin. "But not today," she said
to Stef. "Today, I must perform my duties."

Joy spoke quietly into her collar so as not be heard by the
store owners. "Please?"

Filly snorted and tugged her horse head pendant. Her
leather armor creaked as she bent slightly at the waist as if
to whisper in Joy's ear.

"Make me."

Joy heard the *clink* of Ink's wallet chain, saw Stef draw something on his inner wrist and suspected that Dmitri had just picked up something heavy. Joy held out a hand to stay them and hissed out of the corner of her mouth. "If you don't let us in to see him *right now*, I'll tell him about that little under-the-table fix-up I did for you at Dover Mill. I'm sure he'd forgive the fee, but I'm not so certain that he'd forgive the slight." She raised her eyebrows meaningfully. "He's got this thing about etiquette and decorum, and an awfully long memory, so unless you have another Amanya spell handy, I'd suggest you let us in."

Filly smiled slowly, looking only a little bit disappointed. "Ah. I see they've made you into a politician first." She sighed dramatically, lifted her chin and called over their heads. "Very well, then. Follow me."

She pushed the curtain aside for Joy and Ink, Stef and Dmitri. Joy wasn't sure what anyone saw, but no one moved to stop them as they disappeared behind the clack and clatter of beads. Of course, the noise might have been made by Filly's short cape of finger bones. The sounds were eerily similar.

They followed Filly into the back room, past cartons and crates of stock and supplies to a set of spiral stairs, going down.

"You're kidding, right?" Stef said as Filly began the descent.

Joy shrugged. She was used to back rooms being something more; she'd had enough experience with Mr. Vinh's not to be surprised. Finding a set of spiral stairs winding deep underground was something that bordered on normal. At least there weren't any sharp teeth.

"No big deal," Joy said. "We go in. Convince the King and

Queen to Return. Get out. Go home. Eat pizza. Everyone's happy."

Stef turned back on the first step. "Do you do this a lot?" Joy hesitated. Her brother frowned. "Never mind. I don't want to know."

"I sure hope you know what you're doing," Dmitri muttered as the stairs grew steep.

"Yeah," Joy said, holding on to the railing. "Me, too."

The stairwell corkscrewed beneath the store, the sidewalk, the busy street, past what might be considered a basement level, a cellar, a storeroom and possibly the sewers. There was a chill that came from being far underground, and a smell of moisture and minerals. Joy felt the weight of the world pressing against her skin from all directions, goose pimples glossing all over her arms. Surrounded by the earth...was this a chrysalis? Could it trigger the change? Panic skittered like the heartbeat she no longer had. She grabbed Ink's hand in the semidarkness.

A splash below them made Joy's knees weak, and the *eelet* in her ear translated a bubbling, low rumble under the burble of water, an amphibious burr that could only belong to one person she knew. Filly looked smug as they filed through the doorway into the massive chamber beneath Chinatown. She stepped aside with a flourish.

It was like an underground football field framed in multicolored tiles and gold leaf trim. Stone frescoes lined the walls depicting dragons and phoenixes, rams and tigers, koi fish and cranes, and a key-shaped swimming pool dominated the floor. The design on the deep end depicted two crowned peacocks twined with lilies and flowers and spiraling fish. Soft underwater illumination reflected playful cobwebs of light. Wide, red columns stood in militant rows, and painted scrolls hung from ceiling to floor. The crossbeams were painted in cyans and blues, molded with yellow-gold dragons, yin-yang circles and plum blossom boughs. The room was an impossible montage of green and gold and red and cream, hand-carved wood and hand-cut tiles, mother of pearl and inlaid stones. Ceramic urns flanked the entrance. Painted screens curled around lounge chairs, low tables and *pièces d'art*. A fountain sat in a corner, a waterfall trickling from the mouth of a giant frog into a shallow pool thick with lilies.

Attendants—human attendants, including a young woman and two old men—waited by piles of towels, trays of food and an elaborate, plumed fan mounted on a long pole. Joy kept turning and seeing more intricacies, more details, more wealth, more impossible, elaborate beauty straining to be contained by four subterranean walls. And in the middle of it all, a large shape swam through the water, leaving a strong ripple in its wake; a great beast propelling itself with six strong strokes.

The eyes broke the water first, the rest of the head rising in dramatic disapproval. Water coursed over the ridges and crags, accentuated by the underwater light and the piercing gaze of its icy blue eyes. The frowning mouth opened just enough to show its many rows of pointy, shark-like teeth. Naked and uplit, Graus Claude emerged from the depths like an ancient monster, a demon, a god.

"Ah. Miss Malone, Master Ink." Graus Claude's voice echoed off the chamber walls. "I was looking forward to the time when I would next delight in your presence, which I'd naïvely assumed would be at my discretion." His tone dropped several degrees. "And you've brought...*guests*."

Ink bowed. Joy did likewise, realizing that they were performing for the attendants who obviously held Graus

Claude in high esteem—higher than even that of the Bailiwick of the Twixt. Joy didn't need Ink to remind her. *Respect him. Always.*

"Please forgive us for the interruption," Joy said smoothly.

"Not at all, not at all," he said as he emerged, dripping, from the water. Two handmaidens drifted forward, holding a long scroll of thick cotton towel between them, wrapping the great amphibian efficiently and discreetly in an elaborate dance of tucks, folds and knots. Joy averted her eyes out of politeness, but she'd noticed his *signatura*, emblazoned on his belly—an elegant lotus of crackling blue fire.

He waddled forward and eased himself down in stages, stretching his legs out on one of the sloping benches, the curvature perfectly matching the rolling architecture of his spine. Two hands folded over his chest as the other two clutched the armrests beside him. The handmaidens knelt wordlessly and began clipping, buffing and polishing his claws with tiny instruments and rough bits of cloth. Graus Claude settled in to their ministrations, looking archly at those before him as if daring them to question his right to be pampered. No one did. Joy watched his gaze settle on the unfamiliar pair of young men.

"Bailiwick, sir, you have met my brother, Stef," Joy said. "And this is his friend Dmitri."

"Indeed," the Bailiwick croaked. "I am certain that we all would be more suitably impressed if I were appropriately dressed for the occasion." He glanced sideways at the Valkyrie. "Did I not give specific enough instructions that I was not to be disturbed?"

"You said no one was to disturb you. I count four." Filly shrugged. "Besides, she threatened me."

Graus Claude looked at Joy, impressed. "Indeed?"

"I...came to *request* something of you," Joy said carefully. "As the Bailiwick of the Twixt."

Graus Claude measured her expression and the implied meaning of her words. She hadn't *demanded* entrance as she had once before—to dishonor him twice was absolutely out of the question and to do so before strangers was something she knew she'd pay for in more than blood—but he must have realized how serious this was if she needed to go back into the Bailiwick so soon. The gentle whirring of the miniature buffers stopped. His claws had been painted and set with gold leaf.

A gurgling string of nasal syllables bubbled up from his throat, pinging off the walls like brass cymbals. All the humans—the handmaidens and the older men around the room—turned and moved in an unhurried single file through a swinging door set behind the stone friezes. Joy watched them go, unnervingly proper, steady as clockwork. When the door closed, Joy relaxed.

"Who are they?" she asked.

"They are *mine*," he said, inspecting his nails. "Generations of loyalists from the Old Days, under my auspice and protection, those who know me and my kind for what we are—what we were—and what we have always been." He sighed. "This is a sanctuary, one of many, but alas, one of few suitable for my purposes within my jurisdiction in your world."

"And warded to the nines," Stef muttered, glancing around at the unseen lines of power that permeated the room.

"Yes, that, certainly." Graus Claude nodded, his chin nearly lost in his pillowy jowls. "And staffed by a bloodline whom I know well and who can recognize those whom I associate with as well as those whom I wish to abjure."

Dmitri paled. Joy swallowed. "They could See us upstairs?"

The Bailiwick sighed. "Despite your Eurocentric upbringing, Caucasians are not the only ones who possess the Sight." Graus Claude gazed up at the elaborate ceiling. "This sanctuary was inspired by the Forbidden City as well as the Beibei Wenquan Temple in Chongqing." He spread his toes, drying the webbing between them. His wounds were all but gone. "One would think that they would be disparate elements, but I find there is a harmony to be found in most things brought together for a common purpose," he said to Joy and Ink, his eye ridge lifting. "Even you two."

"And that is why we have come," Ink said. "For our common purpose."

"Aniseed," Joy said quickly. "Aniseed's escaped. She's already tried to kill us and you know she'll stop at nothing to keep the King and Queen from Returning so that she can try to bring about her crazy Golden Age. Bailiwick, once she knows where you are, she'll come after you!"

Graus Claude held up all four of his arms. "Calm yourself, Miss Malone." He demonstrated taking a deep breath. His slit nostrils dilated. "Now. Please explain what has happened from the beginning."

She did. But instead of alarming him, the news seemed to seep what strength he had from his limbs. When she finished, he shook his head, his eyes slipping closed with a sigh. "Miss Malone, I must protest. How many times must she die in order for you to believe that she is dead?" he said. "I assure you, while Aniseed was a remarkable villain, she is not conveniently lurking behind every rock and plot."

"But she *is*!" Joy insisted. "I know she is! It's *her*!"

"It may be that the golem was responding to Aniseed's last instructions before she died, that if something were to happen to the graftling, then the golem should seek revenge upon you—a final, venomous slight, nothing more," the Bailiwick mused. "More disturbing is the notion that someone has pilfered her last remains, perhaps to use as a call to arms? I'd wager the Tide is involved." His voice sank in a sigh. "But if it is as you say, then the Grove Elder is correct—the graftling will not survive. It's over."

"It *isn't*," Joy said flatly. "That's why we've come seeking the Bailiwick. When the King and Queen and the lost Folk Return, *then* it's over."

Graus Claude fiddled with his towel. "Can I get you anything before we continue discussing this theory of yours?" he asked.

Joy glanced around at the others. "No, thank you, I—"

"Good," he said ominously, threading both sets of hands. "Explain."

Joy sighed. *Fair's fair.* "You once told me that the King and Queen spoke the world of the Twixt into being, so whatever they say becomes law, absolute. They are the Makers. They made the rules," she said. "But, since they are also Folk, not even *they* can break them. They've locked *themselves* behind the door, and they didn't even need the Council's *signaturae* to bind it shut, because once they had said that they would not Return until it was safe, those became the conditions of their release. Without the courier to tell them, the King and Queen could never know whether it was safe to come home or not. After Aniseed betrayed the Council and you, making everyone forget about the King and Queen, they were doomed to stay in Faeland by their own Decree. They have been waiting for the courier to fulfill their own conditional rules." Joy shook her head. "But I didn't know that. I erased the locks and opened the door—I broke the rules. That should have been impossible, but I think they *needed* someone who could break the rules. And I think I could do that because I am...what I am," she said carefully, knowing Graus Claude would understand. If she were part-human or part-Elemental, she was born outside the rules of the Twixt. It had nothing whatsoever to do with the scalpel or the Sight, but she couldn't let the others—especially Filly— know that.

Graus Claude inclined his chin, understanding perfectly. "They have been expecting the courier to open the door and tell them that it was safe to Return, in accordance with their own rules." He nodded. "Go on."

Joy nodded. "But it was me."

The Bailiwick exhaled, long and low. "I see."

"So, if the Council's and my theory is correct, it's now *my* job to convince them that it is safe to Return, or they'll be bound by their own words to remain on the other side of the door forever." She checked the Bailiwick's expression, which was still as stone. Joy shrugged helplessly. "Those are the rules."

"A sound, if unfortunate, theory," he agreed. "Without their guidance, I fear both our worlds are destined for war and ruin." He squinted at Stef and Dmitri, his low-slung head regaining some of its palsy quiver. "So what have they to do with this?"

Joy gestured to her brother and the satyr. "I think they might be the proof we need."

"What makes you think this?" the Bailiwick asked.

"Well," Joy said, glancing back at Stef and Dmitri. "If I could prove that Folk and humans can live together, not in fear, but in love, then that should satisfy the conditions of the Return." Why did everything sound dumber when she said it aloud? Joy found her fingers had wrapped themselves in her shirt hem. "Well, I thought it might be worth a try."

"Indeed...it is quite poetic and satisfies the conditions of their Decree," Graus Claude said, sitting up with a groan of effort. It was odd to see him swathed in nothing more than fluffy beach towels on a reclining bench and not an immaculate three-piece suit behind his great mahogany desk. So much had changed in such a short time and yet, Joy realized that Graus Claude still held all the poise and the power he'd had when they'd first met. "It is an elegant solution." The Bailiwick turned to look at Dmitri and Stef. "You are willing to do this? To cross through one world into the next and present yourself as proof to our Majesties, the King and Queen of the Folk?" He sounded doubtful.

Stef paused as if considering. Joy knew that his feelings about the Other Thans were warring with his loyalties and better judgment. The struggle showed on his face. However, Dmitri shrugged his shoulders.

"You're asking us to save the world?" He curled his chin hairs over his knuckle. "Yeah, we can do that," he said casually. "But the world owes us one."

Graus Claude's eye ridge twitched. "And that is...?"

"Back off," Dmitri said, taking Stef's hand. "Let us live together in peace."

The Bailiwick nodded. "Precisely our aim, should you succeed." He leaned back on his haunches and lumbered off behind one of the folding screens. "*Hjalmþrimul?*" he called over the edge.

Filly answered, "Yes, old toad?"

"Ensure none pass," he said gravely. "And this time, heed my words, else risk the lives of these mortals as well as your own."

The Valkyrie snapped a salute and relaxed her stance. "As you say." She nodded to Ink and Joy. "Victory!" she said, raising a fist. Joy and Ink returned the gesture as she vaulted back up the stairs. Graus Claude listened to the echo of her footfalls, waiting until the last taps of her boots blurred on the edge of hearing.

Joy whispered into the pause. "I'm sorry for this." She wished she could erase the indignity of it, reducing him to a thing instead of a person, a title instead of a name.

Graus Claude's head bobbed gently, a nod or a quiver. "Needs must, Miss Malone." He settled his massive bulk on the stones and rested each of his hands, palm-up, fingers poised. "Needs must."

Joy raised her voice. "We demand entrance to the Bailiwick of the Twixt."

Graus Claude stilled, his very breath dissolving like smoke. His mouth yawned wider, the gap growing taller, the hinge of his jaw dislocating with an audible *click*. His eyes misted over, turning milky as cataracts. His mouth grew to the size of a doorway, his tongue curling back to adhere to the top of his mouth, revealing the set of stone steps going down. Joy watched her brother's and the satyr's expressions. There was another soft *click* as the transformation stopped.

The four of them gazed at the end of a long journey. Ink opened his hand to Joy, who took it, threading their fingers together. They stepped over the lower jaw, ducking under the points of sharp teeth.

"This way," Joy said. She felt her brother hesitate as the flash of fire zipped past, changing from blue to red and red to blue as Stef and Dmitri followed.

Dmitri corkscrewed his head, wide-eyed, and spoke through the twist of a grin.

"Down the hatch!"

EIGHTEEN

"I DON'T BELIEVE IT," STEF SAID AS THEY CROSSED THE meadow, slipping on the sliding horizon.

"A little late for that, don't you think?" Dmitri said. Joy was amazed at how well the satyr was adjusting to the pocket world inside the Bailiwick, and his childish glee made her wonder if he believed any of it, or if he was high. He hopped through the long grass, marveling at the sensation. "It's so like the Grove, but—not!" he said through a smile. "It's like I'm at a theme park. Twixtland! Ha ha ha!" He ran through the flowers and kicked up his hooves. He stopped, sniffing. "But there's no scent," he said. "No air. No life." He turned a full circle and looked back at them, bemused. "It's like running through a painting. It's not real."

"No," Ink agreed. "But it was as real as she could remember. As real as it gets after hundreds of years of confinement." He still hadn't forgiven the Folk for forgetting his Maker—his mother, the princess—or her royal family. Perhaps he'd never quite forgiven himself for forgetting, either. He'd had the memories, since the Amanya spell worked only on Folk and not homunculi, like the Scribes or golems, but he hadn't been fully sentient until recently. Inq had waited aeons for her brother to gain the necessary independent thought that would allow him to share half the burden of protecting their creator and hunting down the traitor in secret, which was one of the prime reasons she'd tried forcing him to interact with humans, to learn something about living from mortals who had to live a lifetime in a breath. Joy suspected it was the reason Inq had cooked up the whole *lehman* excuse to cover up Ink's "mistake" back at the Carousel. With Joy having to play the part of Ink's lover, he couldn't help but learn what it was like to have feelings. It was a short skip to learning the meaning of loyalty, passion, betrayal and love.

Ink had learned a lot, knowing Joy. She just wished he hadn't learned quite so much all at once. And there were some things she wished he hadn't learned at all.

"And this is just what's in-between," Joy said, crossing the grassland while keeping her eyes on the door. "The Bailiwick itself is actually a fold in the world, a pocket universe placed outside the Twixt in order to keep it safe from interference." She glanced at her brother. "Human interference. They were so afraid of being enslaved by their True Names, the King and Queen decided that it would be safest to escape this world with most of their people." She pointed ahead and slightly up to where the breach hung in the air. "This is where they placed the door in order to take the Folk out of harm's way and wait until it was safe to return."

"But the Council never sent word," Ink said. "The courier betrayed them."

"Aniseed wanted revenge on the humans but she could not be disloyal to the King and Queen's Edict protecting the humans along with the shared magic, because Folk loyalty is absolute," Joy said. "So she came up with a plan to erase everyone's memory—including her own—figuring you cannot be loyal to something you don't know exists. And she was right. That's when she stepped up her plans to kill off most of the humans with a promise of some fabled Golden Age when the world would be taken over by the Folk."

"She was good at propaganda," Dmitri said. "Lots of Folk sided with her."

"Until they remembered their lost King and Queen," Ink said, squeezing Joy's hand. "By smashing the crystals that held everyone's memory of their own Welcome Gala, they were able to remember that which was forgotten. When magics collide, the older spell wins."

"Unfortunately, the conditions of the Return are like a spell, too," Joy said. "By saying that they would not come back until it was 'safe,' they made that a prerequisite of ever coming back and that is based on the courier telling them that it's so." The doorway gleamed with the promise of Faeland's foreign sun. "So now we have to prove that it's safe to come back."

"But it *isn't* safe," Stef said.

"It is," Joy said. "It is safe for them to come back and not fear being chained to humans by their True Names. That was the purpose of *signaturae.* By binding the magic of True Names to a symbol that could not be spoken, the Folk are safe from human entrapment. That was the whole point!" Joy felt irritated that her brother failed to get how close they were, how much this needed to happen. "It is safe for the Folk to be reunited with their families as well as the King and Queen. The Council may not like it, but they'll respect the rules. The royal family can fulfill the long-awaited Imminent Return and then everything can go back to being... the way it was."

But even as she said it, Joy knew she didn't quite believe it. That's why she couldn't say the last word, *"normal."* Even without the nagging feeling in the pit of her stomach, there was the slight pain—like an ice cube on a sore tooth—that zinged through her whenever she came close to a lie. She didn't need another reminder that she wasn't quite human because she knew even if the King and Queen granted her wish, nothing would ever be quite the same.

Things changed.

Ink twisted direction, and suddenly they were before the door itself, a circular outline of thin, ghostly light against the hazy backdrop of a perpetual summer.

Stef stiffened in surprise. Dmitri inhaled sharply.

"This is it?" the satyr whispered. "This is the entrance to Faeland?"

"One of them," Ink said. "Are you ready?"

Dmitri stared at the door, rapturous. A shiver rippled down his arms, raising the thick brown hair. He smiled eagerly. "Do it!"

Ink pressed open the door and the sun burst through in a brilliant stab of golden light. The sky beyond it was a crystal blue and the rolling hills were impossible shades of emerald green. There were the banners and the tents, the twin thrones and the war machines, and, of course, the gathered army milling about the encampments, but the spun-sugar castles were gone, a lake sparkled to the west and it looked like the sun was coming from another direction, over a misty forest. It was the same place, but also not.

The King and Queen sat in their thrones surrounded by their court. It could have been her imagination, but it looked like the Queen smiled. The rest of the Folk looked less friendly; however, no guards barred the doorway and no army came charging at them from over the hill. That had to be an improvement.

A thousand pairs of eyes took in the two new figures crowded inside the door between worlds. Joy stepped back to allow Stef and Dmitri to be seen by the gathered Folk. Stef stood stiffly, frozen by awe. The satyr tugged off his hoodie and bounced nervously on his great goat legs.

"Your Majesties," Ink spoke across the lengths between them. Light wobbled against the warped bubble film that separated them from the Folk afterworld. Stef inched back when it wavered close to his nose. "We have come at your behest to present that which you requested—proof that it is safe for the Folk to return to the world and rejoin the rest of your people." It was a pretty, proper speech, implying that they did this only to obey their monarch's command. Joy, as one of the Twixt, was expected to acquiesce, and Ink, the creation of the youngest princess, was incapable of disloyalty. The whole thing was tied as neat as a bow. So why did Joy feel like they were making a mistake?

Behold the Destroyer of Worlds.

Joy swallowed. *Not this time.*

She took one of Stef's hands in hers. He was sweating.

"This is your proof?" the King asked. He said it almost disbelievingly, testing them and their resolve. Dmitri reeled back from the voice of his king, shaking and smiling in delicious awe.

"Yes," Joy said. "These two have loved each other nearly all of their lives, despite everything and everyone that kept them apart." Joy found her throat unexpectedly tight, the words meaning more because they were true. Stef turned to look her full in the face and tears wet her eyes, surprising them both. "They have spent years searching and waiting, wondering how they could find their way back to one another and now—" she took a deep breath and squeezed Stef's hand. He squeezed hers back "—they are together, as equals. We wanted you to see that the Folk have nothing to fear from humans." She blinked out at the army and the court of the King and Queen. "This is love. Love is proof."

The Queen dipped her chin. "Love is proof?" she said, as if confirming that she'd heard Joy correctly. Joy felt the razor's edge of doubt touch her spine.

The King's gaze bored into the satyr. Dmitri sucked in his breath.

"Do you love this mortal man, Grove Keeper?"

Dmitri nodded, his face radiant. "I do."

"And you, wizard," he said, not unkindly. "Do you love this buck of the Forest Folk?"

Stef licked his lips. Joy stared at him. Did he love one of the Folk? It seemed obvious, but he'd never said it—never said those words aloud—and Joy was suddenly nervous that he could not truthfully say that he no longer had a hatred of "Other Thans." The moment stretched on a rack before Stef took Dmitri's rough hand in his.

"I do, Your Majesty."

There was a low susurrus as a real breeze tousled the leaves and flapped the banners, toying with the great wings of the King's and Queen's hair.

"Love is not proof," the Queen declared, her voice bitter and biting. "Love is fickle. Transient. Deceitful." Her lips formed the last word as if a marble rolled off her tongue. *"Mortal."* A cleft pinched between her brows. She spoke as if to a simple child. "Hearts are weak, ephemeral, and they can change—" she lifted her wrist, fingertips just touching "—like *that.*"

She snapped her fingers. Dmitri dropped Stef's hand and leaped through the doorway. It was over before Joy could process what had happened. She stared at her brother.

Stef's glasses reflected the alien sunlight as his head turned. His face contorted, the sound of his voice echoed impossibly after the word had shaped his lips. His body was a sharp unfolding of muscles and bones and sinew.

"No!"

Stef dived through the doorway. It popped. Joy screamed.

"Stef!" Joy lurched forward, but Ink's arms held her back. Her feet barely inched toward the barrier, an enticing glow against her shoes. She struggled in his grip, watching Stef fall, landing on the grass and chasing after Dmitri across the hills of Faeland.

She wrenched herself desperately. She screeched. She used nails. "Let me go! Ink! Let me go!"

His voice, crisp and clean, whispered by her ear. "You cannot step into that world," Ink said. "You know that, Joy. You *know* that. But look—"

Her brother breached the swell of the hill, the grass cleaving before him as he scythed a rough line through the verdant hillside, the stalks bowing, snapping, parting as the sun rained down on the back of his neck. Joy could See the aura around him, the shape of wizard light like an invisible wedge as he plowed ahead, clearing a path. Knowingly or not, Stef was using magic. Wizard's magic. Shaking, Joy stared. The world did not crack beneath him. The earth did not crumble or split. Faeland did not reject him. Her brother ran after his love.

Realization twisted inside her like a pin, the shock snapping her still. *How?* she thought. *Is it because he's a wizard? Because he has no signatura? Because he hasn't been marked? Or are we different, somehow?* The next thought swelled to the surface like a boil. *Is it me? Is there something wrong with me?*

Behold the Destroyer of Worlds.

Dmitri was still bounding and jumping ahead of him, zigging and zagging in rapturous glee. From their high vantage point, Joy and Ink could see Dmitri stop before the court and fall to his knees, sides heaving, head bowed. Stef called out his name, but the satyr didn't respond.

Dmitri prostrated himself before his Queen.

"NO!"

Stef crested the hill, rushing forward, eyes wild. The army broke ranks and rushed him. Joy's insides braced as they charged, an inhuman wall against her brother, an army against one lone man. They met with a crash of bodies and limbs; hands clamped on his arms, claws pushing, paws grabbing, tails lashing, pinning him facedown, screaming.

"No! Please no!" Joy jerked and strained, her face wet with furious tears. *"Please stop!"* The Queen gazed up at her, unsympathetic. Dmitri's bare shoulders heaved as he lay calmly at her feet. Joy didn't need to see his face to guess at the adoration that shone there. The Queen had cast her spell to make a point, mocking her brother's love as well as Joy's proof. The King turned away, his profile sharp as glass.

"Your task is unfulfilled, your offer rejected," he said. "Your offering, however, has been accepted."

"No..." Joy whimpered before Ink squeezed her, an unsaid warning to stay silent. She wilted, wondering if her mistake had condemned them all. Her throat cinched as the two young men were dragged before the royal court. The world bowed and wobbled as Ink held her back.

The Queen smiled, triumphant.

The King's voice cut through the void, kind but stern. "Bring us proof that it is safe to Return ere you come again." Lower in timbre but no less biting, he added, "Lead us home."

He made a dismissive gesture. The door swung shut.

Ink and Joy stood on the brink of nothing, deep in the belly of the Bailiwick.

Stef and Dmitri were prisoners of the King and Queen, trapped in Faeland.

There would be no Return.

The world behind Joy's eyes went white. Every hair on her body stood up on end. Her blood boiled, raising a simmer of goose bumps, her arms shook, her skin tightened, tugging her lips back over clenched teeth. She shuddered, burning with the need to reach out, find that place of heat and salt and old, old ice and bury herself inside—but she was far from her world and the soil here was make-believe, and so she trembled, unable to touch anything real.

The last image seared on the back of her brain was the smug countenances of the King and Queen.

Her mind exploded.

THEY CANNOT DO THIS!

Joy grabbed the scalpel and slashed at the door, the blade skipping over the gleaming edges, erasing a great gash of nothingness in its wake. She slashed again and again, ripping through grass and sky and sun and soil, tearing through distant trees and hacking at the horizon, stabbing white wounds through the forever-dawn. The blade cut like wet fingertips through chalk, slicing the grove to ribbons, like scissors through paper. The scalpel flashed, erasing perfect pictures of pebble and brook. She screamed. These were all lies—ALL LIES!—impermanent and untrue. Joy spun, arms flailing, blade slashing, still screaming; her fury echoed, hollow and cruel.

Ink watched her reduce a thousand years of his mother's imprisonment into shreds.

Helpless, furious, Joy tore down the world.

Finally, she stopped, panting, and glared over her shoulder. The door burned defiant against the remains of a piecemeal sky.

Like Maia's door and her mother's abandonment, some things could not be undone.

It crumpled whatever was left inside her. Whimpering,

Joy collapsed, sagging against the ground, caught by an imaginary meadow and the grip of Ink's hands. She rocked back and forth, heaving, gasping. There wasn't enough air in the world. She had to make it stop, make it unhappen, make it untrue. She curled into a ball, her thoughts like dissipating smoke.

Stef... Stef... Stef...

It was every one of her nightmares come true.

"Joy." Ink's voice was close, somewhere outside the pain, but she couldn't bear to look. "Your brother is safe. They will not harm him in any way." His words were urging her to look at him. "He is considered a bond, collateral—the best that we can offer—and they will treat him as such until we return. And we *will* return for him when we bring proof," he said softly, touching her hair. "We will find the answer."

"Very impressive," Inq said, strolling forward. Both Joy and Ink sat up in surprise. "I especially like what you've done with the place." The Scribe nodded slowly, taking in the shredded landscape. "I always felt that it could do with a makeover." She stopped in front of them and knelt down. "Ink is right, you know. Your brother will be fine and so will his boyfriend. It's like how humans used to sacrifice their best, most beautiful warriors to the gods for their favor. They're like treasure now." She rubbed Joy's shoulder. "I told you they liked pretty things. They'll be kept safe."

"No," Joy said, gulping on sobs. "Stef *isn't* safe! He can't be!" She shook her head trying to clear her way through her fog of despair. "Don't you understand? Humans aren't allowed in Faeland!"

"Stef isn't human," Ink said.

"Exactly!" Joy said. "He's like me, part-Folk. Part-Elemental, maybe. But that's the problem—he still has his True Name!" The Scribes exchanged glances. "Don't you get it? He doesn't have a *signatura*! He's vulnerable to anyone—*everyone*—and he's trapped in there, surrounded by Folk! It's his worst nightmare!" She started shaking, wondering what she'd done and what sort of cruelty an army of battle-ready, xenophobic Folk would do with the Queen's new pet.

"He is not defenseless," Ink said, trying to soothe her. "He is a wizard."

Joy shook her head. He didn't understand the delicate balance between Folk and humans who could do magic, but Inq did. The wily Scribe's voice lost some of its edge as she placed a hand on Ink's shoulder. "His being a wizard may make things worse."

"Joy..." Ink said, but his words died off. He couldn't refute it. The confirmation of her worst fears and failures broke something inside her. She collapsed on the meadow and cried.

Ink folded himself around her, embracing her like a set of wings. She sobbed until the tears subsided, anger and guilt giving way to quiet. The wave of emotions crested and crashed. Joy clung to his arms, trembling softly, wrung-out, hollow and spent.

"Come," Inq said tenderly. "We must go tell the Bailiwick." She smoothed back Joy's hair, wiping smears of hot moisture from her cheeks and smiled. "Trust me, Joy—I know this feeling, but we haven't lost your brother yet."

Joy sat up, squeezing her eyes with the pads of her fingers, taking a deep breath and pushing herself to her feet. Ink stood alongside her. Inq stood beside him. Joy picked up the scalpel from the make-believe grass, the glint of silver flashing in the leftover sun. Her breath shuddered as she exhaled. Her lips tasted like salt.

"I'm not going to lose him," she said. "I'm going to bring him back." Joy glared back at the door between worlds and squeezed the scalpel. "I'm going to bring everyone back."

NINETEEN

GRAUS CLAUDE SQUATTED BEFORE ONE OF THE LOW inlaid tables, eating a mountain of rice balls with porcelain chopsticks. Joy waited for him to stop chewing after she'd relayed what had happened to Stef and Dmitri and the danger that her brother was in the longer he stayed in Faeland. She paced by the lounge chairs, burning with resolve.

The Bailiwick raised one set of chopsticks and clicked them together. "What do you plan to do now?"

You. My fault. She was full of guilt and anger and in that moment, she hated him.

"I'm going to go after him," she snapped.

"Aha," he said. "And why is that of the utmost importance?"

"Well, besides being my brother, he's sitting unprotected in Faeland surrounded by thousands of Folk who hate humans and he's *not* fully human, he's part-Folk, but he doesn't have a *signatura*."

"Exactly!" Graus Claude beamed, picking up more rice balls with his other hands. "Your brother is one of the few living changelings who do not yet have a *signatura*. Our proposed method of safeguarding the Folk from humanity postdated the King and Queen's leaving, and they are unfamiliar with it. One of the reasons your acceptance of a *signatura* caused such a stir, Miss Malone, was that the ceremony hadn't happened for hundreds of years." He raised a second set of chopsticks like a conductor's baton. "If your brother could accept a *signatura* of his own, it would protect him from manipulation by his True Name, thus proving to the King and Queen that the system works." He gave a self-satisfied grin. "If the Folk are safe from entrapment, then it proves that it is safe to Return." He popped four rice balls into his mouth and started chewing again.

Joy glanced back at Ink and Filly, who stood silent. Only the lapping of the water and the echo of Graus Claude's words hung in the air. The headstrong Valkyrie smiled at Joy with a knowing grin.

"Oh my God," Joy said. "Oh my God! That would work!" She grabbed the Bailiwick's sleeve, tugging him away from his lunch. "I have to go back! I have to go *now*!"

"Unhand me," Graus Claude rumbled. She let go instantly. He smoothed the wrinkles from the abused silk. "You have an assignment that befits the courier—find the proof that the King and Queen require and all things shall be returned to that which they once were." The Bailiwick glanced at her meaningfully. "And all that should not be will be excised and put right." She dropped her gaze. Graus Claude was genteel enough to let it pass without comment. "Besides," he said. "You would be wasting your time. By now the Court will have hidden both your brother and themselves."

Joy stammered. "Wh-what? Why?"

"It is protocol," he said with a sniff. "Tradition, if you will. The terrain is self-correcting. The labyrinth moves. All the tales speak of it—it is tactically sound."

"So now I have to *find* him in there?" Joy said. "How am I supposed to do that?"

"You aren't," Inq said reasonably. "That's the point."

Ink hesitated by the pillars. "And you cannot step foot beyond the doorway." He meant it literally. Faeland had rejected her. *But not Stef.*

"You're right," Joy said. "But Stef did it. He even used magic." *Wizard magic. Human magic.* She felt the truth of it as the idea slipped into place, like a missing piece. Born with the Sight, they were still human enough—and something else—to slip through the rules. It was who they were. It was the edge she needed. "So, theoretically, I can do it, too." Her fingers grazed the shapes of the dowsing rod in her purse. "If I use human magic, I can find him."

The Bailiwick grumbled. "You will need more magic than you possess to cross Faeland unimpeded."

"I know," Joy said, thinking of Monica and the Wizard Vinh. "But I have some ideas."

The Bailiwick snorted. "Such arrogance," he said in Water Tongue so only the *eelet* could hear it. Joy bit the inside of her cheek to keep from being cheeky.

"You will need a guide," Ink said.

Filly spoke up, "Kestrel?" The inhuman tracker was unparalleled, but Joy shook her head, remembering how the tracker had been used to track *her* down in the Hall. She didn't need to be questioning loyalties out there. "I don't think any of the Folk can help me," she turned to Ink. "You saw what happened to Dmitri."

Ink glanced at his employer. "The Folk's adoration for our monarchs is without question—they would likely prove to be unreliable allies. Anyone could be turned with a word and no human can cross the threshold."

"I think I can get by without a guide," Joy said, wondering if the dowsing rod would work for tracking down siblings. Vinh had told her to track Stef's *mana*, but she didn't know how. "I just need to sneak in, find him, get him to accept a True Name in front of the King and Queen, and bring them all out." Joy shrugged with a little, humorless laugh. "Easy-peasy."

"So you do not need a guide," Filly said, stepping forward. "You need a distraction." She nodded once, decisively. "I volunteer."

"What?" Graus Claude bellowed. "I forbid it!"

"I dare you to try, old squatter," Filly said with a toss of her head. "Ink can swear there's no one better at baiting a trap, and none know it better than he!"

"You know nothing of the pieces at play here," Graus Claude growled through shark's teeth, pointing at both Joy and Ink. "And they shall not tell you." His words served as a double warning.

"Even better," Filly said, hands on her hips. "If captured, I cannot possibly reveal plans that I know nothing about."

Ink considered his brash friend, hands on his hips, fingers just touching the wallet chain as it swayed and caught the light. "Ignorance may be a fine shield, but it won't protect you from what lies beyond the Bailiwick."

"He's right," Joy said. Although strangely touched by the offer and disappointed not to have the warrior woman by her side, she didn't want to put any more of her friends at risk. "It's...another world," she said lamely. "And the King and Queen have every advantage—they know the land, they have all the resources and everyone there is absolutely loyal to their commands."

Filly's eyes sparkled as she grinned. "A challenge!"

"No! An *army*," Joy said, trying to stress her point. "There's a massive army full of war machines and monsters and hundreds of soldiers standing around ready to charge. They're more than ready for anything that comes through that door." She started counting the important points on her fingers. "We'll be outmanned, outmaneuvered and thoroughly outgunned. These Folk have been ready to wage war against the humans for, like, a thousand years!"

Filly's face lost its cocky grin, her eyes gone dreamy, stretching the long blue tattoos under her eyebrows, a quiet awe painting her lips in a silent O. Her voice whispered with wonder:

"Valhalla," she breathed.

Inq glanced sideways at Joy. "Congratulations. There'll be no stopping her now."

Joy leaped out of the breach, running through the condo, looking for something that they might use to help locate Stef. She wrenched open the door to his room, remembering that the place was a wreck and her brother had packed all of his things in his car, which was back at Dmitri's apartment. She tried picking through the mess for something— anything—of Stef's.

"What sort of thing do we need?" Joy gasped as she frantically searched through the rubble. Ink came up behind her and scanned the room with a critical eye.

"It is usually something personal."

"What? Like his watch? Baby blanket?"

Ink picked up the waste bin and looked inside. "Usually hair or tears or blood," he said. "That is what grounds Folk magic, but it will not work in Faeland. You need human magic, wizard's magic, so his master, the Wizard Vinh, will know best. However, there are other preparations that must be made before we go. How will you cross into Faeland, for example?"

Joy ran across the hall to the bathroom, barely listening. "Not even a toothbrush," she said, exasperated. "It's in his car with everything else." She grabbed Ink's hand. "Take me there. We have to—"

The door opened. The alarm beeped off. Dad walked in. Too late.

"Hi, honey." Her father waved from the kitchen as he dropped his briefcase on the counter and his keys in the candy dish by the door. "How was work today?"

"Hi... Dad." Joy fumbled. She'd totally forgotten she'd been scheduled for work today. Ink wasn't using his glamour, so he was still invisible. Joy envied him. "I was just heading out."

He popped the cap off a beer. "Isn't it late?" he asked. "What time is it?"

"Eight?" she guessed. She lost track of time when she wasn't near clocks. Time had become almost meaningless; clocks held almost still in one world versus the next. Enrique had warned her that her body would still know time passing, that was why mortals who slipstreamed would prematurely age—human *lehman*'s lives burned twice as bright if they followed the whims of their immortal lovers, but while Joy was mortal, she wasn't entirely human. *What is time to an Elemental? Do I age like mortals or like one of the Folk?*

She fussed with her purse, tucking the scalpel quickly into her back pocket and trying not to look at Ink. It wasn't easy having her dad and her boyfriend in the same room with only one of them knowing it. This double life was giving her a headache.

"Eight o'clock," her father repeated. He nodded as if that meant something. "Right. So how was your day?"

"Mch." She said the most noncommittal thing she could as she inched closer to Stef's open doorway, blocking it from view. She could feel her father's gaze following her. Ink took the hint and shut the door quietly as Joy said, "How about you? How was your day? Anything interesting?"

He seemed to consider the question as he sat down at the kitchen table. "Interesting," he said. "Yes. That's one word for it."

Joy hesitated. "Interesting?"

"Interesting."

Joy crossed the kitchen. "Like 'may you have an interesting life' interesting or 'wow, somebody must be on some serious drugs' interesting?"

"Your mother called," he said slowly. "She called me at work and asked if she could stop by for a visit."

"Stop by?" Joy frowned. She was having trouble processing this. Her mother lived in Los Angeles with her boy toy, Doug. They were on the other side of the continent from Glendale, North Carolina. The words didn't make sense. "For a visit?"

Her father shrugged. "That's what she said." He sipped his beer. "She's in Chapel Hill for some sort of conference and wanted to stop by."

Joy sat down. "Interesting."

He nodded and took another swallow. "That's what I said."

Joy fiddled with her fingertips, aware of Ink circling the table, unseen by her father, wondering what it all could mean. "So...what did you say?"

"I said of course she could come see you anytime, but I'd have to think about her spending any quality time with me," he said. "She said that she needed to talk to me and I said she could tell me whatever it was on the phone, but she said no, she wanted to talk in person." He let those words hang in the air, dangling with a thousand unsaid things.

"Wow."

"Yeah."

Joy had come to grips with the fact that while her mom and dad would never be together again, her mom still loved Joy and Stef. But Joy still felt her mother's affair and subsequent abandonment like a hole in her chest, precisely where her heart should be. Her mother had been the one with Folk blood, the one who could have told her what to expect or what to do. The way Joy understood it, the Sight could skip a generation or two, and before Stef and Joy, Great-Grandma Caroline was the last McDermott to have had it. She'd been blinded and institutionalized, yet she'd been lucid enough to warn her great-grandson how to protect himself when she'd realized that Stef seemed to possess the Sight. Caroline had died when Joy was only four, and no one had mentioned that girls might manifest later than boys. Joy really couldn't blame her mother for that. She'd been almost seventeen and totally unprepared when she'd seen Ink and Inq that first time at the Carousel, with their weirdly sinuous grace and their all-black eyes. *So much has happened since then.* Joy glanced across the table at her father. *So much has happened for him, too.* Her father had changed from a quiet, workaday homebody into a deeply depressed zombie divorcé and had emerged as a confident, outspoken, middle-aged success story with a promotion, a nice girlfriend and a membership at the gym. Joy wondered what had changed for Mom and why she wanted to visit them now.

"Do you know what this is about?" she asked.

He rested the lip of the bottle against his chin. "I can guess. I can hope. For her sake, anyway. Who knows?" He put down the beer and touched the condensation with his finger. It ran down like tears, streaking the glass. "It only makes what I was going to say harder."

Joy felt her insides clench. She missed the sound of her

thumping heart. Ink cocked his head to one side, curious. "Oh?" she said.

Her father examined his fingernails as they began twisting around his knobby knuckles. "Well," he said. "I wanted to talk to you about how things were going. With Shelley." He squeezed his palms together and nodded to no one in particular. "Things are going...well. Really well. And I know it's only been a short while but, well, it feels like longer." His nods turned to shakes of his chin. *"A lot* longer," he chuckled. "It's been a long time since someone's really cared about what I was doing, what I was thinking—really cared about *me*." His eyes caught hers with a slight panic. "I don't mean you—you and Stef are my rocks. You're my kids and I love you, but...you're my *kids*. There's a big difference between, well, being adults and being kids." He tried a smile. "And I know, you're growing up, but you'll still always be my kids." He picked up the bottle but plunked it down, untouched. "We're all growing up, growing older, growing old—at least I know I am, and that's okay. It's *good* to grow old with people who care about you. I consider myself pretty lucky that way." He was babbling now and he knew it. It was kind of awkward, but also nice. "Anyway. I wanted you to know that things are good. Seriously good." He nodded again. "Things are getting serious...and that's good."

Joy took a moment to sift through the babble and digest the gist. "So...things are getting serious," she repeated.

Dad nodded, not looking up. "Yep."

"With Shelley, you mean."

He kept nodding, tapping his bottle nervously on the tabletop. "Yep."

"Oh," Joy said slowly. "That's good. I mean, great." She tried smiling. It felt weird. She wasn't used to talking about feelings with her dad, but he seemed happy and that was good. She glanced at Ink. *He's here, like a secret.* He smiled, one dimple. She felt herself falling into his eyes, unable to look away. "Things are getting serious with Ink, too."

Two dimples. They danced.

Her father lifted his beer bottle with a ghost of a smile, a ghost of a frown. "Not *that* serious."

Joy shrugged, smoothing her hands over the kitchen table, reminding her of hands, ears, fingers, lips and knowing Ink remembered it, too. "Pretty serious."

Dad took a long swig and placed the bottle down carefully, eyes narrowing. In that moment he reminded her uncomfortably of Graus Claude.

"If you're being serious about getting serious, then we need to have a serious talk."

Ink raised his eyebrows. Joy swallowed. The conversation had taken a precarious turn. The idea of her "serious" with Ink being the same as Dad's "serious" with Shelley was seriously disturbing.

"Um...do we have to do it now?"

Dad shook his head quickly. "No."

Joy breathed, relieved. "Okay."

Ink looked disappointed.

"O-kay," her father said. "So now that we're done being serious, have you eaten yet?"

"I'm...meeting Ink for dinner." She made a note to add grabbing a bite at the C&P as she pointed back over her shoulder. "I just came home to change."

"Figures." Her dad laughed. "Ditched again for a younger man."

Joy stopped. She wasn't sure whether the joke was funny or not—it hit that awkward note between being clever and sad—and she forgot about herself for the moment, about

Stef and Ink and Graus Claude and the Tide. She hesitated on the brink between sister and daughter, family and Folk.

"Stay," Ink said quietly.

Joy frowned at him, confused. Ink stepped back, hovering in the hallway. Her father took another sip of his beer.

"Stay here, with your father, where it is safe," Ink said again. "The ward is still intact on the windowsill and you cannot enter Faeland to search for your brother—not yet. I will make inquiries and return shortly." His logic urged her to consider it, to slow down, to wait. He took another step, leaving Joy with her dad. "We will find Stef and offer his *signatura* as proof, but we can only succeed if we are prepared and I will not go unless I know you are safe." His coaxing smile tipped the scales. He took another step back into the shadows. "I will only be gone for a moment."

Joy whispered, "If that."

Her father glanced up. "What?"

Joy shook her head. "Nothing," she said. Ink waved his arm in a swooping arc and disappeared, gone. She sat down. "What if I stuck around and we watched a movie, instead?" she said, forcing a smile. "We could order in."

Her father looked up at her, his gaze softening. "You know," he said, "I'd like that."

"Okay," she said, taking a deep breath. She trusted Ink. *Patience. Preparation. Priorities.* "Done."

They ate in companionable silence, watching one of the MGM Classics that Monica had returned with gold star stickers on the spines of her favorites. Joy won the coin toss with *Late for Dinner* versus Dad's *Rolling Thunder*. She was loath to admit that the pacing left a lot to be desired. An action flick might have kept her mind off worrying about Stef.

Ink sat invisibly on the floor, mesmerized.

He'd returned with some strategic plans well under way and a message from Mr. Vinh to come by the C&P in the morning. In the meantime, she'd have to wait. Like Inigo Montoya from *The Princess Bride*, she hated waiting. She checked the DVD set, but Rob Reiner's 2006 masterpiece was too recent to be considered a "classic."

Joy texted Monica behind her hip.

Ink loves your movie pick.

Which one?

Late for Dinner.

4 stars, Monica texted back. SOOOO SWEET! G cried.

Srsly? Joy typed. Dad says Somewhere In Time is better & Always. Star casts. Seen em?

YOUR DAD LIKES CHICK FLIX?????

Joy laughed, which gave her away.

"Put down the phone and watch the movie with your old man."

"Yes, Dad," Joy said, typing a final, gtg.

She put down the phone and settled against the pillows, her leg resting gently against Ink's arm. She could feel his stillness and also his nearness, and the awareness that her father was unaware made it almost naughty. She draped her arm off the edge of the couch, her fingertips brushing his hair.

There was a *click* against glass. Ink tensed. Joy sat up. It happened again. First at the kitchen window. Then in the den. Ink stood up and checked the glyphs on the windows.

Nothing should be able to get through the wards. Ink unsheathed his straight razor and began to circuit the house. Her nerves spiked, her skin prickling. She kept her eyes on the television screen and tried to ignore the alarm bells in her head.

It could be a twig. It could be the wind. It could be anything.

Click. Click. Click-Click-Click.

The patter of tiny sounds made her dad turn around.

"Were you planning on sneaking out with Mark tonight?" he asked.

Joy could afford to be completely honest. "No."

"Huh," Dad turned back to the TV, ignoring the last *click.* "Because that's how I used to signal girls to come sneak out of the house and meet me around back. Throw a few pebbles at the window and wait outside."

Joy opened her mouth and tried to look shocked. "You rebel, you!"

He snorted. "You inherited your ninja skills from me."

Click.

Dad kept his eyes on the screen. "You might want to see who it is."

Joy *really* didn't want to—imagining the hairy, peeing sprite or the monstrous Kodama's tongue—but Ink was still here and they were safe. She hauled herself off the couch and went to the window. It was hard to see anything in the wan light. She squinted into the darkness, trying to make out shapes in the shadows. Joy tried to angle herself to peer into the corner where the elm grew by her father's bedroom, but she was on the wrong side of the house.

Click-Click-Click!

Joy jerked as a fine hail of pebbles struck the window. She glared into the darkness. Two reflective green discs stared back. She held her breath. They blinked and narrowed, turning into slits of disapproval. A tiny fire flared, the end of a match, and Avery's pale face and hair lit with gold; shadows carved deep, skeletal hollows into his eyes and cheeks. He tilted his head to the side like an owl and flicked his gaze to the window and back. She shook her head. He glanced again, angrily, around the corner, past the kitchen window to her brother's room...the one with the gaping hole in the wall. She nodded and used Inq's favorite fallback excuse.

"I'm going to use the bathroom," she said.

"Mmm-hmm," her father muttered, not believing it for a minute. "You want me to pause it?"

"No. I'll be quick."

"That's funny," he said, turning up the volume. "My girl thinks she's both sneaky *and* funny. I'm so proud."

Joy shot a wry grin over her shoulder. "Ha ha," she said. "Just give me the recap." She kept an eye on the back of her father's head as she opened the door to the bathroom, but retreated into Stef's room instead. She closed the door and turned around. The wall was still a shattered mess, but the glyph on the windowsill remained intact. Outside, Avery perched on a high branch, level with the second floor and she could tell by the slight shiver of the trailing feathers of his cloak that he'd just landed there, bobbing and swaying in the breeze.

"What is it?" she hissed.

"I must speak with you," he said. "Let me in."

"No," she said. "You can tell me whatever it is from right there."

He frowned. She could see it in the purple shadows. "That would be unwise."

"So would breaking the ward to let you in," she pointed out. "You can see what happened the last time."

His cloak settled about him, almost as if his shoulders had slumped. "You still do not trust me." He said it as fact.

Joy felt unaccountably guilty. The truth was, she didn't, which was smart, and she did, which was dangerous. Despite all that he'd done to help her with Graus Claude and the golems and the Welcome Gala, she could not forget that he was still a member of the Tide and—last she knew—Sol Leander's right-hand aide, although perhaps his plotting with Maia had changed all that. She didn't know. But the way he was always watching over her and rushing to her rescue made it feel like he was trying to be Ink, which made her feel worse.

Joy hedged. "*Should* I trust you?"

"Yes."

"Well, I don't," she said. A twinge lit in her gut. "Not entirely, anyway." The discomfort subsided. "It's hard to trust anyone these days."

"It must be somewhat difficult being the Destroyer of Worlds," he said.

Joy froze, her body gone cold. "Where did you hear that?"

"Let me in."

"No." Joy backed up a step. She touched the doorknob.

"Joy," he said, sounding both reasonable and fed up. "I am not your enemy."

"So you keep saying," she agreed. "And the more you say it, the more I doubt it."

"With good reason," Ink said, shearing his way into Stef's room. "While he may not be your enemy, his intentions are not quite those of a friend."

Avery paused, taken aback by the sudden audience. He

glanced between Ink and Joy. "True," he admitted. "But not for lack of trying."

Ink said nothing. Avery swayed on the branch. The air was heavy with unsaid things.

Joy whispered through the hole in the wall. "Look, call me paranoid, but I'm not keen on lifting the wards right now."

"You are not paranoid," Avery said reasonably. "Everyone really is out to get you." Joy coughed on a surprised laugh. Ink lifted his blade. "But not I," he said. "Not this time." He cast his eyes to the moon. "Now may I come in?"

Ink frowned. "No."

Avery ignored him, speaking to Joy. "You *must* trust me."

"Oh yeah?" she said. "Prove it."

Avery hesitated. "How?"

"Give me your *signatura*."

Avery stilled. Even the leaves on the branch he sat on stopped rustling. His voice hardened—his face a mask of insult and fear. "You're asking too much."

Joy smiled like a fox. "Actually, I'm not. If you want to come in, Ink will have to write it into the ward. He has access to the *signatura* of everyone who has used the Scribes' services, but since you say you haven't claimed anyone, I imagine he doesn't have yours." Joy looked to Ink for confirmation. He nodded. Good guess. She turned back with a shrug. "You want in, we need your True Name."

She watched emotions flutter over his face like the feathers of his voluminous cloak. He knew that she was the Destroyer of Worlds and the Tide claimed that she was the Twixt's greatest enemy—the most dangerous girl in the world. Putting the power of True Names into sigils had been done to protect the Folk from humans and safeguard their truest selves. For her to ask such a thing was ludicrous, and she knew that, and he knew she knew that, so it was a showy sort of bluff. Still, he hesitated. Of course, Joy knew the answer was "no" and was confident that that would end the conversation. Joy opened her mouth to ask him to just tell her whatever it was, but her mouth hung open as he unlaced his collar, pulling the neck aside, exposing where the flesh grew feathers. There was a swooping symbol written into his skin at the knob of his wing. His *signatura*. His True Name.

His eyes glared at her unblinking, daring comment.

"I bequeath it to you willingly," he said. "Now *let me in*."

Ink hesitated. Joy nodded, humbled and unsure. It was still another moment before Ink set the blade to the ward's edge, looping another exception, winding it into the shape of Avery's Name. Ink hesitated over the solid line of protection, and with a last glance between Joy and the snow-haired courtier, severed it. The breach snuffed. The ward reformed, including the newest exception: Avery. Ink stepped back, stiff as glass.

Avery launched from the branch and landed softly with the barest tap of his boots on the floorboards, his cloak settling about him like wings. Ink stepped in front of Joy like a shield or a claim. All she could do was stare.

"I can't believe—" she sputtered.

"That's part of your problem," Avery said haughtily. "One of many. But currently, you have other things to worry about."

"Speak your piece," Ink said. "As you say, we have other pressing matters."

Avery sized up Ink from head to toe as if reconsidering his previous assessments. He spoke over the Scribe's shoulder at Joy. "The Twixt is in an uproar. A veritable civil war has broken out around the scandal of forgetting our King and

Queen and lost kin, thanks to you. While the revelation puts many in your debt, it doubtless also has made many fear the repercussions—our monarchs are not known to forgive treason lightly. This, of course, puts you back squarely in the crosshairs of the Tide, which subsequently puts us back on the outs with the Head of the Council and their supporters. In essence, the truth you have brought to light has plunged us into an unforeseen darkness." He glanced over what was left of Stef's room, disapproval shadowing his face. "You understand the many reasons that the Folk must never war with one another," he said. "Both our dwindling numbers and our obligations to protect the magic of this world prevent us from infighting to this degree." Avery glanced at Ink like a challenge. "We cannot risk further strife. I freed you with the understanding that you would bring an end to it." He was affronted, insistent. "You *must* bring the lost monarchs home!"

She growled back, "I'm *working* on it!"

"Really?" he said. "It looked like you were watching television."

Joy rolled her eyes and stepped from behind Ink. "I don't have to answer to you!"

"No, but you will have to answer to whomever purchases your secret." Avery's statement made Joy's breath hitch and Ink's razor flash in his hand. The courtier noted both with approval. He'd succeeded in getting their attention. "Fortunately for you, once a secret is officially sold, the seller cannot divulge it to anyone save the person who purchased it." His false smile faded. "Unfortunately for you, the fact that there's a secret up for auction means that someone possesses some rather damaging information that they are willing to release, undoubtedly for no good end." Avery whistled through his teeth. "I hope you know what this secret is so that you can take measures to protect yourself."

Joy hesitated. She had a very good idea what the secret might be, but no idea whatsoever what she or anyone else could do about it, least of all Ink. *He doesn't know. I haven't told him. I haven't told anyone. So how can it be for sale?*

"And lastly," Avery said. "There are murmurs that all of this was foretold in the lost times of prophecy and legend, that this, now, is the end of an era—the end of our world—and that you, Joy Malone, are its harbinger, known as the Destroyer of Worlds."

Air dried the surface of her tongue. She closed her mouth with a snap.

He hadn't said anything about Aniseed. Nothing at all.

Avery frowned slowly. "You don't seem surprised."

Ink shifted lightly on his feet. "Neither do you."

Avery ignored him. Ink squeezed the razor's handle, an infinitesimal creak. Joy pushed past them both to stand alone in the middle of the room, choosing her words with care. "I don't think that anything the Folk say would surprise me anymore."

"You claim to know nothing of this?" Avery asked.

Joy shrugged, arms crossed. "You give me too much credit."

It wasn't an answer and they both knew it.

"And this secret of yours?"

She frowned. "Like I'd tell you."

He cocked his head to one side, uncomfortably like Ink. "I showed you mine," he said wryly.

Ink barked, "Get out."

He brushed past Ink, cool as snow. "I came to warn you," he said with a twitch of his shoulders. The feathers fluttered and laid to rest. He stood within inches of Joy. "You surround yourself with those who wish to protect you and at least one who has betrayed you."

Joy was angry enough to dare. "Which one are you?"

Avery stopped, surprised. "Me?" he said, his ocean eyes darkening. "I have wanted nothing but—" He paused, looking at Ink as if suddenly remembering he was there. The edge of his cloak flicked as he withdrew a step. His gaze dropped. "I have wanted nothing from you."

Something about the words tugged at her. Avery seemed uncomfortably evasive.

That's when it struck her: *Wanted. Past tense.*

"You know where he is, don't you?" Avery said, changing the subject quickly. "The Bailiwick."

Joy shrugged, avoiding Ink's stare. "Why do you ask?"

"The Council is after him," Avery said. "And they are after you. You are scattering your resources, which is tactically unsound."

Joy chuckled. "You sound like Filly."

"She's a warrior," Avery said. "She knows the art of war. And make no mistake, Joy, this is war. You should be gathering your forces, for protection if nothing else. 'Keep your friends close and your enemies closer.'" He frowned. "Perhaps then you would be able to discern one from the other."

She turned away. "I don't want to put my closest friends in the line of fire."

His arm shot out and he grabbed her as if to shake some sense into her. Ink's razor appeared at his throat. Avery ignored it, staring at Joy, his eyes burning, intense. "We're already there, whether you like it or not!" he said. "Accept help! Stop pushing us away!"

His word was *us* but his tone said *me.* Joy hesitated, speechless, wondering what she could say. She tore at his fingers, and he dropped his grip. Ink removed the razor's edge by degrees. There wasn't even a line where the blade had been. Avery swallowed, not taking his gaze from Joy. Ink hovered on the edge of the storm.

"You want to help?" Joy said. "Help me bring proof that it's safe for the King and Queen and everyone else to Return! The sooner we do that, the sooner this is over!" Her arms dropped. She swallowed thickly. Saying it out loud brought the reality home—how dangerous their plan was, how impossible, how frail. Joy stepped backward, away from it all. "Then, maybe, it will be safe for me, too."

Avery stared at her, stunned, a moment longer than comfortable. He straightened his swallowtail coat with a snap. "I came to deliver my warnings," he said almost apologetically. "It is up to you whether to heed them or not."

Risking yourself in the process, Joy thought, but she didn't say it aloud. She'd backed into the door again, her fingers sliding over the knob. She felt more than saw Ink's gaze on her as she watched Avery. Falling into the sea was much colder than falling into fathomless black.

"Thank you. For telling me. For coming." She turned the knob, muttering. "Thanks."

He bowed, saying nothing. His eyes scanned the windowsill where his *signatura* burned, woven into the fabric of the ward.

"Thank you for allowing it," he said, perhaps to Ink's shoes. "I will return if I hear more," he added quietly. "Fare well, Joy." He said it like two words, dual meanings.

She said nothing as he lifted the hem of his cloak high over his head and let it drop, erasing himself in a fall of white feathers.

Ink spun around, sheathing his razor and his gloom as if they'd been erased by Avery's leaving. He paused by the door.

"You would do well to listen to him," he said.

"Really?" Joy asked. "I'm surprised. I was pretty sure you hated him."

Ink paused, testing the truth of his words. "It does not matter what I think," he said. "Originally, he may have aligned with the Tide, but three times now he came for you." Ink stepped through the doorway before she could follow. "We will always come for you."

When she stepped into the hallway, Ink was gone.

Joy shut the door quickly behind her and hurried back to the den. Her mind whirled as she flumped down on the couch, staring at whatever was happening on-screen. It was just colors and light and meaningless noise.

"Feeling better?" Dad said with a chuckle in his voice.

"Uh—"

"Tell Mark I say 'Hi' and invite him to come in the front door next time."

"Okay," said Joy, hugging a pillow close to her gut. "I will."

She watched two people kissing on-screen, having completely forgotten who they were.

Joy felt a hand ruffling her awake. She could still taste the mint of her toothpaste in her mouth—she couldn't have been asleep long.

She blinked into the lamplight and Ink's dark eyes. Her playlist droned in one earbud; the other squawked on her pillow. She shut off the music.

"Hey," she said sleepily.

"Hello," he said, hovering by her nightstand. "May I?"

She scooted over as he sat on the edge of her bed. She rubbed her eyes as they came into focus, the soft light sliding off his silver shirt and wallet chain.

"You left."

"I left."

"But you came back."

Ink's face softened. "I will always come back."

It melted something uncertain between them. Joy placed a hand by his arm. "Where did you go?"

A business card appeared between his fingers. "I commissioned something to get you safely through Faeland." He placed the card on her nightstand. She recognized the familiar black squiggle of Idmona's logo. "Your fitting is scheduled for tomorrow, at your convenience, but we should not pursue Stef until then."

"Thank you," she said, tucking one elbow under her pillow. "Have you been standing here watching me sleep?"

"No," he said, sounding curious. "Would you like me to?"

"No," she said, smiling wider. "It's supposed to be sweet, but I think it's kind of creepy."

"I remember watching you sleep," he said, brushing a curl of hair off her cheek. "I did not like it. I watched over you because you asked me to stay." He glanced back at the desk chair. "Your pain was my pain, even then."

Joy remembered the night he'd sat vigil after Hasp had kidnapped her and Briarhook had burned his brand into her arm. Briarhook was one of many nightmares she'd experienced during her time in the Twixt and she had asked Ink to stay as she slept off Graus Claude's medicines and Kurt's healing salves. Even though she'd removed the brand, along with Aniseed's deadly poison, some scars took longer to heal. Ink was the only thing that kept those kinds of nightmares at bay.

She touched his hand, stroking the lines of veins and knuckles, the tiny details they'd made together as they crafted him to look more human.

He inspected her face in the near dark. A smile tugged at his lips. "I like you much better awake."

"Am I awake?" she asked lazily. "I feel like I'm still dreaming."

The bed groaned under his hands as he bent forward. He stared down at her, smiling, one dimple tucked in his cheek.

"I am quite certain," he said, his lips hovering over hers. His eyes grew deeper, beyond the black to the inky substance that made up both Scribes and *signaturae*. A second dimple appeared just before he kissed her. A gentle kiss, the brush of lips that stayed, lingering, on the tip of the tongue.

She opened her mouth and kissed him deeper. The mattress groaned again. Joy let out a sigh that was half contentment, half yearning.

"I've been waiting for you," she said as he lay down beside her. Her hands caressed his backbone, under his shirt.

"I am here," he breathed into her mouth. His breath was warm and sweet, sending shivers under the covers. Her body rose to meet his as he held her close. "I am very, very here."

TWENTY

WEDNESDAY MORNING YAWNED PINK AND GREEN, THE
sun tucked behind a soft down of smeared clouds. Joy rolled
over in a tight circle of blankets. Half of the bed had been
taken over by Ink.

Ink was getting better at feigning sleep. Joy would wake
up all at once, but he would join her in stages; it was turning into a game between them. It would start with peeking
at each other to see if the other person was awake, which
turned into a series of winks and smiles, then blinking and
laughter. Kissing, of course, trumped everything. Joy was
beginning to love mornings with Ink.

Their lips parted slowly. Ink tasted like fresh water and
smelled like rain. He rested his forehead against her temple and laid his arm across her chest. The pillows had rearranged themselves on the headboard and the floor. He
caught her gaze, and she fell once again into those fathomless, midnight eyes like a kid jumping into the deep end of
the pool.

Joy smiled. "Good morning."

"Good morning," he said back instead of his earlier "Is
it?" which had taken some time to explain. Words didn't
always mean what they said and sometimes, Joy explained,
they were just noises humans said to one another. Ink said

that even meaninglessness meant something—it meant that you weren't alone.

He brushed her hair out of her eyes and grinned as it flipped back. He played with her bangs, and she played with his sideburns until their fingers tangled in each other's hair and they were kissing again.

"Your father is home," Ink reminded her between kisses.

"Mmm," she said, kissing him back.

"We are supposed to meet Filly," he said, his words smothered and thick as his legs tangled with hers. "And Vinh. And Idmona. To rescue your brother."

"Mmm."

They pulled closer, tighter, twining together like two strands of yarn.

Joy's phone buzzed. She rolled away, breaking contact. Ink propped up on one elbow as Joy read the ID.

"This you stop for?" he asked.

"Yeah. Hang on," Joy felt a prickle of worry. Monica usually texted instead of called. She thumbed the phone icon. "Hey, Mon."

"Hey, Joy," Monica sounded equally uncertain. "Sorry to call so early, but I think something's wrong." Joy could hear her pacing. "I got a package in the mail, and you know how things have been weird with Gordon lately? I thought he'd sent me a present to, you know, make up or something."

"Uh-huh," Joy said, sitting up. "Okay."

Monica's voice sounded strained. "So it's a necklace. I put it on, but now I can't take it off." There was more than a hint of desperation now. "I don't mean like the clasp is stuck. I mean, when I try to take it off, it gets a little tighter. At first I thought I was imagining things, but now I'm pretty sure and it's kind of freaking me out, so I thought I'd call you—"

"We'll be right there!" Joy said, launching out of bed and grabbing her jeans. "Hang on! Don't move!"

Monica paused. "Wait a minute. *We?*"

"Shut up. Stay on the phone."

Ink was already pulling his shirt over his head. Joy fumbled with her flip-flops. The wallet chain rattled against Ink's hip as he shoved his feet into boots, flipped the razor in his hand and grabbed Joy's wrist. She kept the phone to her ear as they spliced through the void, the feedback squealing and breaking into static as they stepped through the other side into Monica's hallway on the second floor. Joy dropped the phone.

"Monica?"

There was a thump of footsteps. "Down here!"

They nearly crashed in the foyer, Monica's eyes wide as Ink and Joy rushed down the stairs. Her fingers were fastened around a necklace of creamy pearls.

"How did you two get in here?"

"Indelible Airlines," Joy said. "You okay?"

"Do I look okay?" Monica kept her fingers tucked in front of her throat. "As long as I don't try to take it off, we seem to have come to some agreement about whether or not I keep breathing." Her smile was weak. Her lips were chapped. "When I saw a choker of pearls, I didn't think it meant literally!"

Joy took out her scalpel and Ink unfolded his wallet, inspecting the blades. "It's okay," Joy said. "We'll figure this out." She hoped that saying the words aloud would make them true.

Ink circled Monica, inspecting the necklace. "Where did you get this?"

"Delivered via FedEx," Monica said, leading them into the dining room. "Look." She gestured at the cardboard packaging, the brown paper fill and the rich, robin's-egg blue box inside. "It's Tiffany's! Who would suspect something evil from Tiffany's?" Her humor was strained. "Miss Manners *does not* approve."

Joy could see the subtle shifting of glyphs along the pearls. The oozing shapes slithered icy down her spine. "It's enspelled."

"No duh!" Monica snapped.

Ink tucked his razor back into his wallet. "It is resisting being removed in order to give the spell time to infuse," he said. "Once clasped, it activates, closing the circle. It is a contact spell set on the pearls' surface, absorbed through the skin."

Monica shifted uncomfortably. "Fascinating. Really. Can you get it off me?"

"Let me see," Ink said, following the loop of pearls to the small golden clasp at the back of her neck.

"Be careful," Monica said with a quiver. "I tried using the letter opener and the thing shot blue sparks and singed one of my extensions. Burned plastic hair smells the *worst*."

"He'll be careful," Joy said, holding Monica's curls out of the way as Ink swapped his razor for the silver quill with delicately carved fletchings and a wicked-sharp tip. He pinched the clasp and touched the angled shaft to the thread.

Joy saw the flash. The sigils flared and Monica doubled over, gagging and clutching her throat.

"Monica!" Joy screamed.

Ink held the back of Monica's necklace, trying to slip his fingers under the pearls pressed deep into her brown-black flesh. His fingers slid off the tiny globes, scrabbling for purchase as Monica buckled forward, bending over, mouth wide.

"Hold her," he said. Joy grabbed Monica's shoulders, trying to keep her steady. Her friend's tongue stuck out and her eyes were wild. Joy clenched her teeth, whimpering. The choking noises grew thin.

"Ink! Stop it!" Joy begged. "Make it stop!"

Face impassive, Ink struggled to catch the cord between his fingers, calculating an opening, a moment to strike. Joy knew that one mistake could mark Monica the same way she'd been marked, becoming his unintentional *lehman*, but waiting too long might kill her. Joy squeezed her friend's shoulders as Monica pitched to the side. "No no no no...!"

Joy slipped and fell. Ink grimaced. Monica wheezed.

There was a burst of gold sparks outside the window.

Joy looked up. Sol Leander loomed outside the ward. His cloak rippled in the wind, face furious.

"Bring her to me!" he shouted through the magic and glass.

"NO!" Joy screamed back. "GO AWAY!"

"Joy—" Ink warned.

"Now!" barked Sol Leander.

Monica curled forward; a tiny wisp of sound eked out. She collapsed. Joy screamed again.

Ink slashed the air, a complicated loop. A golden cascade disappeared with a zipping noise. The ward was gone. Sol Leander strode through the window as if it wasn't there. Ink drew Joy back in an iron grip, as loving and firm as he had on the lip of Faeland, and just as unwanted.

"Joy," Ink said. "Don't."

Sol Leander lifted Monica in his arms and carried her out onto the lawn through the illusion of walls. The grass was still wet from the sprinklers and caught the sunlight like dewdrops. He sank down on one knee, his cape settling in a blanket of stars as he set his hands along either side of her throat. His fingers fastened like claws.

Joy jerked against Ink's arms. Her voice tore loose. "MONICA!"

The world blurred, a mess of light and stars and robin's-egg blue. Joy could sense the grass through the window—the stones and earth and welcoming soil. She wanted to punch through the foundation, reach through the rubble and rock and ruin and grab the power that was there. Drink it in. Let it fill her. Let it burn her alive. *Let* everything *burn!* And then she would rise up against her enemies and *BURY ALL THAT STOOD IN HER PATH TO HAVE HER REVENGE!*

Joy strained, her head pounding in agony. She ached for the cold and the iron and the blood of the earth, the taste of metal and stone and old, old ice. Her rage was without color, her ears echoed without sound, and it was only because she was trapped in Ink's embrace that she failed to do any of it. He held her back.

"Joy!"

Her eyes snapped open, her fury dissipating, her body dropping to the floor as she watched the tiny white orbs fall into the grass. Sol Leander had severed the necklace.

Monica blinked and touched her throat. Inhaling deeply, she sat up, coughing. She rubbed at the skin of her neck, looking pissed.

"Ow!" she hacked and glared at Sol Leander. "That hurt!"

Sol Leander's eyebrows arched, nearly touching his high widow's peak.

"You can see me?" he said, fanning his fingers before her eyes. "You have the *Sight*?" He whirled about, pointing a finger straight at Joy, his cloak snapping in anger. "You gave her the *Sight*?"

"What?" Joy croaked, her voice cracked and raw. Ink helped her to stand as the dining room tilted. She staggered against Ink. "What just happened?"

"She is under his auspice," Ink whispered into her hair. "He is sworn to protect her, but he could not come inside. He could not get past the wards." His tone was mild censure. "He came to save her, Joy."

Joy pushed him away like a physical denial. Shaking, Joy ran out of the house to Monica's side, placing herself like a rickety shield between her friend and her enemy.

"Are you okay?" she gasped. "Monica?"

"I'm fine," Monica said with a wary edge to her voice. She coughed twice more. "I won't say 'peachy,' but I'll say 'fine.'"

Joy turned to Sol Leander, staring at him, unbelieving. "You saved her."

Sol Leander glared. "And you've damned her," he said.

Joy swallowed her guilt like wet cement.

"Her life was never in mortal danger," Ink said, stepping through the front door. The quill was still in his hand. He cocked his head to the side like a bird. "You know as well as I that the spell upon the necklace was not a noose, but a leash."

Sol Leander declined to meet his gaze, intent on one of the pearls.

Joy held Monica's hands. Her knuckles were pale. "What do you mean?" she asked.

Ink glanced at them both. "It was a trap."

"A trap?"

"A ruse," he amended.

Monica rubbed her neck angrily. The dark, pressurized spots had all but disappeared. "So they're fake?"

Ink picked a pearl from the grass. "No. They are real." He glanced at Sol Leander, then at Joy. "The necklace was not designed to harm, it was merely a delivery method to ensure the enchantment would have time to imbue through the skin." Monica stared at the pearl-littered lawn. Ink smiled apologetically. "It resisted your attempts to remove it, but my using one of the forged instruments of the Twixt forced the necklace to defensively constrict and for that, I apologize. The pearls are safe now that the spell has been broken." He rolled the tiny globe between finger and thumb. Sol Leander said nothing as Ink placed it into Monica's palm. "Restrung, they would make a lovely piece of jewelry."

"So...not Gordon." Monica poked at the pearl.

"It was a *geas*, a spell of obligation," Sol Leander explained. "Once bound, you would have to follow its instructions to the letter. But such an enchantment has to be accepted willingly, hence why it came disguised as a gift."

Monica's lips turned ashen. Joy's fingers clenched. *"You!"*

"Not I," said Sol Leander. "I was forced to wait outside the wards before I could break the binding spell, which placed your friend in considerable danger—something I *expressly* warned you to avoid at all costs." He twitched his cloak closer, a strangely familiar gesture. Avery had likely picked it up from his master. "As I suspected, your friendship proves to be as flimsy as your word."

"Hey!" Monica and Joy chorused in protest.

"Nobody *makes* me do anything," Monica said with heat. "I own my thoughts and my own actions and I don't need to go blaming anybody else for my mistakes."

"A very human sentiment," Sol Leander said. "However, someone went to considerable lengths to make sure you would be more than willing to do anything they wished. *Anything.*" He all but snarled at Joy. "Despite your purported values of freedom and choice, it seems that your actions have robbed your friend of both."

That stole some of Monica's fire and most of Joy's righteousness. The two of them moved a little closer together until their shoulders touched.

"The Sight was her choice," Ink said. "I witnessed its choosing. You, Councilex Leander, are the one obliged to intercede on her behalf. Joy acted out of loyalty, out of love."

Monica stared at the dark gentleman in the cloak of galaxies. "Wait. *You're* Sol Leander? My guardian angel?"

The Tide's representative looked pained. His mouth twitched.

Ink bowed at the waist. "Councilex Leander, may I present Monica Reid, one of your charges under auspice."

Sol Leander's gaze flicked to Monica and then to the Scribe. "As you say," he said with barely a bow. "I had no choice."

Monica's fury simmered behind half-lidded eyes. "Nobody's forcing you."

Sol Leander sneered, "On the contrary."

"Still," Joy said quietly. "Thank you for saving her."

Monica glared at the vampiric representative of the Tide. "Yeah, thanks for that," she said as she knelt down and began picking pearls out of the lawn. Ink sank beside her and helped gather up the tiny, cream-colored pearls, spilling them into her cupped palm. Joy was left standing by the bushes, feeling caught between worlds.

Sol Leander swirled aside. His cloak shimmered, a mass of sparkling, spectral doom. His gaze speared Joy, radiating disapproval. She was hyperaware of her feet touching the grass; although the power seemed enticingly close, she did not dare attempt anything that might expose her. If the Tide ever found out what Ink and Graus Claude suspected, she was as good as dead.

Sol Leander turned so that his cloaked back was like a wall, shutting out Monica and Ink sifting their fingers through the grass.

"You must be more careful, Miss Malone," he growled. "For her sake, if not yours."

Joy nodded. She knew it. She was playing a dangerous game with more lives than just her own.

"Why did you do it?" she asked. "Save her, I mean."

Sol Leander blinked slowly and looked out at the quiet suburban street. "She is under my auspice, which makes her my duty and obligation, both to my people and yours," he said matter-of-factly. "It was the oath I swore when I accepted my place in the Twixt—to preserve what was wrought between our worlds, to preserve the magic...at all costs."

Joy started. "Wait, you mean Monica has magic?"

"Of course she has magic!" he sneered hotly. "Idiot child! What do you think this is all for? Do you have no idea what it means to be one of us, even now?" He gestured dismissively at the lazy neighborhood. "They *all* have magic—they *are* magic!—every one of those hidden places and mortals marked by our kind! They are our sacred responsibility and this one is *mine*!" He turned enough to glance at Monica, almost against his will. "She was an innocent victim of an unprovoked assault like my own—" His words shut off with a tightening of his lips. "It was true of her father before her, and his mother before him, and her sister before her." His gaze flicked back to Joy. "And so it was, so it shall be. They are, all of them, *mine* to protect."

Joy couldn't help it—she glanced at the downward-pointed arrow that slashed the side of his throat, its mirror image bisecting Monica's left eyebrow. Monica was part of this— had always been part of this—carrying a piece of the world's magic long before they'd ever met. A small part of her felt relieved that she hadn't done this to her friend, but she also felt smaller. Whatever was in motion was so much bigger than her, than Monica, than any of them.

The Destroyer of Worlds.

How can I stop it? How can I fix this?

"Do you know who did this?" Sol Leander hissed, interrupting her thoughts.

"No," Joy said. "I mean, it could be anyone—anyone who's after me." Joy glanced over her shoulder, feeling a chill creep down her spine. Her next words came slowly. "Anyone who would think to manipulate her to get to me." *To get at my secrets. To control me. To stop me. To blackmail me to obey.* Joy remembered the slap of cold slush and burned skin and shuddered.

"You suspect someone?" he said.

"Yes." She thought about Briarhook and Hasp and Aniseed.

He mustn't know!

"But you aren't certain," Sol Leander said.

Joy shrugged. "It's a long list."

Sol Leander nodded. "You've made an impressive number of enemies in your short time amongst us," he agreed. "Anyone at the top the list?"

Joy glared at him. "The Tide."

"Ha!" Sol Leander laughed smugly. "Spite blinds you. The Tide may be many things, but we have a strict adherence to the rules. We are considered rather orthodox in our interpretation of the Twixt as it was meant to be, before it was corrupted by the Council after we were abandoned—"

"After you *forgot*," Joy corrected. "After everyone in the Twixt forgot all about the King and Queen and the rest of your people trapped behind a locked door between worlds." Joy tried not to sound quite as smug as he had. "A door *I* managed to open. A spell *I* managed to break."

"As you say," Sol Leander conceded. "But you are still a danger to yourself and others. And now you have managed to place your friend in danger, accusing my colleagues of the crime, all the while refusing to see what is *right before you.*" He waved a hand in Monica's direction. "Someone very powerful, very arrogant or very desperate would dare such a thing at this sensitive time." He cocked an arched eyebrow, his words like molasses—sticky and spoiled-sweet. "Sound like anyone familiar?"

Joy felt like she'd been punched in the gut. *Aniseed! Aniseed had to be behind this!* She knew it in her bones. Joy tried to school her face but could feel the hot flush creeping up her neck, giving away her fears.

"Well," Joy said, trying to match his austere tone. "If we really wanted to know who did this, the easiest thing would have been to let the spell take hold and then simply follow her back to whomever cast it."

As the words left her mouth, Joy gagged. She felt sick. *What am I saying? I'd never do that!* She pressed the heel of her hand to her heart that wasn't there. What was she becoming? More Folk than human? Cruel? Manipulative? Heartless? Was that what she'd need to be to stop Aniseed for good?

Sol Leander laughed, startling her. "You surprise me, Joy Malone," he said, tucking his long hands into his bell sleeves. "You truly *are* becoming one of us. Perhaps that is why the Council has granted you leniency. They must recognize your potential."

Joy paused, biting back her retort. "You mean the motion passed? They're not coming after me?"

His mouth twisted as if he'd tasted something foul. "As the new courier, you are protected under Council law. Your freedom of movement is therefore necessary in order to achieve the Return." He turned his head, spearing her with his scathing stare. "Yet let me make this quite clear—you are a pawn in this game," Sol Leander whispered. "And, through your meddling, your friend is now in play." He clutched the edge of his cloak. "Therefore, I am charging *you* with keeping her safe, as you are most likely closer to the source of this threat than I." He inspected the sky for a moment as if reading words in the clouds. "If she is as important to you as you say, then protect her. Protect her with more than what you have." He leaned closer, the bridge of his nose angling over hers. "And know this, Joy Malone— if my charge is threatened in any way, I am bound by the rules to protect her by any means." His eyes sparked with promise. "So I would be well within my rights to kill you." He stood back with that barest of smiles and adjusted his cloak with sparkles and swirls. "Remember that," he said, and, with a snap, Sol Leander disappeared.

Monica and Ink stared at the spot where the Tide's representative had been.

"Well, he's a charmer," Monica said.

"Yeah. Charming." Joy's mind was a whirl of words and fears. There was a kick of breeze, and Joy saw a flash of orange in the corner of her eye. She spun around, gasping, but it was just sunlight bouncing off the Japanese maple, more red than gold. She shivered in the August breeze. It was a warning. Even subconsciously, Joy knew what she had to do.

"We've got to go," she said. "And you're coming with." Joy grabbed Monica's elbow. "Me. Us. Coming with us. Right now. Bring the pearls."

Monica frowned, cupping her hands together. "Wait a minute. What? Where are we going?"

"We need more magic than we've got and I know where to get it." Joy said, trading a quick look with Ink. "We're off to see a wizard."

TWENTY-ONE

JOY PUSHED OPEN THE DOOR TO THE C&P WITH ITS two-tone *hello* chime. Monica was at her heels and Ink at her side. He must have been invisible since no one in the convenience mart so much as glanced up as the three of them walked down the aisle of pretzels and chips. Joy hadn't had the chance to tell him that his shirt was on backward.

"What are we doing here?" Monica whispered.

Joy grabbed a Clif Bar and a pack of gum. "Making a purchase," she said, winding her way toward the front. "The gum is a code."

Monica pointed at the health bar. "Then what's that for?"

"I'm hungry."

Ink tucked his razor into his wallet as Joy approached the counter, placing her items on the mat along with a ten-dollar bill. Hai barely glanced at them as he rang up the total, tugging the collar of his button-down shirt as he made change for the ten. He handed her a plastic bag and gestured toward the back.

"He's been expecting you," he said to Joy. "And you," he said in Ink's direction. "But not you," he said to Monica. She shrugged and took something from her purse, setting it on the counter with a *click*.

"Behold my passport," Monica said straight-faced.

Hai stared at the ox bone blade before giving her a nod. "Okay, then. You, too."

Monica picked up the knife primly and followed Joy and Ink toward the Employees Only door.

"Why did you bring that?" Joy whispered.

Monica shrugged. "You said 'wizard,' I thought 'magic' and this is the only magic thingie I've got." Joy didn't bother correcting her. Monica pointed the tip of the dagger at Ink. "He could see you?"

"No," Ink said. "But he knew that I was there."

"So is he a wizard?"

"No," Joy said, grabbing the doorknob. "He's a 3-D computer animation artist. His father is a wizard."

"Of course," Monica said. "How silly of me."

Joy walked into the back room and pushed past the stacks of paper towels and flats of soda to grab the hidden lever behind the shelving unit. The back of the closet popped open.

"Hello, busy girl," Mr. Vinh said calmly.

Joy led the way inside. Her shoes crackled on the woven grass mats. "Hello, Mr. Vinh."

"You have been keeping me very busy as of late," he said, sounding pleased. "My services are in high demand." His head turned slightly and he addressed the air. "And how is your glamour holding up, Master Ink?"

Ink flicked his wrist, activating the glamour. "Very well, thank you, Wizard Vinh." He bowed politely, which Mr. Vinh chose to return.

"And how is your tea?" he asked Joy.

"I haven't had it today," she admitted.

"Always follow directions," he said sternly. "Or results are not guaranteed." He stepped over to Monica, who wasn't quite sure how to act. "And who is this?"

"She is my friend, known as Monica Reid," Joy said in

the roundabout way of introductions among the Folk. She hadn't meant to do it—it had become a habit out of necessity, but Monica looked at her as if she'd grown another head.

"Hi," Monica said. "Nice to meet you."

"No tutorials, demonstrations or free samples," Mr. Vinh said automatically.

"It's nothing like that," Joy said. "She already has the Sight—"

"Obviously," he said. "And somewhat else." He slid forward, barely disturbing the matted floor. His fingers traced the air between them, hovering at eye height, then moving down to her hand on the dagger. "I recognize this," he said, his gaze flicking from the blade to Joy, a twitch under thick lids. "I thought this was yours."

"No," Monica said coolly. "It's mine."

Mr. Vinh considered the thing in her hand. "May I?" He reached into the glass cabinet and removed his favorite spyglass, squinting through a smooth stone with a hole in its center as he rotated a tiny dial clockwise.

"Yes," he said, making a few more adjustments. "I believe it is." He looked up. "Interesting."

Monica frowned. "What?"

"Would you be willing to sell it?" he asked, placing the apparatus back in the case. "I can offer a generous price." Joy ignored the casual tone and watched his eyes; he wanted it—the look reminded her of Ladybird once he'd discovered who she was. There might as well have been cartoon dollar signs painted over his eyes.

Monica glanced at Joy, who shook her head. "No," Monica said. "No, thank you. It has...sentimental value."

"It was a gift," Ink said. "From a relative." He murmured a string of syllables that ended in something like *mambo*.

"Ah," Mr. Vinh said, and tucked his hands behind his back. "Well, then, how else may I be of service?"

"Two things," Joy said quickly. "First, can you tell us what spell is on these?" Monica handed Joy the plastic baggie of pearls. Mr. Vinh offered his palm and she dropped it in. He rolled the pearls around with the tip of his finger.

"Yes," he said. "I can do this."

There was a moment's pause.

"We will, of course, compensate you for the information," Ink said.

"Good," Mr. Vinh said, nodding to Joy with mild censure. "Hai has needed recent reminding—no freebies, even for pretty girls."

Joy bit her tongue. Hai had given her the name of the Amanya spell, which had saved Graus Claude, freed everyone of the spell of forgetting, as well as exposed Aniseed's betrayal and illicit coup against the King and Queen—but she knew Mr. Vinh had little love for the *tien* other than as well-paying clients. He would not be swayed by the good it had done for the Twixt.

He wrote a number on the back of a business card and passed it to Ink, who nodded. Mr. Vinh took it back and wrote a single word beneath it. He did not hand it over.

"And the second thing?" he asked.

"I need to find someone—" Joy said.

"Hire a tracker," Mr. Vinh said. "I believe your young Norse friend bartered well for Kestrel's services. I would be happy to make the arrangements for my usual fee."

Monica gasped. "*Gordon* knows about all this?"

"No," Joy said. "He means Filly."

"She's a Valkyrie," Ink said helpfully.

Monica pursed her lips. "O-kay."

"I thought I could use this," Joy said, unzipping her purse and removing the dowsing rod. "We used it for the Amanya spell, but I'm not tracing a spell back to its caster. I thought maybe I could use the human equivalent of an Anvesana spell, but I don't have access to anything like blood so I'm hoping you have a better idea for how to trace *mana* or something."

Mr. Vinh and Monica looked at her with matching expressions of shock.

"How do you know of these things?" he asked.

"*Blood?*" Monica said, glaring at Joy. "Really, Joy? Ew! Do I really have to point out that that sentence has got *'stupid'* written all over it?"

Joy plunked the Y-shaped piece of wood on the desk of painted scrolls. "It's Stef, okay?" Joy said. "My brother, Stef. Your apprentice, Stef. He's been taken by the King and Queen and he's trapped until I can convince them to come out and the only way that I can do that is if I find Stef before they do something to him." As she said it, she wondered if she was already too late. But she needed this spell and she needed Filly's distraction and she probably needed whatever Ink had commissioned from Idmona first. She wasn't about to race into Faeland without being prepared, despite the fact that she desperately wanted to.

If Hai was right, all magic gave off *mana*—ripples of telltale energy—that could be traced back to their origins, which would include a certain wizard-in-training and any enspelled things he might have on him, like glyphed glasses or a frayed iron-bead bracelet. If she was right, she could use human magic to pierce through Faeland. And if her brother was right, all it would take was the right spell.

Mr. Vinh smiled with genuine pleasure. "Very good." He ran a hand over the dowsing rod approvingly. "I see you have been busy, too." Thinking of all the places she'd been dragged around as she sought the origin of the Amanya spell, she could only nod. She wasn't keen about repeating the experience, but she'd do all of it again if it meant saving Stef. Mr. Vinh tapped the side of his cap. "You're clever. Smart girl. This is a good thing for you," he said, turning slowly. "A bad thing, I think, for the *tien*." He chuckled. Mr. Vinh obviously approved.

"You can do this?" Ink said, less a question than a statement.

"Yes," Mr. Vinh said. "Certainly. All I need is blood."

"Again, I call *stupid*." Monica said.

Joy winced. "I don't have any blood."

"Not just any blood," Mr. Vinh waved off their concerns. "Very messy. Unhygienic. All sorts of Health Code violations. No, no—" He paused. "I need the blood of the person you are looking for." He gestured offhandedly toward the door. "It's common insurance among the *tien*, even some humans who are aware of its properties make select deposits, investments against just such an emergency."

Monica glanced back the way they'd come. "You keep blood samples in your stockroom?"

Mr. Vinh frowned. "Of course not!" he said. "They are in the refrigerator."

"He is your apprentice," Ink said. "Do you have a sample of his blood?"

Mr. Vinh huffed through his nose. "Not anymore," he said stiffly and paced the room. "When we learned of your true nature, he returned to me and demanded that we destroy all of his samples." The older man fiddled with one of the boxes on the shelves. "I complied, of course."

"Of course," Joy said slowly, wondering whether Stef had been trying to protect himself or her from discovery? Or maybe keep his master from temptation? What could a wizard do with samples of their blood? Joy had a feeling she didn't want to find out.

Mr. Vinh tapped his stylus thoughtfully. "Do you have

his shaving razor? Toothbrush? Band-Aid? Anything that might have a trace of his blood on it?"

"He was heading off to college," she said. "He took everything. We could break into his car and look..."

"Wait." Ink stepped closer to Mr. Vinh's shelves of dried herbs and things floating in jars. "Is a blood spell like a blood key?"

Joy remembered the term. She flashed back to the illusion of her kitchen and the things boiling in the dark beyond Aniseed's trap, which had been sealed with a blood key. They'd escaped using a blood-soaked coffee cake as a decoy. Joy could still feel the sugary crystals rolling over her open wound.

Mr. Vinh paused, his curiosity piqued. "I believe they work on the same principle."

"Then perhaps it does not need to be as specific as a key," Ink continued. "Perhaps you only need a sample of the shared bloodline."

The wizard considered it. "If your theory applies, then, yes."

Ink turned gently to Joy. "If so, you could find him using your blood."

"Joy—" Monica said, eyes wide. Joy didn't need to hear the words, *No Stupid!*

"It's Stef," she said aloud, to Monica and Ink and Mr. Vinh and herself. It felt inevitable, like Fate unspooling. "I'll do it." Her fingers shook. Ink placed his hand over them. Monica squeezed her shoulder. Joy addressed her brother's master. "Just show me how."

A pinprick and a Band-Aid from the First Aid kit, and it was over. Joy watched as a drop of her blood disappeared into the small divot at the crux of the Y-shaped rod. Mr. Vinh performed the ritual. Ink carefully collected any trash, which he said he would destroy himself. The wizard nodded with professional courtesy and a modicum of respect.

"A wise precaution," the wizard said. Monica whispered a "Thank you" to Ink.

"Done," Mr. Vinh decreed as he wiped his hands on a paper towel. The oil he'd used to seal the reservoir still shone on its surface. Joy's drop of blood was barely a dark patch underneath. "Now, here is your spell—guaranteed for up to three generations." He handed her a rolled piece of scroll paper tied with black ribbon. "The vibrations should increase as you get closer."

Joy's shoulders and elbows ached with residual memory. "Yeah. I'm familiar with it."

Mr. Vinh smiled. "I have always been fascinated by the intersection of technology and magic," he said with genuine delight. "You will tell me how it worked when you both return?" Joy appreciated the unspoken vote of confidence that she would return successfully with her brother in tow. She knew, no matter what he felt about his wayward apprentice, he would not leave Stef to the *tien*.

"Yes," Joy said. "Thank you."

"And you," he said, eyes twinkling at Monica. "Are you certain I cannot convince you to part with your bit of magic stick?"

Monica glanced at Joy again. Her best friend hesitated. "Can it help Joy out there?"

Mr. Vinh's face broke into sly wrinkles. "You are smart to ask. Smarter to stay out of this altogether, but I imagine it's too late for that." He pointed at his own eyebrow. "You are marked. And you can See them. They don't like that, but they should think twice about interfering if you hold on to that." He raised two empty hands. "Keep it. For now. But my offer still stands."

"Okay," Monica said uneasily. "Thanks."

Mr. Vinh dipped his brush back into the pot of paint. "Then our business is done," he said. "Goodbye and good luck."

Joy paused in the door. "Thanks again."

Mr. Vinh paused midstroke. "Do not thank me," he said solemnly. "I expect your brother to do so himself." He pointed the end of the paintbrush at her. "Go bring your family home."

Joy nodded. "I will."

All of them, she promised herself. And, as they all knew, she couldn't lie.

As they exited the back room, Hai paused from straightening the magazines and put on a pair of Ray-Bans etched with runes.

"Done for the day?" he asked. The other customers barely noticed. Hai was just as good as any of the Folk at speaking in code.

Joy nodded. "Yeah."

"Good," Hai said. "Did he tell you that we've sold more in the past month than we have in the past twelve years?" Joy paused, knowing they weren't talking about potato chips. Considering how much Mr. Vinh had quoted her to buy Ink's glamour, she could barely imagine how much money Mr. Vinh was making selling glamours to the Twixt. She remembered the dancers at the Carousel, her head spinning like the glow stick lights. Hai winked. "Yeah," he drawled. "You should have asked for commission." He tipped his chin to Ink. "Come back later and I can put a little more chrome reflection on the chain. It's not catching the light quite right."

Ink nodded as he followed Joy and Monica through the door.

"Artists!" he sighed, sounding exactly like Inq.

TWENTY-TWO

THEY LEFT MONICA AT HOME BEHIND NEW WARDS that included a special dispensation for Sol Leander, should he be needed. Joy didn't like it, but she knew that the Councilex would never harm Monica. Besides, she shuddered to think what would happen if he learned that she and Ink had locked him out a second time.

Monica gave Joy a long hug at the door and pointed a warning finger at Ink. "You watch out for her," she said. "I am trusting you to keep her out of trouble."

Ink gave a gentle bow. "No promises, but I shall try my best."

Monica crossed her arms. "Not good enough."

"I know." He said it quietly, sadly, like a confession. "We are a work in progress."

Monica glanced back at Joy. "Please be careful."

"I will."

"You'd better!" Monica held the door open an extra second. "Now go get Stef back!"

"Will do," Joy said. "Now go call Gordon before he freaks out and buys you something expensive for real. Remember— No Stupid. Talk to him."

"I will."

Joy watched the door close, heard it lock and walked with Ink back down the slope of the Reid's front yard. Ink stopped and examined her face. He looked taller, somehow. Older. He placed a kiss on her lips like a fingerprint and brushed an errant strand of hair from her eyes.

"Ready to go?" he asked.

"Yes." She took Idmona's business card out of her pocket and wrote down the time. The appointment disappeared, reappearing with a confirmation within seconds. Joy took another deep breath. "With a little luck, this plan might work after all."

Ink smiled. "Do you still have your John Melton's boon?"

Joy patted her wallet with the pressed four-leaf clover inside. "Hey, I may be crazy, but I'm not stupid." She glanced back at Monica's front door and whispered, "Remember— No Stupid."

She tore the card in half, and they disappeared.

"Remember, you cannot linger," Graus Claude cautioned as Joy paced the length of the underground pool, attempting to reread the scroll in her hands. The words were slippery and wouldn't stay on the page. It was hard to concentrate with the Bailiwick's constant litany of warnings ringing off the subterranean walls. She'd already heard it all. *Danger. Army. Trespass. Capture.* But there was only one word that mattered to her: *Stef.* At this point, she didn't even care about the King and Queen or her ultimate fate. She just needed her family home, together, safe.

The Bailiwick jostled small ceramic cups on his dinner tray. "Even if we theorize that physical contact is required for you to trigger Faeland's natural defenses, there is no guarantee that the shoes will work." Graus Claude glared at Ink. "You should have consulted me to make the necessary inquiries."

"You have taught me well, Bailiwick," Ink said with a bow.

"Idmona believes that the boots and gloves will protect Joy from direct contact with the soil. Lining the soles with her own silk should fool the magics into accepting Joy's passage as one of the Folk. And, as she is a proper descendant, it should still satisfy the conditions of Faeland." Ink looked up curiously at his employer's concern. "Do you doubt Idmona's work?"

The great amphibian's browridge shot up in surprise. "I would never be so bold," he said. "Or so foolish."

"Then it shouldn't be a problem," Joy said. She wiggled her toes in the unfamiliar soft leather, feeling the spongy give of the pads. She'd needed Filly's help to lace them up to her knees and the elbow-length gloves felt strangely elegant. "She said they'd work and so I trust they'll work." The giant spider-woman had circled Joy's feet, adjusting the leathers and laces for a proper fit, slicing off excess sole with a thin little knife. She'd grown used to the tickle of Idmona's long, stiff hairs and the clunk of her beads, but her many limbs scuttling across the mirror reflections made Joy twitchy. She suspected that Idmona secretly enjoyed scaring her clients. Joy's stomach still felt watery even an hour after they'd gone. "We have plenty of other things to worry about."

Graus Claude smoothed the collar of his silk jacket and grumbled, "Lest we forget."

"Are we ready?" Filly said impatiently. Her blue eyes sparkled and her smile was lusty and wide. "What's taking you so long? The spell's not going to cast itself!"

"Someone is anxious," Ink teased. The young Valkyrie grinned and licked the blue spot below her lip.

"The fun is in the chase," she said, and shot a wink at Joy. "You should know that by now."

"This isn't supposed to be fun," Joy said. "It's about not getting caught. I need you to keep whatever's in there busy until I can track down Stef." She lifted the dowsing rod. It was hard to feel it through the silk gloves. "Ink will stay with me while we get Stef to accept his True Name. When we give the signal, break for the door." She blinked into the unsteady light. "We get out together or not at all." She gave a *hmph* of annoyance as the words of the spell slid from her memory like US History. Joy tried reading the scroll again.

"Give it to me," Ink said gently. "I can adapt myself to read any spoken language."

"Oh?" said Filly, sounding surprised.

"I can shape my tongue."

"You don't say?" She turned to Joy with a smirk. "Is this true?"

Joy bit the side of her cheek.

"I wish that you would allow Mistress Inq and Kurt to accompany you on this adventure," the Bailiwick muttered. Joy knew it was hard for him to feel helpless, left behind.

"Inq and Kurt are our fallback plan," Joy explained again. "If we're captured by the King and Queen, there needs to be someone on this side who can try again." She tried to speak to the anxiety on his face. "Don't worry—we'll give them the proof that they need to come home."

The Bailiwick nodded, a gesture all but lost as his palsy shake returned; his hunched shoulders were more pronounced than usual.

"I know what must be done," he said, his icy gaze made almost radiant in the pool light. "I simply wish that you were not the one to do it."

Joy wasn't sure in that moment if he meant that he regretted putting her in danger, that he wished to keep her safe or that he didn't think that she could do it. She swallowed her anxiety and placed a hand on his arm.

"Trust me."

He patted her hand with one of his own. "I do, Miss Malone. I do, indeed."

She nodded. Ink stepped closer. Filly bounced on her heels.

"I demand entrance to the Bailiwick of the Twixt."

The princess's meadow remained slashed and broken with great swathes of nothing ripped sideways and torn. The pocket world lay in tatters, shredded like a razor blade through a precious painting. Joy stared at her shoes, embarrassed and sorry, remembering how hesitant she had been the first time to step on a perfect blade of grass. In her fury, she'd ruined a thousand years of patient waiting, a thousand years of one person's solace, a world created to both remember and forget.

"What happened here?" Filly said, hand on hilt.

Joy sighed, ignoring Ink's sidelong glance. "I was mad."

Filly gave a soft chuckle, her short cape of finger bones rattling as she surveyed the carnage. "Remind me never to make you mad, Joy Malone."

Joy shook her head. "It won't happen again."

Filly winked. "Your secret is safe with me."

They rolled along the world's surface, sliding until the shimmering portal hung before them in midair. Ink and Joy took up positions on opposite sides of the door. Foreign sunlight eked out the edges, splicing hot rainbows through the sky. Filly crouched in front of the doorway, rocking back and forth on the balls of her feet, her blue eyes fixed on the scintillating light.

"You know what to do," Ink said, his words crisp and clear.

"Yes." Filly grinned.

"Tell me."

"Distraction. Mayhem. Extraction." Her eyes crinkled, catlike and sly. "Preferably in that order."

"Close enough," Joy said. She squeezed the dowsing rod in her hands. It was slippery through the silk gloves. "Ready?"

Filly huffed a laugh through her nose and clanged her vambraces together.

"I was born ready."

Ink flicked the razor and opened the door.

Filly jumped through.

She ran straight through those guarding the door, punching and kicking in a whirl of motion before the soldiers had even registered her presence, but by then she was already gone. Racing past them, down the slope, she threw one of their helmets into the air with a naughty whoop of laughter. Joy saw her vambraces flash as she rained a tornado of blows through an unsuspecting knot of infantry, grabbing a sword from one and borrowing another's shield that was still attached to their arm in order to block a sloppy attack. With a kick, one was down, the other stunned with the flat of the blade as Filly ducked, spun and was off again, casting weapons and assailants aside like a child through a pile of leaves, leaving joyous chaos in her wake.

Ink glanced back at Joy from his side of the door. "I almost feel sorry for them," he said as they watched their friend sprint pell-mell for a saddled creature with a brown eagle head and a lionesque body. It hissed and lunged for her. Filly raised her arms and sang out like a lover, *"Gyrefalcon!"* It reared and brought its front paws crashing down, its sharp claws gouging holes in the turf. It gave an offended shriek as Filly slipped smoothly to one side, grabbed a hold of its bronze harness and launched herself onto its back. She deftly hooked a foot into its stirrup and unholstered a spear in one hand. She yelled something triumphant as the creature sprang into the air, a hundred-foot wingspan snapping a great shadow, and twisted in an attempt to dislodge her. The horde of ground troops pursued.

Ink grinned, both dimples. "Almost sorry, but not much," he confessed.

"Let's go!" Joy urged and Ink followed, pushing through the wobbling membrane of the door into Faeland. She held her breath as she jumped, feeling the filament shear over the surface of her skin. She landed, her held breath punched in her lungs. She stared at her feet. The ground stayed solid.

She took a step. Nothing. Joy exhaled and ran.

The landscape had changed again, as if turning counter-clockwise, revealing strange new turf and a changing sky. Joy didn't stop to admire the thick tendrils of autumn-colored clouds, the spires of green glass in the distance or the enormous mountain caves glowing with dragon heat. They dived toward an outcropping of stone she hadn't remembered seeing before, worn by nothing more than memories and dreams. It was as if it had been created for the purpose of shelter, a shadow of something that might have been in a storybook back on Earth. Joy had a crazy thought, wondering if Faeland itself remembered where they'd come from.

Ink and Joy ducked beneath the lip of stone and looked for the tents and yellow banners snapping over the court-yard from a distance. Joy couldn't see them from here, but she did see the roofs of the sugar-spun castle so she knew where they had been.

"Well, that worked," Joy said. "So far, so good."

"May this work as well," Ink said, unrolling the wizard's scroll and placing Joy's hands firmly on the dowsing rod. She felt his hands as warmth and pressure, missing something through the glove. "Hold firm. This is wizard magic—I am uncertain what it will do."

"As long as it finds my brother," Joy said, "the rest doesn't matter."

Ink paused. "Be careful what you wish for. Especially here, Joy Malone."

"Right," she said, chagrined.

"Do not make me break my promise to Monica," Ink said. "I hear she has thumbscrews."

Joy smiled as he curled his hand over hers and read the words on the parchment. The language was something old and slithery. The sounds dripped from her ears into her limbs down into the wood itself, playing over the worn grain like water through a maze, pooling in the tiny divot darkened with her blood. The droplet deep in the wood pulsed once, twice, like a tiny heartbeat—one which made Joy's own missing heart ache—and then it ignited, flaring along the dowsing rod and shooting a narrow beam of blood-red light out the end, which faded several feet in front of them like a penlight into the dark. The power of the spell shivered under her palms. It tugged like Kestrel, keen for the hunt.

"This way," Ink said as he lifted her elbow up and they started running.

The buzz turned into tremor as they kept going east, if the sun was anything to go by. Joy's eyes locked on her hands and Ink's hand locked on hers, which was locked on the wand. He kept scanning the landscape, directing her by touch. The blood-colored light swerved and Joy's elbows twisted, her forearms wrenching sideways. They wove their way into tall, furry grasses that were like nothing Joy had ever seen before, the scent pouring off them something between wildflowers and wheat.

Ink's hand on her shoulder pushed her down into a crouch. They ducked low under cover of swaying purple grass. Joy could hear voices and footsteps crashing through the field. They waited until the sounds passed, the buzz in her joints growing deeper as the dowsing rod quivered. She held still for a count of ten. Twenty.

Ink squinted up at the sun, his black eyes flashing pale gray. He tapped her gently with the side of his razor and pointed the direction of the spell. "This way."

They skirted a lake, avoiding trees filled with dryads, flocks of pixies that looked like butterflies and cairns of stones that turned out to be hill giants, asleep. As the dowsing rod led them through the odd countryside, Joy realized most of the verdant paradise was alive—living, thinking beings, all potentially hostile and loyal to the King and Queen, all the people that she was trying to set free. Would they help her if she asked? Would they kill her if she were caught?

Joy didn't want to find out.

The light veered again, leading them into a monstrous thicket, like a wall of tangled vegetation, dense and protective. Ink tucked Joy close against him, the vibrations drumming into his chest, echoing hollowly under his voice.

"Stay close."

He lifted his razor and slashed down with great, looping swirls—almost like a dance as they plunged forward, cutting giant swaths out of the hedge. Joy stayed inside the cup of his shoulder as he hacked his way almost effortlessly through the tangle of branches and leaves, praying quietly that nothing in here was alive the way that they were. She kept her eyes averted against potential glares and screaming.

Ink switched hands with a reverse-handled grip as the tremors grew sharper, the light lengthening as if it could reach between the branches and touch a finger through the leaves.

They broke through the foliage into sunlight and laughter. A girl with a blush of blue skin, short hair and pointed ears gasped and dropped her basket of fruit. Startled, Joy let go of the rod. It shot forward, bounced off the girl's arm and fell to the ground, inert.

The girl stumbled back, rubbing her arm. "Ouch."

Ink tucked his blade behind his back and held Joy tight against his shoulder to hide it. The girl stared at them both and then coughed on a laugh. The gills on her throat fluttered. She was a water nymph.

"Ow," she said, pressing a hand to her chest and squeezing out another little laugh. "Oh. You scared me!"

"Um," Joy said. "Sorry."

They stood on the edge of an inlet ringed in jeweled fruit trees, the heavy scent of apples a strange autumn smell in the midst of spring. The fruit itself was yellow-gold and garnet red, the glistening leaves were faceted like diamonds and all around them was the hum of giant, fluffy bees. Waifish children played in the branches, kicking their feet and hanging upside down while older teens gathered the fruit and tickled one another, splashing under a thin, clear waterfall dripping with moss. There was no sign of Stef or Dmitri or anyone over age thirteen. It was as if they'd stumbled into a childhood memory, playful and free.

"You're lost," the girl said, pointing to the left. "The hedge maze is that way. Unless you're looking for the Lovers Lock, which is back the way you came." She blushed a deeper sapphire, her sea glass eyes sparkling and mischievous as she gathered a few of the fruits and shells that had spilled out of her basket. Golden apples with hints of pink and green nested among seashells that matched the color of her hair. She picked up the dowsing rod from the moist carpet of green. "Here. You dropped your—" she turned it over curiously "—stick." She held it out. Joy took it back carefully. Ink seemed at a loss for words. He stared at the girl, at the fruit, at the waterfall, the shells and the trees and the sky. He looked like he was trying to put a puzzle together in his head.

Joy tried not to panic. *Where's Stef?*

"Thanks," Joy said, flashing her Olympic-class smile. The girl smiled back.

"No problem," she said and chose an apple from her basket. "Want one?"

Joy hesitated, remembering the wine at Enrique's funeral. She'd asked whether it was safe to eat or drink, given the old fairy-tale stories. *You are not in Faeland*, he'd said. But now she was, and she was well aware that some stories could be true.

"No, thank you," Joy said quietly. The water nymph wasn't hostile, she was young; not young like Filly or having the appearance of youth like the *guilderdamen*, but genuinely innocent as an ordinary girl of maybe twelve or thirteen. Joy knew that the Folk aged differently than humans, but this was the first time she'd ever met one who might actually be a kid.

A kid who was looking at them with a suspicious twist to her lips. "I don't know you," she said. "I haven't seen you before."

That's our cue. Joy tugged Ink's sleeve. "Probably not."

"Are you from the Hinterlands? Or maybe the Dells?" The girl propped the lip of the basket against her hip. "Everyone's been gathering here since the door opened, but I'm local and so I can tell you we're still not allowed through."

Ink stopped, ignoring Joy's gentle prodding. "Why not?"

"I don't know," the girl said. "The King and Queen won't allow it. They said we have to wait. *Again*." The way she said it convinced Joy that she was certainly adolescent; no one could fake exasperation like that. The girl shifted her feet, her skinny legs planted wide. "And it's not fair! Some of us have *things* to do—" Her eyes narrowed meaningfully, like an unspoken secret between them. "*Important* things."

Ink took a bewildered step closer. The chain at his hip tinkled like bells. "Such as?"

"Like—" Her eyes clouded over, confused and petulant. "I don't know." The cloud lifted, her delicate face clear. "But it's important." Her voice lilted like a question. "Really important. I can feel it—I *have* to go back. You'd understand if you knew."

A creeping calm flowed through Joy. "You mean you can't remember?"

"Sort of." The young girl sighed, trying to find the words. "Ever get the feeling like there's something you're supposed to be doing, but you can't remember exactly what?" She glanced at them, touching the tiny charms piercing her ears. "You know what I mean, right? That's what's bringing most of us to the doorway. Ever since the locks opened, it's like...I've lost something over there and I have to go find it." She rearranged the apples and spoke into the ground. "The Eight say this means I have a responsibility..." She waved her wrist vaguely. "Back there." Her voice changed as the indignation returned. "But I *can't remember what it is*—none of us can! And we can't *do* it if we're not allowed to Return!"

"The Eight?" Ink repeated.

"Well, Nine, I suppose," the girl said, then her eyes brightened. "The youngest princess came back—to warn her family, they said—and so we know that the Middle Land is still out there, still waiting for us, and not destroyed after all, but we don't know if it's safe." She kicked at a clump of moss. "All we want is permission to go home. But until they say yes, we have to stay. That's why everyone's coming here, just wait-ing by the door. There's no breaking the rules." Her voice became dreamy, thick with longing. "I hear it's beautiful."

"You've never been there?" Joy said, but stopped herself. She thought that this was the land of the dead, the after-world of the otherworld, but the tween's blushing cheeks and pointy ears and cowlick curls didn't look dead. She sounded very much alive.

"I'm not *that* old," the girl laughed and pointed off to the bumpy horizon. "I was born in the bay near Cloud Peak."

Ink held up a hand to hush the world. "You were *born* here?"

"But—" Joy swallowed her next words, because they were both telling and untrue. *That's impossible!* She knew that no Folk had been born in the Twixt for over a thousand years—Graus Claude had said so and the Council had confirmed it. It was considered a delicate subject in polite society. Even if this nymph was older than she looked, "that" old would be about a thousand years. Before the Dark Ages. Around the time of the Retreat. About when...

The words slipped out. "When the door closed," Joy said. "That's when it stopped."

Ink stared at Joy. The girl blinked. Her nose twitched.

"Where did you two say you're from, again?"

"You were born here," Ink said, ignoring the question. "On *this* side of the door." He wove his fingers over his wallet chain, each link a separate thought. "The door was closed, locked against any magic coming in—but it also prevented anyone, anything from going out." He pinched a single sil-ver link. "You're here. You are all here," he murmured, his eyes reflected the colors of the world as a smile teased his lips. "You are all very, very *here*."

The water nymph frowned, her fingers pale on the basket. "Um, okay."

But Joy saw it, too. "No one could Return," she whispered. "After death. They were all trapped here."

Ink smiled, one dimple. "A one-way trip."

Joy glanced at the girl. "What are you called?"

The nymph looked frightened now, unsure; her answer was like a shield. "Coral." She squinched her eyes and took a step back. "Why?" Shells and apples wobbled in her basket. "Do I know you?"

"I don't know," Joy said. "Do you?"

"You seem...familiar." Coral confessed. "Ish. Familiarish. Like maybe we've met before, but I think I would have remembered. I think I *might* remember...but I don't." She hesitated, taking a shy doe step closer. "It's like your face is someone else's face, but not your face. It's something else. Like you're someone I ought to know."

Joy swapped a glance with Ink. "Maybe you do." She glanced around the orchard. She pointed the rod around the inlet. "He isn't here, but it led us here—right here—to her. It was pointing right at her." She felt her breath quicken. "Ink—?"

"You know her," he said with certainty. "And she knows you. A lifetime ago and a different face."

Joy's voice hitched. Tears blurred her eyes as she was confronted with sudden understanding.

"Who are you?" Coral asked.

"We're family," Joy said as the dowsing rod dropped to the ground.

TWENTY-THREE

"WE HAVE GOT TO SEE THE KING AND QUEEN," JOY said, pulling Coral's hand. "We have to tell them. Then they'll *have* to Return—Stef, the King and Queen, all of them, right?" She glanced at Ink, who sheared their way through the wilderness. "Right?"

"You can convince the King and Queen to Return? You're *sure*?" Coral sounded delighted. Well, delighted and scared. Joy wasn't certain that the nymph would come with them, but the Folk's natural curiosity had worked in their favor; making daydreams come true pushed them up a notch. "I didn't think that anyone could convince the King and Queen of *anything*."

"Joy is special." Ink spoke over his shoulder, away from the reeds that rimmed the water's edge. Joy could hear distant laughter beneath the bubbles and waves, her *eelet* picking up more as they went. Faeland was pulsing with voices and magic and music. "She is the courier."

"What's that?" Coral asked.

"I'm bringing a message from the...Middle Land," Joy tried the phrase out. It fit on her tongue. It was true. "I have proof that it's safe to come home."

Coral skipped over a log filled with tiny, furry faces that peeped as they passed. "Really? What proof?"

"You," Joy said. "And my brother. We'll have to find him

next. But I can't use the spell until we can figure out how to have it not just point at you."

Ink changed direction, skirting the lake. "Do you think the spell will work?"

"Within three generations," Joy quoted Mr. Vinh. She shook her bangs out of her face, refusing to lose her grip on the scalpel or Coral's hand. The gloves made it feel like she might lose one or both at any moment. "I thought he meant the spell was guaranteed for three generations—like a hundred years or something—not that it would seek out my bloodline through three generations!"

Joy laughed at the mad thoughts whirling through her head. She should have felt relieved or brain-blown or ter-rified, but the truth was that she felt the kind of thrill she'd known only from Olympic training, when everything was on the line and it all came down to trusting herself, her instincts, her hunches and what she knew she could ac-complish.

I can do this!

"I don't understand," Coral said, stumbling to keep up.

"You were born here, but you're not from here," Joy said. "Or maybe you are. Over and over again!" Joy laughed, swal-lowing the taste of pollen and upturned earth. The world tasted like roses and tingled on her tongue. "But last time, you were born human and your name was Caroline."

"Caroline?" the girl said, now more curious than scared. "Who's that?"

"My great-great grandmother."

Coral gasped. Her gills flapped. "And she was human? You're a human?"

"Sort of," Joy said.

"She is a human with the Sight," Ink said, checking their progress. It seemed that Filly had driven her quarry into the lake. They could hear the explosive splashing and barked orders and whooping laughter and smell the water on the wind. "It runs in her family."

Coral stumbled after them, shaking her head full of curls the color of green apples. "But I was born *here*," she insisted. "That makes no sense—"

"It makes perfect sense," Joy said. "When Folk die, they return to Faeland. It's your afterworld, after all, and humans go to Heaven or whatever. *But* if a human has the Sight, that means we have a drop of faery blood—Folk blood—we're descendants, halfings or eighthlings or three-quarterlings, whose souls ends up in Faeland, too. When the Folk leave Faeland to go back to the Twixt, they protect humans with magic—" Joy's voice faltered "—those with the Sight or inherent magic or, maybe, they are Folk reborn. We're family and we look after one another over and over again throughout our lifetimes, protecting the magic by protecting *each other*. Marking people lets you know who was once one of you!" Joy followed Ink, dodging between trees. Joy hoped it was a trick of the light that some of the trees looked like they'd dodged first. "Maybe it's always been that way after death—the Folk come back and then Return." Her feet were flying, her thoughts outpacing her words. "They Return to protect their own!"

"Humans." Ink said. "Humans under auspice. Those who have the magic."

"Yes!" Joy said, crouching under a branch. "Humans go to Heaven. Folk come here. Those in between are—" he flipped her hand "—in between. They Return as the other and cycle anew."

"So you think I have the soul of your ancestor?" Coral asked.

"Maybe. Yes. Or the spell wouldn't have worked." Joy tried

not to think how crazy it sounded, but if the spell on the dowsing rod was correct, then it fit. Coral was Caroline, reincarnated on this side of the Twixt, stuck here behind a locked door, waiting to Return. It explained everything—the dwindling numbers, the endangered magic, the lack of babies and the Folk born here on the wrong side of the door. "If humans under auspice are reborn Folk, then people with magic are part of the Twixt, preserving their magic, their bloodlines, protecting their own—"

"Until they Return," Ink said. "Which they could no longer do when the King and Queen locked the door behind them." Ink redirected them one more time. Joy could see the distant yellow banners over the crest of the land. "They closed off Faeland."

Joy nodded. "A one-way trip with no Return."

Ink was caught up in the momentum. "The magic waned, the tethers grew weaker, their numbers grew fewer—"

"No more births," Joy said.

Ink nodded at Coral. "No more births."

"Are you *kidding*?" Coral said. "There are so many little ones, you can barely take a step for fear of tripping!"

Joy and Ink exchanged a glance. Ink shrugged.

"It is a way to pass the time," he said.

Joy laughed. "For a thousand years?" In her ear Inq's voice whispered, *Halflings happen!* She squinted through the last of their cover, looking down the final hill that sloped into the valley of the royal court's camp. How were they going to approach it without being seen? Joy could almost feel the hum of the doorway hanging in the air off to their left—everything was so close and yet she felt impossibly faraway. Her whole world had turned upside down while she was sitting still. They had to find Stef!

"Can you slice a doorway from here to down there?"

Joy whispered, still staring at the circle of tents outside the court clearing. There were dozens of people, soldiers, guards, armored mounts and more. This was a hive of activity and inside its heart, the King and Queen. If she could plead her case, then maybe they'd agree to bring Stef to her. They could have their proof.

Ink shook his head, the tips of his long bangs hardly moving. "I have never been there," he said. "And my magic will not work here, only human magic—wizard magic—as the Bailiwick said."

Joy glanced at him. "But your blades are working fine."

He shrugged. "Those are not magic, exactly." He tested the edge with the pad of his thumb. "I have been cutting our way with steel and strength."

"Are you kidding?" Joy traced the edge of a branch chopped neatly at an angle; the wood was sheared smooth, the bark sliced through without a splinter. It was moments like these when Joy understood that Ink wasn't human. Joy stared at the straight razor—the edge was jagged, pitted, broken. He'd been destroying his instruments for her. For Stef.

"You know better than most that the magic is not inherent to the tools we use. They are only as strong as those who wield them."

Joy touched his face, smooth under silk, his words brushing past her as she peered down into the valley. Careful not to touch the earth, she parted the stiff grass like curtains with her gloved hands. "So how are we going to get down there without being seen? It's too long to run and too open to hide." She wondered if her four-leaf clover had finally run out of juice.

Ink touched her shoulder, tender and halting. She looked into his eyes, deep pools of black with hot neon light. "Remember the gala—you want to make an entrance. You have already made quite the first impression."

Joy didn't think that should count. "The ground split open."

Coral gasped. "That was *you*?"

"Shh," Ink whispered, crisp and clean.

Joy stared at Ink. He'd never shushed anyone before. It sounded so human.

Ink raised his hand quickly and cocked his head, listening with his Joy-shaped ear. "Do you hear anything?"

Joy hesitated. There was not so much as a breeze in the air.

Ink's boots cracked against the ground as he crouched lower. It sounded so loud in the quiet. He mouthed one word: *Filly?*

He was right—Filly's distracting shenanigans had faded into silence. A warning chill shivered up Joy's arms under the full-length gloves, but then she realized that the tremble was coming from the ground. A quiver traveled up her boots, turning her knees and stomach to jelly. Her mind shrieked, *I didn't do it!* just before Coral screamed.

The hilltop boiled over, unflowering rather than splitting, chunks of earth and grass and root tearing up, rolling back, exposing the brown earth tumbling down. Joy knew she mustn't touch it—mustn't revel in the smell of it, the singing, malevolent power that ached to fill her up, to make everything roil and break and burn...

I AM VENGEANCE AND I WILL BE TRIUMPHANT!

No! She stumbled back. She mustn't let it touch her! She mustn't touch! Mustn't—!

Something snagged her knees, sucking in her feet, her legs, her hips before she realized the earth was pressed against her abdomen, squeezing her like toothpaste. She gave a gurgling scream. Coral fell sideways, still scream-ing a little-girl shriek, as Ink disappeared, swallowed un-derground.

There was just enough time for Joy to take a quick breath before the earth covered her head, shut her eyes and swal-lowed her whole.

TWENTY-FOUR

THEY CAME UP GASPING. JOY STUMBLED INTO INK, solid as stone, holding her steady as she raked earth from her eyes, her hair, her clothes, coughing and sputtering. Coral wiped at her face and sneezed, gills blasting, eyes tearing under the dirt.

Joy had a sudden jolt of panic. She'd been submerged under the earth—dirt caked her face, her arms, her skin. She braced herself to fight the craving, the rush of heat, the thunderous voices, the fury—but there was nothing. No feeling of power or pain. She was simply dirty, tumbled and tired.

They were in a bare circle of earth, the center of the court clearing, surrounded by tall soldiers in banded armor, crosshatched like layers of leaves. They had long beards of grass and stippled helmets like corn, their limbs ending in knotty clubs of wicked, hooked thorns. They'd emerged fully formed from beneath the ground, staring down at the three prisoners. Their eyes were single seeds with flower bud lids, surprisingly delicate in their stern, old-man faces.

"Our Majesties bid you kneel."

Coral dropped to her knee. Ink stood by her shoulder. Joy was too stunned to do much but blink through the grit. She coughed. "What?"

"Our Majesties bid you kneel."

The soldiers repeated the command, accompanied by clawed clubs raised in unison.

Joy hesitated. Ink followed her lead, his hand hiding the blade between his forearm and jeans. She knelt slowly, trying to peek past the lines of soldiers to the guards beyond them. Well, they'd wanted to make an entrance—this was it.

"Interesting," a female voice came from beyond the circle's edge. The soldiers withdrew, revealing guards, posted along the tents, who parted to reveal the King and Queen sitting at ease. Their hair fluttered in the soft breeze, their faces careful masks of beauty and time, with eyes the color of centuries.

The Queen rested like a portrait and only her mouth moved. "Rise."

Coral leaped to her feet. Joy and Ink cautiously stood. The Queen cast a coy glance at her husband, who gave the barest nod.

"Bring them," the King said, and the soldiers swept forward, ushering the three of them through the massive tent enclosure. Joy jostled against Ink and he took her arm, slipping something into her back pocket. The entrance was festooned in ribbons and flowers and plaits of gold. The air inside the tent was hot and still, almost stifling until rope pulls drew triangle flaps down from the ceiling, letting in light and fresh air as well as a cascade of flying critters that circled the perimeter, settling along the seams. There were two thrones on a low dais framed by a half circle of nine curved stools. The stools were empty except for the last two, which were occupied by a brown-haired satyr and a thin man in glasses.

"Stef!" Joy cried, rushing forward, but Ink caught her before the soldiers pushed her back.

Stef jumped to his feet, a thin, gold chain looped about

his neck clinking like Tinkerbell as he moved. The chain was connected to a ring on the dais floor. Dmitri touched his arm. The DJ wore a stiff robe tied with tassels and sat protectively close to Stef. A half-empty bowl of fruit at their feet was littered with rinds and pits. Dmitri smiled at Joy, shot her a finger-gun and winked, which might have been the strangest thing that had happened yet.

"I'm fine," Stef said quickly before a guard clapped a hand on his shoulder and shoved him back into the stool. Stef sat down solidly, adjusting his glasses and adding ruefully, "I'm fine."

"You!" Coral shouted, pointing a skinny arm at him. "I *know* you!"

There was an almost audible creak as all necks turned to Stef. No one was more surprised than he.

The Queen spoke softly, dangerously. "Do you know this child?"

"I— No," Stef glanced between the King and Queen and Dmitri and Joy. Dmitri cocked a wry eyebrow. Coral looked desperate, her gills fluttering. Stef sounded apologetic, both to Coral and the Queen. "No. I'm sorry. I don't."

"Yes, you do!" Coral insisted, pleading eyes turned to the Queen. "I know him!" She struggled to find the right words. "He's *mine!*"

Which sounded familiar and undoubtedly true.

"Enough," the King said. "Leave us." His gaze barely moved, but the cornstalk soldiers sank swiftly into the ground with a dramatic crunch, the upturned earth burying itself closed. The flock of winged pixies took flight, funneling out the open flaps, and the remaining guards filed out quickly and quietly, their shadows remaining like unsaid warnings along the tent's outer walls. A ward sparkled to life, enveloping the room, singing with gold dust and the buzz of summer bees.

The King flicked his wrist as someone from the back of the tent came forward.

Filly walked into the light, scratched and bruised, her arms secured behind her and her armor scuffed and soiled. One eye was puffy and swelling as she shifted her weight, favoring her left foot. She grinned. Her teeth were red with blood.

"This, then, explains your presence here," he said.

Filly shrugged good-naturedly. "Ah, well, couldn't evade them forever." She nodded her head. There was ichor on her braids. "Well met!"

"You have done your deed well, spear-bearer." The King almost smiled. Almost. "It is good to look upon your face once more." He opened his hand sharply, and the bonds that held her disappeared. His gaze slipped past her as she rolled her wrists. "You bring us hope," he said. "Here, at the edge of things. And we do not have much time."

The Queen did not look as impressed or pleased. Her spine was stiff, her manner brusque.

"You have returned," she said, a statement with implied inquiry. "Have you brought us proof?"

"Yes." Joy said, still tasting the grit of dirt in her mouth. "I think so."

"Do you mean this child?" the King said gently.

The Queen's gaze caressed Coral, who fell to her knees, eyes downcast. Her thin shoulders trembled.

"It's not her, but who she *is*," Joy said quickly, trying to spare the girl's terror. "Who she *was*—it means that we..."

"If you think this is the answer," said the Queen. "Then you are asking the wrong question."

Ink flinched. Joy sputtered. The royal couple looked unimpressed.

Joy cried, "Then you *know*?"

"Of course we know," the Queen said, a surprising flare of emotion cracking her mask like an egg. Her ethereal beauty became terrible, a storm of wonders behind jeweled eyes. "We've known for ages what we have wrought! It is the reason above all others why we must Return!"

The King addressed the water nymph, kindly but firmly. His voice had a flavor, a music all its own. "Go now to your family."

Coral peeked at Stef through her apple-colored curls.

"Soon, Water's Daughter," the King promised. "Until then, you will honor us with your obedience."

Coral quietly rose to her feet and bowed, averting her eyes as she scurried from the tent. Joy saw that there were tears and unanswered questions staining her face, not daring to look back at those she left behind.

"Who is she?" Stef asked from his seat. Joy stared at him and he stared back. "Joy?"

"Here she is Coral," she said, glancing at the monarchs. "Back home, she was Caroline."

Her brother's confusion flipped to wonder and then understanding and rage. Dmitri flinched at the look on his face. With the memories of their great-grandmother, the old hate returned.

"You could easily say it the other way around," the King said, placing a gentle hand on his wife's wrist. His manner exuded a preternatural calm of oceans and mountains unruffled by time. "By locking ourselves safely behind Faeland's walls, the cycle was disrupted, our people truly trapped. Once we had discovered our error, it was too late—the door was closed and our courier lost. Our hope was that the Council would determine that it was safe to Return before too much time had passed." His gaze remained focused, but it was as if he was looking through them into a distant past or future. "Unfortunately, the longer we waited, the more convinced we were that our people had perished, that the world had lost its magics and the door would only open in time for us to take up arms in their name." He turned slowly to his Queen, who had composed herself enough that the tears had absorbed back into her flawless gaze. "We were angry—very angry—but have been despondent ever since."

"When the children began to arrive, we knew our punishment was complete," the Queen said, her pain still clear. "Children are not born in Faeland—they are born in the world once they pass through this realm, but with nowhere to go, they were reborn here. This is not a place for us to tarry and by doing so, we condemned what remained of our kin to perish, either by human hand or slow extinction, abandoning that which we swore to uphold forever and always." She lifted her chin. "That was our third mistake."

Joy could feel Ink on the edge of her thoughts, *There are no mistakes.*

"Our second error was to lay foolish conditions upon our release, binding all of us to our word that we would not Return until such conditions had been met—when our people were 'safe' from human entrapment..." The Queen faltered as she looked more lovingly at her King. "We should have known better. With those words, we condemned ourselves and our people to remain on this side of the door until the Council brought word."

"Hence why we need you to find proof—irrevocable proof—that will pave the road for our Return," the King said. "Without that, we are all condemned to wait in paradise, even as we know our faithful few in the Twixt suffer because of our failures." The King and Queen held one another's hands like a single fist.

"And therein lies our greatest mistake," the Queen said. "By insisting ourselves inviolate, we became slaves to order. Without the flexibility of fallibility, we condemned ourselves and all our people." She straightened in her seat. "We destroyed those who chose to disobey our laws, who would not bend to our commands, an act of arrogance masked as righteousness—" She looked back the way that Coral had gone. "The Folk of the Wild, those who eschewed our order, were our other halves and yet, we called them enemies instead of kindred. We broke those who would not bend."

The King settled back in his chair, his hair wafting in intangible winds, catching blues and blacks and iridescent greens. "It was a grave error to declare war on the Elemental Wild." It was a confession that cost him to say aloud. "Our way required rules, and those rules came with a price. And we've paid it. The Wild Folk were our key to this lock, but we did not know that for what it was. Without them, we were lost." His gaze settled on Joy. "But now, you are here."

Filly turned sharply, looking at Joy with new eyes. Suspicious, wary, scary eyes.

"Your ancestors hid themselves in your blood," the King said kindly. "And now you are the answer to the long-awaited question, our broken promise, our penance, our chance to Return." His eyes were a thousand mirrors pointing inward, reflecting forever. She fell into their void, caught up in infinity. "In order to fulfill all of our destinies, you *must* bring us proof to undo the wrongs that are destroying our worlds."

The Destroyer of Worlds.

"She must obey your rules by breaking your rules," Ink said. It was as if his voice broke the spell. Joy blinked her dry eyes.

"Not so simply done, we admit, for it must be someone who can bend the rules, but is also loyal to us." The Queen's voice was just shy of mocking, but her eyes were sparkling, alive. "You are born human, with Wild magic in your ancestry, yet by accepting your True Name, you became part of the Twixt, the land of our Making, and thereby under our rule. You fulfill all the requirements, as I foretold." Her hair fanned around her, a corona of beauty and light. "You, child of Elementals, bringer of destruction, of correction, are the key to our salvation—all of our hopes lie with you."

"But we require our proof," said the King.

"The *signaturae*," Joy said, her voice rusty with awe. "The True Name sigils. That is your proof."

The monarchs wore twin expressions of hope and doubt. "Explain."

"You were afraid of entrapment by humans, afraid what they could do if they discovered your True Names, so Aniseed developed the *signaturae*, which could lock the power of your Names into a symbol, a glyph, that could never be spoken aloud, so that you and all your people would be safe." Joy gestured to Ink. "Your daughter invented the Scribes, who could draw these symbols on humans instead of the Folk doing it themselves, keeping them from risk of discovery and harm. Well, it worked. The *signaturae* work. They keep the Folk from being controlled. Once you accept a *signatura*, your True Name is safe." She chanced a look at her brother. "And I can prove it."

All eyes shifted to Stef. He shook his head. "No."

"You have to," Joy said. "You're like me—we're the same. It's part of us, part of our family." She knew he hated this, knew he hated them, but so much depended on his accepting this part of himself, not just for him but for them all. "You have to accept your True Name—" She glanced at Filly, who looked stern and unforgiving. Joy stammered under her glare. "—t-to be safe, to keep anyone from controlling you."

"I can't—"

"You *can*," Joy said. "And you have to. And if you can do it before the King and Queen, then they will have their proof."

Her breath churned inside her body, hollow without a heartbeat. It all came down to this.

Stef stood up, the golden chain dangled down his shirt. "I know what I am, what we are, and so when I say I can't, you know that I *can't*." He was her older brother, the person she trusted, looked up to, her entire life, and she couldn't doubt him, even in this. Stef turned to address the King and Queen. "Meaning no disrespect to Your Majesties. You know I have given my word to remain here, casting no magic, until the task set before my sister is completed, and you have accepted my word, knowing that here, I, too, cannot lie." He turned to Joy. "As a wizard, I have already taken a True Name—we call it something else, but it serves the same purpose—to protect ourselves and our powers from being manipulated by others of the craft. If that nymph is...who we think she is, then it all makes sense. If humans who have the Sight or magic, or those who are marked by Folk were Folk to begin with, then our magic obeys the same rules. Humans have just learned to protect themselves differently—" He gestured to Joy. "I would have shown you how, if you had told me. But you didn't know." Stef sounded tired, disappointed, as if this was one of his final secrets. "I wish I had told you everything from the beginning. If I had, I could have kept you safe."

Joy's throat tightened, her eyes watering. "So...you can't have a *signatura*?"

"No," he said. "I don't need one."

And what was unsaid was, *And neither did you.* The realization hurt, but she'd made her choices, her own mistakes, and her decisions—even the wrong ones—had made her who she was and, like the King and Queen, there was no going back...unless she broke the rules.

"You could take another oath," she said.

Stef shook his head. "In a paradox, the older spell—"

"—wins out." Joy finished. She knew that all too well, and so did all of the Twixt.

Her brother shook his head. "I'm sorry, Joy."

"I know," Joy said quietly before turning to the royal couple. "Then I can offer you no proof."

The King settled back on his throne. "Then you are dismissed," he said formally. "Until we meet again."

"And you will keep my brother safe?" Joy asked.

"I gave my word that I would stay," Stef said, settling back down in his seat next to Dmitri. "Willingly. Because I trust you." He smiled at her. It was humbling and scary how much he meant it and how much it meant for her to hear it. Stef pointed at her. "You can do this."

Joy nodded, holding back tears. "I know I can."

"Good," the Queen said. "Perhaps next time, you will prove your success."

"Well, you're not making it any easier," Dmitri spoke up. All heads turned. The satyr leaned back in his chair, wry and unapologetic. "She can't keep popping in here with the Bailiwick under wraps and the Twixt in a twist. She's already hedging the odds as is." Dmitri knew what was at stake on the other side of the stairs and Joy was grateful for it. "One whiff of this and she'll be hunted down by the very Folk you want her to save." He tossed a peach between his hands, sliding his thumb over the fuzzy flesh. "You want her to win? Give her some proof of your own that'll help grease the wheels."

"Wise words, Forest born," the Queen said, amused. "And I believe I have something that will suit." She reached up to her coronet and twisted a single, pale jewel that had no color and yet hinted at all of them. It fell into her hand as she flowed off the dais with inhuman grace, her fingers playing silent music as she bent over Joy. Her breath smelled of honeysuckle and wine. She pinched the small stone and drew out a fine gold thread from between her fingers, looping it around Joy's neck. The small stone rested against Joy's skin, tingly and cool.

"Wear this and they will know of me," the Queen intoned. "And I will know of you." Joy wasn't sure how she felt about the gift, but the Queen bent closer to whisper by Joy's ear. "I can watch over you, but I cannot interfere. But know this— there is a traitor amongst your company. Treachery taints the air around you like old perfume. Heed my words and be 'ware."

Joy stared at the Queen's impossibly beautiful face as she slid back to sit beside her King. Joy touched the stone with the tips of her fingers. It felt larger than it looked. She cast a nervous glance at Filly, who had heard everything. The Valkyrie's ever-present grin was gone, turning her chipper face stony and grave.

Wordlessly, the King gestured out the tent. The ward flashed and dissipated in a shower of colored sparks, raining from the ceiling and cascading down the walls. A burst of sounds and smells that had been kept at bay now overwhelmed them, as if to make up for their absence. The flaps peeled away, exposing a straight path to the doorway, lined with armed guards.

They were being sent home.

"Find the answer," the King urged, his words crisp and clear as any of Ink's whispers. "Find our proof, or none of us shall ever Return."

TWENTY-FIVE

"SO," GRAUS CLAUDE SAID AFTER JOY FINISHED RE-
porting her latest failure. "You are the Destroyer of
Worlds." A flash of indignation flickered and died behind
his eyes. "A changeling of prophecy, an Elemental in disguise, one who must obey the rules and also break them
in order to undo the mistakes of our past. An enigma, a
paradox, a near-impossible conflagration of contradiction
and circumstance." He grumbled and nodded. "Indeed,"
he concluded. "I cannot imagine anyone suiting it better."

"Should I be flattered?" Joy asked from one of the curv-
ing benches.

"Are you?" he asked.

"No."

"You should be," the Bailiwick said. "The Folk understand
power in terms of love or fear, and you have demonstrated
a knack for eliciting both. Suffice to say, your mission now
is to find the proof that the King and Queen require before
this secret is discovered and the Folk rally together around
a common purpose to kill you."

Joy twisted her fingers into knots. That wasn't the secret
she was most worried about.

"But if the answer isn't love or fear, then what is it?"
Joy said. "I thought showing them how Stef and Dmitri
could love one another despite everything would be proof

enough, but it wasn't. Then I tried the fear of being controlled, which I wanted to prove was no longer necessary,
because the system of *signaturae* works. But not only can't
a wizard accept a True Name, but the magic wouldn't even
work in Faeland. That's Folk magic, not human magic." Her
brain added, *Aniseed's magic,* but she didn't say it aloud. "I
can't think of a way to convince them that it's safe to come
back, that humans won't try to control them again!" Joy
said. "If I can find proof, then I can save them, and if I save
them, I save all of us, everyone."

I will not be the Destroyer of Worlds!

He shook his great head, a defeated slump weighing
heavily on his deformed spine. Ink said nothing, attempting to sharpen his ruined straight razor, his obsidian blade
having shattered into candy-sharp shards. Filly stared at
Joy as if she didn't recognize her, examining her as if from
a great distance, trying to make out her face from far away.
Joy wasn't sure if she could ever close that distance or if,
given the Valkyrie's expression, she would survive the
experience. Joy might not become an Elemental, but the
potential was enough to change her—in Filly's eyes—and
there was nothing she could do to fix that now.

"I can do this," Joy said, echoing Stef's words. "I will figure it out. Trust me."

Graus Claude stared across the water at the elaborate
tiles and carved walls. "If you cannot, then no one can, Miss
Malone," he said. "But I do not know if I should thank you
for it."

His fear was almost palpable, like the way he avoided
her eyes.

There is a traitor amongst your company.

Fear trickled down her limbs. *Graus Claude?*

No. If the Bailiwick betrayed her, Joy didn't stand a

chance. She depended on him, on his access to the doorway, on his contacts, his resources—yet all this time, he'd been hiding from her, avoiding her, ever since he'd left her home after his rescue from Under the Hill. An icy thought stabbed through her—what if he'd struck a bargain with the Council? What if he'd stayed with her under pretense, as a spy? What if this was all a ruse? What if he'd traded his knowledge of her for clemency? Protection? What if his despair was really guilt?

In fact, that was how he'd been acting—guilty. It hung on his shoulders.

Treachery taints the air around you like old perfume.

No.

Frowning, Joy stood up, her hands balled into fists. She whispered at his back, "Then don't bother, because you cannot lie."

The touch of Ink's hand urged her away. She'd been dismissed. Joy turned toward the stairwell, Idmona's boots making soft scrapes across the floor. Ink walked backward, behind her, covering her exit, shielding her back from her friends, her allies, those whom she trusted the most, those closest to her missing heart.

Joy stopped. Touching the jewel at her throat, she turned back. "Do you know what this is?"

Her question floated through the silence like fog over the key-shaped pool.

"Yes. I know it," Graus Claude confessed.

After a pause, Joy asked, "Are you going to tell me?"

Graus Claude considered the question as the water slapped gently against the tiles.

"No."

Joy sighed, feeling the chasm between them growing wider, darker, deeper, but all she could do was go forward, climb the steps back to the daylight and the human world; the store-front, the garbage-strewn streets of San Francisco's China-town and the lantern-strewn alley where she'd slip through a flap of nothing toward home. She cast one long look back into the depths of the Bailiwick's sanctum, his prison, his fear.

Filly watched them go from her post by the door. Arms crossed, eye swollen, face a mask of determination—to do what, Joy didn't know, but she wasn't eager to find out. She didn't know what to say to the blond warrior as they passed. Filly, for her part, didn't even wave goodbye.

The lack of a brash *Victory!* felt more like *Be damned!*

They appeared in the stairwell to her condo. Joy wiped away tears with shaking fingers. The confidence she'd gained from Stef's belief in her had shriveled under Filly's grim stare and silent dismissal. Ink offered his hand and she threaded her fingers through his.

"What if it's him?" Joy said. "Graus Claude?"

"I cannot believe—"

Joy wrung their hands together. "Then who else?"

"Well, aren't you just the cutest couple?" Inq gushed, pushing away from the wall outside Joy's front door. She tapped one high-heeled boot against the slightly mil-dewed carpet and toyed with a long strand of black pearls. "I would've waited inside, but you've got company."

"Dad?" Joy hadn't yet thought up an excuse for Stef's trashed room. She'd had a lot more pressing things to think about. Her brain stalled.

"Yes, and a lady friend, but that's not important," Inq said. "It looks like I interrupted something serious."

"It seems we may have a traitor in our midst," Ink said. "More than one warning has been issued and more than one coincidence has become suspect."

Inq's mouth became a hard line. "Any idea who?"

Joy sighed. "I think it's the Bailiwick."

"The Bailiwick?" Inq said. "Well, I hope for your sake that you're wrong, but you ought to get inside before we go looking for any boogeymen under the bed."

Joy hesitated. "There such things as boogeymen?"

Inq patted her arm. "Don't be silly," she said. "They're not really called that." She grinned. "Anyway, I need to borrow my brother for a quick trip and wouldn't dream of kidnapping him until you're safe behind wards."

Ink frowned. Inq might have been waiting for Ink to become sentient for hundreds of years, but she hadn't quite gotten the idea that this meant he had a life of his own. Still, Joy knew Ink felt guilty for not telling her about the off switch. He owed her big-time.

"You are very considerate," Ink said with measured politeness.

Inq crinkled her nose playfully. "Aren't I just?"

"Joy—"

"Don't worry," Inq said. "She'll be fine." She hooked an arm through Ink's elbow. "A little recon trip—nothing major. Be back in a jiffy. Oh, and you might want to brush your teeth before you say hi." She winked. "Ta!"

"Stay inside the wards," Ink said as Inq raised her hand. "It will only take a m—"

And they were gone.

For all Inq's lighthearted quips, Joy suspected something was wrong. It pricked her nerves as she fished around for a mint, but only found a pack of gum. The taste of morning-mouth-plus-spearmint reminded her that she hadn't had breakfast or, more importantly, her terrible tea. Shelley might have brought something over, but given Dad's diet, Joy doubted it would be strong enough to blot out the yuck.

She opened the door and quickly shut it behind her, watching the ward settle comfortingly into place.

"Joy," her father said from behind her.

"Hi, honey."

Joy whirled around, eyes wide.

"Mom?"

Her mother smiled at her from the kitchen table. "Welcome home."

Joy missed the beginning of the conversation. The blood rushing in her ears had drowned out all sounds; her head felt cottony and wrong. She sipped her lemon water and forgot how it got there. She wondered if this was some illusion but, in case it wasn't, decided not to start waving around her scalpel as that might be hard to explain.

For now, she just stared.

"So...?" Joy couldn't remember what they were talking about. She had kissed her mother, hugged her and sat down. She could still smell the vanilla flowers of her mother's perfume.

"Your father said you'd be home eventually," her mother said, straightening her skirt. "We've just been catching up."

Dad looked pained, but okay. Things were strange, but civil. How long had they been waiting for her? How long had she abandoned her father to face her mother alone? Joy should have been here. She should have rescued Stef. She should have convinced the King and Queen to Return. She should have been able to fix everything, but she kept falling short across the board.

She got up to make some of Vinh's vile tea. She needed something to snap her out of this weird alternate reality where her mother was in the same room as her father at the kitchen table, eating cheese and crackers like some TV picture of normalcy.

"Well..." Mom smiled, politely. "Now that we're all here, I wanted to discuss something with both of you. I'm only sorry that I missed Stefan before he left. I didn't think he'd be headed back to campus so soon." She shrugged, as if it were simply a matter of bad timing. She didn't know that he was being held for ransom by the King and Queen of the Twixt.

"I've been waiting for her to tell me her news." Dad tried sounding chipper, but it came out strained. "But you know that I've been saving the rack for a special occasion."

"Oh, Jack," her mother said softly. "I wanted Joy to be home. Especially after—after last time." A flicker of doubt, of shame, cracked her sunbaked facade, and Joy knew that whatever was coming was going to be more than she could handle.

She took a drink.

"Gah!" Joy said, scraping her tongue across her teeth. The flavor was impossibly worse each time. Her parents stared at her outburst. Joy's taste buds writhed in disgust. "I need pie," she managed. "You want pie? Cake? How about cake? I can make cake." Joy didn't know where the words were coming from, but she threw them up like bricks. She circled the counter, pulling drawers open blindly, rattling bowls and baking pans.

Her father sighed, "Joy—"

"I don't want cake," her mother said. "Or pie. Please, listen—"

"No, *you* listen!" Joy said, brandishing a whisk in one hand. "You can't just show up here and talk to Dad and have something important to say without Stef being here because *I've been there* and you *can't do that!*" The tears that came now might have been from before or might be fresh and new, special for the occasion. "He should *be here!*" Joy shouted. It meant more than they could know. "You can't just *tell* us something important and have him not *be here,*" she fumed. "We're *family!* That's just *mean,* Mom. That's *cruel.*"

Her mother's face flushed red—Joy had inherited her tell from her mom, and it didn't look good on either of them. "Joy," she said flatly. "I told your father I would be coming. I thought he'd told you both, and I've crossed an entire continent in order to do this right." She glanced at her ex-husband and her daughter. "For once, I'm trying to do it right. Okay?"

"Then say it," Mr. Malone said softly, road-weary and kind. He was stronger now, older, wiser—more generous right now than Joy thought she'd ever be. "Say what you need to say." The unsaid might have been, *and then go,* but he'd never say it aloud.

Her mother straightened her blouse, her lips trembling between a smile and a frown. "I'm getting married," she said. "Doug asked me to marry him and I said yes. I wanted you to know, and I want to have you there."

Joy was glad for the countertop, a physical barrier between them. She didn't trust herself to be as calm and forgiving as her father right then. She watched him lean across the table and open his hand to her mother. She placed her hand in his; neither of them wore rings but the imprint was still visible, even after two years apart.

"Congratulations," he said with his sincerest smile. "I am happy for you both."

Her mother's face broke, tears blurring her mascara. "Really, Jack?"

"Really," he said. "I don't know if I can make it to the wedding, but I'd appreciate a plus one on the invite."

"Of course." Joy's mother sounded flustered.

Joy came out from behind the counter. She left the whisk in the sink.

"Congratulations," she said weakly and accepted another hug. It was surreal. She squeezed her mother tighter, trying to convince herself that this was real even though a part of her prayed for it to be an illusion, a Folk trick, a prank. It *felt* real, it looked real, it smelled real, but it sounded thick and swimmy, fluttering like a tiny, beating heart and that couldn't be real...

Unless.

Joy pushed away from her mother.

Unless.

She pressed a palm flat against her chest. No. Nothing. It wasn't her.

Joy dropped her hand and gawped at her mom. "You're *pregnant*?"

Her mother jerked back. "What? How—?" She glanced worriedly at Joy's father, who sat down heavily in his chair. "It's only been ten weeks. And it's a high-risk pregnancy, so we weren't really sure if, well..." She trailed off and touched her waist. "Does it show?"

"*Mom!*" Joy shrieked, and then she was laughing. Mom was laughing. Dad was getting out glasses. Joy had reached her limit—she'd gone all the way from impossible to terrified to ridiculous and back out again. *This is real!* She could hear the baby's heartbeat through the *eelet* and knew that life would never be the same.

But, maybe, it could be better.

They talked into the night over white wine and brownies. Her mother even showed Joy how to bake them using parchment paper so that the edges still crisped but didn't stick to the pan. It was as if something broken had healed and then broke again to let go, because while her parents would never be together again, maybe at least they could be friends, and if not that, then perhaps live in the same universe with less painful memories between them. Joy tried to believe that might be true for everyone in the Twixt because, despite everything, they were all family.

Somewhere past midnight, Mom called a cab and Joy hugged her at the door. Her father joined her at the kitchen window and waved down into the lot as the taillights faded around the bend. Joy leaned over the sink, trying to catch a last glimpse. Her mother had a red-eye scheduled to get back to LA, her fiancé and her new life 2.0.

"Well," Mr. Malone said, placing the glasses in the sink. "That was exciting."

"Yeah." Joy leaned against his shoulder. "You okay?"

"I'm okay," he said. "But I think I might need to call my girlfriend so I don't feel like a *complete* loser."

Joy mock-punched him. "Dad—"

"Now, now, save the pity party. I'm just suffering sugar crash." He smiled and patted his stomach. "I don't think I've had that much chocolate in the past six months." He pinched the bridge of his nose and rubbed his tired eyes. "Oh, Shelley's going to *love* this."

"My advice? Drink lots of water," Joy said, reaching up to the cabinet to get the Advil. "You're going to get a headache."

"Going to?" he scoffed. "What do you think *that* was?" He laughed a little as he shook a couple of pills into his hand. "Oh, your mother—she sure knows how to make an entrance. But it's over." He swallowed them with a glug of water. "It's finally over. Whew!" He glanced at his daughter, and Joy tried to smile. "And that's good, really, because now I feel like I can *finally* start living my life without waiting for the next shoe to drop." He tucked one arm around her shoulders. "There's a few good years left in your ol' Dad—let's see what he can make of 'em!" He grinned and Joy laughed.

"I love you, Dad."

"Yes, I know," Dad sighed. "Which is why I waited until your mother left the building to bring this up. The super called yesterday."

Joy stopped. She twisted her fingers in her shirt. "Oh?"

"Mmm-hmm. He wanted to know what happened," her father continued patiently. "I said, 'about what?' He said 'to the wall.' And I said, 'What wall?' And he said, 'Exactly.'"

Joy's stomach slid south with a cold, wet feeling. "Oh," she said.

"'Oh'?" he repeated. "That's all you have to say? 'Oh'?" Her father leaned against the cabinet, stress underlining his voice. "Mind telling me what happened to *the wall*, Joy?"

The wall. Her brother's wall. The one with the giant hole.

"Um—"

He brushed past her, reaching for Stef's door. Joy jogged forward, trying to get a step ahead, but the hallway was too narrow and she was too late.

"What wall, you may ask?" he said. "*This* wall, Joy!" He wrenched the door open. Joy saw the gaping hole, the stretched plastic, the blue painter's tape. "I had to have the entire window removed so the contractors could replace the struts."

The window was gone. The windowsill. The sigil. The ward...

And that's when Joy saw what crouched inside.

"*DAD!*"

Joy shoved her father out the doorway. The smiling faces were full of teeth and claws and glowing eyes, and there were at least four of them backlit by open air and street-lights. She slammed the door on a tentacle. Something inhuman shrieked. The door buckled with scrabbly noises and screams.

"Joy?"

"Dad, go to your room!"

Grabbing a can of Lysol from the hall closet, she popped the top and sprayed it into the crack under the door. There was a high whistle-whine. She stomped on another append-age snaking up through the carpet. There was a huge *THUD!* The doorjamb cracked.

"Joy! What is it?"

She toed off her flip-flops and wedged them under the door, kicking them tight for good measure. "Dad, go! Just go!" She pushed her father back. As she ran into her room, Stef's door splintered, exploding out into the hall. Joy grabbed her lamp and a snow globe, diving back into the hall, standing between the creatures and her father. They were blocked from the kitchen and the scalpel in her purse. She lifted her two projectiles and stared down the scaly gargoyle in the lead. A lizard thing made of rope coils hissed and scaled the wall while conjoined twin stick-figures wafted forward on ghostly tendrils, dragging strips of dangling cloth.

Behind her, her father stared right through the Folk at Stef's ruined door.

"Joy—?"

Joy spoke quickly. *"Duei nis da Counsallierai en dictie uel-laris emonim oun!"* As the courier, she should still be under the Council's protection, but it might not be enough to give the monsters pause. The gargoyle dipped its head, its tail curling up and over like a scorpion. The lizard hissed and shied back.

"Dad! Duck!"

Joy dropped to the floor, flattening against her father, pushing them into the wall and down. A volley of spikes buried themselves in the framed photograph above their heads. Glass shattered, forcing them to shield their eyes. Joy threw the snow globe blind, hitting the gargoyle in the face. The globe broke against his temple, spraying stale water and glitter across the floor. The lizard crushed the plastic base beneath its slipknot foot. The coils of its leg unspooled and slithered toward her. Joy felt one loop tie around her ankle and pull. She dropped her weight and shifted as it spun up her calf.

Her father huddled on the floor, staring up at the wreckage, struggling to understand.

"Joy!" he barked. "What's happening?"

The lizard opened its mouth and its tongue shot out, snagging her upper arm like a lasso. Clenching her teeth, she fought against being dragged forward toward the eerie masked pair. Her father shouted something. The air hissed with noise. The walls cracked, the carpet tore, the ceiling crumbled, raining bits of plaster and paint. Joy wrapped her hand around the lizard's tongue, slick with spittle, and sank her nails in. Taking a launch step, she pivoted, driving her knee into the gargoyle and her fist down the lizard's throat. Kicking off the nearest jamb, she gained a few inches and brought the lamp slamming down, smashing the twin leering faces, pulping the porcelain into dust.

The gargoyle grunted. The lizard gagged. The twin floating bodies collapsed in a heap. Joy grabbed the lizard's tongue in the back of its throat and whipped his head hard against the gargoyle's back. The animated twine slackened. Joy quickly wrapped their limbs together. She anchored her bare foot on the gargoyle's hip and straightened, straining, pulling them taut. Both monsters struggled in desperate knots, clawing and snapping as Joy tried to pry her wrist free, but she was too tangled up.

The three of them slammed against walls as they ricocheted down the hall. Joy fought to free one hand, to grab something in the kitchen, but a scaled claw grabbed her shoulder, digging deep, as another sought her eye. Joy grunted, bent her knees, shifted her feet and pushed, bending back as far as she could go, arcing into a deep C. Her head banged against the corner. The lizard scrambled under the gargoyle's hooked feet.

"Joy!"

Stef's shattered door opened, cutting off her view of her father's shocked face.

Ladybird's crimson greatcoat flared behind him as he strode into the hallway, giving a slow golf clap. His hands sparkled with gaudy rings.

"Very impressive," he purred. "Well met, indeed!" He smiled his chitinous grin. "I said we'd meet again, Nightingale. And—lo!—here we are—" he gestured around him "—in your most charming abode!" The small, black spots dotting his hairline and jaw shifted as he spoke. "I confess I felt quite slighted when you could not join me earlier, but this is much cozier." He glanced around the littered hall. "I love what you've done with the place! A little rough around the back entrance, perhaps." He gestured over his shoulder at Stef's room and shrugged. "It's so hard to find good help these days."

His feet kicked up a jig, an unexpected burst of merry madness. The buckles of his boots flashed as a skein of rope looped over her jaw, yanking against her chin. Ladybird swooped so close that she could smell the gritty sharpness of the drugs on his breath. "You'll never guess why I'm here," he leered. "Tick-tock-tick-tock. Ding ding ding! Time's up!" He giggled. "The ante's gone up, my dear, and there are ever so many Folks who want to get their hands and paws and claws on *you.*" His golden eyes narrowed menacingly as his lip curled. "And this time there will be no escape."

He punched her cheekbone hard. Her head snapped back, exploding in a shock of pain and light. Her grunt was muffled under the rope. Her nose streamed. Her eyes ran. The gargoyle laughed—a dry, chalky sound. Its claws dripped a viscous yellow fluid that smelled sharp and hot. Another coil slipped over her throat. Joy redoubled her efforts, straining against her constraints. She could feel the fury building like the ringing echo where he'd struck her in one ear. Her breath hissed through her teeth as Ladybird's gloved fingers peeled the ropes off her lips, scraping her gums, and gently gathered her hair into his fist.

"Come now, pretty bird, before we fly away—let me hear you *scream.*"

An implosion filled the hallway with scarlet smoke. Warding lines shot like lasers, piercing the smog and spraying broken, fractal patterns over the ceiling and floor. There were bellows and shouts, hisses and screams. Joy's head jerked back and her eyes watered as the jagged, ragged pictograms collapsed into a black-white hole on the floor. The viscous smog suctioned to a pinpoint, pulling at her hair and the rope and the red coattails, vacuuming up color and sound, whipping past her face until it disappeared with a pop.

Joy hit the floor. Bits of wood and glass fell around her, bouncing off the carpeting and tinkling against the tiles. She sat up slowly, blinking around the condo and the broken thing on the floor. It might have been a Christmas ornament, full of strange writing and painted swirls, but the blast pattern beneath it was a starburst of soot. A faint crackling green fire licked its shattered, broken edges.

"Joy? Are you all right?" Her father was next to her, helping her up, wide-eyed. "Joy? Did I get it? Did it work?"

She found her footing, but not her train of thought. She stumbled. "What?"

Dad shook her slightly. "Look! Did I get them all?"

Joy's legs buckled, but he was holding her, steadying her, his arms tight and strong.

"Joy?" Her father sounded anxious and angry and unsure.

"Yeah," she whispered, staring around. "Yeah, Dad. You got them all."

He nodded. "Okay. Okay, then. Sit down." Her father placed her on a chair in the kitchen and hurried back to an old tin lunch box, which was now upturned on the floor. He pulled out a large baggie of coarse salt shot with black flakes and poured out a thick line in front of Stef's ruined door. He grabbed an extra handful and threw it into the room. His hands shook as he wiped them on his pants. His shirt collar was stained with sweat.

"That should hold them off," he said, as if it were part of a script, something he'd been told to say. "That's rock salt and ash from a pauper's grave." He looked at Joy for confirmation. "Think that will keep them out?"

Joy gaped at him. "You *knew*?"

Dad coughed into his hand. "Of course I knew!" he said. "I was married to your mother for fifteen years and we dated another three before that so, yes, I knew!" He cursed and wiped his eyes. "She told me years ago. And her mother confirmed it. Heck, her *grandmother* was locked away because of them. The Other Thans. The Fair Folk. Whatever they're calling them these days." He raked all ten fingers through his hair as he staggered into the kitchen. "It's like the McDermott family legend!" he shouted, disbelief and shock adding volume that rang in her ears. "Your grandmother gave me all this crap after the wedding in case we ever needed it, in case they ever came poking around." He shook his head. "I thought she was as crazy as her mother— as crazy as *your* mother—" He paused and gave an exasperated sigh, glancing back at the door. "Your *mother...*" Dad shook his head. "She left, but I kept it. Just in case. Good thing I did." He sat down heavily and wiped salt crystals from his palms. They bounced off the countertop, rolling like knucklebones.

The silence in that moment stretched with a million things unsaid. Joy's world had just cracked open and shattered like that thing in the hall. Everything was upside down and backward and she was pretty sure she'd skipped a step between here and then.

Her father washed his hands in the sink.

"What I don't understand is why you didn't *tell* me." His voice sank into a whisper as he shut off the water. Joy opened her mouth to say something, but there were no words. Her father's face changed. "Oh. Oh. Wait a minute. That night we went to the hospital. The thing with the eye? That's when it started, right?" Joy twisted her fingers in her shirt. She couldn't do anything but nod. Her father sighed again, some of the anger deflating. "And you thought you couldn't tell me."

"I—I wanted to keep you safe."

"Yeah," he breathed. "Yeah, that's what your mother used to say." He glanced around the kitchen as if just realizing where they were. "So, fairies, eh?"

"Yeah." She kicked her feet against the stool.

"And Mark... Ink? He's one of them."

Joy sniffed. Her head hurt. "Yep."

He nodded and glanced back at the ruined door. "I'm guessing this has something to do with why Stef hasn't called to say that he's arrived at school?"

"Yeah."

Dad wiped his hand over his face. "Well, better than a wreck on the highway," he said. "So where is he?"

"In Faeland." Joy couldn't believe those words actually made it past her lips. She couldn't believe she was having this conversation. With Dad. "He's safe," she added. "He's with Dmitri. He'll be home soon."

"Dmitri?" her father said. "I know that name."

Joy shrugged. "It was one of his imaginary friends…"

"When he was five," her dad finished for her and rubbed his eyes with his thumbs. "Oh, this is all starting to make sense now." He blinked up at the ceiling and undid his tie. Pulling it out with a *zip*, he picked up his phone and began typing slowly, pushing too hard. "I am taking a Personal Day," he said while pressing the letters one by one. "Then you and I are going to sit down and you are going to tell me everything."

Joy wiped at unexpected tears. "Everything?" she said. She hardly dared to smile. This was too impossible to be true—a feeling she remembered from their picnic in Abbot's Field, where the impossible became possible, Ink in a glamour shaking everybody's hands. "Everything is…a lot. And it's not all good." She squeezed her fingers together. "You sure?"

"Everything," her father said, and pulled her into a hug. "Nothing you say will change a thing, Joy, because I will always—*always*—love you."

Joy wrapped her arms around him, held on and cried.

TWENTY-SIX

JOY WASN'T SURE WHAT WOKE HER UP THURSDAY morning, but she was still tired; it was either too early or too late. She rolled over, trying to locate the clock and check the time, when she saw the shape of Ink in the dark. She reached out a hand. He accepted it gently. She squeezed his fingers, kissing the inside of his wrist.

"Joy?"

Shocked, she sat up, fumbling for the lamp that wasn't there. Then she remembered: she'd used it to hit twin some-things in the face. She remembered the gargoyle. The slimy-rope-lizard. The smell of Ladybird's breath.

Joy scrambled for the emergency flashlight under her bed and clicked it on. Avery stared back.

"Wha—?" Joy gasped, touching her hair, her clothes, the sheets—all there. She was absurdly glad that she'd fallen asleep fully dressed after her long talk with Dad.

Avery blinked and gestured back into the hall. "What happened here?"

"Oh," Joy said. "Long story. Short version—the ward was removed, we were attacked, we smashed a thingie, every-one vanished, the end." She'd expected Ink to appear by now. Wouldn't he have felt the breach in the ward? Where was he? Was he still out with Inq? Joy checked the clock: 5:20 a.m. She groaned and got out of bed. This conversation was awkward enough without having it lying down. "What are you doing here?"

"I may have found your proof."

Joy yawned. "What?"

"The proof you require to convince the King and Queen to Return," he said. "You said that would help."

"Yes. Right. Hold that thought," Joy said. She motioned for him to follow her into the kitchen. She stepped over the blurry blast pattern in the rug, careful not to step on any missed pieces they hadn't cleaned up from the floor. They'd covered Stef's door with black trash bags that now hung off the door frame by strips of tape. She glanced back at Avery, who looked unrepentant, his feathered cloak gliding over the wreckage like smoke.

She took out orange juice, a PowerBar and Vinh's herbal tea. None of it looked appetizing. She stuck a mug of water in the microwave and turned it on High.

"Okay," Joy said under the whirr. "I'm listening."

"I have been speaking amongst the Tide..." Avery paused at Joy's scowl. "Whatever you may think of them, they are traditionalists and purists and know much about the way things were during the age of the monarchy. I thought it might help to ask them about the glory days." He smoothed the feathers down off his shoulders. "They were quite forthcoming."

Joy removed the water and started mixing her sludge. "And?"

"The Folk are bound to protect this world's magic and that which possesses it—certain plants, animals, the land and its people—and I discovered that there are some remnants of that era that still remain, pure strains of the First Forest, for example, for which this place is named." Joy glanced up. Glendale was originally the Glen, a part of the legendary First Forest. Avery nodded. "I thought, perhaps, if you could show the King and Queen that we have still kept our word, kept those sacraments entrusted to our care, then perhaps they will know we have been successful in what matters most—that the magic has been preserved. Despite their reservations about human entrapment, encroachment or discovery, the Folk have kept the world safe for magic to survive." He gestured through the kitchen window where the sun was just coloring the sky. "We can survive here, together. Therefore, it is safe to Return."

"That's...brilliant," Joy said as she absently drank her tea. The taste woke her up enough to gag and stuff half the bar into her mouth. She raised a finger for him to wait as she glugged down some juice.

"That looks unpleasant," Avery said. "Does it work?"

She gasped for air. "Haven't changed yet."

"You have changed more than you think," he said. "The Twixt changes you, life changes you—people *can* change—perhaps not always in ways that are expected or wanted, but not always for the worse." Circling the counter, he came conspiratorially close. "Unfortunately, I'm not certain if my inquiries have alerted the others. The Folk are understandably nervous and may take precautions. Something is happening—it's in the air—the end of an Age is near. And many believe, quite rightly, that its outcome depends on you." Avery tucked the edge of his cloak in his fist, his snow-white hair fanning over his eyes. "Do you wish to go garner your proof?" he said, glancing at the kitchen table. "Or would you rather wait and take your chair?"

Joy frowned. She knew that she should wait for Ink, but something about Avery's taunt irked her. Did she trust him or not? She still had choices. She could still find proof, but she was running out of time. It was barely unsaid between them: *If you're the chosen one, prove it.*

Joy poured the tea into a tumbler, popped the top and grabbed her purse full of magic. She checked her phone and her scalpel and laced up her spider-silk-lined boots.

"Quickly," she said, grabbing her sludge. "Let's go."

They stood before the Glendale Oak. She shouldn't have been surprised. The giant tree was the town landmark and one of the last traces of the original Glen. A thick canopy of leaves applauded in the breeze as she and Avery dropped to the ground in a sudden rush of silver-blue and feathers. It was almost a shame no one else had seen them—it had been a graceful dismount, a good nine out of ten.

The Glendale Oak's massive trunk was riddled with names and high school sweethearts carved into its bark. It was where she'd often met Ink after school, and the first place she'd seen Aniseed, stretched out naked at its roots. Joy skipped her fingers over the ancient tree and pressed her palm flat against its scars. She tried to imagine when the land had all been forest, the whole of Glendale covered in trees.

"Okay," Joy said. "Now what?"

Avery craned his head back to look. "Bring them proof. How about a leaf?"

"A leaf?" Joy asked. "Why couldn't you have just brought me a leaf?"

"I cannot," Avery said. "This tree is sacred to Forest, and therefore also, to Earth. You have a right to it under your House, but I am of Air. It would be considered profane."

"Really?" Joy said, circling the trunk. Humans, obviously, had no trouble desecrating sacred Folk trees. She wondered which she had been when she'd touched it last—human or halfling? "What's sacred to Air?"

Avery grinned. "There are some places where Folk like you cannot breathe."

"Fair enough," she said. The oak branches were high, but many drooped at the ends, thick with autumn acorns. She stretched as high as she could, but she still couldn't reach. "Are you sure you couldn't just fly up there and shake one down with your foot?"

Avery twitched his cloak closer. "Definitely not."

"Okay," Joy said, taking out her scalpel. "Let's try something else." She tested the handle, feeling the crosshatched texture like an extension of her hand, and looked for a likely target that wouldn't cut close to the telephone wires.

"Tell me it's not true, what they are saying."

She was too busy squinting up at the branches to pay much attention to Avery, but he sounded unusually anxious. "What are they saying, exactly?"

His voice dropped. "That you are not truly part of the Twixt. That you are something...other. Forbidden," he said carefully, and when she turned to him, his blue-green glare cut deep.

"Funny, you calling me Other Than," Joy said without humor. "That's what my brother was taught to call you." She picked out a stray branch waving in the wind and watched it bob and sway, trying to anticipate its movements. "He learned it from my great-grandmother. She'd been warned about Folk like you."

"Like me," Avery said, ruffled. "Is it true, then?"

Joy snapped. "Is *what* true?"

"There are rumors of things Folk have seen, have heard about you, old stories that sound familiar, even prophecies, since your showing at the gala Under the Hill," he said. "They speak of ancient things, creatures of chaos, and say that you may be drawn from them and not the noble Houses. That you do not bend before the rules of the King and Queen." He checked her reaction as she kept her expression neutral. "If that could be proven, it would release you from the protections of the Edict. In fact, it would completely reverse them. And the Tide—" He paused. "The Tide would crush you and have the Council's blessing." Joy shuddered and looked back up at the tree.

Avery placed a hand on her shoulder, speaking low. "Do you understand you would be hunted down as an abomination, not just by the Tide, but by everyone who fears losing our chance to redeem ourselves to our King and Queen, especially when we are so close to reuniting with our kin?" His hand tightened, his voice gone dry. "They see you as the final obstacle to the Imminent Return."

Joy shrugged off his touch. "That's crazy!" she said. "I'm the one who helped them remember the royal family in the first place! I'm the one who's doing everything I can to help bring them back!"

"And if an Elemental stood between them and the door to Heaven, what do you think the Folk would do?"

Joy glared at Avery, who glared right back. This wasn't helping. She was getting distracted. She fixed her gaze on the high branch in the wind.

"Does it matter?" she whispered.

"Of course it *matters*!" he spat, his nearness radiating anger, betrayal. She'd recently experienced much the same thing and Joy reminded herself to be kinder. He spoke before she could apologize.

"No," he said hastily. "You're right. It doesn't matter. You have accepted your *signatura* and your *geas*, and therefore, you are bound as one of us." He raised his head slowly. "The magic accepted you—the Folk must do the same."

Joy hesitated. "That's...very good of you."

"You think so?" Avery asked. "Then you do not know me well at all."

"Not much," she admitted, stepping away from the oak. Avery moved out of her way. Joy wondered if she should be flattered or insulted. A strange thought occurred to her, but she didn't turn around. "Have you come to help me or stop me?"

"I've considered stopping you," he admitted. "But then, I've considered many things since meeting you."

Joy dared not meet his eyes.

Avery stepped back and glanced around the campus. The only sounds were the rustle of leaves and the metallic ping of the rope slapping the flagpole. "You might want to hurry. I cannot fly against the north wind."

"I'm working on it," Joy said. She snapped her wrist, felt the power move, but it flashed past the tree into the air. "Crap. Hold this."

She handed him the hot tea and opened her left palm, giving the branch a *push* and simultaneously snapping the scalpel with her right. The branch shivered in place and the twig cracked with a flick; a clump of leaves came tumbling down. Joy ran to it and picked it up over her head. "Ha!" She hurried over. "Okay, then," she muttered, stuffing the leaves into her purse and taking back her vile tea. "Now what?"

Avery wasn't listening. His eyes lingered on her chest. She felt like slapping him.

"Where did you get that?" Avery asked.

She looked down. The Queen's jewel winked at her throat, catching and tossing the morning light.

"Oh," she said, wondering if it was safe to wear it out in the open. "It was given to me."

"Impossible."

"Shows what you know," Joy said with a lick of sass, the type her father hated most. "The Queen gave it to me when she asked for my help to Return."

Avery flinched. "Do you know what that is?"

Joy shrugged. "Honestly? No."

"It's the Third Eye," he said. "The Crown Jewel of the Queen."

"Oh," Joy said, rubbing the smooth stone under her thumb. It sounded important. She wondered if the Queen thought she'd deserved something with capital letters. "It's pretty."

Avery gave her a look that could curdle milk.

"Legend says that the Queen can see everything that happens through her Third Eye," he said. "There are many who would happily kill you just for that."

"Wonderful!" Joy said, dropping the gem. "Why not add it to the list?"

The wind whipped the American flag into a frenzy and tossed their hair about their faces, blurring their vision. Joy drew a long strand out of her mouth. Avery brushed a hand across his face. "I would not let them," he said.

"Really?" Joy spat out more hairs. "Why not?"

"I promised Enrique."

"Enrique?" Joy remembered Avery's face as he let go of his memory crystal, watching it float up to join the others during Enrique's wake near the Wild.

"Yes. His friendship...meant a lot to me," Avery said.

"Really? A human?" Joy said. *Inq's human?* It sounded like more than just friendship, but she already knew that Inq was not proprietary of her lovers or her love.

"A human with the Sight," Avery said. "And favored among my people. I promised him that I would look after you." He seemed embarrassed at the memory. "He did not yet know of your status vis-à-vis the Tide, but I knew, of course, after the first time I saw you awaiting trial." His ocean-colored gaze sought hers. "And I promised him all the same. Do you know why?"

She didn't want to know. Joy took a hesitant step backward. He stepped closer. His eyes had turned a dark aquamarine, as if they were suddenly diving deep. Goose bumps pebbled her skin. It was suddenly cooler in the shadow of the oak—which split open—as something stepped free.

Tall, was the first thing in Joy's mind, followed by: *Brown. Beautiful. Smiling. Deadly.* And *Dead-dead eyes.*

Her brain screamed. *No! It's not possible! It's not!*

But it was.

"There you are." Her voice was honey-thick, maliciously sweet, and when she moved, it was with the sound of creaking wicker baskets. Fully healed and fully grown, Aniseed smiled, her mahogany eyes whirling maliciously in their sockets. She looked down at Avery. "Hello, little gosling. This worked out quite well."

Avery shrank back. "I didn't—!"

Joy whipped the tumbler sideways, splashing hot tea in Aniseed's face.

"RUN!"

Joy took off across the field, Avery at her side, the wind buffeting against them as Aniseed's shriek wailed behind. Joy couldn't feel her feet touch the ground; she didn't much care if she flew because *nothing* was going to keep her within arm's reach of Aniseed.

Avery followed, purposefully pacing her escape. She wanted to scream at him to move faster, disappear, *fly!*

"Perhaps I was mistaken," Avery shouted. "You're still part-human and dryads have long memories for revenge."

Joy gasped. "You idiot! That was Aniseed!"

Avery staggered, glancing back. "It can't be—"

"It is," Joy said, sprinting. "Trust me!"

The ground buckled and exploded in a tangle of thickets, a great snarl of crooked branches with long black thorns. Joy swerved to avoid them. She recognized the instant brambles. *Briarhook!* Terror crackled over her limbs. *He's here! They're working together!*

"Did you wonder how I did it?" Aniseed's voice carried casually across the wind. "I assure you, it wasn't easy. It was all meticulously planned." There was a crackle and a ripping sound as the earth gave way behind them. "Even before I submitted myself to the graft, I knew that I would eventually need to escape the Grove." Another burst of briars cut off their escape. Joy switched directions, swatting at Avery's cloak as she fled past. Aniseed's voice casually lilted behind her in casual conversation. "I needed to be lost in order to be found."

A mass of wicked underbrush broke through the grass, obscuring the chiseled Glendale High School sign. This time, Joy launched, her legs executing a split leap, easily clearing the briars and a good stretch of earth. She landed and kept running, vaguely aware of Avery's soaring flight. She had to keep moving—keep going—get beyond the hemmed-in maze. She ran knowing that she had no other choice, not knowing whether Avery protected or pursued.

Ink! she prayed under her breath. *Ink! Ink! Ink!*

"It was merely a matter of patience, a matter of will," Aniseed crooned from a new direction—or was it a shift in the wind? Joy couldn't see beyond the veil of hair and fear.

"And I have the strongest will by far because I know what it's like to lose."

A jagged line ripped through the sidewalk, sprouting more bracken, more brambles, more thorns. Joy could feel the closeness of Earth, but didn't dare slow enough to stop, to concentrate. No! She had to *get away*!

Circling the school, Joy and Avery cut across the back lot. Aniseed appeared along the tree line skirting the gym. Naked and shining like polished wood, she slid along the edge of cracked asphalt, loose-limbed and confident, sliding along the intertwined roots. She was younger, stronger, moving with a fluid grace she hadn't had before. But this was a new body, a new life wearing an old face. Now everything had changed.

"Lost in the woods, I knew who would find me," she said as if their conversation was ongoing while Joy and Avery raced to escape. "The Forest Guardian is loyal and hungers for revenge upon a certain young stripling." Her spindly fingers beckoned Joy as she dodged the latest batch of manic plants. "And I grew under his hand and in so doing, I have bested them all." She simpered in maniacal glee. "This is *my* Imminent Return!"

Joy staggered as Avery passed her, a pale blur on her left. She was flagging, gagging, desperate to get away, but the briars were closing, hemming them in. Another wall of thorny branches cut her off. She barely twisted away in time, feeling deep scratches score her arm. As Aniseed rose before them, Joy spied the sigil blazing on the *segulah*'s upper arm—a familiar, spiky flower, seared as if it had been branded there—a wildflower with bite.

Briarhook! The filthy hedgehog had found the tiny graftling and had claimed her under his auspice—those lost in the woods—just as they'd planned. He'd accelerated her growth, like the briar seeds, and now she was fully grown and at full strength. Briarhook was her perfect spy—he knew everything that had happened since her defeat on the warehouse floor, everything about Kurt and Graus Claude, the Council, the King and Queen, Ink and Joy.

Aniseed knew everything, and she'd outsmarted them all.

Joy floundered in panic. Aniseed hated her, but if Briarhook was here, he'd gut her alive.

The dryad raised a hand—the long, thorny fingers stretched and grew. Joy was trapped between rows of briars, exhausted and afraid. Avery pushed her roughly to the ground. He loomed over her, panting, his hair damp with sweat, his feathered cloak drawn about him.

"Your Grace?" he called out. "Is it really you? Have you come to lead your people to glory?"

Aniseed stroked her forearm with fingers like branches, nails like claws.

"I am the Undying Promise," she said. "I am reborn. And I will lead the Folk to war!"

The wind whipped Avery's hair and the feathers at his back. His cloak parted as he grabbed the hilt of his sword in his right hand and unfurled his left wing.

"By the authority invested in me by the Council of the Twixt, you are hereby ordered to stand down and cease your activities immediately, to stand trial for your crimes against the Edict—" he took a few shaky breaths, testing his courage "—or die."

Aniseed chuckled. "I see we will have to teach you a lesson in politics and being politic."

The ground erupted again. Avery unsheathed his weapon and charged.

Joy reacted before she could think, burying her hands in

the upturned dirt, pulling the earth up to her arms. Earth answered, drawing her down.

The suction forced her into the briars, thorns scraping her face and piercing her chest. She felt one tear her cheekbone, just under her eye. Blood and heat and anger trickled over her limbs, the copper-salt taste of it flooding her mouth. She embraced it, skewering herself, shivering, as she reached for the taste of rock and metal and old, old ice.

The dirt flowed over her body, encasing her legs and hips. The ground hardened, clinging to her skin, searing hot and cold and then shearing off in great scabs of clay, broken clods that crumbled apart and steamed. She dived beneath the topsoil, feeling the foreign tendrils of the briar roots and snapping them, breaking their tender shoots and crushing them between fists of stone. She swallowed, leeching the moisture, feeling them shrivel into powder and die on her tongue. Ashes to ashes, dust to dust, adding themselves to her—to her earth—becoming hers.

AND I WILL GROW AND SAVAGE AND TEAR DOWN THE WORLD! I SHALL HAVE MY REVENGE!

Joy's lip split as she grinned.

She crouched waist-deep in mud, shedding broken pieces of earth as she moved. Blood dripped off her chin, salting the ground. She watched the dance of battle, a blur of red-brown and silver on the surface of the world. It no longer mattered. Only Aniseed mattered. Joy felt for where she was—the foreign bark, the oily wood—reaching across the landscape, sliding under the grass, Joy wrapped soil around her pretty ankles and *pulled*.

Aniseed sank up to her armpits. Her arms shot out suddenly, bracing herself against the earth. Avery scored an unexpected hit that bled, sap-like and sticky. The *segulah* screamed in surprised outrage.

Joy smiled wider, salt painting her teeth.

It was almost too easy.

Baked clay flaked off her cheeks. Warmth covered her chest. She felt its pressure on her throat. Earth tried to claim her, but it couldn't—wouldn't—complete. She was trembling on the precipice, so close...so close...!

VINDICATION! ABSOLUTION! VENGEANCE IS MINE!

Joy felt the struggling dryad like a lump in her throat and all she had to do was *swallow.*

Avery grabbed Joy's face. His wing unfurled, obscuring her vision, breaking her concentration with a fan of ivory feathers the size of swords. Aniseed snarled and grabbed the briars. Joy felt her flowing quickly through the black bark with the angry snap of felled trees, disappearing into the grain, siphoning into thorns, branches, the tangled root system, skipping through the subterranean forest network, gone.

Joy felt her enemy slip through her fingers.

NO!

Avery shook her, but Joy couldn't feel it. She focused on the emptiness where Aniseed had been. She sifted through the dirt, scrambling, clawing, seeking, unable to snag even the hem of her gown as her enemy escaped.

NO!

Joy growled in frustration, a grinding noise of mountains crushed into sand. She was half buried, half lucid, her vision hot and streaming and salty red.

"Joy, stop. Please stop. Let it go. Let it fade." Avery chanted a mantra from somewhere outside her skin. "You still have a choice. You can choose not to do this. Please listen. Joy? *Joy!*" Avery snapped, surprising her enough to focus on him. She was still breathing heavily through her teeth. She wanted to pursue, to rend, to burn—she wanted to obliterate everything in her wake and crush it into bloody paste—but she was *stuck* here on the surface in this wretched body, rejected by two worlds, defeated, denied...

"Stop," he said. "Please. It's not too late." He sounded tired. "It hasn't happened. There's still time. It hasn't happened yet." His wing folded around her, covering her shoulders, sheltering her from the wind. He spoke quietly, like a secret shared. "You have a choice right now, and you *have* to take it, or I'll have no choice but to stop you," he said. "It will fade. I promise. Just stop. Don't let it... Don't make me..." He sighed, placing his human hand on her shoulder. "Please, just stop."

She flinched. "Don't—!" She touched her shoulder protectively, surprised at the sound of her own, tiny voice. She was no longer seething, no longer subhuman. She ran her thumb over her Grimson's mark and it brought her back to her skin. Avery relaxed, disappointed or relieved.

"I didn't mark you," he said. It was such a minor detail in the face of what had happened. It was like waking up after a long, confusing sleep.

"Help me up," she said. Taking his hand, he pulled her out of the mound of baked earth, still steaming through fissures. Joy wrenched her legs out, one by one. She staggered onto the grass. Her boots had split. Her nail polish was gone.

Avery dropped her hand and adjusted his cloak. He seemed reluctant to meet her eye.

"That was Aniseed," he said.

"Yes."

"Not a graftling or offspring or any relation—*the* Aniseed. The bringer of the Golden Age. The martyr of the Tide."

Joy swiped the grit from her skin. "Yes. The graftling had Aniseed's consciousness all along. She survived because of Briarhook, who has managed to make her fully grown. She now exists outside of the parameters of the rules, free to do whatever she wants, but she'll keep coming after me in order to stop the King and Queen."

Avery took a deep breath. "I did not know that she—"

"I know you didn't," Joy interrupted. He chanced a glance at her. "I know." Brushing the last bits from her arms, she hugged her shoulders. "It was a good idea to bring proof that the First Forest is still alive." *But how did she know we would come here?* Joy absently checked herself for any new marks, thinking of who might have tipped off the Tide.

"You will never bear my mark," Avery said quietly.

Joy wiped a smear of blood off her face. "Why not?"

"Because I mark those who have been betrayed by their family," Avery said. "And while I know a little of what happened with your mother, hers would not be considered a great betrayal in the manner of which I speak." He draped his cloak back into place, covering his wing. "Although I could probably claim you under my auspice, should I make a case," he admitted. "But I know that you do not wish to bear anyone else's mark."

Joy was curious. "You mean you have a choice?"

"No one has to claim all those who qualify under their auspice, although we realize that someone else surely will." Avery scraped his foot through the dirt. "Everyone who carries magic will be safeguarded by one of the Folk," he said softly. "And I know that you have already been claimed."

The double meaning wasn't lost on her. Joy sighed. "Thank you." She shouldered her purse, checking her belongings and the precious cluster of oak leaves.

He nodded as if distracted. "The wind has changed," he said quietly. "We should go."

He retreated, but Joy snagged his cloak. Feathers bent softly under her grip. She tried to think how she could express that she understood the weight of what he had done, the choice he had made, the choice that he'd given her, that she'd noticed, that she knew.

"Thank you," she said again. "Really. I mean it."

He removed her hand, delicately peeling back her fingers, a gentle letting go. He inspected her palm, considering it, scratched and speckled with dirt and blood. He cradled it in his pristine palm, his fingertips enfolding hers. He stared at it a second longer and then dropped her hand and his gaze.

"Save it for your chair," he said, raising the edge of his cloak.

Standing close as they swept out of the air, Joy wondered what had happened to Ink.

Joy stood in the shower, letting the hot water wipe away the sweat and the dirt and the fear and the questions that were raging inside her head on too much adrenaline and too little sleep. *Aniseed. I knew it. I told them. She's back!*

Being paranoid doesn't mean they're not really out to get you.

She scrubbed herself with soap twice, scouring the crawling panic from her skin. Every time a memory shuddered to the surface, she cranked the temperature hotter, blotting out the thought.

When the water started getting cold, she relented, stepping onto the bath mat and wrapping herself in towels. She reminded herself that she'd have to replace the ones Graus Claude had burned before Dad found out. It was too much to hope she'd get another paycheck. She hadn't shown up to work in almost a week.

After getting dressed, she brushed her hair and picked out a pair of mismatched socks. She placed the sprig of oak leaves inside her open purse. She checked her phone for texts and emails. She put away her laundry. She ate grapes.

She convinced herself that the fact that she could do these ordinary things meant that she was safe, and if she was safe, then she still had a chance.

Her phone rang. She grabbed it.

"Do not answer it," Ink said.

She spun around, first relieved then confused at his sudden appearance. The phone shivered in her hand. Ink barely moved.

"Don't."

Joy checked the caller ID: Cabana Boys. Joy hesitated. Luiz, Nikolai, Ilhami, Antony, Tuan—even Enrique when he'd been alive—she'd always answered their calls, and they'd always answered hers. It was a special bond between them, a secret order. Her fellow *lehman* understood each other in a way no one else could. They were there for one another. Even Raina, Inq's Cabana Girl, had been there for Joy.

"Why?" Joy asked. Ink didn't answer.

She did the unthinkable and let it go to voice mail.

Joy showed him the message screen. "Can you tell me what's going on?"

Ink's thumb slid silently over his wallet chain. "Inq asked me to help her retrieve one of her *lehman*," Ink said softly. "Again."

Joy had one guess. "Ilhami?"

Ink nodded. "She did not want to involve you," he said. "However, this time there had already been an exchange— Ladybird turned him over in exchange for information about how he might get to you, namely your address and the weakest point of entry." Joy's stomach clenched. "Ilhami allowed himself to be lured back and ransomed, even knowing how much he'd stolen from Ladybird last. And, because of that, Inq has decided that Ilhami must live or die by that choice. There will be no rescuing him this time."

Joy twisted her fingers. "That seems...harsh."

"Harsh?" Ink snapped. "He *sold you out*, Joy. He willfully put you in danger, giving Ladybird the means to enter your home!" Ink gestured angrily, helplessness and guilt tainting his words. "Ilhami cares *nothing* for you! He gave you up for lucid dreams, to escape his own skin!" He slashed the air in impotent frustration. "It is Aniseed and Briarhook all over again. This is what these people do! And if Inq had not done so, I would have condemned him myself."

Joy knew he was right to be angry, to be frightened and hate Ilhami—and so should she—but she didn't *feel* it. Her brother *lehman* had placed her and her family in danger, but he was a sort of family, too. Enrique had begged her to help rescue Ilhami last time and they'd succeeded—if only just—and then the eldest *lehman* had died. She felt she owed Enrique, to honor his memory. And now Ilhami was in danger again, and she couldn't let it go.

"Where is he now?" she asked.

Ink turned away. "I do not know," he said. "Hasp told Inq that—"

"*Hasp* has Ilhami?" Joy jumped out of her seat. "We have to find him! Hasp's a lunatic! He'll torture him—"

"Yes," Ink said. "That is exactly what he will do." Ink touched her arms, her hair, as if memorizing this moment. "He will do it because he wants you to come after him. And that is why we must not go—because that is what Hasp wants. He wants *you*."

Her phone buzzed. Text message.

Hey Cabana Girl

...

I screwed up again

...

We're in your old hangout by the river

...

No booby dolls here

Joy's breath quivered with every three dots. She could hear Ilhami bleeding. She could see his hands shaking as he typed an obituary in texts.

Be sure I get a gallery show & get higher than the sky!

...

I'll tell E you say Hi

...

I'm sorry

"Dover Mill," Joy said, grabbing Ink. "Take me there."

Ink covered her hand with his, his face as still as stone. "Do not ask me to do this," he said. "I told Inq I would not interfere."

Joy grabbed her purse, snagged her shoes and slipped the scalpel into her pocket. She couldn't let Ilhami *die*. She wasn't heartless—not really—she was still human.

"I'm not asking you to," Joy said. "Not when I can stop it. Just take me there. Please."

Ink's face hardened. "Do you know what Hasp wants?"

Joy felt her tiny blade bite through denim. "I think I can guess."

It looked the same from the outside—an old, abandoned mill alongside a quiet, muddy stream, its wheel fixed in concrete, and the rough, patchy lawn dotted with hazardous No Fishing signs. It was always windy, but it wasn't always cold. Joy shivered as she and Ink approached the illusion of Dover Mill.

Aniseed could be here!

Piercing the illusion bubble was easy when you knew what to expect, and so when the rickety toolshed became a large wooden overhang over a set of descending stairs, Joy was not surprised, but that didn't mean she wasn't terrified. She knew she was walking into a trap.

Ink checked the wards as he descended the stairs, straight razor drawn, guarding her bodily as they stepped into the underground cellar that had once been Joy's office and Aniseed's hidden cache. It was where the aether sprites had led them months ago in order to turn in one of their own. Hasp.

There were four bare walls, empty shelves, and the ever-present slab of slate. Ilhami lay slumped in a corner and an aether sprite hung upside down above him like a bat.

The yellow-green eyes opened. The football-shaped head split in a grin.

"You came quickly." Hasp's sibilant *hiss* hugged the dark. "Mustn't be kept waiting. You *do* learn, after all." His head rotated as his body unfolded, impossibly long fingers hooking into the tiny holes drilled into the wall where the suspension shelves had been, clicking and scraping as he lowered himself to the floor. One multijointed finger wrapped like a bicycle chain around Ilhami's throat. "This one said you wouldn't come." His eyes flicked between them. "Yet here you are. Scribe. *Lehman* to Ink." He paused thoughtfully, his breath expanding his thin rib cage. "Or is it Scribe and *lehman* to Joy?"

Ink switched his grip and so did Hasp, who bared his teeth.

"Stay back," the damaged aether sprite spat. "You gave your oath."

"I said I would not interfere," Ink said. "But that only extends to your plans for him." He gestured toward Ilhami.

Hasp sneered. Another knuckle slipped around Ilhami's throat.

"Yet you came," Hasp said, his gaze swiveling to Joy. "You care whether this one lives or dies." He dragged the young Turk across the dusty floor. "Monsiegneur Ladybird got what he wanted and then delivered him to me. But the Monsiegneur did not get what he wanted from you." Hasp grinned sickeningly. "So maybe now you have something for me."

She was through playing games. Her vision fuzzed. She needed more sleep.

"What do you want, Hasp?" Joy said, using his name as a reminder that he had not been able to change his True Name no matter how much he'd toadied up to Briarhook and no matter what Aniseed had promised. The crippled aether sprite snarled, and she knew the barb had struck home. Joy wondered if he'd always been ugly, even before the Council had torn off both his wings, or whether he'd been wallowing in human pollution for too long and it had turned the normal fairy beauty foul.

"Business," he said simply, drawing out the *s*. "This is a place of business and I am here as a paying customer to offer trade." He hunched closer to Ilhami's body, farther away from Ink. "Business with Briarhook's gone sour." Hasp's bulbous eyes blinked. "Hasn't the *heart* for this. But you—" His hooked forefinger unwound, stretching toward her. "You know business," he hissed. "And you, Master Scribe, will not interfere, but will bear witness in accordance to the Accords of the Twixt. Proper, legal, binding. *Yes*," Hasp snarled through a maliciously clever grin. "Will it be so?"

Ink gave a delicate snarl. "It shall be witnessed, in accordance to the rules." He lowered his razor as he turned Joy aside. "All you must do is listen to his offer. It is like parlay in the rules of war. You only have to listen. You do not have to obey. I am your witness."

Joy glared at her kidnapper, Briarhook's accomplice. The tip of the scalpel shook with the memory of pain and fear, humiliation and snow. "What do you want?"

"What I have always wanted! What I'll always want!" he spat. "I want my *locqui*." The word shivered down his bare ribs. "I want my birthright, my magic! I want to *fly*! And so, I must be free of my Name that chains me to earth and the Council's damned rules." He tipped back his oblong head, exposing the underside of his chin. Joy's Sight revealed the barbed-hook shape of Hasp's *signatura* carved into the tip of his jaw. His long, pointed finger speared the sigil like a knife. He lowered his face to look at her. "I know what you did within these walls, and now you will do it for me." His breathing quickened. "Erase my mark and everyone goes free."

Joy's surprise was a hiccup of shock. Hasp took another step, dragging Ilhami behind him.

"Well?" he said.

"I c—" She gagged on the lie. She *could*, and part of her wanted to, relishing the chance to finish this, once and for all, but she was very aware of Ink standing witness. What Hasp asked for was possible, but it wouldn't do what he thought. A *signatura* wasn't a mark given to him by any-one else—it was the symbol that he'd accepted along with the power of his True Name. If she erased that, she'd erase him completely. He'd cease to exist. As tempting as that was, Joy was no assassin—she'd learned that the hard way. She cleared her throat and squeezed the scalpel harder. "I don't think you really want me to do that."

Hasp smiled. "Oh, but I do," he said. "As the Scribe is my witness, I most certainly do." His eagerness seemed to feed a desperate strength inside his shriveled limbs. He shook Ilhami by the throat. "You will do it or I will *snap this one's neck*!" Ilhami flopped bonelessly in his grip. He wasn't simply unconscious, he was under a drug or spell or worse. "Do you understand?"

"The bargain is witnessed," Ink said swiftly and turned to Joy. "Do you accept?"

She stared at Ink. He'd barely nodded—it was one of those subtle, human cues he'd learned by watching her. His pulse beat in the side of his neck as he swallowed. Anger brewed in his eyes, flushing his face. He was becoming so human, fingernails and forearm hairs, shades of meaning and shared moments together; now she could almost read his thoughts. Ink believed that she could walk away and Ilhami would die, but Hasp would not hold anything over her and they could leave in peace. Or, if she agreed to his demands, Hasp would be severed from the Twixt, no longer under the rules, and Ink would be free to kill him without the punishment or the guilt of Grimson's mark. But Joy knew if she did this, Ink would see that she had used his gift, his instrument, to commit sacrilege beyond murder—erasing one of the Folk—and that she was, as the Tide always claimed, the most dangerous girl in the world. It would reveal her ugliest secret, her greatest betrayal, and there would be no going back.

If she did this, she might lose Ink, but save Ilhami.

If she didn't, she would never forgive herself.

If she did this, the Folk would kill her.

But she would undo Hasp and he would never torture anyone ever again.

Joy swallowed, gripping the scalpel. Her arms shook. "No."

Hasp's other hand grabbed Ilhami's ankles, like a wishbone. "Then he dies *in pieces*."

Ink appeared in a flash, the razor held just under Hasp's throat.

"Then *you* die," Ink said.

Hasp swallowed, the knobby Adam's apple bobbing under the steel. "You swore you would not interfere."

"I will not interfere if you choose to kill him, but once he is dead, then I am free to act as I wish and so you will die soon after."

Hasp smiled. "Won't bring him back," he whispered. Ink corkscrewed the blade on the edge of his smile.

"Nor you," Ink said. "I can kill you."

"Can you?"

"Yes," Ink ground his teeth. "I have killed our own before."

"Stop!" Joy shouted. She'd caused this. She'd forced Ink here. And she knew how this would end.

Death. Killing. Blood. Guilt.

Remember: he will be learning about everything, watching you.

"It will kill you!" Joy said, her words loud in the cache. "What you are asking for—it will do more than kill you. You will cease to exist."

Ink froze, every muscle caught unawares. Hasp's smile drooped to an uncertain frown. His hands tightened on Ilhami. "You lie!"

"I can't lie," Joy said. "You know that. I am part of the Twixt."

Ink stared at Joy as the aether sprite struggled with the news. She couldn't meet his eyes, staring instead at the smooth slate wall that had once held all of Aniseed's stolen *signaturae*, a map of marks, the blueprint of her plan to cull humanity from the world. Joy had written her own hours of operation on it in chalk before Ink had found her here and found her out. And now this, her last confession. *So many secrets.* These walls knew too much about her.

"No," Hasp croaked finally. "You are *lehman*, ex-*lehman*, half-breed, Earth-claimed, but you are still mortal—I can smell it on you." His slit nostrils flared as if to prove his point. His face had gone pale, his many knuckles white. "You are human and you lie!"

He lifted Ilhami's body with preternatural strength, a meat shield between himself and Ink. Ilhami's head lolled back sickeningly. Hasp swelled with effort, his shoulders straining, gaze locked on Joy, mad, desperate. He was going to tear the Turkish artist limb from limb.

"Stop!" Joy screamed, hands up. "I'll do it!" She held up the scalpel and steadied her breath. "Okay? I'll do it. Put him down. Okay."

Ink blinked, confused, his breathing tight. "Joy?"

"You swear it?" Hasp said, tense, on the brink. "You swear it on your life?"

Joy wiped at her face. "My life. His life. My father's life. Whatever you want," she said. She pointed up the blocky steps. "But let them go," she said, turning to Ink. *Please. Please go.* "Take Ilhami and go."

Ink hesitated, shoulders back, standing tall. "I cannot," he said. It wasn't a lie. "I am a witness." Joy knew and knew it was true. He had pledged to be present in order to fulfill the rules or fate or whatever magic bound them together. Ink was committed to bear witness to this in accordance to the Accords of the Twixt. It was as if everything had been pointing to this moment between them, when all the secrets came out.

"Damn," she whispered, missing her heart, missing her chance. "Damn you." And while she really meant it, it felt more like *Damn me* because she knew what would happen next and there was no turning from it. Fate unflowered like a many-petaled lotus; as if it were happening to someone else, as if it had happened already, and Joy was only just remembering it now. Too late.

Time slowed down for déjà vu.

Tears pooled in her eyes as she nodded. The two combatants eased apart. Ink was chagrined and Hasp was triumphant, but she knew that neither would be so for long. Hasp unwound his fingers, a heady smirk on his face. Ilhami fell to the floor with a *thud*. Ink stepped aside as Hasp squatted on the ground, tipping his head back, yielding his throat to her knife, his tennis-ball eyes slipping closed. Joy remembered Ysabel, her yielding and trust. Freeing her had felt nothing like this.

Joy touched the tip of the scalpel to the edge of the hook, tracing the tightly wound glyph carefully around its many switchbacks squeezed like a button beneath Hasp's pointy chin. She could feel Ink's hot, burning gaze as she watched her own fingers, white on the handle, follow the blaze of undoing, unmaking it—erasing it—as the sigil neared the central point. It was the spot on which Hasp's *signatura* balanced, encompassing the whole of who he was, what he had pledged to be for his people, witnessed by the King and Queen, and that which he'd broken when he'd disobeyed their Decree.

Joy realized she didn't know what his crime had been.

She hesitated. Tears blurred her vision. The scalpel trembled. Furious, Hasp hissed through his teeth.

"Finish it!"

Obediently, she drew the final curve, imagining Hasp on his knees, prostrate before the Council as his great wings were torn from his body. How long had he lived as an outcast? How long had he suffered in the toxic, polluted air? When had Briarhook found him, lost in the woods? How had he been bribed to Aniseed's side as she promised a Golden Age, without humans? How that had happened— no one would ever know.

The *signatura* flared and Hasp, grinning, disappeared.

Joy dropped to the floor on her hands and knees and sobbed.

TWENTY-SEVEN

JOY DIDN'T NEED TO SEE INK TO KNOW HE STOOD BEHIND her. She didn't need to see the naked blade to know that it was there.

"I told him," she whispered again and again through salty lips. "I told him."

"Yes," Ink said flatly. "You did." His voice came closer, barely a breath by her ear. "Now you must tell me."

She didn't face him. Kneeling, penitent, she was a child on her knees confessing her greatest sin to the voice of God.

"I erased his *signatura*," she said. "It wasn't a mark he'd been given or a scar or a glyph—it's his Name." She took a breath that shuddered in the back of her throat. "If I erase a True Name, then that person is erased completely, as if they'd never been." The words themselves were like cracks, truth slipping between the lies. This was her last shred of armor, gone.

Ink hovered just beside her. "You knew this would happen?"

"I *told* him—"

"But you knew," he said. "You knew that this would happen."

"Yes."

"Because it happened before."

Joy nodded. "Yes, but that was an accident. I didn't know."

"The Red Knight?" he guessed.

"Yes."

"You went after him," Ink's voice filled the cache, crisp and clear. "To stop him. To save me. But you didn't know that this would happen then?"

She shook her head.

"This time you did."

His voice was more distant, withdrawn. Joy felt like crying all over again, but the tears were gone. Her eyes were dry and scratchy-swollen. She hadn't known what would happen when she'd trapped the assassin with Briarhook's fast-growing seeds nor what would happen when she carved the Red Knight's True Name into his armor. She'd thought it would lock the magic, keep his incarnations set to one Name; instead, it had negated everything he was and left her alone in the briar.

This time Hasp had willingly given her his *signatura*, demanding she erase it—but she knew it amounted to the same thing. She felt dirty and guilty and wicked that she had wanted it. Wanted it to be over. Wanted him to be gone. What kind of person did that make her? Or was she even a person at all? Was she still human or had she changed too much, gone too far? Without a heart, had she become heartless? Something other than human?

"You've denied him Faeland," Ink said. "Now he can never return."

Joy covered her face, miserable beyond words.

She felt Ink's arms around her, shielding her as if from the *bain sidhe*, his hands on her back and in her hair, whispering fervently into the space between her shoulder and chin.

"Tell me," he whispered. "Tell me something I can believe in."

She knew what he wanted—something that could save her, some sort of proof, something he could use to excuse her crime so that he would not have to protect the Twixt from her. Ink knew what he should do—what he'd been created to do—and what he most wanted to do, which was to love her, to keep her safe. All he needed was a loophole. Fortunately, she knew one.

"Sometimes we must choose immediately unpleasant things in order to prevent greater unpleasantness."

The words hung between them like a string of fairy lights, connecting the past to the present and to a possible future. They had been his words to her, echoed from her mouth to his; it had always been the way between them—his, hers, and ultimately, theirs. Memory wavered in his eyes, testing his resolve; she could see it in the way his face could not commit to one expression. *What would he choose to believe?*

Ink smiled sadly. One dimple.

"Yes," he said, relaxing. "That is true." He cupped a palm against her face. "And you warned him, tried to stop him, and cried afterward in remorse. You spoke no lies, you did not deceive him, but even given the truth, he would not believe you." Ink rested his forehead against hers and took a cleansing breath. "I believe you," he said. "And I believe in you."

Joy flung her arms around him and rocked in his embrace, grateful for him and them, and being together, for honesty, for love and for being alive.

It was over, finally over, and all the secrets between them were over and done.

They returned Ilhami to Inq at Enrique's old apartment. She greeted them with four words:

"The Bailiwick is back."

Ink changed direction, grabbing Joy's hand as they stepped back into the breach, Inq calling out behind them, "I'll meet you there!"

It was strange walking through the brownstone's foyer, but it wasn't the cream-colored walls, the wingback chairs or the fresh flower arrangement that had changed in any way—it was the flat chill Joy felt upon entering the building, a feeling that she was no longer welcome.

Ink and Inq flanked her, arms out, weapons raised—a razor, a scalpel and a dowsing rod. They were following their final clue, confirming the origin of the spell-coated pearls, the last clue to ousting the traitor in their midst.

Inq nodded. "It's him."

Before they neared the ironwood office doors, a booming voice filled the hall.

"Welcome, Miss Malone, Mistress Inq, Master Ink," Graus Claude's calm bass rumbled in greeting as Inq flung the doors open with a ripple of air. The Bailiwick sat composed at his desk, four arms crossed. "Do excuse the impropriety," he said as Filly stepped smoothly in front of them, barring the way. "My butler's gone out."

Joy's stomach curdled in dread. She hated herself for suspecting him, for being fooled, for not being surprised, and hated most the feeling that Graus Claude had been expecting something like this for some time.

She'd never done well with "something like this."

"Well met, Joy Malone," Filly said, fists resting on hips. "Here now, I finally have a secret—" She grinned. *"Yours."*

Ink dropped, ducking fast, fading to one side and launching forward. Filly stepped back, an effortless dodge, punching snake-quick into the inside of his shoulder before Joy could blink. Inq grabbed her and pulled her back into the hall.

The Valkyrie smiled. Ink didn't.

Ink grabbed the outside of her elbow, pushing up and twisting it over, her knuckles ground into his chest as she kicked sharply, collapsing his leg behind the knee and forcing him to the floor. His back bent gracefully, her force swinging past him, her vambrace just tapping him, grazing his chin. Filly's cape of finger bones clattered as she wrenched sideways. Ink shifted to compensate, both of them pitching for balance, forearms braced against one another's, weapons drawn, but neither used.

They were at a standoff, arms locked. It had taken a moment, if that.

Filly grinned. "You capped your off switch."

"Of course," he said. "Why did you do it?"

"Hit you? I know that look in your eye," she said. "That's when the fun starts!"

He switched his grip, clasping her forearm, trapping her elbow and pulling her taut as she drove forward, grabbing his shirt, wrenching a fistful of fabric against his throat and winding it tight. They both stopped, their faces within inches, his razor and her sword reversed, but not forgotten.

A ripple of air hummed an angry wood-chipper whine. Filly slammed her left forearm against her thigh, popping her buckler clasp and grabbing the edge, spinning it like a discus toward Inq's head. Inq ducked back behind the ironwood. The small shield smashed on impact. Joy flinched, still gaping at the traitor, her friend.

"Are we having fun yet?" Filly's question sounded like a last warning. Ink spun, ducking under her arm, loosening his collar and slipping beneath her shoulder, twisting and appearing under her chin. They froze, each with a blade below the other's ear.

"Why did you buy Joy's secret?" he asked.

A crinkle appeared between the warrior's blond brows. "Is *that* what this is all about?" She huffed and pushed Ink backward with a dismissive swipe. He recovered, waiting. There was not even a scratch by his ear.

Filly rotated her wrists and straightened the horse head pendant at her throat as Joy and Inq stepped warily into the office. The Valkyrie snorted, completely ignoring the low buzz of Inq's palm. She pierced Joy with a look. "I did it to protect you."

Joy felt all eyes on her. The Valkyrie's words made no sense. "What?"

Filly rolled her shoulders and tossed her head of braids. "I keep my ears open, which isn't hard hanging with the hags in the Halls, but when your name came up on the black market auction, I paid special attention. But a Black Auction means that no one knows who's at the table until the deal is done, and a bought secret stays locked between the buyer and seller to keep secrets secret and identities blind." She sniffed and licked the blue spot beneath her lip. "Normally, I'd leave such matters to the frog, but since the old wart's been indisposed, I figured I'd keep a hand in the game." She set her feet apart, still wary, still positioning herself between the door and the Bailiwick, still ready to fight or bolt. "And when I heard what you said to the King and Queen, I remembered who was still crawling around out there and I knew she'd stop at nothing to get a hold over you."

Joy breathed, "Aniseed."

Filly nodded grimly. "That sticky witch wants to prevent the Imminent Return," she said. "The moment that they cross through the Bailiwick, the Twixt will recognize their rule and none shall stand against them. If Aniseed wants to seize her second chance, she'll have to do it quickly and so she'll have to stop you first." Filly grinned with pride. "She knows the Return has something to do with you, because you keep tripping her spellwire every time you traipse down the toad's gullet."

Joy stumbled. It made sense. "The last golem came after me once the graftling was gone," she said. "It must have still been connected to the spell on the stairs."

"So you bought Joy's secret so that Aniseed could not have it," Inq said, her hand ceasing its malicious quiver. She flicked her black lacquered nails thoughtfully at the warrior woman. "Well done!"

Filly shrugged at the compliment. "My thought was that she would not be able to make the Market on her own and would have to send one of her lackeys given her pitiful state." She buckled her left vambrace back into place. "It bought me time once we got back. Fortunately, I know the black market well—although you didn't hear it from me!"

"Nonsense," Graus Claude grumbled from his throne. His prominent browridge had furrowed, his hands fidgeting with the things on the desk. "She's dead. Aniseed's dead. The graftling's dead. You're all chasing phantoms, blaming ghosts." He wiped double sets of his hands with a napkin. "Too young to survive and too stubborn to submit—she's lost, I tell you," he said with a hint of regret. "She's gone."

Joy shook her head, unable to begin to say how wrong he was, how deep his denial, but then again, she'd felt the same stubborn disbelief when forced to question his or Filly's loyalties.

"Show me the body," Filly challenged, casting sly eyes back at Joy. "Even then, I'd admit I'd still have doubts."

"Graus Claude," Joy said. "She lives." Her tone was all truth. "Trust me, she lives."

The Bailiwick deflated, speechless and pale.

"There now," Filly said, jerking her chin. "*That* is why I took it off-Market."

"But why didn't you *tell* us?" Joy asked.

Filly shrugged. "I told you politics is not a warrior's game," she said, spitting to one side.

Graus Claude's voice snapped out of shock. "Manners!"

Filly tilted her head back, calling over one shoulder, mocking. "Besides, I knew it was something that no one else should know. Hence why I figured it was best worth knowing!" The Valkyrie sounded quite pleased with herself—she'd managed to get a drop on the comptroller of the Twixt.

"So...you know?" Joy asked, worried, unsure.

Filly's expression became guarded. "Yes."

Joy's body tingled as adrenaline splashed through her. *Which secret was it? What did she know?* Filly had safeguarded her secret as a favor to Joy, but she wasn't reassured by how much leverage the young Valkyrie had over her now.

Filly had been the one to tell Joy that she was part-Twixt. She'd given her the words to take on her True Name. She'd been inside the Bailiwick; she'd even heard the King and Queen say that Joy was a descendant of Elementals, the Destroyer of Worlds. What secrets were left?

I can erase Folk out of existence.

"Who was it?" Joy murmured. "Who sold it to you?"

Filly wasn't the traitor. But the only other person who knew the truth besides Ink was...

Inq cocked her head.

"Kestrel," Filly said.

Both Joy and Inq turned. "What?"

"She said she was there—that she'd witnessed the whole thing."

Joy hesitated, realization hitting her with a one-two punch. It was true—Kestrel had been snuffling in the leaves as Joy had crawled out of the briar patch, alone. Afterward, Inq had placed Grimson's mark upon Joy's shoulder and suggested that they keep mum, but Joy had forgotten that Kestrel wasn't an animal, like a bloodhound or pet, she was a *tracker* who worked and bartered and arranged her affairs through wizards and Folk, alike. She was a professional, an expert, known to be the best. And she'd been a witness to Joy's magical murder.

Filly smirked as if she'd read Joy's mind. "Yes, well, by accepting my bid, she is bound to tell no one else—the secret was sold to me in my keeping." The young warrior smacked Joy in the arm. "You see? I told you that your secrets are safe with me, Joy Malone!"

Joy wanted to hug her, but didn't quite dare. "Thank you."

Filly grinned. "You should!"

She clasped Joy hard around the biceps and pulled her into a laughing, slapping embrace. It felt solid and happy and wholesome and good. Something inside Joy loosened, letting her finally breathe.

"Very well, very well," Graus Claude said while sprinkling plant food into his fountain. "Now if you would be so kind as to fetch a towel so you can clean up your—" his wide mouth puckered around the word "—*secretion*, I would very much appreciate it. Posthaste."

Filly laughed and threw a quick fist-in-the-air salute before dancing out the ironwood doors.

"Well, that's all delightful," Inq said casually. "But we came about a separate matter." She raised the dowsing rod and spoke a word that swallowed itself. The tiny pink pearl strapped to the wood with a rubber band glowed. "Tsk tsk tsk," Inq chirped. "Now you've done it."

Joy's head swam. She stumbled, taking an unconscious step away from Graus Claude. "No." It was all she could say.

He looked mildly bemused, then unhappy, then grim. *Guilty*, she thought. *He looks guilty.* She looked at his silk shirt with its thick collar and its buttons of pearl. *Pearls are a particular specialty of mine.*

The sudden quiet was thick and unsettling. "Tell me," Joy said. "Tell me it's not true. Tell me you didn't send those pearls to Monica." Her fingers clenched into fists. The scalpel felt hot and sharp. "Tell me you didn't betray me!"

Graus Claude paused, tasting the words on his lips. "I did not betray you, Joy Malone."

Joy stared at him, waiting. "And?" The word echoed shrilly. *"And?"*

His icy blue gaze never wavered. He said nothing.

"Why?" Joy shrieked. "Tell me why!"

Graus Claude sighed, steepling his hands. "It was the least invasive option," he said. "The kindest one left, which I pursued specifically keeping your finer feelings in mind." His gaze grew steely, his icy blue eyes bright. "Your friend possesses something valuable of mine." He measured his words carefully. "My efforts to locate or otherwise procure it had thus far proved unsuccessful and therefore I found it distastefully necessary to become more directly involved with its recovery. I wanted the matter resolved with as little fuss as possible, which would have been in everyone's best interests, but, as with all things that have even a passing acquaintance with you, the task proved far more difficult than could ever be countenanced."

Joy gaped at him, stunned. "Are you *kidding* me?" she railed. "She nearly choked to death! You nearly killed her!"

"I did not expect there to be any magical interference," he admitted. "If left untouched, it would have been a painless command. It was never designed to injure Miss Reid, merely ensure her compliance without any further complications."

He wrung his hands, flustered. "By all accounts, she took the necklace willingly! I had arranged for the Bentley to pick her up and transport her to me, and then afterward, she could have happily kept the gift, none the wiser. I could not have surmised that she would have wished to remove it so quickly—fickle female!" He looked further ruffled, tugging gently at his collar. "There was a time when such tokens of affection were accepted with the utmost privacy and propriety. There should not have been a *scene*."

"But you didn't have to do that!" Joy snapped. She couldn't quite believe that he'd been more misguided than malicious. "You could have just asked me to get whatever it was for you. Heck, you could have even asked *her*! She's kind of a great person who doesn't deserve to be *strangled*!"

The Bailiwick sighed, as if Joy were purposefully being very stupid or very naïve. "Don't be droll, Miss Malone," he said. "I could not have made such a request without exposing my position and the object of my interest, which is a poor bargaining point. Better to take it off the table quickly and quietly before anything irreparable occurred."

Joy ground her teeth and clenched her eyes against the threatening headache. Even at the best of times, the Bailiwick's logic could be dizzying, but now he'd concocted an elaborate, paranoid delusion that he might have been suffering under ever since they'd broken him out from Under the Hill. Joy tried to be rational.

"What are you *talking* about?" she muttered, finally. "Monica doesn't have—!"

But she did. Joy knew it. Monica had something—something powerful—that had power over the Bailiwick. She'd seen it happen. She'd been there. Joy remembered him flat on the floor, bloody and beaten and wrapped in a sheet, contrite after

Monica's sudden shout of surprise and her hastily made cross out of the letter opener and a pen.

She'd seen the look on his face, even if Monica hadn't. It was the same look he'd given her when he'd insisted on burning the towels stained with blood.

"You sent Kurt to toss her house," Joy said. "It wasn't robbed—it was searched. And Mr. Vinh—" Joy shook her head. He'd asked the wizard to make an offer. The old wizard must have *loved* that! The ox bone blade may have been enspelled to sever the Amanya at its source, but by stabbing the Bailiwick, Joy had soaked it in Graus Claude's blood. She didn't need Stef to remind her that blood was the most powerful magical substance in both worlds. The letter opener still held power over him, and it belonged to Monica.

Her best friend, Monica Reid, could control the Bailiwick of the Twixt.

Joy felt her hands go numb. "Oh crap."

Graus Claude sighed. "Succinctly, if urbanely, put."

"So I can't—?" Joy started, then stopped. No, she couldn't. The ox bone blade was no longer hers to give. She'd borrowed it and returned it to its rightful owner, Monica Reid. "But can't she—?" Monica would have to give it back willingly, knowing that it was powerful, and therefore risk exposing the fact that it had power over Graus Claude to all of the Twixt. "Can't we—?" Convince her? Bribe her? Explain it somehow? Bring her into the brownstone, where it was safe and no one would know? That's what he'd been trying to do in his twisted, clandestine way. Joy let out a slow breath. "We'll think of something."

"Yes," he said calmly. "You will."

Joy glared at him. He was right—it was her fault—and she'd have to fix it quickly, better sooner than later. If anyone found out about it, Graus Claude, the Bailiwick, and the back door to Faeland would be doomed. Joy touched the jeweled pendant, the mark of the Queen. There was so much at stake.

"Let me try," Joy said. "My way."

"Indeed," he said. "That might be best. I have been trying to avoid steps that might have proved...unpleasant."

Inq raised a hand. "Can we have a hint?"

Joy and Graus Claude said together, "No."

"Well, fine," Inq said as Filly returned, dropping a rag on the floor and rubbing it with her foot. "If we're all convinced that no one is currently attempting to bribe, coerce or otherwise undermine anyone else for the time being, then perhaps we can get back to the little matter of finding the proof that the King and Queen still need to fulfill the conditions of the Imminent Return?" She glanced around the room expectantly. "Anyone?" Inq clucked her tongue and pocketed the pearl. "You're all hopeless," she complained, handing the rod back to Joy. "I'm going to go find some creative brains and see what shakes loose." Her hand widened, fingers spread, as a hole rippled through the air. "Well, this was disappointing. Keep me posted." She sauntered forward and slipped beyond the world.

"Mistress Inq has a point," the Bailiwick said. "Filly, please do me the honor of remaining at your post until Kurt comes to relieve you. I shall be busy determining my current status with the Council and its affairs. Miss Malone, you should return at once to the safety of your abode. And as for you, Master Ink," Graus Claude said, reaching into one of his deep file folders. "My unexpected sabbatical has resulted in a rather impressive backlog that demands your immediate attention." He thumped a stack of paper three inches high. His browridge quirked. "If there is no further delay, then I would suggest adopting Miss Malone's excellent work ethic—" He patted the stack with two of his hands. "There is no time like the present."

Ink, bewildered, picked up the thick stack and tucked it under one arm. Joy stood close beside him; she felt emptied, drained, with more questions than answers. Her phone buzzed in her pocket. She flipped it over in her palm.

"It's Monica," she said dully.

Graus Claude rumbled, "Then you have work to do."

TWENTY-EIGHT

"SO YOU WERE BEING STUPID," MONICA SAID.

Joy threw another wadded-up Kleenex in the trash. "Yes, thank you."

"*Really* stupid."

"Okay. I got it. You're right."

"You went to a hostage situation with a thing that's tried to kill you after a drug lord got Inq's boy toy to give up the keys to your house? And then forced *you* to pull the trigger?" Monica shook her head and tore open another Band-Aid. "That's crazy stupid. Are all Folk terminally stupid? Is it a hereditary thing?"

Joy sighed, patting her clean scratches with gauze. "Can we pick another topic, please?"

Monica took back the hydrogen peroxide and the tiny tube of Neosporin. "Got any plans for college?"

Joy grimaced. "Please. I haven't even gone school shopping yet, and it starts next week." She placed the Band-Aid on her rib where a thorn had broken off under her skin. She'd had to dig it out with tweezers. She drank some more water and wiped her chapped lips. She was dehydrated, she was tired, she was stressed out and she was officially unemployed and back under house arrest.

"So your Dad knows about the whole saving-the-world

thing and he still grounded you for sneaking out?" Monica said. "That's messed up."

"He's just worried about me." Joy said, checking her face in the mirror. She'd say she'd scratched it on a branch during her run. *Not a lie.* "And he doesn't know how else to keep me safe."

Monica twisted her lips. "So you're going to stay home until school starts?"

Joy snorted. "Heck no."

"So what aren't you telling me?" Monica asked. "I listened to your story from Mom's Big Reveal to your latest showdown in Boston and I heard serious editing going on." She raised her hands above her head. "Big edits. Huge." She turned her head against the pillow, smashing her back-to-school haircut flat. "Are you going to tell me what you're not telling me? Because I'm telling you that I can tell you want to tell me."

Joy paused. "I'm not entirely sure what that means, but no."

Joy hadn't figured out how she was going to get Monica to give her the letter opener after she'd already told her that it was hers by right in order to keep it from Mr. Vinh. It was the only bit of magic she had against the Twixt, but Joy couldn't let her keep it. If anyone found out what it could do to the Bailiwick, they could lose their only chance, not to mention Stef, the King and Queen, as well as Graus Claude. Despite what she'd said, Joy couldn't just ask for it, couldn't steal it, couldn't even "borrow" it—the blade would still be Monica's. She'd have to get her best friend to give it to her willingly or give it directly to Graus Claude. And she'd have to do it soon. The thought of Aniseed getting her hands on the ox bone blade made Joy physically ill.

"Okay. So now what?" Monica asked. "We just sit here?"

"Yes. For now we just sit here. Safe behind walls."

It's what she should have done in the first place once Ink reset the wards. Dad had cleaned up the mess outside of Stef's room and they had an appointment with another contractor sometime next week. There was a note on the fridge as well as a bag of seven layer bars, with love, from Shelley. Joy and Monica had been making their way through them. Monica showed Joy how they were better with salt. She sprinkled some more on the gooey chocolate-coconut-caramel square and took a bite.

"We sit here," Joy said while chewing. "And we wait."

"Hoo-rah." Monica said. "I feel like I should *do* something. You're out there, being stupid, and I'm just hanging around waiting to get attacked by FedEx."

"You're doing something. You *did* something," Joy said, pointing to the wax doll. She hoped it wasn't just her imagination that the seed might be open a crack. It was hard to tell through the dye. "It's the nicest thing anyone's done for me to help me get back to normal!"

"Yeah, well," Monica said, "you weren't that normal to begin with."

"Ha ha," Joy said, adding carefully, "But there *is* something you could do—"

A noise clanged in the kitchen. Joy and Monica scrambled with well-trained best-friend instincts, flipping on music, grabbing the nail polish, tossing medicine bottles and tubes in the underwear drawer and stashing the bloody bandages under the bed, flipping a magazine open on the bedspread and stuffing their blades under the pillows. Monica grabbed the wax voodoo doll and tossed it into the ouroboros box for good measure. Joy sat on the bed and read the color of the polish in her hand: Captivating Coral. *Of course.*

There was a knock at her door, which sounded polite, although the babble of voices behind it didn't.

"Joy?"

"You in there?"

"C'mon, kid."

"Let's go!"

Monica frowned at Joy. "What's this? Grand Central Station?"

Inq stepped through the door as Ink appeared outside her closet. Joy sat up. Monica stared. No one looked like they quite believed what was happening right then.

"Joy," Ink said. He glanced at Monica. "I am sorry, but we have to go."

"There's a warrant out," Inq said. "We just got word. The Tide is calling for an immediate dissolution of the Council. Folk are demanding that they stand down as the governing power hindering the Imminent Return."

"What? That makes no sense!" Joy said. "They didn't even remember anything about it until the Amanya spell was broken!"

"The Council agrees with you," Inq said. "That's why they've shifted the blame on you."

Joy gaped. *"What?"*

"The Council has agreed to incarcerate you and charge you with aiding and abetting a known criminal with intent to commit High Treason as an appeasement," Ink said. "They get to retain their authority as long as they can try you for your involvement and build a case that you were manipulating the conditions of the Return to suit your personal agenda."

"I wasn't—!" Joy coughed on the fact that she *had* been after the King and Queen in order to ask them to change the rules for her, to keep her from changing, to grant her a boon. Her tongue stopped swelling and she choked on her spit.

"Exactly," Ink said.

"They're after you and they're on their way here." Inq grabbed Joy's purse and threw it at her. "You have to leave. With us. Now."

"Now?" Joy said weakly, grabbing the scalpel.

"It isn't safe," Ink said. "My wards will hold, but they cannot prevent what is coming."

Joy grabbed Monica's arm. Monica grabbed her dagger.

"Dad?"

Inq shook her head. "Protected by the same familial rules that kept Aniseed's graftling from harm. If the Council is trying to do this by the book, no one will dare touch him." The Scribe searched the room with her fingers spread wide. "They claim that they can track you anywhere you go. They have a dowsing rod, and some goblin braggart claims he's acquired three drops of your blood." Inq shot her a wry glare. "But of course you would never be so foolish as to let anyone do that—why, then they could use the Anvesana spell to track *you*, right?"

Joy twisted her fingers. She'd paid Ladybird three drops of blood for the drug she'd used to knock the Red Knight senseless and forgive Ilhami's debt. Inq swore in several foreign languages.

Monica mouthed, *Stu-pid*.

"Your father will be safe," Ink said. "Your mother is foresworn. You have to leave, but you have sacrificed all armor—all personal protections—save one."

The Cabana Boys pushed through the door. Luiz and Antony, followed by Tuan and Nikolai, Ilhami and Raina, flanked the doorway, guns at the ready. Kurt in his Kevlar and swords stayed in the hall. Raina blew Joy a kiss. Ilhami would not meet her eye.

"Ah." Nikolai smiled at Monica and tossed his caramel bangs. "Hello again."

Monica stared up at the Russian underwear model. "Oh. Sweet. Jesus."

"Jesús is at home with his mother," Luiz said, pronouncing the Spanish. "I tucked him in myself." He gave his buttermelt smile and a quick bow. "We will be your escorts for the evening."

Tuan smirked. "We've come to rescue you!"

"Or pre-rescue you," Antony said holding a Colt .45. "Why wait?"

"There is nothing in your oath that prevents bodyguards," Kurt said. "Especially in the case of a preceding Edict."

Raina shrugged. "We figure if they can use the same argument, why can't we?"

Joy found that she could breathe. She pressed her hand to her chest. "Oh my God," she said. "Oh my God, thank you! Thank you so much!"

"Clock's ticking," Raina said, checking her wrist. "We ready to go?"

"You, too," Ink said, taking Monica's hand.

"What? No!" Joy said.

"She is not your family," Ink said. "And her protections may be insufficient."

What went unsaid was whether Sol Leander would protect Monica against the Tide.

"We'll meet the others at the brownstone," Inq said. "She'll be safer with us than if she stayed here." She wrinkled her nose playfully. "Besides, I like her. She's feisty!"

"But—" To bring Monica along was to drag her into the

heart of danger and Joy felt the flash of hopeless panic, the color of old blood, the memory of the Red Knight reflected in a mall of shattered glass. *I can't let it happen again!*

"Please," Joy said, grabbing Monica. "Please don't. I mean it. Please?"

Monica shook her head. "You heard the lady—I'm safer with you. And, no offense, but I don't trust any of these guys to keep you from doing something stupid."

Raina flashed a golden-gloss smile. "Ooo! I *like* you! You're smart."

Joy stood slowly, overwhelmed with panic and tears. She looked around at the resolve in everyone's faces. "I'm just—"

"Loved," Ink said gently. "You are loved, Joy Malone."

"That's sweet, but we're leaving now." Inq spread her fingers and marched forward, pulling her well-muscled and well-armed harem in her wake. Monica and Joy exchanged glances, Ink took their hands and Kurt covered their backs as they slid through the portal, which wobbled and warped with the scent of dried roses.

Joy, Ink, Monica, Inq, Kurt and the Cabana Boys disappeared through the concentric ripples—gone.

Monica admired the Bailiwick's office, impressed and slightly dazed. Joy tried to see it for the first time with its great mahogany desk and emerald dealer's lamp, its shelves full of art and books, its Roman pedestals, lily fountains and heavy curtains against the sun. But the giant, four-armed frog in the gold-rimmed spectacles was undoubtedly the thing you'd notice first.

Filly clapped Joy's shoulder and gripped her forearm in greeting. The Cabana Boys took their seats. Ilhami flipped his chair ass-backward and draped his arms over the top. Joy was conscious of how Graus Claude tracked Monica's movements, eyes in covetous slits; she would have to keep her friend as far away from the Bailiwick as possible, for everyone's sake.

Kurt entered the room and professionally drew the double doors closed. All eyes turned as the Bailiwick settled himself with a groan of his throne-like chair.

"You never cease to amaze me, Miss Malone," the Bailiwick said. "Each time, you bring me new surprises and you are certainly never one to disappoint." His head quivered as it swung from right to left. "I must confess that I find this current state of affairs rather upsetting on a personal front, and that, quite frankly, is something which I cannot abide. Not being on the Council at present, I cannot verify the claim that Aniseed and the Tide have threatened dissolution, but as there appears to be more evidence than can be dismissed in good conscience, I therefore can only accept the fact that Aniseed has, indeed, returned." His exhalation carried the weight of worlds. "And, knowing her motives as we do, she will no doubt aim her considerable resources at stopping you or, as additional insurance, destroying me. As such, I have a vested interest in ensuring that she does not succeed."

Monica leaned close to Joy. "Does he always talk like that?"

Joy nodded. "Yep."

"My usual position at Court being currently unavailable means that my own not-inconsiderable resources are stretched thin, but my best intelligence reports that Aniseed has reclaimed her seat upon the Council as it stands, subsuming Sol Leander's voting block and assuming his place as representative of the Tide. As such, she has more than enough momentum to move forward with her original plan—or at least its core purpose—to lead a coup against the humans, upsetting the balance between our worlds in order to bring about her misguided Golden Age." He shook his jowls. "With enough well-placed promises of power, wealth, privilege and revenge, I imagine that many will march under her banner, swept up in the fervor of annihilation, which, without the King and Queen to assuage them, will ultimately result in further infighting, division amongst ourselves, and paving the way toward our mutual destruction."

He coughed politely into one hand as a second withdrew his pocket kerchief, a third patting gently at his chest. "The one thing in our favor is that she must accomplish these things before the Royal Majesties cross the threshold back into our world. After that, the Folk will once again be bound by loyalty to our King and Queen, Aniseed's rebellion will end and she will once again be held accountable for her crimes." The Bailiwick's gaze shifted, touching each of them in turn. "Know that all that stands between these two outcomes is Joy's ability to provide the proof that they require, to show our Majesties that it is, in fact, safe to Return to this world. Thus, we must find a way to coax them back, restoring magic and order and balance once more."

"Is that all?" Tuan asked. Nikolai punched him in the arm.

"Not quite," Graus Claude admitted. "Our best option is to buy Joy time and keep her safe until she achieves her task, yet good strategy indicates that nullifying the greatest obstacle might clear the field entirely—removing the immediate threat to her safety would grant us the greatest chance of success."

"Kill Aniseed," Raina translated.

Graus Claude reluctantly nodded. Ink glanced at Kurt, who said nothing.

"It would behoove us to draw her out, alone, and with

every appearance of having the advantage, wherein we take her by surprise, contain her and condemn her," the Bailiwick said slowly. "With witnesses, if at all possible."

Silence strung from glance to glance.

Ink edged closer to Joy. She grabbed his hand and squeezed against the cold, hard weight of her fear. *Aniseed.* Ink stared at a spot on the carpet, as if remembering his defeat and his death at her claws. Joy kissed his knuckles. He did not respond.

"I'll do it," Filly said.

Graus Claude rumbled, "No offense, *valkyrja*, but this time it will take more than you."

Filly shrugged with casual arrogance. "I have no delusions of mortality, old frog," she said. "It is my auspice to escort warriors from their final battle, so if Aniseed dares to take up arms against you, I am sure to be there as well." She smiled lazily, like a cat, stretching the blue spot below her lower lip. Her eyes danced in anticipation. She was more than a little frightening just then.

"I must ensure that it is final," Kurt said, arms crossed. He seemed to take the return of his nemesis as a personal affront. Joy couldn't blame him; he'd lived a dozen lifetimes in training and servitude for the chance to kill her. The butler-bodyguard turned to his employer. "You may deny me many things, but you cannot deny me my fate."

Graus Claude lowered his gaze, but said nothing.

"Well, then," Inq said, crossing her feet. "We need to lure Aniseed to a remote location with something powerful enough and personal enough to make her forget to be cautious, then contain her, distract her and let Kurt kill her." She snapped her fingers. "Simple enough. Any suggestions?"

"Yes," Joy said, surprising herself. She glanced at Graus Claude. They knew how to do this. "We use bait." She nodded to Ink. "And we cheat."

TWENTY-NINE

JOY STOOD IN THE SUN, OUT IN THE OPEN, ON THE clean, even turf with the smell of mowed grass thick in her nose. Her feet, wrapped in Idmona's repaired soft, padded boots, itched to run, to leap, fly, flip and soar, but that was part of the reason she'd come here; even though the temptation to touch the Earth was terrible, she'd never felt more capable, strong, unbeatable or alive than right here at Abbot's Field.

"This is a strategically poor location," Graus Claude grumbled.

"You said I should choose a place that I knew best," Joy said. "Well, outside my home, this is it."

"Was it too much to hope that you felt safe within, say, a military compound? Or perhaps an abandoned underground nuclear power plant?"

She patted his third shoulder. "Too late now. Everyone is already in position. Now it's only a matter of waiting."

"I know," the great toad murmured, squinting under the blaze of the sun. "That is what I find most disconcerting."

"Has anyone ever said that you're kind of a control freak?"

Graus Claude slid his gaze sideways. "Not in my presence."

Joy knew she should have been worried, anxious, nervous, nauseous, but the truth was that she felt great. She craved this feeling—anticipation—like a drug. This was how she weighed her own growth and progress, measuring herself against a skilled opponent, moments before the big event. Without it, she'd been floundering, wondering, waiting to be judged, but she'd always been her harshest critic as well as her greatest coach. She didn't need someone to tell her that she could do this. She already knew, deep in her missing heart, that they'd already won.

Joy just had to get everyone else to see it, too.

"By the Swells," the Bailiwick complained under his breath. He mopped his sweaty brow with a monogrammed kerchief. The *eelet* translated his growing unease.

"Is everybody ready?" Joy asked Inq. The Scribe spread her fingers, scanning the field and forest, and nodded.

"Your furry friends have all arrived," she confirmed.

Ysabel's werewolf pack had been all too willing to be their scouts and formal witnesses to the oncoming clash. Joy had pulled in every favor and friend she had on this side of the Twixt.

"Sound off," Raina said into her earpiece.

The Cabana Boys and all of her friends answered in curt bursts like gunfire at a range. It made the quiet seem quieter after they'd finished. There was only the lonely crunch and skitter of leaves across the gravel drive.

"May I ask what those are for?" Graus Claude indicated the clump of oak leaves by her feet.

"Backup plan," Joy said. "From the Glendale Oak. In case this doesn't work."

The Bailiwick groaned, his palsy quiver more pronounced. "Let us pretend that I did not hear that and that you did not, under any circumstances, *intentionally damage* the Glendale Oak, which, aside from alerting every Forest born within a hundred leagues, would no doubt insult the King and Queen, who happen to be the ones that *planted it there!*" The last words were hissed between rows of shark teeth. Joy inched away from the offending twig. Graus Claude grimaced. "Exactly who was it that suggested this brilliant idea?"

Joy twisted her fingers. "Um, Avery."

"Who received his information from—?"

Joy swallowed. "The Tide."

"Who, I might add, take their orders from—?"

"Sol Leander," Joy whispered. "No! Aniseed."

The great amphibian nodded. "You are learning."

"Great," she said weakly. "So much for Plan Z."

"I wouldn't concern yourself overmuch," the Bailiwick sighed. "If this doesn't work, I'm afraid we won't be around to try anything else."

Joy wrapped her finger around the thin gold chain at her neck. "I get the sense that you're less than enthusiastic about our current plan."

"Forgive me. I find myself quite anxious at the prospect of confronting my ex-lover and political rival as well as my mentor, all of my clients and professional colleagues while completely exposed on all sides standing in the middle of an empty football field!"

Joy rocked on her heels. "If it makes you feel any better, it's a soccer field."

The Bailiwick's eyes narrowed dangerously. He huffed. *"Americans."*

Monica walked over to Joy and whispered in her ear. "What's with Mr. Toad?"

"He's feeling a little nervous," Joy said.

"*He's* feeling nervous?" Monica said. "What about me? I thought Goth Girl Friday said I'd be safer with you, but this feels one hundred and eighty degrees south of safe."

Joy eyed Graus Claude, who glared at Monica with calculated interest. "Well, in a sense, you are much safer here." She hesitated to add the truth that tingled on her tongue. "And, in another sense, you're also bait."

Monica's glare narrowed to a squint. "Say that again?"

"Incoming," Ink said. Everyone tensed like a fist.

This is it. Joy knew she should feel her heart hammering, but it wasn't there. There was only the hollowness and the one question: *Who would be first?*

A moment of nothing and then there he was—starlight cloak blazing, eyes furious.

"What manner of idiocy have you orchestrated this time?" Sol Leander growled as he stepped closer to the ring of combatants. The deposed representative ignored the weapons as well as those who held them, glaring directly at Joy and Graus Claude. Joy hesitated to answer. She honestly couldn't tell which of them he was talking to. "I am expected elsewhere, as I am certain you know, and have therefore come to collect my charge." He reached a hand toward Monica. "Miss Reid, if you please."

Joy turned to Monica. "You could go with him, you know," she said. "He is sworn to keep you safe."

But Monica planted her Jimmy Choos firmly in the grass.

"Forget it," Monica said. "I'm staying."

Joy felt a little bit proud and very, very guilty, but Joy needed all the help that she could get, and this was one way to get it. Joy felt horrible and triumphant that her best friend had accepted her role as part of the plan. Joy told herself that she was being honest and cautious, manipulative and sneaky, underhanded and conniving and no-holds-barred-cruel, but it was ultimately for the good of both worlds.

It still made her feel Other Than.

"Disobedience is not an option," Sol Leander said.

Monica cocked a hip. "I'm not going with you."

Sol Leander strode forward. Several guns shifted to train on him.

"You *must* leave!" he said through clenched teeth.

Ink appeared next to Monica with his straight razor. "Why?"

"Because," Avery said, materializing in a swirl of feathers and coattails. "If his charge will not withdraw from the danger, then my master will be obligated to remain at her side." The pale courtier sounded positively delighted by the prospect. "And then I, of course, would be thus obligated, too." He bowed. "In deference to my master."

Joy and Graus Claude shared identical smiles full of teeth.

"You are welcome to join us," the Bailiwick said, "provided you agree to allying with our cause, adhering to the wishes of your charge that she remain, and to provide aid toward her purpose, namely, protecting Miss Malone, defeating Aniseed and bearing witness to the Imminent Return."

Sol Leander shivered, a ripple of disgust shuddered under his cloak. He calmed himself with visible effort, his hands wrung into fists. He glared at Monica, who matched him, stare for stare. The *signatura* through her left eyebrow wrinkled as it raised in question.

"I swear it," he said hotly. "By the sun and the stars and the infinite skies." He snapped his cloak and tucked his hands neatly into his sleeves. "May I join your doomed company?"

"Indeed," Graus Claude said graciously. Raina whistled a sharp noise through her teeth and the guns lowered to let him pass. Avery took a similar oath and stepped into the circle of Folk and humans.

"Doomed, you say?" Luiz piped from his post. "That doesn't sound promising."

Sol Leander primly straightened his cloak. "She will crush you, all of you, if the Tide doesn't get here first."

"We're kind of counting on it," Joy said. Sol Leander scowled.

"I warned you what would happen if you placed your friend in danger."

"She didn't," Monica said. "I volunteered."

Joy reached out and squeezed Monica's hand, a chocolate-vanilla swirl.

Ink stood by the two of them. "That is everyone."

"Okay, then," Joy said. "Ready?"

There was a chorus of "ready"s punctuated by popping clips, clicks and snaps, and a low, buzzing drone.

Joy fished inside her pocket. It had taken a lot of searching, but she had found what she wanted on the pavement at school: a single, tiny seed. She pinched her fingers around it, picked a direction and threw.

The seed landed outside the circle, hitting the dirt. It erupted into a thick bush of wicked black thorns, marring the smooth perfection of Abbot's Field—something Joy felt like a punch to the gut.

Sol Leander sneered. "I fail to see the purpose of these theatrics."

"It's a message," Joy said, carefully. "To let them know where we are."

She glanced back at the trees surrounding the parking lot and lining the edge of the field. If they came through the forest, it would be from that direction. If they came through Earth, she would feel it underfoot. If they came by Air, they had a clear view of the sky. If by Water, both she and Graus Claude would hear them come.

One way or another, Joy doubted they'd be waiting long.

The thorn bush shuddered, branches rattling, dark spikes morphing into quills as something manifested, taking shape, uncurling, rolling backward and out, standing up suddenly on bulky, clawed feet. A snout poked out from the furry flesh. A rat's tail flopped. Piggy eyes blinked. Briarhook still wore the remnants of his disguise from Under the Hill, stained, muddy, bloody and torn—it was as if the giant hedgehog *preferred* to wear rags and reek of half-dead meat. Tuan pulled his shirt collar over his nose. Briarhook smiled with rotten teeth.

"Waiting for you, I," her tormentor said in broken English. "Long for this. End this. Promised you, I!"

"You did," Joy said past the lump in her throat. "We have an arrangement." Kurt wordlessly lifted the iron box. It contained the last of Briarhook's heart. "Consider it insurance to stay just where you are."

He scratched at the scabs around the metal plate in his chest and chuckled with the sound of rusty saws.

"Maybe let *segulah* tear pieces, you," he said. "Rip skin, chew flesh, crack bones, you, eh?" His long quills bristled, claws digging into the earth. "What think, you?"

There was a yelping snap behind them.

"A fine idea," Aniseed said, flowing out of the woods. She dropped the body of a broken wolf like a discarded shawl.

Several weapons swung to face her. She was easily eleven or twelve feet tall. It was impossible to believe that those without the Sight could miss her—she was a towering presence, gleaming and glorious. An enormous gown of forest green velvet hung from her shoulders, its edges lined in gold and copious orange fur. A generation of vixen tails curled around her neck and her dark wooden eyes whirled as she smiled. She ignored the growls of the circling pack as they melted out of the woods, lips curled, teeth bared.

"I see you've made this easy for me," Aniseed purred, stroking a hand down her stole. "Or perhaps this isn't what it seems—could it be a trap?" The dryad's face contorted into a frown, and even that was beautiful. "Oh dear, I expected more from you, Graus Claude. Administrational duties have dulled your edge."

"You speak with false knowledge and a tongue that isn't yours," he said mildly. "Neither it, nor you, are as sharp as you think." He wore his samurai suit of armor and carried a weapon in each hand—two ancient polearms, a sword and an automatic rifle. He squatted, holding them at cardinal points. "Your thoughts are secondhand, your parent's goal, a sham." He sighed. "Aniseed was intelligent, passionate, gifted beyond peer—I knew her well." His icy gaze pierced. "You are nothing more than her shadow made flesh."

"No, Claude. I am here. This is me," she said, creaking closer. "You have pearls to store your memories, I have *seeds*." She stroked her foxtail ruff. "I've survived the Council's petty Edicts, your pet assassins and my ill-promised Fate. I have *cheated death*, old pollywog, and no one knows better how rare that can be. Look around you—do you think that shall happen with any one of you?" She tilted her head coyly. "We are not ones born to submit, you and I—we know better—we *are* better. We make our own rules." She became strangely earnest, her madness sounding more like a plea. "We defied them once before—do you remember, my love? And it almost destroyed us. It could be different this time."

"No," he sighed, apologetic, sincere. "There is no 'we,' because you are not her," he whispered. "For good or ill, you are not her."

She shrugged a shapely shoulder, her polished skin flecked with blood. "So be it."

Joy swallowed. "Now."

Ink sank his blade into the ground, igniting a spark that raced along the curve of a ward that flared into life, surrounding them all. It crackled with waves of incandescent light.

Aniseed frowned. "What is this?"

"You once asked me for my *signatura*," Ink said crisply. "Here it is."

The ouroboros flamed, a dragon swallowing its tail, its scales, a thousand tongues of lapping yellow-gold, encircled all of them in its infinite waves; its eye was a single, yellow crystal, a golden clasp that once held a precious double strand of pearls. The energy of the ward was turning the gemstone sooty black. It cracked with a sudden *pop*.

Aniseed tipped her chin back and laughed. It seemed unfair that Kurt's killing stroke had left no scar on her graftling's throat. "Poor dumb creature," she said. "You are defective, defunct. You have no more magic than you have a soul. Do you think you've trapped me inside this ward with you? You think that will save anyone? I'll simply tear you all to ribbons," she said, smiling. "I've done it before."

Briarhook's quills quivered in anticipated pleasure. His claws scratched the soil.

"On the contrary," Graus Claude said. "The ward is less to keep you in, than to keep them out."

Everyone craned their heads as the winds changed. The barometer dropped. Ionic static licked the air. Massive clouds gathered in layers overhead. The field suddenly reeked of pine and brimstone and rain. The ground trembled like distant thunder, a shudder under their feet. Joy felt every hair on her body stand on end. Monica's mouth dropped open.

"Oh no, sir!"

A shadow the size of a 747 snaked across the field. Trees bent in the sudden gale, spraying leaves and seeds and fairy Folk. The Forest Folk stepped lithely out of branches or through broken bark. The ground spat out brownies, dwarves and rocks that formed shapes, pushing their way blindly forward. Pixies and sprites, nagas and djinn, banshees, basilisks, gargoyles and gryphons flew out of the sky by the dozens, soaring low on outstretched wings, curls of smoke and rolls of colorful carpet. Giants squatted near dryads, elves stood by lizard kings, ghostly wraiths slipped through phookas and bunyips, and nixies dismounted from dripping hippocamps while geysers of fire erupted, spewing handsome, long-limbed warriors with glowing pet salamanders perched on their backs.

Then the mighty dragon, Bùxiǔ de Zhēnzhū, landed with all the Council members gathered along his length. His smoky mustaches undulated along his thick mane, his teeth dripped saliva down his thin chin beard.

Councilex Maia held up her right hand; the tip of her forefinger was sooty black.

"Ye summoned me, Councilex Claude?" she asked.

"Indeed," the Bailiwick said. The Cabana Boys kept the *segulah* trained in their sights. "I have summoned the Council and the members of the Twixt here to bear witness to the charges brought against the graftling, Aniseed, who has—with full intent and foreknowledge—adopted her parental memories and mission to actively forestall the Imminent Return by reinstating herself on the Council through coercion, usurping the monarchy by collusion, and pursuing the annihilation of four-fifths of the human population, in direct violation of the Accords, to further her private agenda of revenge. I therefore charge the graftling, Aniseed, a traitor and self-proclaimed autocrat bent on genocide, regicide and the premeditated attempted murder of the changeling, Joy Malone, and myself, as the Bailiwick of the Twixt—" If any of the Council were surprised by Graus Claude's claims, none showed it. Joy held her breath, waiting for the frog's coup de grâce. "—As witnessed by all those present as well as the King and Queen of the Twixt."

There was a tumult of murmurs, screams and shrieks, clicks, grunts and squawks, but none of the horror matched the expression on Aniseed's face.

"You *lie!*" she spat, reeling, off balance and afraid. "They are not here! They haven't Returned!"

Folk loyalty was absolute—betrayal was impossible, which was why the original Aniseed had cast a spell to make everyone—including herself—forget the King and Queen. One could not be loyal to that which no one could remember. Her crime, if known by them, would be unforgivable.

"They abandoned us! We can rule ourselves!" She appealed to those beyond the ward. "We will take back this world and claim our rightful place as gods!"

Graus Claude shook his head sadly, jowls swinging. "Alas, that is precisely the sort of myopic inanity I referenced when I said that you are a mere shadow of your predecessor," he said. "Aniseed would never have accused anyone, let alone me, of such an absurdity, and would have paid careful attention to my phrasing in order to glean my true intent." He leaned forward, head bobbing between the halberd and the rifle butt. "I did not say that they were here—I said that they were watching you."

Joy hooked her thumb under the gold chain and lifted the Third Eye pendant.

Recoiling, Aniseed screamed.

She lunged for Joy through the sudden rain of bullets. There was a mad scramble as Joy and Monica backpedaled to the farthest side of the circle as the rest of them closed in. Ink leaped forward, straight razor flashing, as Inq sheared her blurred hand, gouging a great buzzing gash in the *segulah*'s side. Sludge gushed from the wound, but it only made the dryad seethe, eyes rolling, as she continued to charge.

Sol Leander stood transfixed, caught between his leader and his human charge. Avery spun, a whirl of feather and blades, slicing through her upper arm, bisecting Briarhook's mark. The wild rose brand wept amber blood. The front line, Antony and Raina, concentrated their fire on Aniseed's face, a rictus of bloodlust and fury. Her ear snapped off. A bullet pierced her cheek. Shrieking, her hand shot forward, spearing Raina through her torso and slamming her bodily into Antony and Tuan. Joy screamed, grabbing Monica, and wrenched them back from the line of shimmering fire. The ward pulsed and repulsed, a warning shiver not to cross. Joy and her best friend huddled together, shielding their eyes from the horror of death.

Kurt unsheathed his blades, glaring up at the dryad who was tearing weapons from arms and arms from sockets amidst screams. Avery danced aside, snapping his left wing like a matador's cape. Ink dived into her blind side, shearing a sharp line, cracking ribs. Her madness turned to laughter and then tears as Aniseed twisted, corkscrew-tight within the ward.

Joy scootched back. The ouroboros was shrinking, swallowing its tail, as per the plan.

"Out!" shouted Inq, tapping her sternum.

An answering pulse flashed on the *lehman*'s chests. Antony grabbed fistfuls of Raina's and Tuan's shirts, yanking them through the ward. It let them pass. Ilhami gave a rebel yell, covering their escape, scooping up Tuan's weapon and shooting both barrels at everything above head height. Nikolai bodily tackled him as Aniseed hissed, spinning, splashing the contents of whatever vial she'd had hidden under her stole. Her fringe of fox fur smoked black and the earth around them sizzled. Both Nik and Ilhami writhed like wounded animals, their skin bubbling and bursting, their limbs contorting into broken shapes.

"Out!" Inq shouted.

Another flash. Both men struggled to obey their mistress, rolling and crawling desperately, clawing their fingers in the dirt. Nikolai screamed as he dragged his belly through the burning ward, agonizingly slow. Ilhami, half-blinded, face melted, flailed in the grass. Joy moved to help him. His hand shot out, warning her off.

"No! Joy! Get back!"

Monica yanked her behind Sol Leander.

Flopping, heaving, Ilhami panted, straining forward, face pressed into the green, as Aniseed's giant fist hit his skull with a sickening crack.

"NO!" Joy screamed. Monica's fingernails dug into her arms, holding her back.

"Joy! *Don't!*"

Inq howled. A burst of atomized sap exploded from Aniseed's chest. Kurt landed a solid kick followed by a punch of steel. Avery vanished in a sweep of feathers, appearing moments later beneath the witch's chin, slicing sideways as Inq buried her arm into Aniseed's gut. The dryad screamed, choking, and clawed at her middle, catching nothing but air. Another ripple, Inq appeared and Ilhami was thrown outside the ward.

"I'm done playing," Inq said. "Just watch me—"

"Down!"

Graus Claude jumped, extending his impossibly long legs, crossing two of his weapons before him, simultaneously throwing the halberd and squeezing the rifle's trigger, catching the recoil against his chest. Aniseed staggered. Her wrist snapped. Sharpened claws flew like arrows, catching the armored amphibian in the stomach, chest, arm and throat. He hit the ground behind them like a wet sack.

"No!" Joy dropped to her knees and crawled beside him. "No no no no—!" Monica crouched next to her, the letter opener quivering in her fist. Inq spun around quickly, her buzzing hands swift as scythes. A gash exploded across Aniseed's face, dragging from clavicle to breast.

"Graus Claude!" Joy said desperately, pressing her hands against one of the bubbling wounds. "Bailiwick!" The four-inch wooden talons were buried deep. Blood gushed absolutely everywhere and his flesh was spongy and slack. Monica pressed hard around the stake in the Bailiwick's belly. He sputtered, a strangled sound. Joy's hands slipped off the bloody armor as she fumbled with the ties. If she removed Aniseed's thorns, there was no doubt he'd die before she cut the wounds closed, but if she didn't do something, he'd certainly die in her hands.

Unlike Aniseed, who refused to ever die.

This can't be happening! I can stop it! I can make it untrue!

Graus Claude wheezed thinly, his sharp eyes beginning to fade.

"They will come," he panted through bloody lips. "They will come."

Joy's hands flailed, her brain screaming, *Graus Claude! No! Stef!*

There was another bloodcurdling scream as Aniseed lunged, but Sol Leander stepped between them with a burst of negative light, erecting a ward like the corona of an eclipse in reverse.

"Stay down!" he commanded.

Joy screamed, "Can't you stop her?"

Sol Leander pushed back grimly on the force of his spell. "I can hold her at bay for a short while," he said, glancing down at the skewered body. "But I do not have the Bailiwick's power."

Joy squinted, shielding her eyes. The Bailiwick *was* powerful, both as Graus Claude and as the door between worlds. Joy needed that power to save him, and her brother and everyone else, right now! Her Sight caught the faintest blue light—a tiny *signatura* of a flowering lotus in the heart of the ox bone blade.

Joy grabbed Monica's hand and yanked her closer. "We have to get him up!" she shouted. "We have to get him standing!"

"Are you crazy?" Monica shouted, pressing bloody hands down. "That'll kill him!"

"No!" Joy said. "It's the only way to save him!"

Another assault battered the black hole shield. There was the *shing* and clatter and roar of battle just beyond Sol Leander's spell.

"Use the knife! This knife! Command him! Here!" Joy shook her friend's hand. "Order him to stand up! You can make him! Do it! Try!"

"What do you mean I can *make* him?" Monica asked.

Joy hissed a low whisper; afraid of being overheard, afraid it was already too late. "You can *control* him. With this. It's got his blood on it! It's magic! Do it! Tell him! Command it! Now!"

"*That's* what you did with this thing? You made him into a puppet? And you *knew*?" Joy's best friend looked very much like she wanted to slap her and storm off. "Do you have any idea how WRONG that is?"

"Yes, I do," Joy said. "Just use it!"

"No!" Monica shouted. "No, I won't, Joy. I can't!" She stared down at the dying frog. "It's not right!"

This wasn't the time for an ethical debate—Graus Claude was dying by degrees.

"Monica—!"

Her friend shook her head. "Is that what's been going on—the house? The pearls? The surveillance? For this?"

"YES!"

"NO!" Monica shouted. "I can't believe you'd do this to me! You made him a slave and gave me the whip?" Joy was terrified, speechless. Monica, for her part, seethed. "I can't do that! I can't make him do something against his will!"

Joy shook her sticky fists, helpless, furious. Monica didn't understand; she couldn't—wouldn't—use magic, but Joy could and would and did.

"Fine," she snapped. "Give it to me."

Monica glared daggers at her. "No."

"Bequeath me the knife!" Joy said. "I can use it to save him! To save us!"

"No," Monica said flatly. "You can't hold power like that over someone—that's slavery! That's..." She struggled for the right word. "Inhuman!"

Joy choked back tears, recoiling. "But he'll die!"

Monica was beyond angry, her blotchy face matching Joy's flush. "It's not your life! It's not your choice! And it's not mine, either—" She grabbed one of the Bailiwick's loose hands, claws and all, and slapped the ox bone blade into his palm. "It's his!"

Joy knelt closer, willing for there to be a miracle, wishing that he would heal himself, hoping that he could hold on.

Her mentor's breath rattled in his chest. He was deflating like a balloon. She shook her head, dripping tears. "Graus Claude," she whispered into his eardrum. "I can save you, but you have to stand up! *Please!*"

But he barely moved. Even if she could take the ox bone blade and use it like the scalpel, she needed time. He needed time. And immortality did not mean No Return.

"*Bailiwick!*" Joy screamed.

Three arms pushed forward. His eyes were rolling as he coughed up blood. He wheezed through his teeth and dragged his feet through the dirt, squatting forward on his belly like a toad. His head nodded, quivering, eyes glazed, mouth dripping. It was enough.

"I demand entrance to the Bailiwick of the Twixt!"

At first Joy thought she was too late, but then his glassy eyes filmed over, his breathing slowed, his broken jaw clicked as his mouth grew wider, taller, stronger, stiffening as his body lurched into position—his head yawned open, mouth upraised, hands curled into familiar perches on his hips and knees. His tongue adhered to the top of his palette, exposing the stairwell down into darkness beyond.

Graus Claude, the Bailiwick, was safe as stone—an immortal thing, outside of time.

Joy collapsed in relief, her body's tension cut in two.

"What the hell happened?!" Monica shouted.

"He's the entrance to the Bailiwick," Joy said. "The doorway to Faeland—I opened it. He's safe, now." She glanced down his throat, wondering if they could hear her. "But we *can't* let Aniseed get through before the Imminent Return!"

Monica wiped her hands in the grass as the battle raged behind them in a shower of sparks and blood. "How long is that going to take?"

"I don't know," Joy said. "It's supposed to be imminent."

Monica stared at Joy. "Are you kidding me?" She grabbed Graus Claude's discarded rifle and dragged it over by the butt. She propped the recoil pad against the statue's knee and dug the stand into the grassy ground. Joy edged away from the weapon. She was far more scared of guns than magic.

"Do you know how to use that?" Sol Leander asked.

"No," Monica said, trembling, adjusting the grip with shaking fingers. "But don't tell them that!"

Sol Leander shifted his shield with a ghost of a smile. It looked like pride.

"You should go," Joy said. "Get outside the ward. The Cabana Boys will protect you. You can ask for asylum from the Court of Earth."

"Air!" Sol Leander snapped. "She is *my* charge!"

"She's my friend!"

"She's standing *right here*!" Monica pulled on the cartridge, leaning back until she found the safety, which surprised her by flipping with a sharp *clack*. She smiled uneasily, lips quivering. "And I'm staying," she said. "Because if I'm staying, he's staying and you need him to win this thing—you need both of us—so that's that." She shrugged. "Just call me Stupid."

"Okay," Joy said. "Okay. Thank you."

"If she dies, I will kill you," Sol Leander swore impotently at Joy's back.

She barely glanced away from the battle. She muttered thickly, "Get in line."

"You wish to save her?" Sol Leander said, grunting with the effort of holding off the death match. "Do you wish to save him? Yourself? Anyone? Then you need more—" He broke off, sternly apologetic, almost fatherly. "I am sorry, but you must be more than what you are."

Joy understood. If she could not have a human heart, she was willing to sacrifice it to save two worlds. She would sacrifice the chance to be human to save her friends, to save Stef, to save Ink. She knew what had to happen next.

Monica said, "I've got your back."

"You always do." Joy smiled. "Just don't shoot me in the head."

Monica nodded but didn't laugh. She knelt, hands shaking, next to the Bailiwick, prepared to defend him for her friend. There was an explosion of stars as Sol Leander's ward collapsed. The first thing she saw was Ink, standing before Aniseed, his face splotched with black blood. His head turned away from the dryad's, shrieking and writhing, catching Joy's eye as the eclipse light winked out. He saw what would happen. He couldn't stop it. He knew.

She fell into his eyes. They said *No* and *I love you* and *Goodbye*.

Joy stepped in front of the Bailiwick and placed her hands on the ground—the earth she knew better than any other rose to meet her, thick, rich, well-seeded and firm. She spread her fingers through the grass, letting her eyes unfocus, tuning out the tumult into a quiet blur. Shapes softened, becoming colors; swirls of black, blue and silver against green and orange and brown. Sounds dimmed to a hum and the world unfolded under her feet.

Salt. Minerals. Water. Earth. Blood. She felt herself touching everything—everything alive—because all life came from the oceans, the earth, the blood, the salt. It tasted of metal and glaciers, rock and sand, sea water, copper, iron, and old, old ice. It burned up her arms, lit up her hamstrings, fired her legs, her hips, filling her up from the core of her world, *this* world, and the one she'd inherited from her ancestors long ago in the Wild. She'd been fighting it, afraid of losing herself, but the truth was that she'd found herself, her True Name, her power. *Her.* Even if the Earth scared her, changed her, there were some things worth protecting. She let go, becoming what she was born to be— what she had always been—

No mistakes.

The ground broke upward and outward, fountaining dirt and mud and icy ore, enfolding her, embracing her, hardening, collapsing, trying to complete the transformation, the merging of two worlds into one body, the instrument of an entire people buried, hunted and forgotten, waiting to arise. Joy embraced Earth and called it home.

I AM THIS WORLD. I AM ITS MOTHER. I AM ITS ANCIENT DAUGHTER.

WE ARE LIFE, INVINCIBLE.

I AM WOKEN. I AM FREE.

Her body convulsed, half-buried, burning; her skin baked, merging, melting into rock, into steam. Plates of earth kept hardening into crystals that shattered, flaking away in shards, pieces rolling down the slopes of her massive legs and buried hips that disappeared into the ground. Incomplete, at the edge of things, it was still enough.

Aniseed's roots tore through the surface, salting the ground with blood and gore. Joy's buried fist drove up, bursting in a tidal wave of earth, great slabs of stone shooting up like a wall—a prison, a cage—pinning Aniseed, trapping her long enough for Ink to sever her leg with his blade. She screeched. The others swarmed upon her, those few that were left. Sol Leander grabbed his aide by the feathered scruff and tossed him inelegantly through the shrinking ward.

Aniseed stared at the half-formed creature that was part-Elemental, the thing of Folk nightmares, the scourge of the

Twixt. The gathered Folk howled in terror at the sight of their ancient enemy. Ink's ward kept them locked out, at bay. Joy was distantly both grateful and grim. She had just been outed as the most dangerous creature in the world.

Aniseed laughed within her stony prison, even as she clutched her severed leg. "Ha ha ha! Look, stripling—" she gasped. "Do you see? See all those you meant to save? They will kill you! They hate you! They want to tear you apart and toss the pieces like flower petals at the feet of their King and Queen." A growing light was crawling up the Bailiwick's throat. "No matter what happens to me, I will know that I had my revenge!"

"As have I," Joy managed through her clattering teeth, the ground slowly closing over her head. The clay helm kept breaking off and falling apart in crumbles, exposing hot chunks of her human face. Joy blinked away the chalky dust while staring at her foe.

"Oh no," Aniseed chuckled. "I know the face of my death and it is not yours—my death was fated, foretold in the Dark Days—but I did not submit! I chose to make my *own* destiny! I am undying! I am triumphant!" She pointed at the crumpled mass to her left. *"I have cheated death!"*

Kurt was splayed on the ground, an inelegant smear. Everyone in the Twixt knew what Fate had held in store for him—it was well known the Bailiwick's manservant had been spared the Black Plague and offered to Graus Claude in exchange for his life, having lived for one purpose: to bring about Aniseed's death. It was both his Fate and his fondest wish.

Joy blinked, unbelieving. Her breath chugged in her chest, coughing through puffs of dust. "Is—is he dead?"

Ink staggered on unsteady legs, pale as a shadow, eyes flat. "He is dead."

"Aha!" Aniseed cackled with mad relief. The light from the Bailiwick etched her face in stark shadow. "I win!"

Kurt's head lolled sideways. His body flickered. His mouth moved.

"Not exactly," he said.

The glamour died, revealing Filly laughing, coughing blood across her cheek.

"Victory!" she said and spat at the witch.

Kurt stepped out of the Bailiwick, hale and hearty, both swords held high as he broke into a run, racing purposefully, joyously, malevolently toward his fate. Aniseed lunged back, her mouth a snarl of horror. Joy let go, the stone slabs of the dryad's prison parted, falling, as Kurt ran through the breach, undaunted, slashing both swords in unison and plunging them deep into her back. It was the crack of an ax. A clap of thunder. With a guttural scream, he wrenched them lengthwise, scissors slicing, severing her spine.

The great tree witch toppled, broken, slapping heavily against the ground. Joy felt the impact through the soil and in the roots of her teeth. Aniseed's body crumpled in stages, her broken limbs shuddering death whispers, her blood slowly soaking into the grass—to Joy, it tasted like honey. Disgusted, Joy withdrew from Earth...and what remained behind was human. *Part-human. Part-Twixt. Part-Earth. Me.*

Joy's stony carapace crumbled, flaking off great scabs of dirt. Ink appeared beside her, holding her, helping her out, running his fingers over her hair and face and arms and back, convincing himself that she was whole. Joy leaned on his forearm and managed a smile.

"I am here," she said with shaky breaths. "I am very, very here."

Aniseed's fading gaze slid over them as if slipping off a far horizon. Her mahogany lips creaked as she spoke her last.

"How?" she whispered.

Ink glared down at her, stone-faced. "I lied."

Her eyes rolled slowly in their sockets, a one-quarter turn. The air seemed to leave her lungs as she sagged against the ground, her torso collapsing, sprouting moss and mushrooms that bloomed and blackened, withered and died, as her body dissolved, emptying, joining the earth from which all things come and go and come again—but this time, in this life, it was Aniseed's final Return.

"Wait," Joy mumbled, wetting her lips and staring at Ink. "What did you say?"

Ink brushed her shoulders, lingering a moment on Grimson's mark. "I lied," he said. "Remember, I was made, not born. So, technically, I am not one of the Folk, and therefore I am not bound by their rules. It is what the princess intended and the Folk required—that Inq and I would be loyal and yet have the freedom to choose to whom we give our loyalty."

Joy gaped at him. The words took longer than they should have to come out. "You *lied*?"

He nodded. "Often."

"But...you said you never lied."

He cocked his head, smiling. One dimple. "Also a lie."

Joy stepped closer. He caught her arm as she swayed. "Have you lied to me?"

"Not intentionally," he said, black eyes demure behind long lashes. Two dimples.

"Liar," she said, and kissed him.

THIRTY

THE HONEYED LIGHT FROM THE BAILIWICK SWELLED and burst into golden radiance as the King and Queen emerged and everyone dropped to their knees. Joy knelt, head bent, because she chose to—not because she had to—she was not Folk, she was a part-human changeling, and she was mourning what it was to be mortal.

Their entrance preceded a sudden flood of Folk; soldiers and courtiers and wide-eyed children walked disbelievingly onto the grassy field, squinting up at their long-lost sun. Their awed murmurs transformed into screams of joy, a clamor of names as the Twixt raised their eyes.

"Mama!" A tiny antlered girl ran toward the line of flame.

"Drop the ward," the King commanded. "We are not separate any longer."

Ink obeyed, slicing through the ouroboros, which collapsed in a shower of sparks as the crowd of Folk converged in a laughing, crying, hugging, keening, jumping, flying, barking, cawing, roaring, singing, breathing, glorious mass of family, kith and kin.

The Council bowed before their monarchs, begging forgiveness and offering fealty; many of the Folk lay prostrate as others kissed the hems of their gowns, crying grateful tears. Children yelped and laughed and cried and squealed the way that only small children do, and Joy searched the crowd for a certain sapphire nixie she'd know upon Sight.

Strange music radiated in every direction, like Inq's ripples through the world. Wherever it touched, the world looked brighter, fuller, more saturated with color and light.

Something was changing and everything had changed.

The Folk crowded Abbot's Field. Ink held her arm. Joy hung on to him, looking for her brother and Dmitri, Inq and the Cabana Boys—she needed to know who was safe and alive. Ink's hand was on her back, steadying her against the warring tides of hope and sadness, relief and dread, knowing and not. She didn't know what to feel until she could see them all again. Joy turned, trying to find their faces in the crowd, when the Queen appeared suddenly within a hand's breadth.

"Release him," she commanded, pointing at Graus Claude.

"I formally withdraw from the Bailiwick," Joy said, tripping over the words. His features began to color, his mouth retracting, shrinking, as bloody patches bloomed over his skin. Aniseed's wooden talons had broken off during the change—but what would happen when he started breathing, bleeding? How much time had Joy stolen? Had it been enough?

But as his eyes changed from white to ice blue, the Bailiwick stretched languorously, all traces of wounds and damage gone. Joy would have run and hugged him if not for their formal audience and the grisly state of his armor. *Etiquette and decorum.*

Graus Claude tugged his bloodied armor and bowed before his Queen.

"Your Majesty," he rumbled. "I humbly beg your forgiveness for my lapses, for my failure to act, for my weakness and willful ignorance that brought us to this brink, but I would have you know that I remained loyal and in your devoted service in the hopes of realizing this glorious day."

"Nonsense," the Queen said. "You are our chosen vessel and the best of all those maintaining the Twixt in our stead. Ironshod could not have chosen wiser. He always spoke highly of you and with the utmost respect. You honor us with your loyalty and the love you've shown our people." She turned her terrible, beautiful face to Joy with the barest hint of a smile. "You have done well by us, courier, although your predecessor had little to offer as praise. Yet you fulfilled your role admirably, Joy Malone."

"Thank you, Your Majesty."

"And thus, you are absolved of any wrongdoings concerning the oak." Joy swallowed audibly as Graus Claude shot her an icy glare.

"Was that your proof?" Joy blurted. Graus Claude coughed with a scandalized scowl. "Your Majesty?"

The Queen did not deign to acknowledge the lapse. "Our proof was this." She gestured to Monica. "We witnessed a human willingly and knowingly decline to claim ownership over one of the Folk, bequeathing onto him his own freedom, his own life, rather than abusing that power to save herself." She fanned her fingers as if caressing Monica's cheek through the air between them. "To you, who granted us our safe Return, you have our eternal gratitude."

Monica blinked as the Queen herself inclined her chin and everyone around them, including Joy, bowed before Monica—the most powerful human in the world—the girl who saved the world simply by being *human*.

Satisfied, the Queen withdrew. The crowds stood. Monica swooned on her feet.

"Miss Reid." The Bailiwick addressed her formally with

every ounce of dignity. "To you I must also offer my humblest apologies," he said, bowing again. "May I extend our gratitude to you, as members of the Council of the Twixt, as well as my own, personal, appreciation that you are a person of wisdom, integrity, honor, compassion and enlightenment." He glanced up at Joy from beneath his postorbital ridge. "Best take notes, Miss Malone."

He took a hand from each of them and pressed a sincere kiss across their knuckles in turn. He hung on to Joy's a moment longer, covering her hand with his own.

"Thank you," said Monica. "And may I suggest you do likewise."

The Bailiwick stiffened. Joy felt a sick stab in her gut. The icy blue eyes blinked once.

"Pardon?"

"You said how much you appreciate my granting you your freedom," she said. "How about paying it forward?" Monica turned pointedly to look at Kurt, who stood with Inq and the remaining Cabana Boys in a quiet huddle. Joy had told her Kurt's story, but Monica, being Monica, pushed it one step further. "I'm *certain* your King and Queen would approve."

Graus Claude's stillness cracked along the edges. All four hands twitched. Even freed, he could deny her nothing— she'd just been honored by royalty.

"Indeed," he croaked. "You are quite correct." The Bailiwick placed his hands across his belly and, with a double-slashing motion, crossed an X through where his *signatura* burned. Across the field, Kurt jerked—a hand pressed hard against his abs—and his eyes cut to his master, who was his master no more. Graus Claude gestured, a soldier's salute, and Kurt returned it, placing a hand on Inq's shoulder.

"There, now, doesn't that feel better?" Monica said with a self-satisfied smirk.

Graus Claude grumbled, shifting his enormous feet. "You could have commanded me to do so before you released me."

"Yes, but then what would have been the point?" Monica said. "You have to have the choice to do what's right—*that's* the point."

The Bailiwick nodded and then took Joy by the arm, steering her quickly aside as if to forestall her getting any new ideas from her best friend.

"I expect I will be seeing you again shortly," he said, his authoritative tone returning. "Now that my theory about your change has proven out, we must invent an entirely new category of Folk and establish the proper protocols—if the Return is any evidence, the magic has already adjusted to suit and now our work can truly begin."

Ink slid into step alongside them. "And what theory is this?"

"Why, that there was no possibility of Joy completing the transformation," the Bailiwick said as if this were obvious, which it wasn't. Not by a long shot. Joy stopped walking. Graus Claude raised a manicured claw. "Miss Malone foreswore all armor in exchange for accepting a True Name. Did I not explain that in order to become an Earth Elemental, you must be entirely subsumed within your element—in a cocoon, if you will—until the change can complete?" He spread his four arms wide. "Well, there you have it. Without ability to suit yourself in Earth's embrace, no transformation is possible. Thus you are now as you always shall be—wholly and completely 'incomplete' until we all Return, ashes to ashes, dust to dust." He smiled knowingly. "I am afraid this condemns you to remain part-Twixt and part-human, after all."

Joy could have kissed him and did. As she pressed her lips against his jowly cheek, he blushed a brilliant emerald green. He smiled and patted her arm as she let go.

"Now I know that you must have many questions and decisions to make concerning your upcoming future, but you are the first human-Elemental changeling we've identified since the purge and, as such, you are granted certain responsibilities that must be formally included within our governance in order for your status to be sanctioned." He paused, considering. "I am thinking 'ambassador' has a fine ring to it. Ambassador to the Twixt. Of course, this will elevate the Scribes accordingly—given their ties to both the princess and yourself. Mistress Inq, in particular, should be quite pleased with that!" The Bailiwick draped an arm casually over Joy's shoulders. "Have you ever considered majoring in Political Science?" His eyes fairly glinted with imagined opportunities. "Yes, Miss Malone. We have much to do!"

"As do we all, good sir Bailiwick," Ink said, gesturing toward Bùxiǔ de Zhēnzhū, a dragon no longer, and his Council of loyalists speaking to the King.

"Ah yes," Graus Claude said, straightening his spine to his impressive height. "I must go present myself formally to my colleagues on the Council." His grin was full of shark teeth. His pink tongue flicked with a snap. "I shall deeply relish watching them squirm."

And with that, the hunchbacked Councilex lumbered resolutely toward the gathering Courts. Ink and Joy exchanged a glance at the pomp in his step.

"Will you look at the Frog Prince strut," Monica muttered over Joy's shoulder.

"Monica!" Joy grabbed her best friend, squeezing her in her arms. "Oh my God! You did it!" she crowed. "You are the *best*! You're *amazing*! You saved the world!"

Monica laughed. "I did! You did! We so totally did!"

They clung to each other, laughing with effervescent glee. This was it—what Joy had always wanted, but never hoped could happen—friends, family, kindness, forgiveness, happy endings, new beginnings, all together. *This!*

"Joy!"

Stef pushed past a knot of sasquatch and grabbed her bodily, smashing her against his chest.

"Stef!" she cried, her eyes tearing.

"Oh my God," he whispered, squeezing her tight. "You did it, Joy! I knew you could!"

Burly arms wrapped around them both, knocking them sideways. Curly horns butted against her head.

"Hey," Dmitri said, scratching his beard against her cheek. "Did I hear something about someone saving the world?"

"Not me—it was Monica," Joy said, pointing at Monica, who joined the group hug. Joy felt Ink's arms come around her and he tucked his chin on her shoulder.

"You deserve some credit," he said.

She wrapped her arm around him. "I'm just happy to be me!"

As they turned in their huddle, Joy spied Sol Leander staring at them over a young lady's sparkling shoulder. She might have imagined his nod, but she did not imagine the kiss he pressed against the maiden's starlight hair. He held her tenderly as they walked off together, exposing the snow-haired figure standing behind him.

Joy shouted, "Avery!"

He turned, stumbling slightly under his thick cloak of

feathers. Even wounded, he looked happy. He kept glancing around at all the Folk dancing and laughing, kissing and clasping hands, embracing one another lovingly in their wings. The courtier smiled, looking lighter despite the heavy weight on his shoulders.

"Well met, Joy Malone," he said. "And an honor, Miss Reid."

Joy asked, "Do you have family here?"

"No. All my family were human," Avery said. "They died long ago." He didn't sound sad when he said it. It must have been years, decades, centuries. "Sometimes, when we find ourselves alone, we will cling to any kindness." It was almost a story—betrayed by family, joining the Tide, condemnation, redemption—it showed on his face. "Do you see now why I wanted to save you?"

It seemed too public a place, too private a question, too unsaid a secret, especially with Ink standing by.

Because you love me? she guessed. Instead she said, "No."

Avery gave a rueful smile, a gentle chiding as if he'd heard her thoughts. *So human.* "Because of what you represent," he said. "That magic chooses justly, that right will win out, that we can be kind as well as cruel and that there are no mistakes." His wing shifted, curled protectively against his side. "And that if you belong, well, then, so do I."

"Avery," Joy said. "I know it's a curse, but you've given me your *signatura*—if you want, I can negate the spell by erasing its mark on you." She glanced at Ink and her brother. "But it may mark you as one of mine."

"Really?" Avery said. "Have you discovered your auspice?"

She nodded. "I can erase the mistakes of the past."

Avery blinked, and a flush of pink rose to his cheeks. "Well," he said. "That is something to consider. And I will consider it most seriously." He bowed to each of them, pressing a bandaged hand to his heart as he left. "Many thanks to all of you and very well met."

"Hey, Cabana Girl," Luiz whispered timidly behind her, and then Joy was in his arms, holding him, grateful and sorry and mournful and alive. It felt like Enrique's funeral all over again, and she knew that Ilhami and Raina were dead without even having to ask. Her eyes filled with tears as she squeezed him harder. Knowing wasn't better than not knowing for sure.

"Inq?" she said.

"She's mourning," Luiz said past her ear. "But we'll light fires and have a party and paint ourselves gold."

"And have an art gallery showing and get higher than kites," Joy said. "They would have loved that."

Luiz started crying. "Now you get it, Cabana Girl." Antony hugged her next, stoic and solemn, then Tuan, who clung to her and openly sobbed, but it was Nikolai who brought out the laughing tears, because Ilhami was right—he *did* smell like beans.

One by one, the Cabana Boys melted into the throng.

"Joy," Ink said, accepting her back into his arms. "I am sorry."

"It's done," Joy whispered. "It's over."

"Not quite," Ink said, tugging her closer. "I must now give you back what you have given me."

A sudden fear crept over her. *What is he saying? Is he leaving? Am I losing him* now? Joy blinked back startled tears. Her fingers tightened in his sleeves.

"I—" she began, and swallowed, mouth gone dry. "I don't—"

He smiled, both dimples. "You gave me your heart," he said slowly, shyly, drawing his fingers down the silver wallet chain, back to the trifold wallet in his pocket. He lifted out the silver quill, its every fletching etched delicately by hand. Tilting the point above his heart, he swept it expertly in a graceful design—a looping circlet with a hook at its center, a pictograph in profile: a flame-winged bird taking flight. Joy recognized it instantly. *My signatura. My True Name.* He slipped his hand through the sigil, passing from one plane to the next, and drew an object out of thin air, placing it in her hand. "I kept it safe for you."

The wax simulacrum was warm to the touch. Joy stared at its brown hair and the red bump at its heart. She almost said, *How?* but then remembered Monica stuffing it in the ouroboros box, her birthday present from Ink—their private way of sending each other letters full of *I love you* and *I miss you*, exchanging distant secrets across time and space.

It had sent him her heart. And he'd kept it safe.

Ink's fingers traced the tiny face, the curl of hair, and the tiny red flower bud waiting to bloom.

"You!" Briarhook's snarled. Joy jerked in Ink's arms. The fetid hedgehog stood in his tattered rags and dirty chest plate, bits of leaf and mulch sticking to the ends of his quills. He squinted piggy eyes at her and curled his lip from rotted teeth. "Have business, you, I. Promised you. Know this promise, *mine!*"

Joy could feel the nearness of the Cabana Boys and Monica, Dmitri and Stef, and Ink steady at her side. Inq slipped through the masses, the Folk parting to make way, and behind her, Kurt, her lover, followed carrying an iron box. He presented it formally to Joy. It felt lighter than ever. Briarhook hissed, drooling, his quills quivering as he watched it exchange hands.

She knew what she had to do. The nightmares were over.

"You're right," she said. "I understand." And she did. "I

know what it is to be without a heart." She offered him the box. "Take it. It's yours."

He hunched back, wary, sensing a trap. "My *heart*—?"

"Yes."

"Price, you?"

"No," Joy said. "I give it to you, willingly." Her arms shook slightly. The box wasn't *that* light, and Briarhook was still scary. "Let us finish this between us."

Briarhook snatched the box greedily in both hands. Flipping the lid, he grabbed the last morsel of his heart and stuffed it into his cheeks, barely chewing, gobbling, swallowing it down. His eyes closed for a moment. Joy waited, patient, tense. His body shuddered and he stood a little straighter. He no longer looked quite as grubby, quite as pallid, quite as ill. His eyes opened slowly. Wiping his sticky hand across his belly, he smiled.

"Ah. Promised you, I," he said, coyly. "When my heart, mine, then you die *slow*."

Several weapons appeared as their small circle tightened around Joy. Ink shoved the wax doll into her hands, the jagged razor reappearing with a flick of his wrist. The hedgehog glanced at them, past them, then around the joyous chorus of the Imminent Return. He shuffled forward, raising one hand, spreading his claws like an umbrella; a strange heat blossomed, stirring the thing in her hands. Joy felt something wriggle beneath her thumb.

Then, all at once, her doll's heart *bloomed*.

Joy gasped. The tiny flower had pushed itself out of the wax and opened. She pressed her palm against an answering thud in her chest. Joy inhaled like she'd been underwater, her cheeks flushing with heat, her eyes sparkling, her ears pounding: *Thump-thump! Thump-thump! Thump-thump!*

"I can feel it!" she said, tears spilling out her eyes. She

grabbed Ink and pulled Monica close. She felt both of them laughing. "I can feel you! I can feel my heart!"

Ink pressed her to him, smiling. "Now you know what it is to feel Joy!"

Briarhook gave a dismissive sneeze and swatted the air with his claw. "Is done. Promised you, I." He scratched at his snout. "Die, you, old age," he muttered. "Mortal death, eh? You die *slow*." Hunching, turning away, he curled into a tight, prickly ball. Briarhook rolled past the others and crawled into the briar bush, melting among the thorns, and vanished with a rattle of quills.

Joy stumbled on her feet. She could breathe again! She could *breathe*!

"Well, now, that one certainly knows how to play his cards!" Filly quipped, stepping up with a clatter of finger bones. She grasped Joy's forearm, giving an extra squeeze. "Well played, indeed!"

"Well played, yourself," Joy said. "Ink scared me to death when he said that Kurt was dead. I wasn't sure if he meant the glamour or you!" Kurt nodded politely. Filly laughed.

"Oh, I'm *fine*," the Valkyrie said with a wink. "No worse for wear after walking around looking like this ugly brute." She cocked a thumb at Kurt, who didn't even flinch. Filly's face split in a slit-eyed grin. "I wonder how much fun I'll have with a glamour that looks like you?"

Kurt smiled. It was scary. Inq chuckled.

Oh boy.

The King and Queen raised their arms, their long hair fanning behind them like wings. Ink and Joy turned with everyone else to hear their twined voices, crisp and sharp and clear as a sword cleaving the sky:

"And so it has come to pass that all those gathered here bear witness to the miracle of an ending, the joy of reunion, the chance of rebirth—" and Joy might have imagined their ancient gazes seeking her out, smiling in Ink's arms "—as has been prophesied, the Old Worlds of Man and Folk have been destroyed—they are divided no more. That Age is past, its blemish gone. Now our futures shall be forever entwined, for today begins a new era, a new magic, a new Age. Together, we shall explore our world and its wonders, discovering what our children and our children's children can dream beyond imagining."

Their faces were rapturous, their voices raised in song: "Behold the Age of Miracles!"

EPILOGUE

"I DON'T UNDERSTAND," SHELLEY SAID AS SHE TOOK the roast out of the oven. "Where is all this coming from?"

"Joy decided she wants to major in Governmental Law at Georgetown," Dad said with a shrug. "She says she's interested in diplomatic relations or something and qualifies for some obscure scholarship, so who am I to argue?" He tossed the roasted Brussels sprouts and grabbed the pepper. "She's excited about it, and I'm just glad she's made a choice."

"Sounds wonderful," Shelley said, setting napkins around the table. "Has anyone heard from Stef since he got back?"

"He lost his housing placement," Joy said. "But he and Dmitri found an apartment off campus." Ink handed her cups and she poured the lemon water. He was mesmerized by the cascade patterns splashing against the glass. "They said we can come visit once they're settled in."

"We just got back from traveling," Dad said, sitting down. "And now this trip to California?" He speared a sprout with his fork. "Some of us still have to work around here."

"Hey," Joy said, pointing at herself. "Paid internship girl."

Ink sat down and passed the potatoes like a pro. "She is doing very well in her new position," he said with a smile. "She is already indispensable."

Dad smiled, "That's my girl."

Joy laughed and Ink took her hand under the table,

threading their fingers together. She leaned forward and kissed him full on the lips. Her heart pounded happily.

Ink caught her sleeve, tugging her closer. "Again, please."

She kissed him again—an everyday miracle.

And he tasted like rain.

* * * * *

ACKNOWLEDGMENTS

THIS IS IT—THE END OF MY VERY FIRST SERIES, MY OWN Age of Miracles. Thanks, as always, to my editor, Natashya Wilson, for allowing me to share my journey through the winding, wonderful world of the Twixt, my agent, Sarah Davies, for wisdom and support, and everyone in my life who volunteered to help keep me sane as I struggled to keep track of just how many characters, plots, subplots, red herrings and loose threads I'd written over the course of three books, including Jenny Bannock, Nicole Boucher, Maurissa Guibord, Shari Metcalf and Kate Smith. My wall of Skittle-colored Post-its would be lost without you!

Deep, sweeping bows and heaps of roses for the Harlequin TEEN Dream Team who made the dream of the Twixt a reality (on paper, ebook and audiobook!)—kudos to Shara Alexander, Evan Brown, Bryn Collier, Ingrid Dolan, Kristin Errico, T. S. Ferguson, Amy Jones, Siena Koncsol, Margaret Marbury, Ashley McCallan, Suzanne Mitchell, Bradley Myles, Kathleen Oudit, Reka Rubin, Anne Sharpe, Mary Sheldon, Lauren Smulski, and Anna Baggaley of the UK Mira Ink team.

Finally, to the people who made all of my dreams come true from infancy to parenthood and whatever passes for adulthood these days: my parents, Holly and Barry, who filled my life with love and words and play, my other parents, Marilyn and Harold, who always support their crazy daughter-in-law with laughter and open arms, my siblings by birth and marriage, Corrie (Crunchy Parent), Richard (Suave Sir), Adam (Music Man), Michelle (Awesome Aussie), David (Gamer Mensch) and Shari (Riddle-Me-Miss) and to Jonathan, my beloved partner-in-crime in the starched pajamas who whacks people with pool noodles for a living and whom I love beyond words—thank you for your patience, your humor, your support and love...and for not whacking me with a pool noodle while I was busy typing. And, of course, to my two greatest contributions to the world: Maestro and The Pigtailed Overlord—I am so proud of who you are and who you've been and who you are becoming; I love you more and more each day! (And thank you, my darling daughter, for being old enough to be my very first, very best beta reader!)

And to all of you who have read this saga from beginning to end—my crazy only exists inside my head until I write it down, and then you read it, and now it exists inside *your* head! Treat it well. Pay it forward. Eat more chocolate. And thank you.

AUTHOR'S NOTE

WHEN I'VE BEEN ASKED WHAT INSPIRED THE TWIXT, I remember Richard Peck saying of book ideas, "As if we can't think of them ourselves?" And although I'd love to claim credit for the whole kit 'n' kaboodle, I'm a big believer that the best ideas are cocreated, inclusive and influenced by the brilliant, creative, insightful and oddly weird and wonderful people who share our little blue planet. So, bottom line—there are lots of things that inspired the Twixt.

The idea for the books themselves began with a rant, which seems to be where I get a lot of fuel for my fires. I had been getting a little tired of the glut of stories that featured an immortal guy falling for a sixteen-year-old girl and sweeping her off her feet to "show her the way to love." (Cue eye-roll here.) I thought, "Why not flip it?" I remembered how much I loved my literary crush, Peter Pan, and later Johnny Depp as Edward Scissorhands and Brad Pitt in *Meet Joe Black*. Wild, boyish and innocent, these otherworldly heartthrobs were clueless, cocky and a little bit dangerous. There was something sorta sexy about the mysterious, guileless guy with both power and principles who wore his heart on his sleeve! These were the first seeds of Indelible Ink. (And, of course, I flipped every single one of them to create his sisterly foil, Invisible Inq.)

I named my main character "Joy" because, while she'd

been through a lot, at her core she was a happy person who was gleefully expressive. I wanted her to be very physical, and aware of herself, someone who belonged to something bigger—a group that she'd lost along with her mother—and have that be a huge part of her identity. Her journey back to that place of happiness is a return to who she truly is, as well as a decision about who she'd like to be—as always, it's a choice. Additionally, as Wendy to Ink's Peter Pan, I wanted Joy to know the difference between "a thimble and a kiss" so she wasn't as innocent as some of those other clueless characters out there. I think of Joy as being like a lot of real girls; someone who knows something about herself before she goes looking for another person to tell her. And I hope that the whole prude/slut dichotomy burns a horrible, fiery death.

As for, "Why gymnastics?" I'd had experiences being on a sports team with soccer and basketball, skating and martial arts, but I decided to give Joy something different so she didn't come off as too "Buffy" aka "every other paranormal heroine on TV who just happens to know kung fu." I spoke with a lot of young gymnasts, instructors and an Olympics-level coach in Australia who helped me translate Joy's world into something I wanted to use and Joy Malone sprang out of those initial conversations and multiple links on YouTube.

Most of the other characters were made up as I went along, coalescing out of the weird, twisted miasma of my brain; notable exceptions being Avery, who was inspired by Hans Christian Andersen's *The Wild Swans*; Filly, the youngest Valkyrie, whose bravado was heavily influenced by Zeetha of *Girl Genius* by Phil & Kaja Foglio; and the Bailiwick, Graus Claude—whose name sprang fully formed out of nowhere—who is an amalgam of an old RPG character, the voice of James Earl Jones and Baron Von Greenback from the British cartoon, *Danger Mouse*. (I never claimed these made sense, it's just the way my mind works.)

The world of the Twixt is a collection of all the myths, legends and fairy tales I know and love; everywhere I thought magic might exist in the world was a part of it, strung together like an archipelago, inhabited by everything other-than-human so that everyone's Other Thans had a toehold in truth. The Loch Ness Monster, Bigfoot and the Emerald Isle's "fair folk" coexisted on the same plane as Romanian vampires, Japanese Kodama, Danish mermaids, Hindu Rakshasa, Greek satyrs, Islamic djinn and ancient Egyptian gods—I wanted all of our stories from all over the world to conceivably originate from the Folk of the Twixt because this is *everybody's* world, and therefore this is anybody's story. For this series, I focused on one local chapter anchored in a place that had special meaning for the Folk, so I invented the Glen, a small patch of the sacred First Forest, that later became known in America as Glendale, North Carolina. (Apologies to all North Carolinians if I messed up the geography. I invented the entire city and all surrounding environs with the exception of Lake James State Park. Sorry, folks, there's no Carousel. Pity.)

Nods and/or blame should be shared with early influences including, but not limited to, Jim Henson, Spider Robinson, Neil Gaiman, Joan D. Vinge, Connie Willis, William Gibson, Tim Burton, Wendy & Richard Pini, Phil & Kaja Foglio, Brian & Wendy Froud, Alan Moore, Nick Park, *Cirque du Soleil*, *Monty Python*, Guillermo del Toro Gómez, Hayao Miyazaki, and, of course, my parents, siblings and friends, which should come as no surprise to anyone.

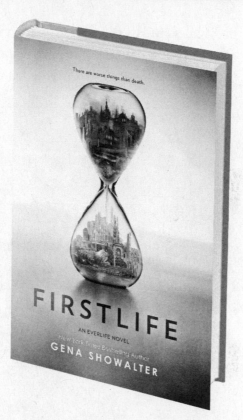

From the critically acclaimed author of
The Paper Gods

AMANDA SUN

Don't miss this sweeping fantasy novel of a kingdom of floating continents, and the girl who falls from the edge

Available now!

HTASHTTSTR2